Dani Wade astonished her local librarians as a teenager when she carried home ten books every week—and actually read them all. Now she writes her own characters, who clamor for attention in the midst of the chaos that is her life. Residing in the Southern United States with a husband, two kids, two dogs and one grumpy cat, she stays busy until she can closet herself away with her characters once more.

USA TODAY bestselling author **Catherine Mann** has won numerous awards for her novels, including both a prestigious RITA® Award and an RT Book Reviews Reviewers' Choice Award. After years of moving around the country bringing up four children, Catherine has settled in her home state of South Carolina, where she's active in animal rescue. For more information, visit her website, www.catherinemann.com.

Discover more at millsandboon.co.uk

TAMING THE BILLIONAIRE

DANI WADE

THE DOUBLE DEAL

CATHERINE MANN

MILLS & BOON

First Published in Great Britain 2018
by Mills & Boon, an imprint of HarperCollinsPublishers,
1 London Bridge Street, London, SE1 9GF

Taming the Billionaire © 2018 Katherine Worsham
The Double Deal © 2018 Catherine Mann

ISBN: 978-0-263-93595-0

51-0318

MIX
Paper from
responsible sources
FSC™ C007454

This book is produced from independently certified FSC™ paper to ensure responsible forest management.

For more information visit: www.harpercollins.co.uk/green

Printed and bound in Spain
by CPI, Barcelona

TAMING THE BILLIONAIRE

DANI WADE

To Charles Griemsman, aka Awesome Editor…
You've taught me a great deal over these years
about writing, communication, story and self-worth.
Thank you for helping me grow in confidence
and style. I'm truly blessed to work with such
a kind, considerate (yet constructive!) editor.

One

Sabatini House. Finally.

Willow stared up at the imposing, impressive castle-like residence through the windshield of her car. The thunderstorm raging around it was only appropriate. A structure as mysterious and unique as Sabatini House deserved an atmospheric introduction.

Unfortunately, since the intercom hadn't worked when she'd stopped at the gates, Willow now had to figure out how to get inside. It took concentrated effort to relax her fingers on the steering wheel.

The rain pounded her little car, at times completely obscuring the view. Willow had been fascinated with Sabatini House for several years, since she'd discovered mention of its owners, the Kingston family, in her great-grandmother's journals. But they contained very little about its history, which had only whetted her appetite for more.

According to the rare articles she'd found about the house since then, it was said to have been built by a Spanish pirate for his lover. It featured underground caves that allowed the ocean to actually flow underneath the house to create a swimming cove. In her journal, Willow's great-grandmother had described the cave from her one and only time sneaking into a party in the house, declaring it a truly magical tie between the land and the sea. As a descendant of pirates herself, that would be something her great-grandmother would have appreciated.

From the outside it still looked like a magnificent castle, with turrets and peaks and arched windows. But Willow was dying for a glimpse of the inside. She hadn't been able to find any photos or documentation in her research. The current reclusive owner had never allowed anyone else inside besides his caretaker, Murdoch Evans, and the occasional trusted workman.

Until today.

Taking a deep breath, Willow pulled her raincoat around her as best she could. There wasn't any point feeling wimpy about the rain. She needed to get inside. The sooner she settled in, the sooner she could start looking for clues. As much as the house fascinated her, the secrets it held were what truly drew her here. Secrets about the Kingstons, and one fateful night generations ago, that could change her own history forever.

Her umbrella would be useless in the strong winds blowing off the water. On the count of three, she jumped out of her car and ran for the side door where Murdoch had told her to enter.

With Murdoch gone to Florida to visit his daughter after she'd had a baby, there was no one to cook and clean for the current resident of Sabatini House.

She and Murdoch had gotten to know each other well in the year she'd been pestering him for information about the house. When he'd known he was leaving for the summer, he'd hired her to come in on her summer break from teaching at the local college to take care of the place.

Hiring on without even meeting her employer hadn't seemed that odd at the time. Right about now she was second-guessing that choice.

She'd been due to arrive midafternoon today, but the thunderstorm had blown in early. Packing and driving had become a complicated mess. Living in required she take quite a bit with her, even if she'd be going home to visit on Sundays. Loading the car in the rain had left her and her luggage soggy.

The island would normally have been about a forty-five minute drive from the house where she lived with her sisters in Savannah. Instead she'd been struggling with poor visibility and winds rocking the car for a good hour and a half. So she was now arriving after dark with no warning, since the weather had knocked out the power and phone lines on the island, preventing her from letting her new employer know of the delay.

The rain pelted her with angry pellets as she ran. The flashlight in her hand was her only guide. Reaching the small covered porch was a relief, although not much of one. She fumbled for the key Murdoch had given her.

Excitement shimmered in her belly, even as the effort to get inside exhausted her. She was about to walk into Sabatini House…and hopefully discover all of the mysteries it held.

She knocked hard as she inserted the key and turned it, eager to get out of the rain blowing in under the small porch awning overhead. Giving her new boss a heart attack wasn't on her agenda, but the heavy streaks of lightning splitting the sky didn't encourage her to linger. Fumbling with the keys, flashlight and doorknob, she finally got herself inside and out of the blowing rain. Conscious of the unlit alarm keypad on the wall to her right, she allowed herself to lean back against the now-closed door for only a brief moment. Her heart raced.

"Hello? Mr. Kingston?" she yelled.

Considering the constant barrage of thunder and rain, the odds of him hearing her were slim unless he was close by. She hated to burst in like this, but what other choice had she had? The lines had been down when she'd tried to call earlier in the evening, and there wasn't a cell tower close enough to allow them to work out here. Murdoch had warned her about that. The house was huge, and with the power out there were no lights to guide her.

But that uneasy feeling in the pit of her stomach told her to find him quickly, announce her presence, and make sure he was safe and sound. The fact that he was out here by himself only woke her curiosity. As she tip-toed through the empty room, she wondered where his family was and why he was all alone, even though that was absolutely none of her business.

"Mr. Kingston? It's Willow, your new housekeeper."

Her voice seemed to be swallowed up by the darkness and rain, though the sounds from the storm were muted in this part of the house. The flashlight illuminated the path out of the mudroom where she stood. Thank goodness she'd grabbed a good, sturdy one on her way to the car.

Even inside, the smell of the ocean permeated the

air. It mixed with the rain, salty and wet with a slight undertone of some kind of flowers.

She dripped on the tile floor as she made her way through a modernized kitchen, narrow and long like an oversize galley with all the amenities. Murdoch had mentioned the kitchen had been updated about five years ago.

Lightning flashed outside, brightening the entire room through the long row of arched windows along one side. Willow winced, trying to concentrate on her surroundings so she didn't get spooked. Sweeping the flashlight around, she noticed more arches. Every doorway, every window. Some were outlined in brick. Some plaster. Hopefully cleaning the windows wasn't her purview, because there seemed to be a lot of them.

Determining that the room was empty, Willow pushed forward through the kitchen and found a wide hallway at the other end. The whole time she called for Mr. Kingston. The darkness, as well as the thought that he had no idea she was in his house, left her with antsy feet and a churning stomach. And she was increasingly uncomfortable not knowing he was okay.

Hopefully he would forgive her intrusion. Murdoch hadn't said anything about her boss being incapacitated, but in a storm like this anything could happen. A fall. A bad cut. A concussion. All alone, he could lie on the floor injured for hours with no help. He could bleed to death. And there was no way to contact the outside world because the landline was down.

She cautiously made her way down the wide hallway. Everything here was built on a majestic scale. She flicked the beam of light over the various rooms as she went, checking for Mr. Kingston.

Most of the doors were open, some of them revealing empty spaces. Other rooms held furniture covered in sheets. Only a formal living room boasted carefully placed antique furniture, but it still lacked a lived-in look.

If she hadn't known better, and the kitchen hadn't appeared to have been recently used, Willow would have suspected the house was unoccupied. Empty of all life. But she knew Mr. Kingston had to be here somewhere.

Her uneasy feeling grew until Willow's stomach cramped. Yes, the house was huge. Three stories that she knew of, though the turrets suggested more. Still, what more could she do to be heard? The storm seemed to absorb her calls and footsteps.

The hallway finally opened into a large, two-story rotunda-style room centered on an incredible staircase leading upward. The sound of the storm outside now resounded in her ears. The staircase drew her eye as far up as she could see in the darkness. No lights shone on the upper floors, offering no clues as to where her employer might be.

"Mr. Kingston?" she called again, her voice suddenly echoing loudly back from the walls. Guilt snaked through her. Even though she needed him to hear her to answer, it felt wrong to yell in a house that wasn't her own.

A noise, like something small had fallen, barely reached her across the rotunda. "Hello? Is anyone there?"

No response. Only the sound of the rain beating at the house.

Willow swung the flashlight around in a circle, taking note of the numerous doors leading off this room and on the upper floors. A strong sense of uncertainty crept over her. She had no idea where to look, and no idea which direction to go. With this many rooms, she could look all night and possibly never find this man.

Had she made a mistake coming here so late?

Her excitement at finally being inside the house had now given way to more uncertainty, mixed with rapidly rising fear.

A metallic rattle came from the hallway opposite her, ramping her pulse to high speed. Was that a normal noise for the house? She had no idea. Her light reflected back from the ocean-blue tile outlining the bottom of the plaster walls. She took a tentative step forward, struggling to think logically.

The bedrooms were probably upstairs. She'd start on the second floor. He would most likely be there. If she could just find some light. Surely, given how often the power went out on the islands, he would be well equipped with lanterns.

Or a generator. Though if he'd already gone to bed, he might not have bothered starting it. She couldn't remember if Murdoch had mentioned one in his instructions.

Her wet tennis shoes squeaked on the tile as she made her way to the bottom of the staircase. Reaching out, she grasped the wooden balustrade. Her light trailed upward, showcasing the stairs' brilliant blue tiles with a mother-of-pearl glaze. The silver filigree in the blond wooden rail looked delicate but remained firm in her grip. As her light reached the next floor, she caught a shadow move out of the corner of her eye.

Startled, Willow dropped the flashlight from her hand. The clatter echoed through the massive room.

"Hello?" She tried to project her voice, but fear made it tiny. She almost couldn't hear it herself over the rain and rumble of thunder.

Just as she bent forward for the light, a strong arm snaked around her neck, forcing her back against a hard wall of muscle and heat that she recognized as human... and huge.

The size and strength of her attacker told her it had to be a man, but she was too busy trying not to wet her pants to figure out more than that.

The arm around her neck tightened, almost cutting off her air. Then she felt the man's face near hers, his breath harsh in her ear. "Want to explain what you're doing in my house?"

Tate Kingston felt a surge of adrenaline like he hadn't felt in years.

He'd thought there was a burglar. When he first heard the sounds, he knew they didn't belong in the house where he'd lived his entire life. His brain had automatically drifted down dark alleys with nefarious characters. Not surprising for a horror fiction author.

Then again, he'd never experienced an intruder in this house. Just to be sure, he'd slowly made his way down the back stairs. Spying what he thought was a young man, he stalked him as he came into the center rotunda. A teenager, he'd thought. Maybe someone who'd been dared to sneak inside Sabatini House, the place of legends.

Instead, Tate found a woman pressed against him in his tight grip.

She came only to the hollow of his throat, even though she had to be taller than average. She froze in fear. Not that he blamed her. He'd be scared stiff, too, if he'd just broken into what he assumed to be an empty house.

Only this one was occupied.

He pressed his forearm down against her collarbone, careful to avoid the more fragile area of her neck. Though his knowledge of this hold was completely cerebral, he wanted to instill simple fear. Not find himself with a lawsuit on his hands.

"I asked you a question," he said, letting his voice drop even deeper. He carefully emphasized every word. "What are you doing in my house?"

"Your house?" she squeaked, trying to get her words out even though he could tell she was short of breath. From fear? *Good.* When she walked back out that door, he didn't want her or her friends to even think about coming back here.

"What are you talking about?" she gasped.

He loosened his hold, giving the impression of leniency even though he had no intention of giving in to whatever she wanted. But if he wanted answers, he needed her to talk. "How about *you* answer the questions?" he demanded. "Who are you?"

Her sudden lunge forward took him by surprise. He loosened his grip and let her go, not wanting to injure her just to keep her contained. After all, she couldn't escape. There wasn't a place in this house he couldn't find her.

But she went only as far as the stairs, sinking down to grab her flashlight. From her crouch against the railing she let the beam slowly travel up the length of him. "You can't be Mr. Kingston," she breathed as the light paused right below his face.

"Clearly I am."

"No…" That breathless quality distracted him more than he cared to admit. "Mr. Kingston is…um…"

"Is what?"

This time she didn't answer.

"Look, I don't care why you're here. But if you leave right now, I won't contact the police."

Behind her flashlight he could barely make out a frown.

"But I'm supposed to be here," she said.

What? "I don't think so."

"I am," she insisted, her voice quickly firming up. "I'm the new housekeeper."

For a moment Tate's very active brain froze. Somehow this scenario had never occurred to him. "Absolutely not."

Now it was her turn to ask. "Why?"

"You cannot be my new housekeeper."

Murdoch would not have done that to me.

Tate let his own powerful flashlight travel up her body, till the beam hit her full in the face. His author brain kicked in automatically, narrating the view. Pale, creamy skin. Hair that glinted fire, even in the strong light. And a thin, soaked T-shirt that outlined her curves perfectly beneath an open rain jacket.

She eased to her feet, blinking to adjust her sight. "I am the new housekeeper," she insisted. "Murdoch hired me."

"You can't be. The new housekeeper is a man. Will Harden."

She slapped her hand on her hip. "Uh, no. It's me. Willow Harden."

Damn Murdoch.

"I know I was supposed to be here earlier," she explained, "but things got pretty complicated with the storm moving in early. The power was out here and I worried, um, that you were okay."

"As you can see, I'm neither old nor in need of assistance." Yet. Though some days he felt every one of his thirty-eight years and more. He ignored the discomfort of that thought and continued, "I'm perfectly prepared for the weather. I certainly didn't need you to break into my house to check on me."

"I didn't break in. Murdoch gave me the keys."

Of course he did. "And the codes?"

"Yes, sir."

As her voice grew small, Tate recognized that the bully method of questioning wasn't helping anything. Obviously he'd been fed incorrect information on purpose. Murdoch knew Tate would view a woman as a threat. An unwanted intrusion to a life spent making amends for his mistakes. Deadly mistakes.

Heck, that was probably why Murdoch had done it. He'd been different since finding his daughter again, since deciding to visit her for the first time. But that didn't mean Tate had to live with his friend's decisions.

This woman had to go.

They stood there in the dark, flashlights trained on each other like weapons. Tate would have found the situation amusing if he wasn't faced with the complications she represented. There was no way he could tolerate this intrusion.

"Well, I appreciate your concern, Ms. Harden—"

"Willow."

"—but I'm well equipped for this kind of thing. If you're a Savannah native, you know that the power goes out on these islands quite easily. I have lanterns, a portable cookstove, stored water, a generator—everything I need."

Her light dipped. Tate wondered what she was thinking. Why the hell would Murdoch hire a woman to come in and take care of Sabatini House while he visited his new grandchild? Granted, Tate hadn't specified gender when they'd discussed Murdoch's stand-in, but it should have been a given considering his history.

When she didn't speak further, he figured he needed to spell it out. "Well, *Willow*, since I'm not what you wanted. And you aren't what I..."

He caught the lift of one eyebrow. Somehow he could read the warning for him to choose his words carefully. The fact that he understood that unspoken communication, and the earlier joy that had streaked through his body as he'd been pressed against her softness, convinced him she definitely had to go.

Joy was the last thing he deserved...and having her in this house would be nothing more than a temptation.

He continued carefully, "You aren't what *I expected*, so I think it would be best if we called this whole thing off. Don't you?"

He wasn't certain, but he thought she mumbled *Are you sure about that?* under her breath. The sound of the rain doubling down outside made it hard to tell.

"Obviously Murdoch made a mistake," he said.

"Nooo," she countered, shaking her head. "No, he didn't. He was very specific in his instructions. And after all this time, he knew I would follow them to the letter."

Tate tried to squelch his curiosity, but the words slipped out anyway. "How long have you known Murdoch?"

He could see her muscles loosen a little, softening her stance. "We met early last year. He's such a sweet man, once he lets you get to know him."

That's exactly how Tate would describe the man who'd been with him through the last twenty years of self-imposed exile from most of the world. Murdoch had been with him through the death of both his parents, the sale of his first book, but mostly he'd been there for Tate as he dealt with the grief that seemed never-ending. Murdoch had mentioned on more than one occasion that Tate's lifestyle wasn't healthy, but that simple opinion wouldn't change the choices Tate had made.

Couldn't change them.

Then Murdoch had said he was leaving…and now here Tate was facing the only woman to be in this house since his mother died.

"Look," she said, taking a step closer. "Murdoch would never forgive me if I walked away after all of the trouble he went through to make sure this place was taken care of while he was gone. Please. Just give me a chance."

Tate let his eyelids slide shut. The first thing that came to mind weren't words, as was often the case, but the memory of her body against his. The close heat. The sweet scent. The softness of curves.

Nope. Bad idea. He crossed his arms over his chest, knowing full well his bulk could be intimidating.

Probably reading the rejection in his stance, Willow continued, "Besides, how will you hire someone else? Phone calls. Interviews. How many will it take before you find the right person?"

"No."

No more intrusion. Anger rose as Tate tried to think, quickly. This woman was way too smart, and well-armed with info. Uneasiness slithered through him as he wondered what else Murdoch might have told her.

But the aggression in his tone didn't seem to faze her. "Or you could just accept the inevitable," she continued.

"And that is?"

"Without me, you're gonna have a ton of people tromping all through this place. From what Murdoch said, that's not something you would enjoy."

"Or I could settle for just you?"

He caught her sneaky smile on the outer edge of his flashlight glow. Then she asked, "Besides, have you driven in this stuff recently?" She flicked the flashlight toward one of the massive windows behind him. "I thought I was going to die trying to get here. I have no desire to go back out into this weather."

"A little melodramatic, aren't you?" Even he cringed at his condescending tone. Defensiveness didn't sit well on him.

But on her... The way she stiffened her spine put other attributes on display. Tate tried not to notice.

"Are you kidding me?" she demanded. "You obviously haven't tried driving a tiny car over that bridge in fifty-mile-an-hour wind gusts. Have you?"

Tate felt himself automatically shut down. No, he hadn't driven in this kind of weather...not for many, many years. And he never would. Certainly not over the narrow bridge that connected the island to the mainland.

"I made a lot of effort to get here. It's at least common courtesy to let me try to do the job."

Tate clenched his jaw, frustration tightening his tone. "If you stay, you won't find courtesy to be one of my strong points."

This time she didn't respond, but adopted a stance that mimicked his own. In that moment, Tate recognized her.

Oh, he'd never met her before, but he'd described her type over and over in his work. She was the embodiment of the heroines he wrote about in his horror stories. Women with grit, determination and smarts who made it out alive when lesser mortals rarely survived.

That tingling awareness he'd been doing his best to

ignore multiplied. All the more reason to get her out of here.

A flash of white lit the room as lightning suddenly streaked across the night sky. Tate saw her jaw clench and shoulders straighten as she braced herself. Admirable. It was a little clue that told him a lot about her. Heck, the fact that she'd made it here in the first place in this weather signified a strength and determination some people never displayed in their lifetime.

The flash was followed closely by a hard clap of thunder. The storm was picking up again. But it was just starting for Tate.

Somehow he knew giving in on this point meant he would lose this battle…and lose the war. But she was right. As a long roll of thunder shook the house, he knew he couldn't send her back out in this weather. His own feelings about her presence aside, he refused to make an impulsive decision that cost someone their life.

Again.

"Let me show you to a room, then."

Two

At least he had let her stay instead of forcing her back out into the weather.

The consolation was mild as her overactive brain was assaulted with emotions. First the drive and the storm, then the dark house, and now being led up this magnificent staircase by a tall, brooding man carrying an old-fashioned lantern. If she wanted atmosphere, she'd received it in abundance.

Actually, more than she'd hoped for.

She shivered, though she couldn't tell if it was because of her still-damp shirt or the continued uncertainty of this entire situation.

Tate led her only a short way down the hall before pausing beside a closed door. As with the ones she'd seen downstairs, there were intricate carvings, swirls and maybe leaves and vines that gave the wood dimension. Even in the gloom it was gorgeous. "This will be your room for the night."

So, he still wouldn't concede that she was right?

"Where's yours?" she asked, only to clamp her lips together in regret.

In the light of the lantern she watched one thick, dark brow rise. "I'm in a suite at the end of the hall," he answered simply.

Right.

The darkened room beyond slowly came to life as Tate lit candles from a fireplace match. Willow stared in awe as the historical setting came to life. A large silver candelabrum on the dresser provided most of the light, with smaller candlesticks dotted around the room. As Tate's big body moved through the shadows, fear and fascination mingled inside of her.

A four-poster bed with drapes and some kind of fabric topper dominated the space, the white fabric with navy filigree pattern lending to the old-fashioned feel of the room. Add in the tall man with shoulder-length disheveled hair and she had the makings of a regular *Wuthering Heights* on her hands. The thought sent another shiver over her.

As he turned to look at her, she became all too conscious of her body's reaction. She'd love to blame it on the cold, but she feared the tightening of her nipples had more to do with the man standing before her than the temperature. She quickly crossed her arms over her chest.

Let him make of that what he wanted.

"It's beautiful," she murmured. Even in the shadows, there was no mistaking the intricate designs on the furniture and fabrics.

His gruff command grated on her nerves. "Don't get too attached. We will discuss this situation in the morning."

"Really? We're still not over that, are we?" She wasn't sure what gave her the gumption to say it, but as she stood there shivering with cold, she was over his attitude.

He raised those dark brows again. "I may require more patience than you possess."

There was almost a literary quality to his pronunciation that sharpened the edge of his words.

Maybe he was right, but… "I have more patience than you could imagine. After all, I teach history to eighteen-year-old freshmen who think being at college gives them the freedom to do whatever they want."

Her response seemed to surprise him, lightening his expression a little. "The fearlessness to enter a dark house, the patience of a saint… Is there anything else Murdoch didn't tell me about you?"

I'm attracted to tall, dark and mysterious men? "Um…a classroom of eighty of those monsters has made me efficient, organized and slightly entertaining?"

"Do you really call them monsters?"

This time she didn't hold back a cheeky grin. "To their faces—with the utmost of affection, I assure you."

"Then I can only imagine what you'd call me."

Before she could come up with a clever response, he was at the door. "Good night," he said as he left the room, closing the door behind him.

At least he didn't lock me in.

Willow half grinned, half whimpered at the thought. Her sisters would take away her modern-woman card if they knew she'd been seriously attracted to the dark brooding man in the darkened house on the isolated island. Somehow she'd been cast in her very own Gothic mystery with a leading man who would fit right in with Hollywood's most gorgeous heartthrobs.

But she had a feeling he saw her more as a nuisance than a leading lady. She'd do well to remember that.

Despite wanting to get out of her damp clothes and shoes, Willow took a moment to slowly turn around in the middle of the room. This place was incredible. The furniture she'd seen in the other rooms had been antique, too, but this was an incredibly high-quality fairy-tale look that she'd seen only in photographs.

The bedroom was fit for a royal prince, even if Murdoch had only been the hired help. Willow jumped as lightning flashed through the sheer window coverings, then giggled as she glanced around. The dark furniture was offset by the creamy color of the bed draperies that almost matched the ivory walls. There was a heavy chifforobe, a dresser with an oval mirror hanging above it that reflected the light from the large silver candelabra and matching bedside tables. A large navy carpet mimicked the pattern of the drapes. It looked so soft, Willow couldn't wait to dig in her cold toes.

Conscious of how damp she was, she glanced in the chifforobe for anything to cover herself with, but it was empty. Well, she wasn't going back out in this weather for her suitcase, and Tate hadn't offered. She would just have to make do.

At least her current dilemma took her mind off the man sleeping in the suite at the end of the hall.

She flipped the cream-colored duvet down to the end of the bed, grateful to find another blanket beneath it. As she removed her jeans and wet shoes, she tried to think of ways she could convince Tate to let her stay. This was a short-term gig. Murdoch had chosen her personally. She could prove she was good at the job... if Tate would just give her the chance to show him.

She blew out all the candles except a couple right

beside her bed. The urge to search out the dark corners of the room still irked her. But even crawling under the warm blanket didn't relax her. Exhaustion lurked just below the surface, but her overactive brain wouldn't let it take over.

Maybe she could make him her special French toast for breakfast? They said food was the way to a man's heart. Maybe showcasing her cooking skills would at least soften his.

As she reached for her phone to set an alarm, a noise caught her attention. The deep creak of old wood sounded above her, reminding her of her mission and renewing her courage. She needed this job. She needed to find out the secrets her great-grandmother had hinted at in her journals.

Just remember that, little miss!

More creaking, then a thud overhead had Willow sitting up. That sounded like more than just an old house settling in. Had Tate gone upstairs before going to bed? She hadn't heard any footsteps, but—

Bam!

Willow tucked herself down in the bed, instincts insisting those few inches would save her. But when nothing else happened, she giggled a little. Boy, tonight's atmospheric adventures were sure affecting her.

Drip. Drip.

Willow bent over to inspect the water droplet that had landed on her now-bare calf. Where was that coming from? She glanced up at the material above her. The heavy drapes were gathered in the middle, creating myriad folds that revealed nothing. The lack of light wasn't helping. Curiosity getting the better of her, she lifted up onto her knees for a better vantage point.

That might be water droplets hanging from the fabric. Maybe?

Then the world went dark as the creak became a crash.

Tate debated whether to go back to work or give it up for the night. He'd been moving along at a fast clip when he'd heard Willow downstairs. But the conflicting emotions of the last hour had left him growlier than a grizzly bear. He usually didn't write well in that state. Working out would be better, but with the electricity off he'd better not be wandering around in the basement.

Also he probably needed to keep an ear peeled for his houseguest for a little while. Something told him she needed supervision. A feeling that had nothing to do with wanting to get his hands on her again. *Absolutely nothing.*

Suddenly he could feel the approaching crash on the final lap of his adrenaline rush. Yeah, writing would be impossible in a matter of minutes. His brain would fog over and the words simply wouldn't be able to break through. Better to rest now and write tomorrow—after he'd dealt with the problem lurking in Murdoch's bedroom in the form of one sexy redhead.

Tate strolled into the office to shut off the battery-operated lantern he'd left in there earlier. Before he cut off the light, he paused, staring at the shutters closed tightly over the windows. Heavy rain beat against the house, but here the sound was muffled. The last thing Tate had wanted to see was the choppy waves of the sea below, stirred up by the storm.

Haunting memories rose despite his mental protest. Maybe he wouldn't be able to sleep tonight, after all.

As he flipped the switch on the lantern, another noise

joined the rest. It was so faint he almost missed it. Moving back toward the hall, he wondered if his guest had come to find him. He hoped not. He had willpower like a suit of armor, but she seemed to be able to find every weak point.

Then he heard the booming crash. He hurried down the empty hall until he reached her room. A commotion was in progress behind the door. What the hell?

He swung the door open, then froze. The door slammed against the wall. Before him…he wasn't even sure what was happening. A writhing mass of wet bedclothes, splintered pieces of wood and dripping water occupied the bed…instead of the slightly damp housekeeper he'd left here thirty minutes before.

For a moment, the scene captured his artistic imagination. Despite the urge to rush in, he had to catalog it for future reference. And frankly, he was enjoying the show.

The frantic wiggling granted him glimpses of nicely rounded calves. He should help untangle her, he really should. Then she froze. He could just hear the quick intake of breath before she screamed, "Help me!"

That galvanized him into action. He struggled to find an opening as she thrashed about. "Be still," he snapped.

His low command seemed to make it through to her because she paused long enough for him to snag the edge of the fabric. With a heavy tug, he divested her of the soggy bed curtains.

Then had the immediate urge to cover her back up.

As her bare calves had warned him, she'd taken off her jeans. And her bra. She now crouched, breathing hard, in the middle of the bed wearing nothing but a wet T-shirt and panties. Her wild auburn hair flew in every direction, including over her lightly freckled face.

If he'd had twinges of attraction earlier, they were nothing compared with now.

Finally she reached up and tossed her hair back from her face. Tate quickly directed his gaze up to the ceiling. Whoa. Leaning over, he got a better angle to see what had happened. The substantial hole over her bed revealed only the darkened room above and the steady drip of water that he suspected came from dislodged tiles on the roof.

Straightening, he then let his gaze track back to the woman in the middle of the mess. "Don't guess you will be sleeping here tonight. There must be some damage to the roof. In this part of the house, there's only the one floor above you. It was fine during the last inspection, but something might have hit it or the wind must have ripped something loose."

Reaching out, he plucked her from the bed. Her squeal echoed around the room. The distinctly feminine sound jump-started his heart. He hadn't heard someone make a sound like that since he was a teenager. The women he met now didn't squeal. They wouldn't consider it sexy.

"Let's get you settled somewhere else," he said.

She was already shaking her head, sending her hair flying once more. "We need to clean up first," she insisted. To his surprise she started gathering the mess into the middle of the bed.

While the thought was appreciated, her movements afforded Tate an even better view. The T-shirt barely covered her upper thighs. The expanse of smooth skin was mouthwatering. "I'll get something to catch the water," he murmured.

Escape was a relief, but a brief one.

When he returned with a large plastic tub, he found

himself eye level with a pair of silky panties he'd have been better off not seeing. "What are you doing?" he growled.

Willow jerked, her shock unbalancing her and the candle in her hand as she stood on the bed.

"Woman," he snapped. "Let's not catch the bed on fire, too."

She frowned at him. "This isn't my fault. I was just trying to see what had caused the leak."

"I'll investigate in the morning." He glanced over the now-stripped bed and soggy mattress. "And get this all replaced."

There was no helping it. His gaze snagged on creamy white thighs below the edge of her T-shirt. She might not have realized how she looked before, but now was different. Her delicate hand came into view, tugging the hem down. He flicked his gaze up to her face, only to see a red stain spreading across her skin. Yep, she was fully aware now.

"Let me help you," he murmured, then had to clear his throat as his voice deepened without his permission.

Still she accepted his hand for balance as she climbed down. The shocking chill of her skin as it met his made him shift gears from lust to more practical matters. Like where she was going to sleep...

He placed the tub carefully in the middle of the bed to catch the dripping water. Good thing it wasn't coming down heavier. "This should halt the damage for a while. It should stop raining in a couple of hours," he said.

Willow offered a brief nod, then skirted around behind him. "I've got to see about some clothes," she said, her voice sounding strangled.

He shouldn't have made her uncomfortable, but the rest of the night would make matters much worse.

"Where do you think you're going?" he asked as she scooted toward the open doorway.

"I guess I'll have to go out to the car to get my bags." She paused, then inched back inside. "I should probably put on some shoes for that."

"You aren't going out in this weather." As if to back him up, lightning flashed outside, then thunder rumbled loud enough to rattle the windows. "We will find something else for you." He gestured for her to go out into the hall, but she hesitated.

Tate had a feeling this was where living as a single man and not as part of a family was going to bite him in the ass. He turned smartly on his heel and headed back the way he'd come, silently gesturing for her to follow. He ignored her questions, trying to get everything straight in his own mind first. With a sense of trepidation that he kept well hidden, he walked straight into his bedroom and opened the top drawer of the bureau, pulling out a well-worn T-shirt. He turned back to see her hovering in the doorway.

"You might as well come inside," he snapped.

"Why?"

Her obvious hesitation reminded him that the situation wasn't her fault and was completely out of both of their control. He tempered his tone.

"Because this is where the only other bed in the house is," he said with a voice full of resignation.

She stepped through the doorway, her eyes wide with shock. "What?"

He spoke a little more slowly. "This is the only bed... And the only decent sofa is right there." He pointed back toward the living area that comprised half the large master suite. "We're going to share a room tonight, I'm afraid."

Even in the dim light he could see her eyes cataloging everything she'd seen tonight—which wasn't much. Still, she tried. "But there are so many rooms—"

"Which have been stripped. Or I assure you the mattresses are nothing but dust and springs by now."

He held out the oversize T. "Your attire, my dear."

Three

Even with the sound of heavy rain outside, Willow could still hear every squeak of the leather when Tate moved on the couch. And he moved a lot.

Too bad it wasn't thundering still.

As the furniture protested yet another turn of Tate's big body, Willow contemplated their current situation in the dark. She knew Murdoch had said they never had visitors, but she never imagined a big house like this wouldn't at least be set up for the possibility. This was the South. Hospitality was an actual way of life down here. All these rooms lying dormant would be unheard of.

It was a type of isolation Willow couldn't imagine.

She should be sound asleep right now. Between the tense drive and the stress of meeting her new boss, exhaustion weighed down her bones. But her unexpected dousing in cold water and ceiling tiles had her hyped.

And every squeak of the leather told her Tate was in the same boat.

As one particularly restless move was followed by a long sigh, Willow finally gave in. She sat up and projected her voice above the noise of raindrops hitting the windows. "This is ridiculous. Come to bed."

Hmm…that probably wasn't the right way to put it. Now that her vision had adjusted somewhat to the dark, she could see his head and bare shoulders rise above the back of the couch. "What did you say?"

She should have been intimidated, but she was over that by now. "Come sleep in your own bed. You're never gonna get any rest over there. And neither am I."

"What's that supposed to mean?"

"That every time you move that couch creaks. It's even noisier than the rain outside."

He slowly got to his feet. To her relief, he wrapped a blanket around his shoulders, covering the light skin that she wanted so badly to see. To cover her awkwardness over having her gorgeous new boss approach the bed she was sleeping in, she said the first thing that came to mind.

"At least the one good bed left in the house is the size of a football field." Frankly, she felt a little lost in all this yardage.

"I'm not a small guy."

To that, she could attest.

"But I don't think this is a good idea," he said.

"*I think* we'll manage," she said, her sense of humor asserting itself. "I won't think less of you if you put pillows down the middle. After all, I want you to feel safe."

Even in the dark she caught his pause. "Shouldn't that be my line?" he asked. She detected a touch of amusement. Probably the best she could hope for with him, especially since his progress had slowed considerably. Did walking toward her on the bed have to resemble a death march?

Not that he should be too eager, but still…

"I'm not the one who needs convincing," she reminded him. "And if I don't get some sleep soon, I'll have trouble proving my worth to my new boss tomorrow."

This time she was granted a chuckle, and he finished making his way across the room. The bed shifted a little as he lay down, but he seemed to stay as close to the edge as possible. Heck, her arm fully stretched out wouldn't come close to reaching him.

"No pillows?" she finally asked.

"I think I'm safe."

You wish. She tried to relax, tried to sink into the most comfortable mattress she'd ever lain on, but it wasn't happening. Then he suddenly spoke.

"Considering how well you've taken everything that's happened tonight, I think you might have earned a point or two in your favor. Hopefully your new boss will agree."

She huffed out a little laugh, then consciously forced her muscles to clench, then relax. It was the only thing she knew of to distract herself from his presence. So close, but still a good distance away.

That's the way she should want it, but a niggling desire wouldn't be smothered. If what he'd said was true, she'd have to learn to live with lusting after her boss in the quiet recesses of her own mind.

Though she'd thought sleep wouldn't show up, considering the thoughts running rampant through her brain, the steady sound of the rain, the exhaustion she couldn't fight any longer and the even breath of the man a few feet away eventually lured her under.

She woke to a different environment altogether. Instead of rain, sunshine peeked through the slats that protected the windows. Heavy covers kept her warm. Her body, her muscles, felt languid, almost liquefied in her relaxation. Then something shifted against her leg and sleep was immediately a thing of the past.

Suddenly the weight against her back and lower body made more sense. It wasn't a heavy blanket. It was a man.

Her heart picked up speed. She lay on her stomach. His chest seemed to be covering part of her back. Now that she knew what to look for, she could see his fingers against the covers on the opposite side of her body. His warm, musky scent clung to the sheets, tempting her to draw in a deep breath.

But would even that slight movement wake him up?

As incredibly sexy as this was, and as much as her body throbbed its approval, the last thing she wanted was to face him knowing his leg had slid between hers. Why hadn't he stayed on his side of the football field?

He shifted, rubbing a warm, hairy leg against the sensitive skin of her inner thighs. The shirt he'd given her hung almost to her knees, but now she had a feeling her panties were exposed...and probably a little damp.

She needed out now. But how did she do that?

Above her hair, she heard a heavy sigh. The big body half covering hers stretched, pressing harder against her. A certain part of him was making its approval well-known. Willow bit her lip to keep a groan inside. Why did he have to feel so good?

Then he went absolutely still.

She squeezed her eyes shut. *I don't want to deal with*

this. And she certainly didn't want him to see how much she enjoyed waking up to his body pressed against hers. But as he shifted infinitesimally, she braced herself for the inevitable awkward confrontation.

"Oh no," he groaned softly behind her.

Oh yes. The only thing to do was guard her expression as best as possible and brave this out. Twisting around, she tried to blink innocently. "Sleep well?"

"Not my usual," he said, his voice deep and gravelly enough to send tingles along her nerve endings.

She tried to ignore his heavy eyelids, sleepy expression and tousled black hair. But this whole "barely awake" look was short-circuiting her overloaded brain. "Pardon me?"

"Sleeping is usually a solitary experience."

Even though the past twelve hours had proved that guests weren't an option around here, she had a difficult time believing this hot, virile male only slept alone. "Seriously?"

Pulling away, he sat up on the edge of the bed. With him facing away from her, she couldn't read his expression. She had a feeling that was on purpose.

His voice was low when he spoke, though not as gravelly as earlier. "I haven't slept in the same room with another person since I was a teenager."

As he walked away, Willow marveled for a moment. Considering how good it had felt to lie with him in this bed, she'd have thought he'd had plenty of experience in this area.

Or any area related to the bedroom.

Tate was glad Willow had disappeared by the time he came out of his dressing room. The tremor in his hands as he'd washed up and dressed had startled him.

The desire had hit him hard and fast.

Not since he'd been an untried youth had he been near a woman he had to have. His casual liaisons focused more on one-night stands to scratch an itch. He could appreciate a beautiful woman, even desire one. But urgency was definitely a thing of the past for him.

Yet his body's response to Willow had been all-consuming. If it hadn't been awkward enough to curb him, they would still be in his big bed—a whole lot more naked than they'd been upon awakening.

He breathed through the sudden surge of his body, waiting until his response died down before making his way out the door and downstairs. Instead of the sound of crashing thunder, the rooms now echoed with the rumble of waves beneath the house. The sound was muted as he moved down the hall to the kitchen.

There he found Willow bent over, inspecting the contents of the fridge. His body pulsed, responding to the sight of feminine curves encased in still-damp jeans.

His body was happy. His brain was not. This response was downright unsettling.

"What are you doing?" he asked, a little too gruff.

He felt bad about his tone when she jumped, bumping her ginger head into the lower edge of the freezer door. Her low moan made it worse, because it brought to mind things he shouldn't be thinking about around her. He'd never had sex with anyone in Sabatini House since he'd become an adult. He hadn't been lying when he'd told her that he hadn't slept with anyone. Though why those words had come out in that moment, he had no idea.

Just say what you need to say and get out of here.

But words escaped him as she turned to face him. Seeing her in full sunlight was like living color compared with the black-and-white of last night. Willow had the classic pale skin of a redhead with just a fine dusting of freckles across her cheeks. She had emerald-green eyes, which was what he favored for the female characters he wrote about, but in person hers were so vibrant. She was tall for a woman, just as he'd noticed last night, but now he could see all the sexy curves he hadn't had a chance to truly savor this morning.

He cleared his throat, glancing out the window behind her to steady himself. Which wasn't as effective as looking seaside. That would have reminded him of exactly why this woman was off-limits to a man like him. But at least the view of the barren hill leading to the gates below calmed the resurgence of desire that thrummed through his veins.

As if his silence was an invitation, Willow jumped right in. "I'm just checking to see what the inventory is like." Crossing to the island, she picked up a pen and tapped it against the pad of paper lying there. "The landline is still out, but when we can get through, here are some places I'll call about the roof and repairs—with your permission, of course."

Though he'd prefer to direct this discussion himself, focusing on action was a very good idea right now. "Why wait? I'll get the satellite phone from my office."

She raised a brow. "Murdoch didn't mention that you had a satellite phone."

"I prefer to forget I have it. My editor, Charles, insisted I get it because he got tired of my being out of reach and ignoring his emails. The landline goes down all the time out here. I only use it to call him and my agent and for emergencies."

He could tell by her face that this little explanation puzzled her, but Tate wasn't going out of his way to explain his eccentricities. That was the way he operated. She could take it or leave it.

He glanced over the list. "These two," he said, pointing to a couple of companies he'd worked with in the past. She had good taste. "I'll get your luggage while you put in the calls."

"What? So you were serious—"

"If you haven't slapped me yet, I guess we're pretty close to compatible. And it saves me the time of searching for a housekeeper to hold me over for just two months."

Willow started a little happy dance on her side of the island. Tate did his best to ignore the sway of soft body parts.

This decision was probably a mistake, but it was expedient. And after accosting her in his sleep he felt obligated to be rather generous.

"So let me know when they arrive, and I'll show them around."

"I can handle it," she quickly countered.

Tate adopted his sternest expression. "But I know the house, so I will. Got it?"

"Yeeesss…" The drawn-out word made it clear she didn't understand, but she would soon enough.

"I'll give you a chance to clean up, then we'll go over a few things," he said, eager for a break from his unrelenting response to her presence.

"We can now," she said, eagerness practically vibrating off her in waves. "I'm good."

Maybe getting it over with was a good choice. Like ripping a bandage off a particularly sensitive patch of skin.

"Let's start with the rules."

She blinked, as if trying to comprehend what he was saying.

"What did Murdoch tell you?"

Her smile opened her face up, revealing a pleasure that sunk straight into Tate's darkened heart. He couldn't catch his breath for a moment. Luckily she didn't notice as she bent over to pull a notebook from her backpack. Guess she wasn't a designer purse kind of girl.

"He gave me a whole notebook on house procedures. Let's see, gate and alarm codes, chore schedule, your favorite foods…"

But no real rules? Somehow at this point he wasn't surprised. Yesterday he would have been. Not today.

But Tate was a big believer in start how you mean to go on…

"Rule number one. I am not to be disturbed."

That seemed pretty self-explanatory, but Willow still asked, "You mean when you're writing?"

Tate refused to show the jolt of surprise that shot through him. "So Murdoch told you what I do for a living?"

"Actually, the fact that you're an author is pretty well-known and speculated on in Savannah. Though no one has been able to crack the answer to what you actually write."

"And Murdoch didn't share that."

The solemn shake of her head didn't dampen the curiosity in her expression. But he wasn't about to satisfy her with an answer. Instead he ignored the whole line of questioning.

"Actually, when I'm in my office at all, I'm not to be disturbed. I'll come down at the set mealtimes I'm sure Murdoch gave you."

Willow quickly moved on. "What about mail? Do you want your mail when it comes, or for me to wait for a meal and give it to you then?"

As she opened her mouth to say something else, Tate raised his hand for her to stop. "Do. Not. Disturb. Understand?"

He could see another question brewing in those green eyes, but he forged ahead. "Rule number two. No talking about me or anything that happens here or that you see here outside of these premises."

"What about with my family?"

That wasn't an issue Tate had ever run into with Murdoch. He and his family had been estranged for the first ten years he had worked here, but even after the reconciliation Murdoch hadn't shared important details of his job with them. He'd simply gotten into the habit of keeping Tate's issues private.

But Willow's family might be a different story.

"I think that rule is self-explanatory," he said, injecting a stern note into his tone.

"Actually, it's not," Willow said. "I mean, I'm guessing you want me to keep quiet about who you are, since Murdoch did. What about the house? Can I talk about it? Am I supposed to keep quiet about everything I see? Where's the line? Can I tell my family how to contact me?"

"Of course."

She'd asked more than one question, and the litany confused him. Murdoch was a quiet, loner type. Willow was not quiet…at all.

"Of course you can tell your family the landline number, as long as they don't abuse it or share it," he amended. "But my home, my business, are to be kept private at all times."

"Do I need to sign a nondisclosure agreement?"

"I don't know. Do you?"

The rapid shake of her head sent wisps of red hair flying. Man, that was gorgeous. This woman was all living color. He looked back out the windows.

"Certain rooms in the house are off-limits to everyone but me."

"Murdoch mentioned that, but how will I know which ones they are?"

"Good God, woman, do you ever stop asking questions?"

Tate looked back at her just in time to see her blink hard. For a moment, he feared he might be facing tears, but no. Just a sad "Sorry. I guess I just want to do it right the first time."

Man, I'm such a jerk.

Tate's brain scrambled to rectify the situation. He heard himself say, "I'll take you around and show you." Until now, he'd had no intention of doing any such thing.

And the way her eyes lit up made him think what should be a simple thirty-minute walk would turn into hours of her asking questions he didn't want to answer. "Later," he added.

He might need to fortify himself with a drink...or two...beforehand.

Four

Willow wasn't stupid.

She knew her curiosity tended to get on people's nerves. A lifelong learner—that's what one of her professors in college had called her. The insatiable curiosity and hunger for knowledge made her annoying to some people and boring to most.

Her sisters loved pretty dresses, nail polish and all things feminine. And while Willow had a good enough eye to help them pick things out, she had no desire for those things herself. Instead she was excited by books, old houses and antiques. If there was a mystery to go along with them, all the better.

She seemed to get on Tate's nerves more than most. Which was too bad. Because he was a hunk.

All those glorious muscles, that messy hair and brooding intense stare. He matched the mysterious house to perfection… But he wasn't well matched with her. She could tell he'd enjoyed her much more in his sleep—when she wasn't talking.

After a morning spent inspecting the kitchen and fixing his lunch, she waited impatiently for him to finish eating. He took his time in the breakfast nook, while she struggled not to eagerly bounce from foot to foot in the kitchen. She'd snuck a peek at some of the adjacent rooms, but she was eager to see the rest of the house... even if it was just a tour for him to show her what she wasn't allowed to touch.

Finally he brought his plate back into the kitchen.

"Is it time now?" she asked, then pressed her lips together, inwardly chastising herself for her impatience.

He raised one dark brow, but this time seemed rather amused by her enthusiasm instead of annoyed.

He gestured toward the hallway leading to the rotunda. "Shall we?"

As they walked down the hall, she once more glanced into the open rooms. For the most part, they were bare. Some were decorated with boxes and sheet-covered lumps that could have been furniture. Intricately carved doors and elaborate lighting fixtures coated in dust reinforced their lack of use.

As they reached the rotunda, Tate paused. He braced himself in the middle of the round room, staring up the magnificent staircase as if he were challenging it. A multitiered chandelier that Willow hadn't been able to make out in the dark hung from the very high ceiling. A row of small windows around the top of the rotunda let in light that bounced off the chandelier's crystals.

"Sabatini House was built by a pirate," he started, his voice echoing slightly off the walls. "It took over ten years to complete, though he brought his bride here after only three. It's built to celebrate the spot where the water forges its connection with the land."

Willow started to open her mouth, started to question whether the stories of the underground caves were true, but then she remembered the cut of his reprimand this morning. She quickly closed it again.

The last thing she needed was to aggravate Tate at the moment. She'd hold all of her questions as long as she possibly could. After all, she wanted him to be able to at least tolerate her. Maybe there would be a time to ask her questions later, after he got used to her being around.

Or maybe she could settle for something benign? Like "How long have you lived here?"

"The house has had a long and varied history," Tate said. "My family were direct descendants, so I've lived here all of my life."

She thought of how much her own little house meant to her and her family. It wasn't anything as magnificent as this, but it was a direct link to their people. "Wow," she said. "That must be an incredible feeling."

The indistinct noise Tate made drew her gaze away from the impressive rotunda to his face. He stared at nothing with a deep frown. "Both a blessing and a curse," he said.

She ached for him to explain, but he simply turned away. Where was his family now? she wondered. Why did they leave him all alone? These were definitely questions she should *not* ask.

And he certainly wasn't volunteering that information.

Instead he kept to the general. "The house was built to withstand the rough weather of the outer islands. Tropical storms, hurricanes, flooding—they all pose a threat. But not to Sabatini House. After a lifetime living on ships at sea, that pirate knew exactly what he was up against. Even the erosion of the ocean was guarded against when building the foundation."

Curiosity burned in Willow's throat. He had to be referring to the flood of the ocean beneath the mansion. Were the rumors true? Murdoch had refused to deny or confirm the existence of caves beneath Sabatini House, stating it wasn't his place to say.

Tate's strong legs carried him up the stairs. "Sabatini House doesn't have an elevator. All the upper floors are reached through this staircase, or the one on the opposite end from the kitchen. If a room is locked, it is off-limits to you. That includes the third floor."

Panic swallowed up Willow's reserve. "But what if—"

Tate paused, twisting around to stare down at her from a few steps above. "Off. Limits."

"Right," she mumbled as they continued up the stairs. She struggled not to show her unease. Her personal reasons for taking this job included finding the answer to a family mystery...an answer that probably hid in one of the third-floor rooms, if Murdoch's information was correct.

Resolving to find a way, Willow focused once more on the current tour.

As they traversed several hallways, Tate gave short explanations about architecture, molding and carvings in the plaster. But nothing personal. Nothing meaningful. He could have been a boring docent in a beautiful museum for all the enthusiasm he infused in his words.

Many of the rooms were dusty. Some were completely empty. He hadn't been kidding when he said there wasn't another mattress in the place. One of the downstairs living areas had been decorated with "more modern" furniture from the fifties or sixties. Any bedrooms had empty bed frames—beautiful, but achingly empty. While Tate obviously understood the history of the house—the why and how it was built—that didn't translate into pride of ownership.

Willow's hands itched to work on some of the antiques that they passed. A large grandfather clock. Leather-bound books. Incredible pieces of furniture covered in dust cloths…or simply dust. Restoring antiques was a passionate hobby of hers, but she doubted Tate would appreciate her efforts.

They came to the wing on the second floor that Willow remembered from this morning. It was closed off from the main hall with heavy wooden doors carved with intricate swirled designs.

Tate paused. "This wing holds my suite of rooms," he said. "If these doors are open, you may come down the hall. You'll of course need to clean and gather laundry. But my office is absolutely off-limits."

He pulled the heavy floor-to-ceiling doors open with a loud creak. Guess there was no sneaking in here… She smothered a giggle. Tate didn't seem the type to appreciate her subversive brand of humor.

This hallway was darker than the others. Most of the adjoining doors were closed, cutting off the light from outside. Tate pointed to the far end. His face was grim as he said, "My bedroom suite. You can go in there to change the sheets or clean the bathroom. But cleaning only."

He pointed to a long table on one side of the hallway. "That door there is my office. If any mail comes that needs to be attended to, you can set it on the table and I'll get it when I'm ready."

He turned to study her, his expression almost expectant. She knew he was wondering why she didn't ask any questions. Her earlier behavior had proved her curiosity. But the questions she wanted to ask weren't appropriate. Like, why are you keeping these rooms off-limits? What is it you have to hide? Why can't I bring the mail to you, instead of just leaving it on the table outside?

None of his secrecy or demands for privacy made any sense.

Finally he continued, "The third story and turrets are off-limits."

It was a struggle not to roll her eyes like a smart-alecky teenager, despite the unease that resurfaced. She was beginning to think the word *off-limits* was his absolute favorite.

"There's nothing up there that you need to be involved in, and some of the rooms could be dangerous from disrepair. As evidenced by the roof caving in last night."

"I thought you said the roof had been inspected?"

"It is, yearly. But as you can see, in a house this old, anything is possible. Even when you're careful."

She trailed behind him as they went back down the stairs, only this time he curved around behind the staircase and down another, much smaller set of stairs. Her heart started to thud as the sound of the ocean grew louder in her ears.

"Down here you'll find the laundry room, and some storage areas where we keep extra supplies."

He walked down the hallway. The floor seemed to be carved straight out of rock. The laundry room was industrial-sized, but obviously converted from something else that had been there for many, many years.

The storage room was lined with shelves. The cool atmosphere was perfect for storing a variety of items and keeping them fresh. She could just look around these rooms and see the history of them, feel how integral they had been to a huge busy household that had many mouths to feed. The history buff in her shivered with excitement.

The other side of the hall had one large, long room with a door open at each end. The space was full of exercise equipment. Guess she now knew where Tate's bulk came from.

"I work out every night." Gesturing toward a phone at one end of the room, he added, "You can reach me on the intercom here if necessary."

At least he wasn't *off-limits* when he was working out. Although seeing him half-dressed and sweaty might be more than she could resist. After all, that might make her forget his current attitude…

They made their way back toward the bottom of the staircase. Willow kept expecting him to mention the sound of the ocean and the underground cave that was rumored to be part of the house, but he never did. She'd been a good girl, keeping herself focused on the essentials and not plying him with questions. But as he took that first step up the stairs, she couldn't hold it in any longer.

"Is it true?"

He turned to stare down at her, his brooding look almost daring her to ask the question. But she couldn't help herself.

"Are there underground caves here beneath Sabatini House?"

His stare turned into a glare, and for long moments she thought he wouldn't answer. Then he came back down the steps to stand uncomfortably close. He pointed down the opposite hallway.

"Yes, it is true," he said, his voice low and rumbly. She could almost feel the vibration in her core. "The caves are actually natural, with parts that are hand-carved beneath the house's foundation. But they are completely—"

"Off-limits?" she supplied.

It was all she could do not to giggle when he glared down at her. "The swimming cove is not safe," he insisted. "Don't ever go in there."

"Why? How is it not safe?"

If nothing else, she just wanted a peek.

The question changed his tone from stern to downright cold. "I don't need a reason. Just stay away."

She shivered at his intensity. But that didn't kill her curiosity. As he turned to leave, she couldn't help but stare at the hall leading to the most mysterious part of the house.

What was it he was hiding?

If Willow had any doubts about Tate's determination that she stay away from the third floor, they disappeared when the repairmen arrived that afternoon.

She didn't even have to call him down—he simply appeared in the doorway to the kitchen as she watched the repair truck drive up the winding road and around to the side of the house. Tate had used this company before, so they knew where to enter.

Tate completely bypassed her, focusing all of his attention on Mr. Hobbins, the company's owner. Only the best for Sabatini House. Despite the need to help rising up in her, watching both the men was amusing in its own way.

Mr. Hobbins was obviously used to dealing with Murdoch. He glanced back and forth between Tate and her with a bemused expression, then looked behind Tate for good measure, as though Murdoch might be hiding there. He quickly recovered and offered Tate a "Good afternoon."

For his part, Tate exuded control and authority. But he didn't indulge in small talk. In fact, he didn't reach out to shake the man's hand, either. He launched into an explanation of the current issues that needed addressing. Mr. Hobbins's expression quickly transformed from polite to all business. They discussed what would need to be done, and Tate waved away the offer of an estimate. "Just do it right, whatever that costs. And quickly. We've got some more rain coming in later this week. We don't need new damage."

They walked away, Tate passing along instructions about reinspecting the entire roof. He never looked her way, increasing the *keep away* vibes, but Mr. Hobbins threw her a perplexed look before walking out the doorway. A whole wealth of confusion and curiosity resided in that glance, but he didn't say anything.

"Yeah, you and me both, buddy," she murmured, conscious of her own confusion and uncertainty. Which seemed to grow with every encounter she had with Tate. Close or not.

Tate's refusal to let her help only increased her curiosity about the third floor. Unfortunately, that was the one area where her impulse control had always been weak. She was smart enough to stay in the kitchen until he had finished barking orders and retired to his office. Now the sound of the ocean waves was punctuated by the pounding of hammers and grating of saws. Only when she deemed it clear did she grab the handle of her suitcase and drag it up the back stairs.

Chagrined at how out of breath the task made her, Willow paused just inside the door to her bedroom for a bit of a rest. The bedroom was not so temporary now, thank goodness. Hopefully Mr. Hobbins would at least raise the room's safety standards by that night. Tate would want to avoid a repeat of this morning just as much as she did.

Next time she might not be able to brush it off as well.

The bed frame had been moved and a ladder set up beneath the hole in the ceiling. A stack of tools and stuff lay nearby. She hefted her suitcase to the dresser top so it wouldn't be in the way. She took out the clothes on hangers, which she'd packed on top, and put them in the closet.

On her way back to her suitcase, voices from the upper floor caught her attention. It was just the workers talking, but it was a reminder of where she wished she was instead of down here unpacking. After a paranoid glance behind her, Willow inched under the damaged ceiling until she could see into the room above.

Her view was limited, but the first thing to catch her eye was an antique rolltop desk. The dull wood left the impression of years' worth of dust coating it and the slatted chair pulled up close. A couple of boxes occupied the space in front of it, blocking access. Slowly Willow rotated to the right, as if moving too fast might give away her intent.

That was when she caught sight of the trunks, which brought a smile to her face. They weren't new plastic and metal pieces. Oh no. These were the real deal, genuine antiques. Leather and handmade nails, if she was seeing correctly from this far away. That was exactly what she had hoped for…exactly where she needed to look.

If she could just find some paperwork proving how the Kingstons had been involved in the tragic historic event that ended with her family being driven from town, her heart would be satisfied. Her discovery wouldn't be for public consumption, but would serve as validation for the Harden sisters, who were all that was left of their family. If what her great-grandmother suspected was true, their mother's insistence that their family was innocent of the crime would be justified… at least to them.

Her frustration at not being able to go right up burned in her, but greed wasn't very ladylike. The trunks looked like they'd been sitting in the same spot for decades. A few more days wouldn't hurt anything. But if she could find what she was looking for, it would clear her family name. Not that anyone would care but her and her sisters.

Still, it was the principle of the thing.

"Ma'am?"

Willow quickly controlled her instinctive need to either yelp or jump or both. After a deep breath, she turned to the workman who had appeared in the doorway. "Yes?"

"We're about to start cutting the ruined parts out of this here ceiling. I need to get this stuff covered."

"Of course. Let me help you."

He protested, but she kept right on working. At least he couldn't order her to stop like Tate. Between the two of them they quickly tarped the remaining furniture and the antique rug. He did insist on moving her open suitcase into the walk-in closet for her, then left her to continue unpacking with a closed door to keep the construction dust out.

She pulled out a couple of changes of clothes. The rest could wait until her bedroom was complete. But the ticking clock in her head told her to hurry. The new mattress should be delivered within an hour, and she needed to be back downstairs to unlock the gates.

Grabbing a couple of T-shirts, she walked to some empty shelves. She'd gone only a few feet when she heard a light thud on the carpeted floor. Bending over to get a better look in the dim light of the closet, she quickly straightened back up in shock. An unreasonable fear kept her still for long moments. Logically she knew she was being ridiculous. Still her heart thudded hard in her ears.

Finally she forced herself to bend over and pick the object up from the floor. A ring, to be exact. One she recognized all too well. It had been in her family for generations. Blessed, her auntie called it. Given by a pirate who'd turned respectable to the most desirable woman in all of Savannah. The founding couple of their familial line.

A ring said to bring the woman who wore it true abiding love. So why the heck would anyone think Willow would need it at Sabatini House and pack it in her suitcase when she wasn't looking?

Five

"So…" Willow paused for dramatic effect. "Whose brilliant idea was this?"

She slid the antique emerald ring onto the dining room table at her family's weekly Sunday dinner. Each person sitting around the table received a moment of intense study, except Rosie, who, at only nine months old, couldn't have been involved.

When her older sister, Jasmine, pressed her lips together as if suppressing a smile, Willow had her culprit. "This isn't funny," she complained, wincing at the slight whine in her protest.

Jasmine's fiancé, Royce, had to add his two cents' worth. "We just want to see you as happy as we are," he teased.

"Since when are you buying into this pirate legend business?"

He hugged Jasmine to him. "Why not? I've got the proof right here. After all, your sister wore that ring almost the entire time she worked on planning the masquerade event for me."

"Well, the last thing I need to do is romance my boss," Willow said. Their youngest sister, Ivy, scoffed before pushing back from the table and crossing to the stove. Her back was stiff, giving her a closed-off look.

"You okay, Ivy?" Willow asked.

Her sister didn't respond, which worried Willow. She had always been close with Ivy, even more so since Jasmine had adopted Rosie. Their oldest sister had taken on a huge responsibility and gone through a lot of changes in the last year. Willow and Ivy had turned to each other as confidantes rather than add to their sister's stress.

As she watched Ivy, it occurred to Willow that it had been a couple of weeks since she'd had a good talk with her younger sister. First she'd been preparing for her new job, and then living at Sabatini House had cut back on the time they spent together. She should see if she could have her sister out there. Maybe seeing the awesome house would distract her from whatever was bothering her or give her a chance to open up about it.

Of course, it might take a miracle to talk Tate into letting her have a stranger in the house. She'd better hold off on that conversation for a while.

She turned back to Jasmine and Royce. "He definitely has his own ideas about how things should be done," Willow said. "Where I can go and what I can do. I mean, I realize this is his home, but I'm beginning to think Tate is überparanoid."

Except he didn't give off a paranoid vibe. So she couldn't quite grasp what the issue is. "And being in control is the be-all, end-all for him."

Jasmine cast an arch glance at her fiancé. "Well, men tend to be that way."

"That doesn't mean we're wrong," Royce said, "for all the good it does us." His smile was amused instead of defensive, though.

Jasmine and Royce had clashed about how things should be done from the moment he'd hired her to coordinate a charity event for him. As Willow watched them now, she was amazed. For two people who had often butted heads, their love for each other and Jasmine's adopted daughter, Rosie, was palpable.

Of course, they'd overcome a lot to get that way.

"It's just…" Willow struggled to put her feelings about her new job, and her new boss, into words. Though not all her feelings—the last thing she wanted to discuss with Royce was the disturbing amount of lust that colored her every interaction with Tate. "I don't understand. Why is he so defensive? What's he hiding in all those rooms? And what does he do with himself all day? I mean, I know he's a writer. Is he writing all day? About what?" The frustrating lack of answers left her antsy.

Ivy turned away from the stove, where she was putting the finishing touches on the marinara sauce, to ask, "What do you mean?" Her earlier stiffness seemed to be gone.

"Well, after we did the house tour, he went upstairs and I didn't see him again. He just silently appeared almost the minute dinner was on the table."

Ivy snickered. "I can see that driving you crazy."

Meanie. "I just want to know!"

He had to have been locked up in his office all afternoon. She'd never heard him moving around and hadn't seen him the few times she'd gone up to check on the workman in her bedroom. He'd never been in the workout room when she'd gone into the basement to wash the dirty bedclothes. "What was he doing with himself for so many hours on end?"

"Why do you care?" Royce asked. Then he glanced around as the other women laughed. "What?"

"Willow is notoriously curious," Jasmine explained. "So the more Tate Kingston tries to hide things from her, the more she's gonna want to dig."

"I can't help it," Willow protested. "He's just so secretive and closemouthed and..."

"Sexy?" Ivy teased.

"Yes." Willow sighed, lured into the answer by her sister's lighter expression. Then Willow shook her head. "No, no, he's not."

Auntie threw in her two cents' worth while she supervised Rosie in her high chair. "Methinks she protests too much..."

"Auntie!" Willow's cursed pale complexion flushed hotly. "He's frustrating, that's what he is."

"Because he wants to keep his privacy?" Royce asked.

Willow could tell this whole conversation had him confused. Trying to explain it to him when she felt she couldn't be completely open was confusing for Willow, too. The sisters and Auntie had long been on their own and weren't used to male input yet.

Auntie wasn't really their aunt at all. She'd been their mother's nanny when she was little and their grandmother's best friend. Auntie and the Harden sisters had all lived together in this house since their parents had died in a car accident. Until Jasmine had fallen in love with Royce. Then she and Rosie had moved out.

Since the sisters had come to live with Auntie, they'd never had a man in the house. Not a boyfriend or lover or spouse had lived there. It had just been the girls.

Royce's presence changed things. Though Jasmine and Rosie had moved into his penthouse in historic Savannah, they were here as often as not.

Ivy grinned at Willow as she carried the pot of sauce to the table and set it on a trivet. "You know that secrecy means he has some kind of tragic past," she said.

"You are so melodramatic," Willow scoffed, but deep down...

Ivy took her chair with a knowing look. "But I'm right."

Jasmine gasped, theatrically laying her hands over her heart. "I bet if you wore *the ring* you could get him to fall in love with you," she teased. "Then you would know *all* his secrets."

Ivy groaned. The out-of-character response caused Willow to cast her a worried glance. "What's the matter, Ivy? I thought you were a believer in the family ring?"

Jasmine piped up. "I definitely am."

"Oh, hush," Ivy said, and left the room.

"What's the matter with her?" Royce asked, though her disappearance didn't stop him from digging into dinner.

Jasmine smiled, but her expression was a little sad around the edges. "She's a little testy at the moment. The legend of the ring starts with a pirate who found it and used it to win over his true love. She was an upper-class woman who never would have been within his reach before that. But he married her and started our family line."

Royce nodded. "What does that have to do with Ivy? You wore the ring the whole time we were working together, right?"

"Yes, sir." The furrow between Jasmine's brows deepened. "But Ivy wore it the night of the masquerade."

They all fell quiet for a moment. Something had happened between Ivy and her boss on the night of the masquerade ball that Jasmine had planned as a charity fund-raiser for Royce and his company. Only Jasmine and Willow knew that her boss had taken Ivy to his bed. The next morning, he had left to deal with a problem at one of his manufacturing plants. That was three weeks ago. *Bless her heart.*

"I think I'll hold off on wearing the ring," Willow said, turning it over and over in her hand. The lighting caused the teardrop-shaped emerald-and-gold filigree to glitter and spark. Almost to herself she mused, "I've gotten myself in enough trouble already."

"How so?" Jasmine asked.

The last thing Willow wanted to talk about was ending up in Tate's bed or waking up to him wrapped around her body like a real lover. Or what a hard time she was having forgetting those heated moments before he'd woken.

So she chose a safer topic. "My whole purpose in going to Sabatini House didn't have anything to do with Tate. If he keeps everything locked down, I'll have wasted my whole summer on a wild-goose chase."

Not that the memory of Tate's body against hers could ever be considered a waste.

"What are you talking about?" Jasmine asked.

Willow caught Auntie's gaze. "I read the journal."

Out of the corner of her eye, she saw Jasmine and Royce exchange a glance. She figured she better explain before the questions started.

"Auntie gave me our great-grandmother's journal."

"I found it in the attic, in the same trunk as the ring," Auntie interjected.

Willow had spent many a rainy afternoon prowling through the old trunks in their attic with Auntie. It was how she'd come by her love of antiques and mysteries.

"While I was reading the journal, I came across some speculation from great-grandmother about who was really responsible for the tragedy that eventually drove them out of town."

Royce jumped in. "This is about the sabotage of the rival company's ship, right?"

Willow nodded. "The accusation was that our great-grandfather, a direct descendent of a pirate, sunk the biggest ship of a rival by setting it on fire to give his own shipping company an advantage. That family's eldest son and heir was on the ship the night it caught fire and died."

"Great-Grandfather vehemently denied any involvement," Jasmine added, "but no one believed him. The rival family threatened first his business, then his wife and child. He felt he had no choice but to skip town."

Willow drew in a deep breath before saying, "But Great-Grandmother knew there were other shipping companies that would have been happy to get a lead over that same rival. Possibly even the Kingstons."

The others stared at her with wide eyes. Even Rosie seemed to focus in on her, as if sensing something wasn't right in her world.

"Oh, Willow," Jasmine finally breathed. "Please be careful."

Willow shrugged off her concern. "It's just a piece of history now. At least, to most people. But it's our history. I, for one, would like to know the truth."

"I don't know about this," Royce said.

"I do," Willow said. "Our family history means a lot

to me. And that truth just might be hiding in a trunk on Sabatini House's third floor. I want to find it."

The question remained, was she willing to defy Tate Kingston to find her answers?

Willow set his plate in front of him on the table in silence. She didn't offer any pleasantries with the food. Of course, he didn't, either.

Tate had gone out of his way to get this situation back to strictly business. It didn't help him forget the feel of Willow's body against his, but at least a professional attitude kept him from reaching for her whenever she walked by him.

He kept all answers precise and as short as possible. Small talk wasn't an issue...he wasn't good at that anyway. And he certainly never addressed anything personal. She probably thought he hated her—and that was best for everyone.

So why did the thought unsettle him?

There were other things that also left him off-kilter. For instance, he'd started to notice little touches around the house—homey touches. A pillow here. A new picture there. Yesterday he'd come across a little clock that had been his mother's, fully restored, on the mantel in the living room. Whether Willow believed it or not, he did actually prowl the house. Usually in the dark hours of the night.

There it had sat, pretty as you please, right below his eye level. He'd wanted to curse Willow for the memories she'd evoked, but he couldn't stop himself from walking over to it. Touching the little clock that had been his mother's had been beyond him, but he had to check for dents, chips in the delicate paint. Any signs of the years of neglect he'd allowed to occur.

All had been well…but not with his soul.

He'd wanted to fire her, but by morning the feeling had passed. She'd be gone at the end of the summer… and he'd be free of the temptation to kiss those freckles on her face. Or spark that redheaded temper so he could see the tension enter her body until it radiated from her.

Until then, he'd stay far, far away.

So why, when he saw her pass by the doorway with a covered plate and a book, did he ask, "Where are you going?"

Her glance his way was too brief for him to get a good look into those glassy green eyes.

"To eat lunch. Don't worry. I'll be back."

He wasn't worried—exactly. And her cautious tone would have been funny if he hadn't been the one to put it there. The word *cautious* just didn't seem to describe Willow. Tate saw her as more of a free spirit—a fiery, determined sprite who knew exactly what she wanted and would plow right over anyone in the way…or when the situation warranted, sneak around the boundaries anyone set up for her.

But he had a good view of the rest of her…and the book under her elbow. His heart started pounding out of his control.

"You don't seem like the horror story type," he said. The words slipped out before the "business only" side of him could kick in.

She paused, then turned back to him as if she wasn't quite sure he was speaking to her. She offered a half grin that looked sad on her full lips. "I get that a lot." She mimicked a high-pitched tone. "What would an innocent-looking thing like you want to read that scary stuff for?" She shrugged her delicate shoulders. "I love it, though."

"Me, too." More than she would ever know. Yep, this could end up very bad.

"Really?" she asked, her eyes going wide and finally meeting his. "I love it. Horror, mystery, suspense. Anything that keeps me guessing."

His smile was genuine for once. "You aren't one of those obnoxious people who guess the ending all the time, are you? And ruin it for everybody else?"

"Of course not. And if I can guess the ending, then the author isn't trying hard enough."

He shouldn't ask. He knew he shouldn't. "What about him?" he asked, nudging his chin toward the book. As he waited for her answer, his stomach did a slow roll that brought on a surge of nausea.

Maybe it was a sign of weakness, but it wasn't every day that he got to meet one of his fans. Okay, he'd never done it on *any* day. Except for his agent, and then his editor, Tate had never spoken face-to-face with someone who enjoyed his writing. They were professionals. True fans were a little different.

Willow was his first.

Luckily she didn't notice anything unusual. "Oh, Adam Tate is one of my favorite authors. He combines historical facts with suspense and supernatural horror elements. All of the books are set in famous places where major events have happened, with all these fascinating details. And he's pretty accurate, I might add."

"Oh?"

"Yep..." The smirk on her lips drew his gaze. "I'm a history teacher. Remember?"

"Right!" But Tate was having trouble concentrating.

The excitement on her face was utterly fascinating. Why was he doing this to himself? "And the stories keep you guessing?"

"Definitely." She frowned, wrinkling her normally smooth forehead. "Tate, are you okay?"

He swallowed against the nausea. "Of course. Why?"

"You look funny."

Uh-oh. "No. I'm fine."

He turned back to the table. Reclaiming his seat, he forced himself to keep his gaze trained on his plate.

Luckily, Willow didn't say anything else. A minute later he heard the door open, then close. He'd probably offended her by abruptly cutting off their conversation. It was the best thing, though—keeping her at arm's length.

Now he knew he had even more he needed to keep from her. He'd never shared his pen name with anyone except his publisher. Even his parents hadn't known. Tate hadn't sought publication until after they had both passed away. Writing was Tate's one pleasure left in this world—the only indulgence he allowed himself.

Besides, if Willow ever knew the real him, the real secrets he hid, she would hate him. Just like his parents had. And it had been every bit deserved.

He glanced out at the sea crashing on the beach within sight of the house. It was his anchor, his reminder. Not in a good way. Oh no. The sight of it, the sound of it beneath the house's foundation, was an eternal reminder that pleasure was something he didn't deserve. Neither was friendship, love or fulfillment. His brother would never have any of those things…so neither would Tate.

He'd been fine with that until Willow came. His parents had never forced him outside of his self-imposed prison—probably because they agreed with him. Oh, they'd never come out and said it. But he knew.

After all, they'd lost two sons that day, all because

of his selfish pride. Adam. Then Tate. After that, they'd stayed away more than they were home, though, so Tate hadn't had to come face-to-face with their accusations often. Murdoch had simply followed in his mother's footsteps, never questioning Tate's decision or boundaries.

But Willow did.

Tate turned back to his plate, trying to concentrate on the food. Normally it wasn't a problem. Willow was a great cook. Most of the food was simple and hearty, but delicious. Today, though, too many thoughts distracted him.

Out of the corner of his eye, he saw a movement out the window. A movement that didn't belong to the normal sway of the sea grass and barren tree limbs. Turning his head, he caught sight of a slim figure crossing the sand toward the water.

No!

Willow carried her plate and book, along with what looked like a small blanket. So benign. So innocent. Walking right into dangerous territory.

Tate stood, his heart pumping as fear tried to take hold. *Don't go near the water. Don't get any closer.*

To his relief, she spread the small blanket well away from the water line. But his heart didn't stop racing, even though she picked up her paperback and started to read. Every so often she'd put some food in her mouth. Tate's lunch sat forgotten and cold on the table. He couldn't take his eyes from her, afraid of what might happen if he moved away.

Twenty minutes later, just as he'd come to accept that she was okay, she set the book on top of the already-finished plate.

She'll pack up and come inside. She has to.

Only she didn't. Leaving her stuff there, she dug her bare feet into the sand as she stood. Stretched. Tate's hands curled into fists.

Don't. Don't do it.

Defying his mental commands with just as much attitude as she showed when defying his verbal ones, she took step after step toward the water's edge. Tate pressed his palms tight against the glass, not sure whether he was actually yelling or if the sound was simply reverberating in his head.

Completely oblivious to his shouts and banging on the window, Willow paused to inspect something in the sand before continuing forward. His voice went hoarse with the strain. He was caught in a slow-motion nightmare despite the daylight.

As her delicate toes met the edge of the rushing water, images flashed through Tate's mind of a young man built strong and utterly familiar with that beach. A young man who rushed the waves as Tate watched from this very window twenty years ago. He had run against the tide until knee-deep, then dived under the incoming waves, seeking the exercise that would cool his anger.

His strong-armed stroke through the choppy sea had been Tate's last glimpse of his brother.

As Tate stood at that same window, his body replayed the terror and fear that had filled him in those last moments of his brother's life. He couldn't block it out, couldn't ignore it. He simply pressed the heels of his hands hard against the glass as he endured. Sweat broke out on his brow. His stomach churned. Desperately his mind sought a way out of the maelstrom. And then it came to him. A whisper at first. A tendril of peace that grew until it formed a hazy wall between him and the tragedy in his mind.

The feel of a woman. A body close against his, the contradiction of contentment and excitement when waking wrapped around Willow. In this memory there was no dread, there was no pain. Nothing had ever done that for him before. *No one* had ever done that.

A different kind of adrenaline rushed against the current inside him, redirecting the river of pain in his memories. Building, turning the tide to an energy Tate didn't want to acknowledge, but truly couldn't resist.

Suddenly he was running out of the house and through the rough sand to Willow. The feel of the grains against the soles of his feet brought back thoughts of another panicked run to the water's edge. Forcefully he blanked his mind and focused on the woman knee-deep in the water ahead of him.

He had to reach her. He would reach her. He would save her.

His low growl carried to her on the wind. Just as he reached the water's edge, she glanced over her shoulder. Surprise opened her features but couldn't save her. Her sudden surge deeper into the water was no match for his long stride.

Somehow he found his arms around her waist. Without further thought he lifted her, draping her waist across his shoulder. His instincts brought his arms across her thighs, pinning her to him. On the outer edge of his consciousness he could hear her protests, but they didn't register. All he knew was that he had to get her away from the water.

And he had to be close to her.

He slashed back out of the surf. He stomped back across the sand. Now the memories couldn't reach him. His emotions were too strong. He embraced the surge of adrenaline and desire, letting it overtake his primal mind and crowd out the painful images that lurked in the shadows.

He followed a different wave this time, the wave of instinct that drove him to her. He carried her through the door and into the kitchen. Deft movements pulled her back upright and plopped her bottom onto the marble top of the kitchen island.

He recognized the look on her face as one that many a professor over the years had adopted. A *what the hell do you think you're doing?* expression that many people get when working with freshmen at college. Only this time Tate was the one in for the reprimand.

"What the heck was that?" Willow demanded.

Honestly he thought she showed remarkable restraint, but language wasn't a working function of his brain at the moment. He couldn't talk about this right now. Instead he acted.

He buried his hands in that thick auburn hair and pulled her forward until their mouths met. Her body went still against his. Not stiff, but still, expectant, waiting for what was to come. As if she had been waiting for this moment just as much as he had.

Deep inside Tate searched for a thread of restraint, but it was now out of his reach. His mouth opened over hers, his tongue plunging deep. Taking what he wanted, taking what he needed. No more words. Only every ounce of what she could make him feel.

Six

Willow's rational brain demanded an explanation. After all, this was the least professional behavior that she could imagine. Being slung over her boss's shoulder like he was a caveman carrying her back to his cave was completely inappropriate.

If utterly thrilling.

But the anger and determination on his face when he reached her in the water had nothing to do with his being her employer. Frankly, the emotions on his face had been so intense as to scare her.

Then he carried her back here and kissed her more thoroughly than she'd ever been kissed before. She should have resisted. But all too quickly the feel of his mouth against hers drowned out all logical thought. Until the only thing left was her body's desire to pull him closer. Her mouth's desire to take all that he was willing to give.

Suddenly she felt the light scrape of his nails down

her back through her thin shirt. Shivers radiated out from the contact. Without permission, she began to squirm on the marble countertop. Tentatively she stroked her tongue over his.

With a low growly noise, Tate clutched her closer. Her breasts crushed against his chest. His firm hold allowed him to rub against the front of her body. Somehow her knees had parted and Tate now stood between them. The ache at the apex of her thighs told Willow she wanted him closer, then closer still.

No thoughts intruded on the fiery lick of passion. No recriminations nor regrets. Only the driving need for this man, unlike anything she'd ever felt before. Willow wasn't led by her passions. Instead her brain normally ruled the roost, yet somehow in this moment it had taken a permanent vacation.

The whole lower half of her body throbbed. No matter what was going on here, she only wanted to experience the feel of Tate against her once more. And the feel of him inside her for the first time.

He must have wanted the same, because suddenly there was a whoosh of fabric and her thin cotton top was cast aside. Clad in only her underclothes and a light skirt, Willow should have felt self-conscious. Instead she was all too glad when Tate's strong hands explored her heated skin. She clutched him closer as his fingers roughly explored the muscles in her back before making deft work of her bra clasp.

Only then did he allow even a hint of space between them. Their moans filled the kitchen as Tate slid her bra up so he could massage the firm mounds of her breasts. The feel was exquisite, causing her nipples to tighten. Greedy, she wanted more, but couldn't find the words to ask.

Tate seemed to be in too much of a hurry to ask, too. Just as he had with her shirt, he burrowed his hand beneath her skirt. The rough glide of his calloused fingertips against her thighs made her gasp. Sparks radiated from the point of touch to sensitize the skin all over her body. He didn't slow down until he found his way blocked by the elastic edge of her panties.

Then he stilled. The only sound in the room was the mingling of their harsh gasps for air. Though how Willow could hear even that over the pounding of her blood in her ears was a miracle. The last thing she wanted was to face reality, but the longer Tate refused to move, the more self-consciousness crept in. The more Willow became aware what she was doing was a big mistake.

Tilting her head back, she forced her eyelids to open. The face before hers was a frozen picture of anguish and need. Tate's classic dark features were a study in the struggle he obviously felt. Suddenly his jaw clenched hard. Down below, his fingers dug into the sensitive juncture between her thighs.

After long moments, he finally tilted his head down. When his eyes opened, she gasped at the intensity of the passion within their dark depths. Even as his mouth returned to hers, blotting out reality, his fingers grasped her panties and tore them with a harsh tug.

Her core melted as he jerked her forward to the edge. The V of her legs left her exposed and vulnerable. Not for long. She felt a vague fumbling between them, then Tate stepped forward those last few inches. His big body forced her legs even farther apart, but there was no time to feel vulnerable. Instead a determined exploration of his fingers gave way to blunt pressure at her core. Her body resisted for long moments, moments that reminded her just how long it had been since she'd accepted anyone into her body this way. A slight pumping motion helped him gain headway, spreading her juices over the smooth head of him.

One hand snaked behind her, pulling her closer, gaining him access. He buried the other in her hair. His mouth covered hers, his thrusting tongue mimicking the movements of his lower body. Willow's mind overloaded on bliss. The repeated thrusts conquered every inch of her passage, stretching her tight. Friction sparked electricity that tingled in her nipples and tight nub. She cried out with every stroke, her hands clutching his biceps. Urging him closer, faster, harder.

His entire body pressed up and then back. The feel of him saturated her consciousness from her thighs to her palms to her breasts. She sucked his hot, masculine scent deep into her lungs. Each thrust brought him close enough for her to press her lips against his neck and taste the steamy essence of the Tate he'd hidden from her all this time.

With a roar, he ground against her. The hard pulse of him inside her caused her own ecstasy to explode. They strained against each other, draining every last ounce of pleasure they could draw from the connection.

Until neither of them could do anything but gasp and groan.

Only long moments later did Willow become aware of the change in Tate's body. He stiffened, and a half groan, half self-deprecating choke came from his throat.

Reality had returned in an instant.

Unfortunately it found Willow with her naked bottom on her employer's kitchen island and no dignified way to extract herself from this situation. Because that wasn't a sound someone made when they were happy and satisfied. Oh no. At least he hadn't removed all of her clothes, so she had that small dignity.

"That was incredible…" Tate groaned.

What? Just as Willow relaxed, he went on. "Incredibly stupid."

All the tension of the last few minutes coalesced into a ball of nerves setting up a protest inside her stomach. Without thought, Willow pushed hard at his arms. Tate released her immediately, not trying to contain her. He backed up willingly, with no protest.

Willow slid from the high counter with difficulty, struggling to keep her skirt down out of a belated sense of modesty. Then she backed slowly away, step by step. She fumbled with her bra, struggling to get it back down over her breasts. Her mind, heart and body were too caught up in turmoil to even form coherent thoughts.

She couldn't look up at him, not even when he whispered her name. Her back bumped against the door frame, and she fumbled behind her for empty space. A quick glance at his face revealed the same wide-eyed surprise mixed with chaos that she felt inside. But she didn't stick around to share.

Acting completely on instinct she threw herself out the door, racing for the staircase.

Well, that hadn't gone according to plan.

Tate's goal had been strictly professional behavior. He'd been aiming for almost cold, almost impersonal. How he'd gotten from that to his current conundrum was a complete mystery to him.

A combination of dismay and satisfaction swept through him as he glanced down to see the ruined remains of Willow's panties on the floor. Chauvinistic though it may be… Hypocritical though it definitely was... Tate had to acknowledge the heat that rekindled inside of him with the knowledge that he would keep that small reminder.

He picked up the scrap and slid it quickly into his pocket, as if it didn't really happen if no one saw him. Then he circled the island to clean up at the sink. He didn't want to think about what had occurred. And he didn't want to think about how much he wanted the proof that it had.

It wasn't until he held the towel in his hand with his unbuttoned pants still around his hips that he realized something was very wrong.

The adrenaline that coursed through him now was true panic—pure and simple. As he turned and raced down the hall and up the stairs, he clenched his hands against the unwanted emotions.

I can fix this. I can fix this.

He stormed through the door into Willow's bedroom, only to find it empty. So much chaos churned inside him that for a moment he couldn't grasp the fact she wasn't there. He crossed to the bathroom door, only to find just enough self-control not to blow it off its hinges. Pressure built inside as he pounded on the wood separating him from Willow. The bitter taste of regret flooded his mouth.

"Willow!"

Just when he thought about breaking the door down, he heard the click of the latch. The door swung open on a woman whose auburn hair was in disarray and red-rimmed eyes burned with fire. Tate refused to register with that might mean.

"What the hell—" she started.

"We made a mistake."

Apparently that was the wrong approach.

"We?" One brow arched high as she glanced down at his crotch. Her sharp tone brought him up short.

Old instincts immediately kicked in—a lifetime of protecting himself against the aggression of others. It was the way his family had operated since the beginning, from what he could tell. The turmoil and uneasiness of this unusual situation gave Tate permission to slide right into the comfortable role.

"If you think this is all on me, you're mistaken," he asserted. "I didn't hear any protest from your direction when I had you on the kitchen counter."

A bright pink flush started at her neck and quickly spread up and over her cheeks. Tate actually felt the urge to step back. He didn't know Willow as well as he should, but he had a feeling that was a very bad sign.

But she didn't yell as he expected. Instead she set him straight through teeth clenched so tight she'd have a headache later, he was sure.

"Are you seriously banging on my door so you can make sure I know this was my fault?"

Her escalating volume urged him to move, to speak, do something. He opened his mouth, but she didn't give him a chance to defend his stupidity.

"I *did* protest," she insisted. Striding forward, she actually crowded him back across the room. And he was gentleman enough to let her...this time. "Long before we ever got to the kitchen. All the way back to the house. *You* are the one who wouldn't listen. *You* are the one who pulled the caveman act."

"*You* shouldn't have gone in the water. It's off-limits for a reason. You should have known that."

Willow cocked her head to the side. "Let me get this straight...all of this happened because the ocean, the very body of water that surrounds this island, that this house is actually built on, is *off-limits*?"

The rising anger in her voice and the use of air quotes edged her into dangerous territory. The redheaded temper was a real thing. A lifetime of fighting back urged Tate to retaliate, but he had just enough intelligence left to realize he'd get nowhere. He had to calm her down before she'd listen.

Unsure of his next move, he simply let her blow off steam.

"I protested plenty while slung over your shoulder, he-man." She poked his chest with a short finger. He let her because he was not proud of that behavior now, outside of the haze of desire. "You are the one who kissed me, remember?"

Finally Tate grasped her hand. Without intending to, he curled his fingers around hers until some of her stiffness melted. Quietly he admitted, "I remember."

How could he forget? The taste of her, the smell of her. He would swear everything about Willow was designed to be his own personal kryptonite. He didn't want to notice how her breasts moved with each breath, or how full her lips were after she'd kissed him. So why did he?

And the situation they were in now was the very reason he needed to stay far, far away. He released her and deliberately moved closer to the door, to freedom.

"Look, I didn't come here to make accusations or blame you for what happened."

"Could have fooled me."

Tate tamped down his instinct to tear into her. She didn't deserve that. And he was better than that, better than his ingrained family traits. "We have a problem, Willow."

"I'm sure you do."

Tate was done with the hysterics. It was time to figure this out, to find a solution. He looked her straight in the eye with a stern expression.

"Willow, I didn't use a condom."

Seven

Tate would hate for her to lock herself in the bathroom again. But Willow couldn't find it in herself to care. She needed time to process how to fix the mess they'd landed themselves in. As far as she was concerned, the conversation was over when he harshly insisted on knowing if she was on birth control.

As if that demand was the response she'd been expecting after the most incredible sexual experience of her life.

She also didn't expect him to go away and leave her alone, but that's exactly what he did. After half an hour of silence, she poked her head out of the bathroom to find her bedroom empty, the door closed.

Miracle of miracles, as Auntie would say.

Willow flopped down on her bed, but her body remained tense. She was waiting for Tate to come barging in again. She couldn't think about the lack of a condom, or the possible consequences.

Instead she focused on the practical. What should she do now? Leave? Stay?

Facing Tate every day after making love to him and pretending it never happened wasn't something she could handle. Knowing he saw it as a mistake, a complication, when she'd experienced something far different would be unbearable...

No, she couldn't stay.

She allowed herself the luxury of a few tears before dragging herself from the bed. The pounding headache brought on by the rapid flux of emotions only added to her misery. But she forced herself to start opening drawers and emptying them onto the bed in neat little piles. She'd go home...even if that was the immature thing to do.

After about an hour, she heard steps approaching from Tate's wing. He paused outside her door.

She stared at the handle, anticipating the turn. The nerves tightening her stomach only made her headache worse. There was almost a feeling like any noise from her would cause him to barge through that door. She didn't dare move. But long minutes later he continued on, leaving her to collapse on the last available space on her bed in relief.

She'd just started to drift off when the sound of a motor disturbed her. It was so unusual on the island that her foggy mind struggled for a moment to identify it. Dragging her weary body to the window, she saw Tate drive the house's Jeep out across an unknown path instead of down the drive. From Murdoch's notes, she knew the unfamiliar road led to the airplane hangar on the other side of the island. For some reason Murdoch hadn't explained, Tate didn't take the car on the rare occasions he left the island. His only method of transport away from Sabatini House was his plane. Murdoch had used the Jeep to handle all of the travel to Savannah for household necessities.

Was Tate going to blow off steam by working on his plane? Or fly for a while, the way some people would go for a drive? Her answer came about thirty minutes later when she heard his four-seater plane take off. She reached the window in just enough time to see it lift over the trees, curve in a graceful arc, then disappear out of her line of sight.

Where was he going? Especially this late in the evening. But Willow was too tired to figure it out. Instead she sprawled on her bed next to her packed suitcase and let sleep obliterate all the questions and her headache.

When she woke, darkness had fully arrived and the clock said it was just after eight at night. Somehow she knew Tate wasn't back, but she padded out to the garage and confirmed the Jeep wasn't there.

As she walked back to the house and glanced up at its grandeur, even in the darkness of the summer night, her heart spasmed. In all the drama, she'd forgotten one of her main reasons for coming to Sabatini House.

The third floor.

She rushed back inside. Why, oh why, had she fallen asleep? She needed to find the keys.

Where had Tate gotten them from the other day to let the workmen up to the third floor? The utility room off the kitchen. She remembered seeing him come out of there. She only hoped he'd put them back where he got them from and not dropped them in his office or something.

After fifteen minutes of searching the drawers, she opened the cabinet and found a pegboard with several sets of keys. She quickly grabbed the one marked Third Floor, then rushed for the stairs.

As she worked the key into the lock, she glanced to the side to see an open door. Light from the hall showed letters stenciled onto the wall. Not a poem or a quote, but the ABCs.

Like for a nursery.

She shouldn't open the door. She really shouldn't. But still she reached out to push it back, letting the hall light spill into the darkened room.

She flipped the light switch, but only a single bulb in the huge room lit up, leaving lots of gray shadows clouding the space. Gorgeous built-in bookcases with filigreed edges lined one wall. The shelves were filled to the brim with hardback books, but no pictures or personal memorabilia. Large toys that would now be considered antiques were scattered throughout the open space. Some of it was covered like the furniture downstairs, but she could make out a couple of handmade rocking horses, a large wooden playhouse shaped like a pirate ship and two tricycles. An open chest under one window overflowed with painted building blocks. Bins marked Toys or Clothes were stacked in one corner, partially concealed by a tarp.

Willow wandered farther in, fascinated by the abandoned nature of the space. Even though it was filled with stuff, there was no sense of any of the occupants who had previously lived and played here. Even though the items were personal in nature, the arrangement was more of a storage area. Yet some things looked as if the owner had simply walked away from them one day. Weird.

She passed a large oversize bassinet filled with neglected stuffed toys. Involuntarily, she rubbed her hand over a fluffy elephant dressed in a sailor suit.

The sight that stopped her short was a crib. No, not one crib. Two cribs, pushed together so their sturdy hand-carved railings almost touched. She stared for a moment, trying to figure out the puzzle. A quick glance into a second open area of the room revealed two twin beds and dressers on opposite walls. The beds were neatly covered with navy comforters decorated with sailboats. As if someone had simply gotten the children up, made their beds and walked out yesterday, except for the layer of dust covering them and more boxes lining the wall.

From what she could tell, Sabatini House hadn't had children in it since, well, Tate. Had it? Crossing to one of the dressers, she picked up a simple photograph, the only one she could see in the entire space. For having so much stuff, the room was oddly stark. No family photographs lining the mantel: no baby pictures, no cute little bathtub photo ops. Were the mementos all packed away?

Only this single framed photograph still remained. She rubbed the dusty glass to get a better look. It had been taken in a photography studio and showed two little boys in smart white sailor suits with navy decorations. Two dark-haired, dark-eyed boys with the same full, definitively shaped lips as Tate's.

"What are you doing in here?"

Willow twisted around to find Tate behind her, his face tight and menacing.

"Tate! You scared me."

Something about being in this room, seeing everything that had meant so much to him and his brother, and knowing the eventual outcome, deepened the darkness of his mood.

"I told you to stay out of the rooms." He almost said she knew the rooms were off-limits, but the last thing he wanted was to bring back the memory of her teasing him about the use of that phrase.

Thoughts of their lighter moments, thoughts of the easily lit attraction she held for him, made him want to rage at the universe. As if he hadn't martyred himself enough, the world saw fit to bring him this incredible temptation. He knew good and well he was supposed to look and not touch. As usual, touching hadn't turned out so well, had it?

Not realizing just how dangerous he was, she quickly fired back.

"Actually," she said, adopting the stubborn look that made her sparse spattering of freckles stand out. "You told me to stay out of the third floor. I'm not on the third floor."

"Touché."

He stared directly at her, almost afraid of what he'd find in this room. He probably hadn't been in here in a good five years if not more. Though it was easier than going into his brother's last bedroom.

But that door was currently locked, unlike this one.

When she raised her brow, Tate knew he'd stretched the moment too long. Forcing himself to glance around, he noted as if for the first time that everything had been stored in sets of two. A dead giveaway. Had she divined his secret already?

"And what did you find so interesting in here?"

She hesitated only a moment before answering. "Honestly, it's hard to imagine Sabatini House with a nursery." Her voice softened as she, too, looked around, the framed photograph in her hand forgotten for the moment. That was one thing Tate refused to acknowledge.

"It should be. The Kingstons have never been well-known for their softer side."

"What do you mean?"

Her voice seemed to come from the very shadows of the room. Under normal circumstances, the last thing Tate would do was indulge her curiosity. But maybe letting her in on some of Sabatini House's secrets would be for the best. She should know exactly what this family was like—it would help win her over to his way of thinking regarding the encounter they'd had in the kitchen.

"Every last one of us was born from the loins of a pirate. Not the well-known kind here in Savannah. Not the watered-down version who loved to drink, enjoyed women, and roamed the seas far and wide. Oh no."

Tate swallowed hard, stomach churning as he contemplated his heritage. "We come from the bloodthirsty, ice-cold kind. The kind that roamed the seas to kill for sport, to take what didn't belong to him. For my ancestor, that included his wife, who belonged to someone else."

He wasn't sure why he smiled. Surely the expression looked as grim as he felt. "He brought her here to this island and started his dynasty, determined to be the best in the shipping industry that was rapidly growing. He wanted to be a respectable man—but had not-so-respectable practices. He was ruthless and went after anything he wanted, staying just on the right side of the law. He was exceptional at not getting caught.

"His wife gave him three sons, a single and a set

of twins. Each generation since has had another set of twins. My brother and I were identical."

"Where is he?" she asked, her voice barely more than a whisper.

"Adam is dead," Tate said starkly, "and it's all my fault."

"Why?"

He liked that she didn't protest…didn't throw out platitudes to try to make him feel better.

"Because I did what we always do. I took what I wanted without caring how he felt about it. And he died. I lived."

His father and grandfather would have called that survival of the fittest. Tate saw it as perpetuating the bad things in the world…drowning out the good.

The atmosphere in the abandoned room drew out his next words. "Some days I wonder if the universe took him on purpose. Regardless, his death taught me something. There will be no marriage, no children, no future for me. When I die, this family is done."

He stubbornly shook off whatever hold the memories had over him and focused hard on the woman in front of him. "That's why I want you to take this." He pulled a flat packet from the back pocket of his jeans.

Willow squinted in the dim light. "What is it?"

"A morning-after pill."

Even in the shadows he could see her eyes go wide, exposing the whites. "Are you serious?"

"As serious as possible." She needed to understand the gravity of the situation.

"I'm sorry, Tate. I can't."

He didn't get mad, didn't rage. But she'd soon learn he could be as stubborn as her.

The emotions inside him urged him forward, deliberate steps that carried him closer until he loomed over her. "Then you will stay here until you see why this is necessary. Because the Kingston family ends with me."

Eight

Unease over the whole situation stalked Willow, leaving her to toss and turn in her bed the entire night while she tried to think through her options. Morning did not find her happy or any closer to a decision. Tate's stoic, almost silent pressure didn't help.

After his declaration, she'd expected him to badger her into doing what he wanted ASAP. Instead he'd rarely said a word to her today. He simply watched her, but that pointed gaze spoke everything he wouldn't say out loud.

If he'd known anything about her—which she was starting to doubt—she was a woman with a need to know. She liked facts, history and knowledge for its own sake. If Tate thought she was swallowing a pill without any other information, he was sadly mistaken. She simply wasn't sure how to tell him this. The reasons were pretty private. And though she'd shared her body with him, Tate's arm's-length attitude didn't encourage her to share her thoughts.

Dates had been few and far between for Willow. She was a little too bookish for most men, or so she gathered. At least compared with the party-hearty college students she was surrounded by on a daily basis.

Few dates meant even fewer sexual partners, which was why she'd never bothered taking a birth control pill. Why mess with Mother Nature if she wasn't bothering anyone?

Willow had always insisted on a condom before because she was practical, after all. The fact that she'd never even thought about it with Tate left her deeply dismayed. What had happened between them was different, far more explosive than she'd ever experienced with the few other men she'd allowed that close.

Considering their current stalemate, she couldn't believe that part of her wanted to repeat the experience. But the fiercely passionate and possessive Tate had been so much more dynamic than the one staring balefully at her across the kitchen island the next morning. Or should she call it the scene of the crime? She'd never see this kitchen quite the same again.

Not that she would be seeing it again. Not if she had anything to say about it.

"I'm not arguing with you. You're not leaving."

She glanced over at the suitcase she'd brought down from her room. "Tate, I think it's for the best. This is… uncomfortable."

"It won't be forever."

His brutal disregard made her temper flare and face flush, but she clenched her fist to regain control. "I won't be bullied, Tate."

"Honey, if I was a bully, this conversation wouldn't

be nearly this civil. It really wouldn't be a conversation at all. Instead, I'm simply demanding you stay until we've come to a mutually agreed upon conclusion."

Though the words sounded conciliatory, Willow had a feeling he still meant his way or else. Why, oh why, had she let herself be put in this position?

He stepped closer, bracing his hands on the island. She wouldn't think about what had happened on it just yesterday. Or how good it had felt to have him inside her. Since she now had to live with this churning chaos in her gut that wouldn't give her the answer that would fix everything.

"This is not a family you want to bring children into, Willow," he insisted, as if that were the only issue on the table. "My ancestors laughed while they ruined their competitors in business, took women they wanted without thought or permission, cheated their employees out of their wages. Hell—my parents weren't above using those same psycho games with their own children—pitting us against each other until one of us was dead. Not that they noticed he was gone."

Willow watched Tate wide-eyed, her attention snagged by the return of real emotions to his expression. She almost gasped from the intensity of his words and the anguish on his face. How did he live every day with all of that hidden behind his usual tightly controlled facade?

She was beginning to realize that was exactly what it was—just a facade.

"How did he die?" she whispered. For some reason, it was important for her to know. As if the answer was a key that would unlock the puzzle before her.

Tate's gaze flicked behind her to the window in the breakfast nook. For a moment she thought he would avoid answering her. Then she realized he was giving her a clue as he said, "In the same water you so innocently waded into yesterday."

Willow's chest tightened, cutting off her breath for a moment. She remembered dipping her toes into the cool, lapping waves. Heaven help her.

"We'd had an argument," Tate continued, his voice low and intense. "Adam went swimming—alone—to blow off some steam. He never came back."

His brother. His twin. How awful. She wanted to ask how it felt to lose someone who was literally the other half of you—but she didn't dare. Tate shouldn't have to relive the emotions, the pain. Though his expression told her he relived it more often than necessary.

His pain made her own heart hurt. She couldn't stop herself from reaching over the island to cover his hand with her own. "I'm so sorry, Tate."

His eyes widened for a moment, as if he didn't know what to make of this simple offer of comfort. Or, heaven forbid, he had never been offered comfort before now. What kind of family left a young man to suffer the guilt of his twin's death without trying to reassure him that it wasn't his fault? That he didn't make his twin go into the ocean alone, and certainly didn't cause whatever had led to his drowning, no matter how angry he'd been at the moment.

As a child she'd spent many nights crying over the deaths of her parents, but she'd been surrounded by a family that cared about her, talked through these things with her and helped her process the tragedy. Obviously no one had ever done that with Tate.

Sounded like he knew his family pretty well when he warned her about them.

He'd bared his soul to her...or as close as she'd imagined he could come to it. She at least owed him an explanation. "I don't just want to leave because of—"

She glanced down at the cool marble of the kitchen island. What should she say? *Because we had sex? Because you want to force me to do what? Prevent further consequences?* Her cheeks burned over all of those options, but she ignored her reaction. Maybe he would, too.

She noticed he'd dropped his dark, brooding gaze to the counter and his right index finger tapped heavily against the surface. Was he thinking the same things she was?

He didn't make her wait to find out. "Do you think I can't control myself? Is that why you want to leave? After yesterday's display, that's understandable. But I can keep my hands to myself—I assure you."

Willow didn't want him to, but that was a desire she would keep to herself. Instead, despite her embarrassment, she would suck it up and talk to him about her misgivings. She discussed difficult subjects with her students all the time...it was just easier because it wasn't personal. Still...she could do this.

"Tate, do you realize you are demanding I do something to my body that I have no clue about?"

He cocked his head to the side and frowned. She was fascinated how his entire face was involved when he let down his guard—brows lowering, eyes narrowing, forehead wrinkling. She usually had to search for clues about his emotional state.

"It's perfectly safe," he said.

Willow took a deep breath, choosing her words carefully. "I'm sure it is, but I don't know that—for certain. I've never looked into this—well, I've never needed to know before. But now I do." When he continued to look at her with that confused frown, she shrugged. "How does it work? What are the side effects?"

"Doesn't it come with all of that information?"

Was he really this dense? He looked genuinely perplexed, but she had to wonder. "Have you ever tried to read the inserts that come with medicine?" she challenged.

She could tell he hadn't but wouldn't admit it.

"Most of the words don't make any sense…and I have multiple college degrees."

"So, look it up."

His stubborn nonchalance had her slapping her hands on her hips. "On what, exactly?"

Comprehension finally dawned. She could see it come over his face like a sunrise. Without warning, Tate left the room, leaving her to fume over his lack of realization that she'd been taken back to the 1980s, technology-wise. Yes, they lived in an age where the most common way to find out what she needed was to search the internet. But she hadn't counted on being held captive in a house where the only computer was in his office—and thus, off-limits—and her Wi-Fi wouldn't work.

For an author, he sure hadn't thought this scenario through.

The sound of his footsteps allowed her to track his movements through the house. The tide was out for the day, muting the sound of rushing water that served as the soundtrack for everything here at Sabatini House. She lost track of him on the second floor, but heard the slam of his office door after a few moments.

It wasn't long before he came back to the kitchen with a small stack of papers, which he'd obviously just printed from the computer. He held them out to her. "Here you go."

She glanced down at the top page. The headline was about the medication followed by several paragraphs of text. Looked like she wasn't the only one overly fond of research.

She stood there, staring down at the papers, and realized how awkward this entire situation was. But now that most everything was out in the open, she felt better. Then she thought about all that he'd told her in the last day. "I'm sorry, Tate," she said, barely able to look up at him. "No one should ever have to grow up like that."

His expression immediately closed down. "If it's in my power, no one else will."

A few days later, Willow very casually picked up her covered plate and book, then headed for the outer door.

"Where are you going?" Tate demanded.

His gruff tone made her want to jump, but she wasn't about to give Tate an edge. She refused to meet his gaze just shot a smile in his general direction.

"I'm eating my lunch."

Then she confidently strode out the door. For the last several days, she'd silently insisted on returning to the beach to have her lunch every day. Tate never tried to stop her, but she could feel his gaze on her most of the time.

Some people would think she was simply torturing him, but Willow disagreed. From what she could gather, Tate had closed himself off from moving forward, based on his past. No more family. No more friends. No swimming, even though he was surrounded by the ocean. And no driving...though her suspicion that he feared going over the ocean bridge leading to the mainland was simply speculation at this point.

She wasn't going to get in the water again. No way

would she risk a repeat of her last little wade-in. And forcing him to see her in the water now seemed cruel. But there was no harm being on the sand. He needed to accept that and stop making demands and refusing to talk things out with her like adults.

Somehow she knew she could help Tate break free from the boundaries he'd let his past impose on him—but that meant she had to stay.

Of course, the tension was even higher now than when they'd had sex. And some tiny stubborn part of her refused to tell him she had finally taken the pill. But that was mostly his own fault. Once their last personal conversation was over, he'd retreated back behind the wall of cold professionalism. She knew it was for the best, but it didn't ease any of the heartache she felt.

Her pride—and to an extent, the female part of her that still wanted to be more than just his employee—insisted he had to come to her if he wanted an update.

But all the hyperawareness and tiptoeing around did make dinner with her family tonight a welcome prospect.

By the time early evening came around, Tate didn't stop her from leaving, but again she felt his watching her as she guided her little car down the drive. Her tension faded as she crossed the bridge to the mainland. When she arrived home, she was immediately comforted by the presence of her family. But she also found herself uneasy with all the secrets she was keeping from them.

"It's so wonderful to have everyone back here," Auntie said. "I miss having all of you under one roof."

Jasmine grinned at her as she settled her daughter into her high chair. "You see us almost every day when I drop off Rosie."

"And what am I? Chopped liver?" Ivy asked.

"It's not the same, though," Auntie said before she frowned at Ivy, who was the only one currently living at home, "and you spend all your time at work or in your room."

Ivy's creamy skin flushed when everyone looked her way. "I'm working a lot."

Willow sympathized. "Your boss still out of town?"

Ivy gave a short, stiff nod, but kept silent. Willow made a note to catch up with her younger sister in private.

"How's your job going?" Royce asked.

"Just fine," Willow replied. Maybe too quickly. "A little boring actually."

Jasmine narrowed her eyes, apparently not sold on Willow's lie. "Is Mr. High and Mighty off his high horse yet?" she asked.

"I'm not sure that's possible," Willow answered, giving a silly smile.

Everyone laughed, as she'd planned, but Royce's expression was serious when he added, "As long as you're okay."

She and Jasmine exchanged a look. It felt weird to have a man looking out for them, but in a nice way. "I'm good," she assured them, ignoring the hitch in her voice. Maybe Jasmine would, too, but Willow doubted it.

Later, when Royce took Rosie to the other room to clean her up and change her, Ivy finally opened up. "I have to find a new job."

"What?" Jasmine asked.

"Why?" Willow added at the same time.

Ivy's gaze met theirs in turn, her big beautiful eyes filling with tears. "I'm pregnant."

They each froze for a moment, shocked into silence. Then they all rushed from their various sides of the table to surround her, a wall of feminine comfort that would surely protect Ivy from the outside world.

Auntie was the first to offer a coherent question. "Honey, is that why you've been moping?"

Ivy grimaced. "That and I can't handle the smell of, well, pretty much anything." She glanced at the stove with its half-empty pots and pans.

All of them were aware of how this had come about, so there was no use asking silly questions like who the father was. Willow, sensitive from her own struggles with the man who was her employer, asked, "And he's never said—"

Ivy shook her head. "Not a single word. Every phone conversation since he left has been strictly business. After the first two weeks, I was afraid to bring our… night together…up myself. Now, I'm petrified."

For the first time, Willow was very grateful to Tate. She would not enjoy facing this. Their conversations might have been a strain and not gone in the direction she wanted, but she was glad they'd had at least that much.

"But you can't just walk out," Jasmine insisted. "You're having his baby."

Ivy's look was a little wild-eyed. "Do you seriously think he's up for this after a month and a half of silence? And what about his family? The McLemores are extremely close. There's no way they would accept me." She met each of their gazes in turn. "I've never talked about my family with him—for a reason."

Jasmine and Willow eyed each other for a moment. Willow's heart sank. Grudges lasted a long time in Savannah, especially within the upper classes. Sometimes over stupid, insignificant stuff. After all, rich people could afford to be a little eccentric.

But not this. Never this. Ivy's boss belonged to the

family that had run theirs out of town three generations ago. The McLemores. The fact that the Harden sisters' last name was now different due to their grandmother's marriage was the only thing that allowed Ivy to get her executive assistant job for the highly recognized Savannah shipping exec or allowed Jasmine to run an event planning business for Savannah's elite.

No one could immediately connect them with the family wrongfully run out of town after the McLemores' prize ship was torched, with their beloved son inside. But the McLemore family was still run by a matriarch who remembered those days all too well, and the Hardens had to be careful.

Being able to prove that their ancestors weren't responsible for that horrible tragedy would have given them a measure of protection. Willow felt a twinge of guilt over how little progress she'd made in her mission. Her struggles with Tate had taken up her every waking thought lately. The truth about their past would have helped so much in Ivy's current predicament.

Willow and Jasmine had advised Ivy not to take the job in the first place, but she had a deep desire to provide for herself after being taken care of by her sisters for so many years. It had been a huge promotion, and she'd excelled.

It had been well worth the risk—until now.

"You knew who he was. Why did you go home with him?" Jasmine moaned.

Ivy's eyes filled with tears. "I love him."

Willow was sure Jasmine's heart melted just like hers.

"I know—it's stupid and impractical. I thought, in hopelessly optimistic fashion, it would all work itself out." Ivy buried her face in her hands. "I was so naive."

They all were—to think they could mingle with Savannah's elite and never have their past revealed. Jasmine hugged her sister, offering comfort, but Willow was formulating a plan. Her own recent experiences in mind, she asked first and foremost, "Do you want to keep it?"

"Yes." Sincerity showed through Ivy's tears. "I just don't know what to do. If he wanted me, wouldn't he have said so by now?"

"Who knows what men think," Auntie said. Though her one husband was long deceased, she spoke with a note of experience.

Jasmine nodded. "They're supposed to be the less emotional sex, but their actions don't always make logical sense."

All people were influenced by their pasts, as Willow well knew. "The best thing for now is to get you out of that office before he gets back. Don't turn in your resignation yet. Just request time off through HR."

Willow knew Ivy had plenty of vacation time to cover a two-weeks' notice. The important thing was not to alert her boss that she was leaving before absolutely necessary.

She continued, "We'll worry about everything else later. Let me see what I can find at Sabatini House before we make any further decisions." Willow's mission had just turned from interesting to urgent.

"Thank you," Ivy said.

Then Willow saw her sister's normally porcelain skin take on a literal green tinge before she rushed for the powder room in the hall. Jasmine quickly followed.

Willow watched them go, momentarily grateful she'd swallowed that little pill.

Nine

Filled with determination after learning of her sister's plight, Willow didn't waste any time in searching Sabatini House further once she got back—only waiting long enough for Tate to get good and settled in his suite.

As she picked her way down the hall, she carefully avoided the areas of the floor she'd learned were creaky in an effort to make as little noise as possible.

The keys she had slid in her pocket when Tate had discovered her earlier now rested in her clasp. But as she approached the door to the third floor, she felt the pull of the nursery once more.

She justified her return by telling herself she could look for clues that she'd missed before—lame as that might be. The dual sets of toys and furniture still fascinated her, but she forced herself past them to the bureaus in the second part of the room. The miniature flashlight she used to get around the house at night helped her find and go through the drawers.

The first bureau held only clothes. The second was more interesting, though not helpful in her mission.

An entire drawer held loose photos of the twins—their mischievous grins and black curls making her heart ache. They all seemed to be professional shots rather than candid photos. And if she guessed right, the woman in the photos when the boys were babies wasn't their mother...she was too young. Maybe a nanny?

Willow slipped one of the pictures of the boys as teens into her pocket without thought.

The next drawer was filled to the brim with books—everything from picture books to Hardy Boys mysteries. Unlike the uniform hardbacks on the shelves, these were mostly paperback, tattered and worn. Had Tate's love of the written word started young? Had it served as an escape for him? For his twin?

A book in one of the right-hand stacks drew her eye. Willow picked it up and flipped through. It looked like a pictorial history of the Kingston family. Obviously handmade. Willow didn't take Tate's parents for artsy-craftsy types. Maybe the nanny had made this?

Unable to resist, Willow sank to the carpet and opened the book properly for a closer look. There weren't pictures in the front, but a story written in graceful, curvy lettering that described a pirate who came to the island, staked his claim and built Sabatini House—just as Tate had said.

It was the whitewashed version, of course. Whoever had written the book to teach the little ones their family history had kept the audience in mind.

Willow could relate. She remembered discovering their own family was descended from pirates. As children, she and her sisters would dress in long, oversize raincoats their mother had bought at the thrift store, tied with sashes, and spend long days pretending to fight with swords and walk the plank.

Their father had relayed stories of how their ancestor had established himself as a good man, stressing the importance of pride and respectability in their family.

Willow's research had born those stories out—theirs was a legacy of integrity for generations. She refused to believe those values had failed enough to allow her great-grandfather to burn down that ship.

But what about Tate's?

When Willow got to the part of the book with the actual photographs of Tate's ancestors, she could actually see some of the qualities he'd mentioned.

She was used to studying historical photos for her own research purposes—personal and professional. The progression of the camera and photo development technology was a familiar concept to her, but these images went beyond simply having to hold still for a long exposure.

Both the men and women were stern-looking, almost dour in most cases. But it was more about the look in their eyes—the hard way their gazes were trained on the camera. Aggressive, almost forcefully suspicious.

In the group shots, she could see the same manner in the children, who were always held by servants rather than a relative, giving the impression of a hands-off, impersonal form of childrearing.

Willow found herself holding her breath as she turned the pages, hoping to be surprised by a portrait with a more familial casual arrangement. But it never came.

There were only more stiff suits and strong postures and direct stares. Definitely not the friendliest group, even as the cameras had improved over time enough to not require the more somber expressions.

Which left Willow even more curious as to whether those unfeeling looks translated into the ruthless way of life Tate had described.

Had they feuded with the other local shipping barons? Had they settled one of those feuds with death and destruction? Murdoch had hinted that might be the case.

The chime of the grandfather clock in the upper hall jarred her. Time to move on. Willow dropped the book back into the drawer and gathered the flashlight. Back at the door to the third floor, she juggled the flashlight while trying to jiggle the key in the uncooperative lock.

Suddenly she heard a noise.

Unable to place exactly what it was, Willow strained to listen. She quickly flicked off the flashlight. Standing stock-still, she studied the darkness of the hall over her shoulder. She did not want a repeat of the last time.

When nothing happened, she turned back to the door. The decision had barely been made when the sound came again.

This time she could clearly hear a person's voice, though not what they were saying. Fear exploded inside her. A voice in the house could mean only one thing— Tate was awake.

Backtracking, Willow rushed to get back near her room while she listened out for the source, because she had no doubt now that someone was there. No way would she make it to the third floor tonight.

Sure enough, when she reached the door to Tate's suite, she heard a muffled voice. Was he on the phone? Not good.

At least he hadn't caught her first. He wasn't the type to retreat from a confrontation. So what was he doing?

Unable to quell her curiosity, she dropped the key and flashlight in her room, then crept back in the dark to stand outside his bedroom door.

She'd barely been there sixty seconds when she clearly heard a shout. She froze. It came again. Was he being attacked?

Willow rushed inside before giving herself time to think. A quick sweep of her gaze over the deep shadows of the room indicated she and Tate were the only ones here. He thrashed on the bed, throwing off his covers as he called out. As she crossed to him, hot memories of the last time she'd been in this room flashed through her brain. She didn't want to remember, didn't want to ache to have Tate's skin against hers once more. But the memories wouldn't completely recede.

She tried to focus on the present instead. The sadness and sympathy brought on by the combination of his earlier description of his parents and the pictures from the book pushed her forward until she could lay her hand on his brow.

He didn't have a fever, but she could feel the tremors that racked him in his sleep. Leaning forward, she started whispering nonsense the way she did to Rosie when she was sick.

It took several minutes, but eventually he began to settle down. He seemed to be sleeping deeply despite the ruckus, so Willow slowly pulled her hand back. Retreating was harder than she'd anticipated. She fought her natural desire to help and her ache to be close to Tate when his guard was down. Still, she forced herself away from him. Back one step. Two.

Just when she thought she'd get away undetected, she found herself grappled into a bear hug that cut off her breath and toppled her to the bed.

* * *

The nightmare slowly faded as Tate squeezed down hard on his pillow. Only his pillow felt flesh-firm and warm. The shaking he hadn't experienced in years slowly dissipated as his nostrils filled with a sweet vanilla fragrance. The scent mingled with the heat beneath his cheek. It seemed to surround him, hotter at the base of his neck and along the side of his temple.

He welcomed the invasion of sensation and scent. Anything would be better than reliving his brother's death over and over, but this moment was especially sweet. Somehow he knew that if he could focus on it, then the nightmare would fully recede.

Then he realized his pillow was moving…breathing. *Willow.*

Her presence didn't surprise him. He simply accepted it, welcomed it. He had just enough awareness to ask.

"Willow?"

"It's okay, Tate."

A shudder ran through his body. He clenched his fists as desire washed over him like a wave. In this one thing, he needed to be sure. "You know what I want."

"Yes…" she murmured, "and I'm still here."

Then the forceful surge of need inside his body drowned out all the questions. No thinking. He simply twisted until she lay flat beneath him, then buried his face against her neck.

It was the only bit of bare skin he could find—but it wasn't nearly enough. He nuzzled, eager to taste what smelled so good. He sucked in the vanilla-scented air. Would she let him eat her up?

The way she sunk her fingers into his hair seemed like an invitation. Tentatively he licked her. The taste was even better than he'd imagined. Warm sweetness. Musky woman. And something he could describe only as life.

He indulged in a slow glide of his tongue from the ridge of her collarbone up to the tip of her chin. His entire body pressed into her as he moved, craving complete contact. Her pulse throbbed beneath his tongue, picking up speed until he lost count of the beats. Her moans filled the air around them.

Never had he felt as alive as he did in this moment. Every stroke of his body against hers was both a relief and fuel for the fire. The blood pounded through him, his body demanding to take what it wanted. She arched into him as if she needed the same.

Tate lost himself in the sensations. He'd never wanted anyone like this before…shouldn't want her now. But logic seemed to have no influence over his body. He wanted her. He would have her.

Again.

Just as he moved to slip his fingers beneath the hem of her shirt, a deluge of emotions and anger washed over him. It was a realization that had propelled him through the last week of living with her. He couldn't take her again. That would be the utmost in stupidity.

But you have a box of condoms. Sure he did. He might have been convinced he would never have sex with Willow again, but he wasn't stupid. He'd bought condoms when he'd bought the pill. No way was he risking impregnating her. If he hadn't already…

His body throbbed hard, as if telling him he should take her any way he could get her. It was that primal urge to show the world that this woman was his. Only she wasn't. She could never be.

And it wasn't fair to lead her on just so he could satisfy his body's urges.

But this wasn't just about his urges. Her racing pulse wasn't the only clue as to how much she wanted him. Her gasps were enhanced by soft, sweet moans. Her hips lifted to cradle his. Her hands clutched at his forearms, pulling him closer instead of pushing him away.

All he had to do was press his mouth over hers and it would happen. He'd be slow this time, thorough enough to learn every inch of her curvy body. An experience neither of them would forget...

Which was why he forced his body back, pulled his mouth away from that delectable skin. He couldn't do this to himself, and he wouldn't do this to her. Words wouldn't come. He simply rolled to his feet and stood with fists clenched in an effort not to change his mind.

She lay frozen on the bed for a long moment. The only sound in the room was the two of them struggling for air. Was she confused? Afraid to provoke him? Working her way back to sanity right along with him? From the incredible response of her body to his, probably the latter.

Please let it be the latter.

Finally she propped herself up on her elbow. He could sense her gaze, even though he couldn't see more than a faint outline in the darkness of the room. This wasn't like the mainland. There wasn't any ambient light to turn the shadows gray. It was pitch-black, especially when there was only a sliver of moon like tonight.

"Are you okay now?" she asked.

Like the instant a match meets its striker, anger flared. At himself...for caving in to weakness. For letting the nightmare in. At her...for being the very thing he needed. For being the very thing he shouldn't have.

"You shouldn't have come in here," he said, his voice low and gravelly. The desire that burned so close to the surface transformed easily into the aggression he needed to keep himself from taking her. He didn't know how else to burn it off, so he let her be the object of his desire…and his rage.

He wasn't the only one who was angry. She shot up off the bed onto her feet. "I shouldn't have come in here? When I heard you yelling behind a closed door? Excuse me for caring."

"Why would you?" While he said it as a challenge, part of him truly wanted to know. He was fully aware of how callously he treated her. The constant hot and cold. Why would she care about someone like him being in pain?

"I have no idea." Exhaustion seemed to weigh her down. But she tossed one more retort over her shoulder as she made for the door. "Next time I'll just leave you to be strangled in your sleep."

"It would be better than the alternative."

She froze. His eyes had adjusted to the dark enough that he could see her stop, though he sensed the lack of movement more than anything. Her next words told him everything he couldn't see in her expression. "I didn't realize that being close to me was so repulsive. I'll do my best to help you avoid this situation in the future."

Her deliberate misconstruction of his statement only added fuel to his temper. "That would be helpful," he snarled. "It's all your fault. If you hadn't come here with all your questions and prying and stubbornness…"

He dropped onto the edge of the bed, grateful the pitch-black hid the moisture that welled in his eyes. Still he rubbed his palms against them for good measure. "I miss him. I'd blocked it out for years, remembering only what I had to and now—" he pounded his fist against the mattress "—this. I haven't had this nightmare in forever. Why did you have to come here?"

Despite his accusations, she edged closer. "It shouldn't stay locked away, Tate. He was your brother."

"He was my biggest mistake. Losing him should have marked the end of my life."

"No."

The pressure inside him reached explosive levels. "It has to," he yelled. "I can't live like this. With the memories and emotions and pain. I want to go back to being numb."

"But was that really living?"

Ten

I wonder what kind of mood His Highness is in today.

Willow knew she had an attitude, but it was beyond her to do anything about it. Tate might have finally pushed her past her limits. Either that or she had the worst case of PMS known to the history of womankind.

Still, the man was driving her nuts. As she climbed the stairs to collect the laundry from his dressing room, instances from the last few days played through her mind. Tate had literally skulked like a schoolboy after their last confrontation. Willow would know—she'd dealt with this type of behavior all the time in her freshman classes.

Tate should have grown up by now, but the isolated lifestyle he'd set up for himself kept him from having to evolve his face-to-face communication skills.

That was only her opinion, of course. Possibly influenced by her bad mood, but still justifiable based on his actions.

Several times each day, she asked herself why she didn't just leave. Or why he didn't send her away. She couldn't speak for him, but she still had things she needed to accomplish here. If she could just find the opportunity... Even though he spent so much time in his office, she was afraid to breach the third floor with him so close. She'd never been the person who got away with things. Somehow, she always ended up getting caught.

She had explored the entirety of the first and second floor rooms, though. Her lack of findings told her that what she really needed, if any evidence remained at all, was hidden in the historical wealth stored on the third floor.

She refused to let her sisters down. Willow had always been one to go the extra mile for others, even if she was too afraid to do something for herself. Maybe that's why she stayed. Having seen the man behind the angry facade, some of the pain and fear Tate carried around with him on a daily basis, Willow didn't feel comfortable simply walking away. Tate needed someone...even if he refused to admit it.

The sound of typing as she walked back past his office distracted her from her gloomy thoughts for a moment. Tate's bad attitude didn't seem to have affected his work. But the fact that she still didn't know what that work entailed only irked her further...

She carried the laundry down into the basement, none too eager to get any of her chores done today. The main drawback to living in was that her job didn't end. And she had a very difficult time justifying spending a couple of hours in bed with a good book when her boss could clearly see she wasn't working.

What she needed was a good night out with her sisters. Margaritas, chips and salsa, and lots of juicy gossip. That sounded like heaven right about now.

Especially after the brief, brittle conversation she'd had with Tate yesterday. She'd been cleaning up after dinner, looking forward to a night spent reading her newest novel once Tate retired to the isolation of his office, when she'd felt him pause behind her in the kitchen.

"Did you take it?"

Willow didn't pretend not to know what he was talking about, even though his question was short to the point of rudeness. He had a right to know.

"Yes."

To her surprise, he went still instead of immediately walking away. She turned to him, feeling that he wanted to say something more. It was an ethereal connection, as if they both wanted to acknowledge what had happened but didn't have the words to reach out to each other.

Then he left.

Willow sorted her loads and got the washing machine started, then shuffled her way back toward the stairs. Enthusiasm for the mundane tasks of her job had completely fled at this point. She couldn't quite figure out a way to resurrect it, except to continue her exploration of the house that had proved to be even more full of surprises than she'd anticipated. It just refused to give her the one piece of information she, and Ivy, desperately needed right now.

As she paused beside the door to the mythical underground cave—she refused to believe it was actually real until Tate let her see it in person—Willow leaned against the door and tried to let go of the unusual exhaustion that plagued her. The sound of the rushing waves soothed her. A swim would be nice, but she couldn't bring herself to do that to Tate right now.

Despite her current irritation.

As much as she resented his attitude the other night, she realized a lot of it was born of pain. He'd settled into a cocooned way of life that allowed him to keep the memories and emotions at bay. Until she'd started digging all that stuff out, dragging it into the open and forcing him to acknowledge it once more. That couldn't be comfortable. Some days she wondered if it was even safe. If she'd opened a Pandora's box she should have left alone.

But there wasn't anyone here to give her an answer to that. So she had to make her best guesstimate and move on. As much as she might resent his attitude, knowing where it came from made her want to stay, to see whatever this was through to the end.

She'd never been a quitter just because things got difficult.

Opening her eyes after long minutes of simply standing, breathing and listening to the waves, Willow was surprised to see a door toward the far end of the corridor that she'd never noticed before. Not all the way on the end, which she would have seen each time she entered the hallway. This was a slim door about three-quarters of the way down that occupied a shadowy area, in contrast to a bright patch of sunlight let in by the window right before it.

Sabatini House was full of all kinds of cool nooks and crannies. She'd found odd closets, weirdly shaped rooms and all kinds of architectural goodies that either came original to the house or had been modernized over the last few generations. So as she walked down the hallway, excitement lightened her step for just a moment. Even if it was just an empty room with a couple of spiderwebs, it would be interesting to see and speculate on its use.

Except, as she should have come to expect by now, the door was locked. She knew where the downstairs keys were and had never been officially told these rooms were off-limits. She huffed a little laugh as she ran upstairs to the utility room for the keys. She ran back down and in no time was turning the handle to get inside.

At first glance, the little room served as straight storage. Slightly larger than a walk-in closet, it was over three-quarters full of plain brown boxes, all uniform in size. That, in and of itself, struck her as odd. The house had a few rooms that housed old furniture and odds and ends. Her glimpse into the third floor had shown lots of trunks and cabinets and such. Even the nursery's contents were either covered with tarps or stored inside drawers.

But so far she hadn't seen uniform packing boxes like this anywhere else in the house.

So what made the contents of these so special? Taking a few steps closer, she could see that some had the tape broken on the top, but most of them had never been opened. Definitely odd. Willow reached for the nearest open box and pulled back the flaps.

Granted, the one lighting fixture in the small room didn't do a fantastic job, but even then she wasn't sure she was trusting her eyesight. Because all she could see was books.

Actually, multiple copies of the same book. *The Secret Child* by Adam Tate.

Willow wasn't sure how long she stood staring, trying to resolve what she was seeing with the truth it had to represent. No one was enough of a fan to have twenty-five copies of the same book. Publishers had those…and authors.

How could he have kept this a secret from her?

Just to make sure, she sped from box to box, checking to see that they were all the same. *The Red Light. The Encroaching Sea. The Third Floor.* All Adam Tate books. And with each title she read, excitement and irritation grew inside her. Finally she ran out into the hall, leaving the door open behind her. She rushed up the stairs and down the passage until she reached Tate's office door.

She felt vaguely surprised that the door wasn't locked, but couldn't stop long enough to analyze why that might be. Bursting through, she ran in a few steps before skidding to a stop before his large black desk. Tate stared at her in shock, mouth open, eyes wide. The same emotions echoed in her own mind, but she couldn't focus on him. Behind the desk were gorgeous floor-to-ceiling bookshelves that covered the entire wall. Light from the large, arched windows shone across the beloved titles that took front-and-center stage. If she wasn't mistaken, the shelves contained every Adam Tate title ever written, along with many other books by her favorite authors, what looked like nonfiction research books and several rows of white binders.

Her gaze swept across all of it in an instant, then back to the man who looked like he was still trying to process her presence.

"You jerk. Why wouldn't you tell me that you're Adam Tate?"

In shock, Tate reverted to his natural response. "What are you doing in my office?"

"Answer my question."

Her hands-on-hips stance did not bode well for brushing her off. "Willow—"

"We aren't talking about just any author here. You knew how I felt about those stories. You talked to me about his—your—books and just decided that it wasn't worth mentioning that you wrote them? Seriously?"

Frustration tightened Tate's muscles. Shutting down his computer screen, he shoved back his chair to pace around the room, pulling at hair that was way past the need for a haircut.

The sudden breeze reminded him of his open button-down shirt. He glanced at Willow, only to see her force her gaze from his abs back to the books.

"Tate, this is incredible," she said, waving her hand at the overflowing shelves. "Why would you keep this a secret?"

That had him raising a brow. "I'm a little bit of a privacy nut."

Her expression told him she was fully aware of that.

"Look, I'm not even sure how people found out I was an author. I never wanted it to be known. Making up stories is my escape. I don't want the recognition."

Willow shook her head. "But...you're Adam Tate. I'm a fan. I live here. Why keep this a secret from *me*? I mean, you know I'm not gonna turn into a creepy stalker, right?"

Looking up, he realized the true issues underlying this conversation. The point was not his secrecy, nor secrecy in general. The point was how he viewed her.

Tate had given her mixed signals since she first came to Sabatini House. A lot of them were twisted up in his own idiosyncrasies, as he fought against all the things she made him feel. She deserved better than that.

Now that he was truly looking, he could see the hurt

dulling those gorgeous green eyes. It shouldn't be there. He'd done his best to keep her at arm's length, but pulling her close was too damn tempting…and he was too damn weak.

They'd shared too much, more than he ever had with anyone else.

Oh, he and Murdoch talked, but unless they were both drunk the conversations were at best on the surface—just the way men liked it. The few serious discussions he could remember involved his parents' deaths and Tate's decision to clear out their stuff.

He and his editor were friendly, would have a meal together outside the office when Tate was in New York, but the conversation was either business or story, which they could discuss for days on end without tiring of the subjects. That was the way book nerds were. That was their bond. Neither of them attempted to bridge that gap, because that was how Tate wanted it.

But with Willow? They'd gone deeply personal. Fast. He'd not only shared his body with her, but his nightmares, his brother, his fears.

Now this.

As he watched her, there was no getting around the stubborn set to that tiny pointed chin, or the determined look in her eyes. He'd learned that much by now. He might as well fess up. Otherwise she'd find a way to drag it out of him.

That might not be pretty for either of them.

"Honestly, I'd never told anyone before. I very rarely meet new people who are interested in discussing what I do for a living. I'm not even sure how to bring it up."

And that was the God's honest truth.

Willow cocked her head to the side. "Well, it's time you got some practice."

Tate almost laughed. Leave it to Willow to be practical rather than sentimental.

"You're not a typical sympathetic kind of girl, are you?"

Willow shrugged, but lowered her lashes as she tried to hide her reaction. Tate had a feeling he'd hit a nerve.

"I feel just as much sympathy as anyone else," she said softly. "But sometimes that isn't what the situation calls for. I grew up in a house full of women. There's always been enough emotion to drown us all in it. Somebody has to be practical if we're gonna actually get moving."

Why did that attitude frustrate him while making him want to kiss her at the same time?

Tate was more than aware that she challenged him, was moving him away from his comfortable status quo to a new level. He shouldn't like her—should push her far away. Fire her, even.

So why was he still aching to do the opposite?

He watched as she circled the desk, her body moving with unconscious sensual grace that hit him right in the gut. It took everything in him to keep from reaching out.

Her long, delicate fingers stroked over the books' spines. "So who did you base the woman on in *The Train*? She was seriously creepy," Willow asked.

"No one," he answered automatically. "She's made up, though the story idea came from an article I read."

"Cool. About what?"

The conversation started just like that. Tate was honestly amazed at how easy it was to suddenly talk about his work. He'd never done it with anyone but his agent and editor before today. Why didn't he resent her intrusion? Rebuff her questions?

Because the whole thing fascinated him. He had to admit, her observations were insightful. Even as they moved on from his books to others on the shelf, Willow brought up points about the stories he'd never even thought of before today. Her brain worked in fascinating ways.

And that was how Tate found himself falling in love with the woman he should never want.

Before he had time to absorb the realization and panic, the house phone rang. Tate gratefully crossed to answer it.

"Hey there, young man," a familiar voice said. "How's today treating you?"

Murdoch's standard greeting was never more welcome. The familiar words had kept Tate grounded and focused on the present for years. Tate needed them now more than ever. "Good as always. And you?"

Tate's ears tuned in to Murdoch's tales of meeting his daughter as an adult, the new grandbaby and this whole new family he had found, but Tate's gaze couldn't be torn away from Willow, who took the liberty to explore his office while he was distracted. He should stop her from invading this last vestige of private space left to him, but her expressive face and the way she reached out to touch everything captured his imagination.

So much so that he lost the flow of the conversation. "I'm sorry, Murdoch. What did you say?" he asked, trying to catch up.

"I said, I hate to do this, boy, but I'm not coming back."

Eleven

Willow wasn't sure what the sound was that caught her attention, but she turned back from the window in the office to find Tate white-knuckling the phone. His normal olive skin was pale beneath the color. Willow had the distinct impression that his sheer will was the only thing keeping him upright.

She took a tentative step toward him. Then another. Tate wouldn't want sympathy, but she had the urge to hug him, just the same.

What was wrong?

When his eyes opened, even they seemed paler versions of themselves. He held out the phone.

"Murdoch wants to talk to you."

Though eager to catch up with her friend, Willow couldn't forget Tate's look, even after he turned away. With no answers from that corner, she jumped into the conversation headfirst.

"What's wrong?" she asked Murdoch.

A long sigh met her over the airwaves. "I'm sorry, Willow. I'd hoped this would be easier, but I couldn't wait much longer to tell him."

"Tell him what?" Willow's heart pounded in her ears while she waited for his answer.

"I'm not returning. My place is here, with the family I've finally found."

There was a long pause as Willow tried to muster a response. In the background of the call she heard the faint sound of a baby starting to cry.

"I have no idea how much time I have left, so I need as much time with them now as I can get," Murdoch continued. "I let my daughter down. I won't do it again…to her or the little one."

Willow certainly understood. From the first day she'd met him, she'd sensed the utter loneliness inside Murdoch. Finding out he had family out there, especially a daughter starting a family of her own, wasn't something he would turn his back on. She should have realized that as soon as he'd offered her this job.

"I know this is a shock to Tate, but I have to do it," Murdoch said.

At the mention of his name, Willow turned to see how Tate was doing, only to find herself alone in the room.

"Oh, Murdoch. What is he going to do?" She sighed, free to ask anything now that she was alone. That didn't stop her from worrying.

"I know this will be hard," Murdoch admitted. "But I've devoted my life to the Kingston family. Tate, in particular. He's the only one of them who deserved it, in my opinion." He paused, sighing. "But it's time to devote myself elsewhere, Willow."

She could sense he was trying to convince himself as

much as he was her. Bless his heart. "I understand that, Murdoch. It's what you need to do…what you should do. It will just be hard here."

"I was hoping having you there would make it easier."

Huh? "By giving me a summer job?"

"Is it just a summer job?"

Willow could hardly wrap her brain around what he was saying, but was actually surprised she hadn't suspected this before. After all, Murdoch could have easily hired a man for this position, since he knew all of Tate's issues firsthand.

"Murdoch, did you set me up?"

"Not you so much as Tate."

"You could have at least given a girl some warning." So Murdoch had had this in mind all along. Had he known the difficulties it would cause both of them when he'd played matchmaker? She wanted to ask if he was aware Tate didn't keep condoms on hand…but even she didn't have the gall to say that.

"Willow, you're the smartest, most insightful woman I know. Granted, I don't know many, but sometimes you just know things about a person. I knew without a doubt that if anyone could break Tate out of his self-imposed prison, it would be a woman like you." Silence filtered down the line for a moment. The baby wasn't crying anymore. "He needs you," Murdoch finally said.

No joke. Willow had known that from the beginning, though she hadn't been prepared for what breaking him out of his shell would entail. "But that doesn't mean he's ready for it, Murdoch."

"Or that it will be easy," he agreed. "I'm fully aware that Tate has some unhealthy boundaries in place. Hell,

I stood to the side while he planted the line and dug in deep. But he needs to let go. You can do that for him, Willow."

"No, I can't. Only Tate can make those changes for himself."

Murdoch wasn't budging an inch. "But he never will with no one to challenge him."

That got her ruff up a bit. "So you sent me here because you thought I would be difficult to live with?"

"In your own way." He chuckled. "Tell me you haven't shaken things up already."

"More than you know," she mumbled before she thought about the implications of letting that out into the open.

Murdoch grew silent for a long moment. She could almost hear him thinking, but she was afraid of saying anything further. Afraid of bringing her fears to life. After all, Tate wasn't the only one who was scared of something.

"Then I only have one question," he finally said.

"What's that?"

"Are you okay?"

No. She thought back over all the strange symptoms she'd had since taking the morning-after pill, all the ups and downs of her interactions with Tate, and her own fears about what Murdoch was telling her. She wasn't ready, was she?

"I'm really not sure."

"I'll tell you the two things I've learned since coming here, Willow." His voice was a deep mixture of happiness and regret. "One, love can make even the most fearful thing worthwhile. And two, nothing will ever make loving someone completely easy. You might never be ready...but you've got to take the leap sometime."

* * *

Tate sensed Willow's presence even before he heard her. He wanted to go to her, take her, but too much had happened. There was too much to process. Every inch of him, mind and body, felt oversensitized.

"It's not a good idea to be here," he said, wincing at the density in his voice.

He didn't want to scare her off, but the river of emotions and need bubbling up inside him were too deep not to find their way to the surface. Especially in the room that held such sexy memories of her. Where her scent still lingered on the pillow. His imagination could paint the perfect picture of her laid out on his bed in the heat of the afternoon sun.

She needed to stay far away from him.

But she didn't heed his silent warning. Instead she moved closer. "Murdoch needs to be with his family right now, Tate."

He waved off her words with a rough gesture. "I know that! I'm not a selfish teenager anymore, expecting someone to cater to my wants and needs."

If anything, her voice softened further. "That doesn't mean change isn't hard. That it doesn't spark resentment."

In the mirror, he saw her sink onto the edge of his bed. The sight of her vibrant beauty against the navy comforter drew his eye. But he refused to turn, knowing he'd do something rash.

"You know, Tate—" she said, tilting her head to the side. A wash of auburn hair swung into view. "I lost both of my parents when I was a teenager."

Shock froze Tate's entire body for several seconds. "You did?"

She nodded. "Both of them. Car accident."

Though she'd talked about going home for family dinners, Tate had never asked her whom she met with or any of the details. Normally functioning families weren't something he could relate to...in fact, very few of the characters in his books had them. He was more likely to kill off any close relatives or orphan the characters in some way. That isolated lifestyle was one he knew far more about than being part of a happy family.

"Congratulations on turning out far more normal than me," he said, only a touch of bitterness tainting his reply.

"Unlike you, I had a very loving family left even after they were gone. I have two sisters—one older, one younger. My little sister was still young enough to need extra care. We came back to Savannah to live with Auntie."

He shouldn't want to know, but he asked anyway. "Who is she?"

"Not a blood relative at all, actually. Auntie was my grandmother's best friend, and nanny to my mother when she was little. Though she'd moved back to Savannah, they remained close. She adopted all three of us girls and raised us like her own family, even though she'd never been able to have children of her own.

"So losing people I loved was a lot different for me than it was for you. None of that made it easy, just bearable. But if I had my sisters ripped away now, I don't know that I'd survive. They are my support system. I can't imagine losing them."

Tate's voice was raspy as he struggled to speak from tightening lungs. "What will I do?"

"I don't honestly know, but we'll figure it out."

Tate sensed her approach behind him and inhaled at the press of her body against his back, as if she were bracing him for the changes ahead. "Murdoch has been your family, even more than your blood family, for many years. It's okay to grieve," she said.

It had been one thing to have Murdoch leave for a while, hard to accept but doable. To know he wouldn't be coming back, would no longer be part of Tate's daily life... That was something for which Tate was completely unprepared.

Closing his eyes, Tate breathed deep and soaked in the heat of her against him. Oh so slowly, her arms moved up his sides to anchor her against his shoulders. Almost as if they were one, braced against the world. As much as he shouldn't want it, he couldn't turn away from the incredible feeling of her melding with him.

When the need grew too strong, he moved toward her instead. Chest-to-chest. Face-to-face. He buried his hands in that fiery hair. He had to have her, had to savor this incredible woman who had come into his life so unexpectedly.

Having made the decision, Tate refused to hurry. If this was the only taste of heaven he ever had, he wouldn't rush it.

Using his hands to tilt her head back, he traced her lips with his tongue. Memorizing every part of her became his top priority, no matter how loudly his body demanded he take her right now.

Her perfectly full lips had a slightly salty taste. He couldn't hold back a groan as he pushed deeper. So hot. So responsive. Her tongue reached to meet his. Something about holding her like this, demanding entry and receiving her surrender, spiked his pleasure. He massaged her scalp. Her neck muscles loosened, her head falling back into his palms. Knowing he brought her pleasure, too, made his head spin.

He could barely move far enough away to pull her
shirt over her head. The sight of the soft upper curves
of her breasts in the dappled light made his muscles
tighten. He could almost stand there looking all night.
Cupping them in his hands, he squeezed lightly. Her
breath caught. The material of her bra was thin enough
for him to feel her nipples peak against his palms. Rubbing across them in short circles had them both moan-
ing. She swayed. Willow's hands returned to his biceps,
her fingers pressing into him in search of stability.

He loved that his touch made her body go weak.

How much longer they could both stand, he wasn't
sure. Quickly he lifted her, then laid her out on the bed
like a feast for his senses. Gorgeous pale skin. Sweet vanilla scent. Fresh, vibrant taste. And hot, burning touch.
What had he ever done to deserve such a precious gift?

He removed each piece of clothing with exquisite
care. He pulled her shorts down over long, shapely legs.
Panties followed the same path, revealing the neat patch
of red hair that protected her most delicate skin. She
arched so he could unhook her bra, allowing him to
see the dark pink nipples he'd so insistently aroused.

His own clothes came off with more speed and efficiency. Even though he was in danger of being carried
away by his passion for her, Tate didn't forget to reach
into his bedside table for a condom. This time he would
protect *her*, even more than he'd tried to protect himself.

Her body welcomed him eagerly. Tate gasped as her
muscles made way for him, bathing him in her liquid
heat. He squeezed his eyes shut. Somewhere deep inside, he found the control that kept him from pounding into her. From finishing before they'd both milked
every ounce of pleasure from this moment.

Instead he thrust lightly into her, relishing every lift

of her hips for more. The feel of her nails scraping down his chest jolted him closer to the edge. He bent low, licking and sucking at the delicate skin of her neck, feeling her cries against his lips. When she squeezed those supple legs around his hips, he could hold back no longer.

Now thrusting hard, Tate drove them both higher, seeking that ultimate explosion. For the first time, he felt as though they were seeking together with a need that transcended physical release. Somehow he knew this moment with Willow was a unique promise...a bond that would never be broken.

Twelve

Willow rolled over on her back, sure something wasn't right. It took her a moment to realize that she wasn't in her own bed. And another moment to realize that she was alone in Tate's.

While she was trying to banish the fog from her brain, she heard the rare sound of the plane as it gained altitude, climbing away from the island. Despite the gray darkness before dawn, Tate was already on his way.

Willow tried not to be hurt but found it hard to keep her emotions on an even keel. Yesterday and last night had been incredible. Though she tried to remind herself that Tate was probably just reaching out for human contact after learning about Murdoch, that didn't mean he had to take off without telling her. But the very fact she felt that way told her everything she needed to know about herself in this situation—as much as she might try to be a modern woman taking things one day at a time, she was really more of a relationship kind of girl.

Which meant in the end, she was probably going to end up hurt.

She padded downstairs in Tate's shirt, because she could. As she reached for the coffeepot, she found his note.

Wasn't sure you remembered. I have a meeting with Charles today. See you later tonight.

Oh, right. Willow laughed a little, glad Tate hadn't been here when she overreacted. Now she felt a little silly getting upset over something he'd already told her about. He was meeting with his editor to discuss the first book on the new contract today.

But things were always unsettled with Tate. One minute off; one minute on. No wonder she jumped to conclusions.

Staring out the window, she inhaled deeply. The dark, smooth scent of coffee filled the air. She took a couple more breaths, searching for calm. Rain started to sprinkle outside the window. They were supposed to have some showers, then a couple of overcast days before a major storm came ashore. She'd hoped to swim while Tate wasn't here to hover, but she didn't want to risk it in the rain.

Then again, she knew what she could do…

She smiled as she poured herself a cup, then added a substantial amount of cream. Just the way she liked it. That first sip was always heavenly, but today it made her frown.

After a minute, she tried again. Ugh. Her creamer must have gone sour. She'd get some more tomorrow. With the storm developing, Willow wanted to make sure they had everything they needed to be off the grid for a few days. Also, lunch with her sisters was always a plus.

Eager to do what she'd put off too many times already, Willow changed her clothes, then headed to the door to the third floor at the far end of the hall. She worked the key in the door, finally getting the tough lock to turn. The stairs beyond were crusted along the edges with thick dust, but the centers were clean from the recent treks of the workmen who made the repairs.

The first couple of rooms were disappointingly empty. Another one had an empty bed frame and a chifforobe filled with women's formal clothes that could date back to the twenties and thirties.

Then—jackpot.

The door was still open to the room directly over hers, giving her a clear view of the trunks and rolltop desk she'd seen that night. It felt like forever since she'd watched the ceiling fall down on her that first night. So much had happened since then.

A quick peek showed the room across was almost identical, but even more loaded with stuff. It would be hard to walk in there without tripping over something.

Goodness, there were enough storage trunks that she could be here all day. After a good look around, she started with the first room because everything had been carefully moved to one side during the work, making it tidier. Maybe that would make it easier to search through.

But the more she looked, she realized the dates on the papers in the boxes and trunks were too current to be relevant. For what she was looking for anyway. Unfortunately, as a history buff, all of it was interesting, so she was slow in making her way through the materials.

Finally she moved to the next room. When she was barely halfway across a loud boom shook the house. Willow jumped. A shaky laugh escaped her. The shutters were all closed, so she hadn't realized a bigger storm had moved in. Rain, too. The drops suddenly came down heavy and hard on the roof. She hoped Tate had been able to fly clear of it.

Now to the task at hand.

The thick layer of dust in this room suggested it had been untouched for years, possibly decades. Fortunately, everything was neatly boxed. Unfortunately, there weren't any labels to give her a preview of what was in each trunk...and they weren't all easy to open.

She could sure use a handy crowbar right about now.

Practical planner that she was, she started at the wall by the door and worked her way around. Before long, crouching had her thighs screaming in pain, so she just plopped herself down on the dusty hardwood floor.

The first thing to slow her down was that she didn't know exactly what she was looking for. She wanted proof that exonerated her family, but didn't know what form said proof would take. That meant looking at a lot of pieces of paper so she didn't miss anything.

But the dates on the documents were close to the period when the crime took place—if she could just find the exact year. That much, at least, she knew.

Tate's family hadn't been big on personal accounts, it seemed, but they were big on business. There were no diaries or cards or letters but lots of ledgers and files and dust. Eventually she seemed to hit the sweet spot—a trunk of dated ledgers. At one time it seemed to have been padlocked, but someone had unlocked it and simply slipped the lock back into place without forcing it closed.

Bingo! There was the year she needed.

Only a few pages in she realized Tate had been telling the honest truth about his relatives. His ancestor, Joseph Kingston, had been a bad, bad boy.

These weren't your typical business ledgers—they contained everything that couldn't be kept with the "official" records.

According to the neatly written pages, repeated payment went to the same four or five individuals throughout the year in question. Probably local troublemakers, if Willow had to guess. Though the entries didn't list exactly what the men were hired for—which was a big warning sign in Willow's brain—they did list locations, times, special supplies needed and either a company or family name.

Willow's heart pounded over both the historical and personal significance of what she was reading. Joseph Kingston had systematically waged war on others in their regional community. Not a week went by without an entry.

How much property damage did this thick ledger represent? And how many lives were lost when people carelessly got in the way?

Like the McLemores' heir.

Willow wondered if she could link these dates to incidents reported in the local newspapers at the time. The researcher in her was excited. Quickly she flipped through to the date she most needed.

There was an entry. She scanned through and found the memo line—McLemore.

For a few seconds, Willow savored the elation of discovery. This could make a big difference for her sister—just the confidence of being able to cast doubt if Paxton McLemore's family accused her of anything was huge. Now they would be prepared for the conflict they all knew was coming.

But what about Tate?

For the first time, Willow thought about him in all of this. As she carried the ledger downstairs to her room, she thought over all that he'd been through lately. As private as he was, how would he feel about this part of his family history becoming known?

As Tate let himself into Sabatini House after midnight, he was curious in what state he would find Willow. Though they'd both known he'd be gone today, he was pretty sure she would have forgotten by morning—hence the note he'd left. He'd been trying to keep himself out of the doghouse, so why had he still felt like he was bailing when he let himself out before dawn?

As Tate walked through the empty, dimly lit kitchen, he was at least grateful she didn't jump out and start lecturing him…though his mind's picture of Willow in full-on irate-professor mode was pretty entertaining. Realizing the lower levels of the house were quiet, he climbed the stairs, his body growing hard at the question of whether she would be in his bed.

He didn't have the right to demand it. He didn't even know if she thought she belonged there. After all, he'd never given her reason to believe it was where he wanted her all the time. He only knew the ache for her had been constant all day, but now it ramped up to screaming level.

He shouldn't be so greedy, but his body was tired and his psyche was stressed. He wanted the balm he knew Willow could grant him. Besides, he knew what the next few days held, on top of the roller-coaster ride of the last few.

Which brought him full circle. Would she want him again? Or would she want him nowhere near her?

Nerves ate him up as he rounded the corner for the hall to his suite…and hers. Willow had slept every night since the first in her bed with the door closed. Part of him was resigned to finding his access cut off by the door to her room. Instead his gaze was drawn to a square of light on the floor.

Her door was open. The light was on. Tate set his briefcase and carry bag against the wall, then unbuttoned his shirt as he strode toward her door.

She lay curled away from him facing the lamp that put out soft light on the bedside table. Eager to see her, he moved to the end of the bed with soft steps. One of her hands cradled her cheek as she slept. The other rested over one of his paperback books, as if she'd fallen asleep reading.

The softest of feelings wrapped around Tate's chest like a thick, plush blanket. It wasn't the same as the spark of passion or the sting of regret. Nor the heat of anger.

Softness had never had a place in his life. What little he'd experienced he'd had no use for. So why did he embrace whatever was happening now?

He had no answers but was grateful when the warm glow was swept away by a heated wave of passion. This he was familiar with. This he could handle.

Not soon enough he was stripped to his boxers and slipping into the bed beside her. Every time he was with Willow brought new experiences to him, new insights. But tonight, of all the things he remembered, that first moment when she opened her eyes and smiled sleepily at him hit him square in the chest and stayed with him to the next day.

Her gorgeous welcome allowed him to fall asleep, but the unfamiliar bed and all-too-familiar thoughts pushed him from her way too early. He didn't sleep well at the best of times, but this time of year it was impossible for him to get more than a few hours at a time. Thoughts of his brother, of his guilt, made rest illusive.

Like a beacon, the water lured Tate downstairs, past his forgotten briefcase and carry-on and the coffee he needed to start each day. All the way to the door he opened only once a year. It had started calling a few days early this year.

Tate stood for long time with his palm pressed against the door that led to the underground swimming cave, as if testing the temperature. This was the place his family had seen as a symbol of their life force. They had started on the water. Made their home on the water. Made their living on the water. They'd had enough hubris to believe they controlled it.

Tate had learned better.

He forced himself to grasp the handle and turn it. When the door opened, the sound of rushing water filled his ears.

What so many had called an amazing creation didn't inspire awe in him. The dim break of dawn spilled into the deep, low room from the mouth of the cave, allowing him to watch the push and pull of the waves against rocky surfaces long worn smooth. It was not magical. Not to him. Tate considered the place evil incarnate. The source of his family's power…and with his brother Adam's death, it had become the source of their demise.

Never again would Tate trust the water. It might have been the source of his family's successes, but they'd failed to acknowledge its power to destroy. Now, when he looked at the beach and the waves, or even considered driving across the bridge to the mainland, all he could see was the deceptive calm that hid the malevolent power beneath the surface.

He hated the weakness that came with the fear, but the power was real...and far from benevolent. Tate gripped the door frame hard enough for his hands to ache. He needed the strain to keep him anchored.

Suddenly a delicate hand covered his, a lithe body pressed against his back. Willow didn't try to peek around him. Didn't ask any questions. Instead she rested her cheek between his shoulder blades to once again offer him comfort.

His body shuddered as the tension flowed from him. Her gentle touch reminded him that he wasn't alone.

"Are you okay?" she finally whispered against his bare back.

He wasn't. But for once, with her, that wasn't an insurmountable problem. So he told her the memory that kept him from sleeping in her bed. "Tomorrow would have been his birthday."

Thirteen

Tate's words haunted Willow as she headed to town for supplies. He would spend the day prepping the house for the incoming storm. She'd make sure they had everything they needed—along with a little extra.

That attitude felt a little too close to homemaking for her comfort. Less like a job and more like a desire to take care of someone on a personal level. She tried not to think of it that way, but the association lingered around the edges of her consciousness anyway.

If she could get up the nerve, she planned to throw Tate a little well-deserved celebration. He'd been pleased that his contract negotiations had gone through and had asked her to get something for a special meal, but she was more interested in celebrating his personal milestone than the professional one.

Hopefully he'd enjoy it. From what she'd learned from Murdoch, no one had celebrated Tate's birthday for a long time. Not since his brother's death. Which was beyond sad. She knew he loved his brother, but Tate's life hadn't ended. The fact that his parents had acted as though it had was beyond cruel.

Now she could see how it played out in so many ways in Tate's life. But to her, this one was significant. Letting someone know they were special, that their presence here on earth was appreciated and welcomed, was important to the building of self-worth.

Tate's family got a big fat F for failure in many areas, but especially this one in particular.

Besides, spending some time together, showing him how much she appreciated him as a person, might soften the blow she could feel approaching. As much as she wanted to deny it, she was terribly afraid that his nightmare was about to come true. Her odd symptoms were getting too frequent to ignore.

With that in mind, she turned to her sister Jasmine as they walked together down the aisle at the large, local shopping center. "How is Ivy?"

"Bless her heart, she's miserable," Jasmine said, shaking her head. "The nausea is just killing her. And I don't see how she's going to look for work every day, she's so tired."

"Poor thing," Willow added, but she was turning the information over in her mind as she pushed the cart down the aisle.

"She's a nervous wreck, too," Jasmine added, oblivious to Willow's distraction. "She only left work a few days ago using her leave, and the replacement keeps calling her, telling her the boss is asking more and more questions."

Willow imagined he was...after all, he knew more than anyone that there was unfinished business between himself and his executive assistant. "She should quit answering the phone."

"That's what I told her. She's putting in all these applications because she insists she should support herself." Jasmine rolled her eyes.

"She's been that way since her first job, you know that. It's a hang-up." They all had them in some form or another.

"Yeah, but she's struggling. I think maybe a job would help her feel like she has some control in this situation. But I really wish she'd give herself a break. I think she's afraid if she waits too long, it will be harder to get work because she'll be closer to term."

Willow shook her head, but she completely understood Ivy's concerns. An employer would have to really want to hire her to overlook a large pregnant belly at an interview.

Getting back to her own worries, Willow asked, "So she's tired and nauseous?" Willow had only one of those symptoms. Did that mean she'd dodged a bullet? Were the other things she'd experienced just an odd coincidence?

"What's that look on your face?"

Willow brought her attention back to Jasmine. *Uh-oh*. Her sister had stopped midaisle to study her...a little too closely. She tried to blank her expression. "What do you mean?"

Jasmine's gaze narrowed. "Don't try that innocent look on me. That hasn't worked with me since you were a little kid with gangly legs."

This was her sister. Willow knew she could trust Jasmine to keep her secrets. It was just—the thought of saying her suspicions out loud scared her. Heck, whispering them even… But Willow really needed someone to talk to.

This wasn't a subject she'd paid any attention to over the years. She could have looked it up, but until now she'd been afraid of confirming that her suspicions were true. And besides, the last thing she wanted filling her brain were all the horror stories floating around the internet.

So Jasmine was her best option.

Willow tried for her most matter-of-fact tone. "What exactly are the symptoms of pregnancy? Besides nausea, of course."

Jasmine gasped, her voice notching up an octave. "Girl! Are you—"

"Would you hush?" Willow demanded, glancing around. It would be just her luck to run into a student while her sister was grilling her about the consequences of her sex life.

Jasmine frowned, but lowered her voice. "What are you trying to say, Willow?"

"Nothing," Willow said, feeling contrary. "I'm trying to ask something, in a subtle way."

"I don't think it worked."

"I noticed."

They stood there staring at each other in stalemate until they both began to giggle… Jasmine was the first to sober up. "So I'm guessing you have reason to believe you might be pregnant?"

"I shouldn't be."

Jasmine simply raised her brows at that. How did she look so elegant all the time, even when she was in interrogation mode? "Would you stop beating around the bush and tell me what's going on?"

Willow lowered her voice even more. "I took a morning-after pill, so I thought everything would be okay. But I've felt weird ever since."

Jasmine's frown echoed her own.

"But I'm not nauseous. So that's good, right? I'm just exhausted. And things taste weird. And sometimes I feel dizzy—"

Jasmine started walking. Willow stared for a few seconds, then hurried to follow. "Where are we going?" she asked.

"For someone who is so smart, you can be incredibly dumb at times," Jasmine said over her shoulder.

Willow should be offended, but she knew her sister was teasing her. "What did I miss?"

Jasmine marched determinedly through the store, leaving Willow confused and a little out of breath as she tried to follow with her full shopping cart. Seeing Jasmine pause to scan the pharmacy section gave her concern, though.

"You do realize that the morning-after pill has a failure rate, right?" Jasmine disappeared down one aisle, then came back with a small box. "Just use this. Then you'll know for sure."

Willow stared down at the pregnancy test, almost afraid to touch it. Then came the nausea...right on schedule.

"Come on," Jasmine urged, nudging the box in her direction. "We can buy it right now and have answers in less than three minutes."

"No," Willow said, appalled at the idea. "I'm not doing that here."

Jasmine's small smile infuriated her. "At the house, then," she countered.

"I'll..." Willow swallowed hard. "I'll take it with me. Then we'll see."

Jasmine quickly snatched the box out of her reach. "As long as you promise to call me when it's done," she insisted.

"Oh, trust me. I'll let you know."

"ASAP. After telling the father, of course."

Now, didn't that sound like a pleasant prospect?

Tate squeezed his fingers into fists, forcing himself to ignore the ache that told him to continue writing. He'd been in the flow for several hours now. As much as he wanted to continue working, he needed to attend to other matters.

Still, it felt strange for writing to not be the most important thing in his life anymore.

But the clock told him that Willow would be starting dinner about now. They'd talked about something special to celebrate his new contract, but Tate had a few ideas of his own that he hadn't shared. So he saved his document and shut down his computer before heading down the stairs.

As he walked by, he could hear Willow in the kitchen. He smiled. She didn't give herself props for how good of a cook she was. Tate looked forward to every meal, and often came down early for a glimpse of the menu items. But today he kept moving until he reached the front formal living room.

The furniture in this room was from the early sixties, as far as he could tell. He'd never bothered to change it out, because the space wasn't in use. If a family lived here, the large area would be perfect for a leather sectional, a couple of recliners, a large television and maybe a game area, but for just Tate and Murdoch, all that wasn't necessary. He walked through, noting the clean floors and lack of dust. Willow had obviously cleaned the room, even though no one was ever in here.

His steps gradually slowed as he approached the opposite wall. He slowly pulled back the floor-to-ceiling curtains to reveal French doors leading out onto a covered deck. The outdoor space had been used for parties and long summer days by the ocean.

At least, it had been by his parents.

Tate hadn't set foot out here since they died. He hadn't had any use for it. The very thought of returning to this incredible space where he'd spent so much of his childhood and teenage years always had him breaking out in a sweat. Just like it did now, but this time he refused to let it stop him.

Despite years of disuse, the door unlocked and opened easily. Tate had to grin. This was probably as a result of Murdoch's efforts. They'd never talked about it, but Tate knew Murdoch did many things to maintain the house and grounds. He'd disagreed with how Tate had cut himself off from others and the beauty surrounding them. Murdoch had handled upkeep on the underground cave, the beachfront and nursery. Until he'd left, he'd handled the inspections of the third floor, too. Tate had no interest in all the "history" up there. Murdoch's attempt to keep Sabatini House in livable condition was his way of voicing his opinion without having to deal with direct conflict.

The way they both liked it.

Sure enough, the furniture on the deck had been carefully covered and secured. Tate kept his gaze trained on his task without letting it stray to the water nearby. He made quick work of the preparations. Soon he'd taken the tarps off a table with two chairs and strategically placed them for viewing the approaching sunset. He prepared another side table to hold the food. When he'd told Willow they would have a nice dinner, he hadn't told her exactly where.

Tate wasn't necessarily ready to talk about commitment or permanence over the salad course, but he could no longer ignore what was happening with Willow. The emotions and sensations he experienced when they were together—both in bed and out of it—were unique. The feelings Tate had around her both scared the spit out of him *and* left him wanting more. He had to acknowledge whatever this was in some way—for his sake and hers.

He returned to the kitchen right on time. Willow already had the tray loaded to carry the serving dishes into the breakfast nook where he normally ate alone. Without a word, he relieved her of the burden. Then he loaded their place settings onto the tray as well and headed out of the kitchen.

"Where are you going?" Willow asked.

After a brief pause, he finally heard her steps as she rushed to follow him. When she caught up he stood to one side of the open French doors. Then he stepped through and led her to the seating area he had set up.

When he didn't hear her follow, he put the tray down on the side table and glanced back. She stood just outside the doorway, looking confused. He tried not to smile as he returned to her, took her hand, then led her to her seat, which faced the ocean.

"I thought you never came out here because of the bad memories," she finally said.

"Surprised?" he asked.

Her smirk was extra sassy. "You're enjoying this, aren't you?" Then her expression sobered. "But honestly, Tate, I can't believe how well you're dealing with your fear of the water."

Tate glanced at the sun as it slowly sank into the horizon, leaving the sky various shades of pink and purple. "It's time, don't you think?" He shifted his gaze to her. "I know you do. But to answer your first question, yes, I'm enjoying some of it."

"Especially shocking the pants off me," she teased.

"Oh no," he said, letting her playful tone distract him from his darker side. "There's better ways to accomplish that goal."

Her grin made him light up inside. For the first time since she'd come to Sabatini House, he served her. He set their places, then filled their plates. As they ate, Tate found he was okay as long as he didn't stare directly into the ocean and didn't allow himself to remember those heart-wrenching moments from so long ago.

Sometimes the monsters get bigger if we let them hide in the dark. One of the protagonists in his books had said that. Tate should have listened to himself a long time ago.

"Are you going to tell me what brought this on?" Willow finally asked after about twenty minutes of small talk.

Tate allowed himself to savor his bite of beef while he formulated his answer. "You've been good for me, Willow."

"Are you sure?"

Sarcasm wasn't what he'd expected, though he should have, considering his audience.

"Yes. We both know I don't express my gratitude very well—"

"Humph."

He ignored her for the moment. "But I do appreciate all you've done here and wanted to show you I'm making an effort."

"Don't do it for me," she insisted, shaking her head. "Do it for you."

"I will. I—" For a strange moment, words failed him. "Willow, these last few weeks have been incredible—"

Her distressed squeak caught his attention.

"What is it?" he asked.

Her wide green eyes were full of worry. "Did you serve me dinner, then show me you're making positive changes, so you could tell me you don't need me anymore?"

"Is that what you want me to say?"

Now she looked confused. "No."

"Then it's a good thing that wasn't my plan."

She sat, chest heaving, face flushed. Part of him felt bad about her distress, but the other part was amused. And flattered. At least she wanted to stay, even though he'd been a jackass on occasion.

"Then what was your plan?" she asked.

He couldn't help teasing a little more. "If you'd stop jumping to conclusions, I might be able to finish."

She gave a short nod, but he'd swear her eyes were teary before she lowered her eyelids. Time to get down to business.

"Whatever this is," he said, gesturing between the two of them, "it's different for me. Unique."

Now Willow looked up, pinning him with that green gaze. "Really?" she whispered.

Tate nodded, reaching out to finger several strands of her fiery hair. Not only did he want to touch her, but it felt weird to say this stuff without touching her. "Thank you for being here."

Somehow Tate knew the look that they shared said way more than either of them was ready to voice. "I—"

He swallowed, unsure how to put these exact feelings into words. "I—"

She cut him off. "Me, too."

He knew she was getting his message, but he had to finish.

"You're incredible. And I don't really know what to do with this, but I don't want it to end." Not his most suave speech, but Tate wasn't a very suave kind of guy. Written words were much more his forte than spoken. But at least he was honest.

As his reward, she leaned forward and pressed her lips tightly against his for a few seconds.

"Is that a yes?" he asked after she pulled back.

She grinned. "You bet."

"See," he said. "I knew we had something to celebrate."

Suddenly Willow gasped. He barely had time to raise a brow before she was up and running back into the house.

He couldn't help but call out, "Did you change your mind already?"

Fourteen

Willow rushed around the kitchen, anxious to get everything ready before Tate came inside to find out why she was acting so weird. After as little time as possible, she headed back to the deck with a small tray at a much slower pace.

Tate stood to one side of the table, staring at the sky. How long had it been since he'd watched the sun set over the ocean out here? From the tight set of his shoulders, he wasn't necessarily enjoying it, and he kept back from the edge of the deck, but he was here. That was a step in the right direction. An important step in taking his life back from the shadows.

Willow hoped her surprise would be a positive step, too. "Happy Birthday, Tate."

As he turned, she looked into his eyes, then watched as his gaze dropped to the miniature cake she was carrying.

He didn't move for so long she started to panic inside.

Was he angry that she'd acknowledged the birthday he hadn't celebrated in years? Then suddenly he strode toward her, took the tray and set it aside.

Just when she thought he would recant everything he'd said earlier, he cupped her face and kissed her. Unlike earlier, this kiss was slow and very, very hot.

All too soon, Tate drew back and barely whispered, "I just might love you."

Willow didn't respond, couldn't for the fear and excitement rushing through her, but she smiled before brushing her lips back across his. She wasn't ready to say it out loud, but this was enough, for now.

"Time for cake," she finally said.

To his chagrin, she made him go through the whole blowing-out-the-candle thing. No mention was made by either of them of a wish. Willow didn't want to push Tate too far. She made a silent one for him instead, in hopes he could find the happiness he deserved.

He did seem to enjoy it as they cut through the checkerboard exterior to the cake layered with chocolate ganache below. Afterward they cleared the dishes from the deck together and left it in darkness.

Willow made quick work of loading the dishwasher, anticipation sparkling in her veins. Tate only exacerbated the situation. He touched her every time he passed close until her skin grew tight, her body wet with need.

Just as she finished, he picked up the stack of clean trays and stored them back under the island, knocking her purse off the counter in the process. He bent over to pick it up.

Willow didn't realize anything was wrong until he stood and asked, "What the hell is this?"

He was holding the little white box from the pharmacy.

His voice turned hard, accusing. "You told me you took the pill."

Willow's heart pounded. Her stomach twisted so hard she thought she might be sick. "I did." She could barely get her voice above a whisper. "I just—I haven't felt right."

Tate stared at the box with what Willow could only describe as horror. For a moment, she swore he swayed. She immediately reached for him, but at the last minute he backed away and straightened. Willow wasn't sure if he was bracing himself or deliberately pulling out of her reach.

Based on his behavior since she'd met him, she assumed a bit of both. Tate had spent a lifetime alone. Isolation seemed to be his defense of choice. After the evening they'd just had, the fact that he would pull away hurt more than she wanted him to see.

But she couldn't change him.

Willow found herself frozen, unsure of what to do. Then Tate blinked, visibly trying to get a hold of himself. "I don't understand," he murmured. "You said you took the pill."

She could accept his saying it once, but repeating himself… "Are you accusing me of lying?" she demanded.

"No," he said, drawing out the word. "I just don't understand."

She opened her mouth to tell him to get a clue, but then closed it again. "Is it that you don't understand, or that you don't want to understand?"

For the first time, he really looked at her. "What?"

Yep. Sometimes it was hard to face reality. "So I'm guessing I'm not the only one who glossed over the failure-rate information in the literature."

"I guess not."

He was too calm, speaking in a completely detached, logical tone. That was probably not a good sign, but Willow could see the first beads of sweat against his temples. He might just be human after all. Somehow it felt good to have someone else sweating over this issue, instead of just her.

"Let's do it."

Wait. What? She frowned at him as she said, "I don't understand."

Tate held up the box and shook it. "We need to take this."

"Don't you mean *I* need to take it?" she pointed out.

"Are we going to argue about semantics or pee on the dang stick?"

Oh, she could argue all night long if it meant not taking that test. "Do you really want to know?" she asked.

"The truth is there, whether we know it or not." This time his gaze was much steadier, but she had to wonder if he was hiding more extreme emotions. She knew she was.

Fear. Anger. Sadness.

"Come on." There was resolve in his voice. Clearly he wasn't shying away from the action required.

He headed down the hall, and for a moment she couldn't get her feet to follow. Part of her could have stood in the kitchen forever, rather than take the test. Finally she managed to reach the stairs just as he made it to the top. Then she trailed him into her room.

She was glad they were doing it there. For some reason, she needed the comfort of the familiar right now. And frankly his suite held too many memories for her to handle on top of this situation.

To her dismay, Tate walked straight through to the

bathroom. Willow paused to take a deep breath. She needed to take control of this situation—ASAP. Otherwise Tate would think he had the only vote…and she'd find herself at his complete and total mercy.

She stopped short behind him as he stared at the box on the counter. "Out," she said.

Tate glanced up, meeting her gaze in the mirror. "But—"

"Out."

He obeyed, but stopped only a few inches outside the doorway. She had to close the door carefully but firmly. She briefly wished to use the lock, but figured it wouldn't stop him if he really wanted back inside.

At least he didn't have to break it down five minutes later when she didn't respond to his knocks. She simply couldn't make herself move, even after he let himself in. She faced the counter, hands braced, eyes squeezed shut. He closed in until his heat bathed her back. His chest brushed her as he leaned over her shoulder to look at the test on the counter.

"Okay, then."

Willow opened her eyes to see him walking away. Her stomach dropped. Glancing down, she felt her world tilt.

Can't sleep. Hot. Grumpy.

There was so much on Willow's mind—the baby, her family, the ledger, Tate. She'd only taken the test last night and already the chaos was overwhelming. In an effort to try to make some sense of any of it, she looked back through the book to make sure her dates and impressions were correct.

Unfortunately, the answers weren't waiting there on the parchment page.

What was she going to do? There was no mistaking the dates, or that this entry was somehow tied to the McLemore family. Circumstantial evidence, but the court of public opinion didn't care about those niceties. Only, if she were to reveal this, instead of just diverting blame to a family that might not care, she would be destroying the reputation of the family her child would be a part of.

Her child. She laid her hand over her stomach. It was still kind of hard to comprehend.

No longer able to lie still, Willow headed out of her room. She'd kill for some coffee. Knowing that it wouldn't taste right put her in a very bad mood.

The light in Tate's office was on. She paused but heard no sound. Had he truly been working or simply avoiding her? Should she rush inside and demand to know what he was thinking or give him his space to process, like she was doing?

It was just too hard to guess.

She wished she was like Jasmine or Ivy. They dealt with high-powered men every day. What would they have done? Willow was more suited to recalcitrant boys or know-it-all freshmen. She had logical conversations that dealt with schedules and term papers and historical facts. Not power plays or emotional issues.

Tate was a whole different animal that she'd shown very little skill in handling. So she continued on her way, figuring it best if she didn't poke the lion in its cage.

There was no point going to the kitchen. And she didn't need to start breakfast for Tate for several hours yet. Would he even come down to eat, or wait until she'd moved on to something else so he didn't have to confront her?

Antsy and anxious, she continued to the lower level. Maybe she'd start some laundry. Instead, she found herself stopping before the door to the underground cave. In the same way she'd seen Tate standing there the other night, she pressed her hand to the door, soaking in the sound of the waves. They sounded a little choppy right now with the storm arriving today. By midafternoon they'd be crashing against the shore outside, the sound drowned out by the torrential rain they were supposed to receive.

Which only served to remind her how hot she was right now. Without too much thought, she opened the door and walked through. The incredible sight drew her in. What had probably been a natural cave when Tate's ancestors first arrived had been reshaped to great effect by human ingenuity. The ceiling was low but long, with a man-made stone and copper-orange tile arch marking the front of the pool. Flicking a nearby light switch, she stepped down hand-hewn stone steps into the cool, damp room.

The few working bulbs were just enough light to let her explore safely. The light shimmered over the lapping water. With each receding wave, she could see wide long steps leading down into a roughly rectangular pool. The far end was an open frame, offering glimpses of the sky beyond, which was still dark gray before the dawn.

Fascinated, she sat on the edge, dangling her legs in the water. It felt like her entire body cooled down a degree or two. Her muscles started to relax. This had felt like the hottest summer, but especially the past few weeks. Her brain gave a mental pause before she laughed.

She wondered if being overheated had anything to

do with those pregnancy hormones at work again. She guessed the next time she went to town, she needed to buy a book, huh?

The water felt so good. She'd grown up with the beach and was a strong swimmer. It felt weird to have been near a beach so long this summer and not swum at all.

Without thinking, she stood and stripped to her bra and panties. The cool water sent chills over her as she waded into it. It felt so good. She loved to swim. She missed it.

Cautiously she waded a little deeper. The cave was so large that the water was already chest high about three-quarters of the way out. There Willow started to swim from one side to the other.

Not knowing what to expect, she didn't risk getting too close to the opening to the ocean. The cave's structure slowed the water down just enough to keep the waves gentle. Willow felt her stress melt away with this simple, cool exercise. Here in the gently lapping water she didn't think about old feuds or tragedies or what to call these feelings for Tate—just about breathing, moving and the feel of the liquid chill against her skin.

Until a loud bang broke her concentration. Willow jerked upright to see Tate in the open doorway, fury on his face. She barely registered how angry he was before a cramp running down her side took her under. Her immediate panic wasn't for the water closing over her head or for the doubled-up position that kept her from standing.

It was for the vicious pain that stole her breath and her peace of mind.

Then a hard grip pulled her above the surface. She quickly found herself pressed against a fully clothed male. Tate seemed to be yelling as he dragged her back to the pool's edge.

Willow wasn't sure. She was too busy struggling to process what had just happened—oh, and suck in air.

Only when Tate plopped her butt-first on the edge did she finally start to listen. By then, the pain had disappeared. *Thank goodness.*

"Why would you do this? You know how I feel about this place. So you decide to come swim in here alone and would have drowned if I hadn't happened to walk by at that moment?" His loud voice echoed off the cave walls. Willow started to shiver.

"Why would you do this, Willow? What possessed you? I told you this place was *off-limits.*"

In that moment, Willow decided she'd had enough. Those last two words made her want to scream. Instead she clenched her teeth and ground out, "I don't know, Tate. I guess for a moment I thought I might be more than just a hired employee. You know—a woman capable of making her own decisions for a change."

"How did that work for you?" he asked, his face tight with anger. "Your foolishness could have killed our child."

Fifteen

"Don't I have any say in this?"

Tate knew he looked like a prison guard as he stood over her, legs locked, arms crossed over his chest. But he couldn't seem to soften his position. "Don't you want to know if everything is okay?"

"Is that why he's here?" Her green gaze seemed to hold an accusation that he wasn't quite catching.

"Yes, he's a doctor."

"Well, the last time you brought home a medical surprise, my well-being wasn't what you had in mind."

Light dawned. Man, they had some serious communication issues. Tate knew it. He should have talked to her instead of rushing to the phone to call Dr. D'Ambrosio. But the shock had him more than a little off-kilter.

About everything. While Willow spent the night sleeping—in her own room—Tate had spent it pacing his office while his brain ran through all of the possibilities. Life could be such a mess sometimes.

As much as Tate argued with himself that he'd vowed never to have children, the fact was, Willow was pregnant. Obviously fate had a completely different plan from his. The question was, what did they do now?

For Tate, this was completely foreign territory. But the only emotion absent in the gamut he'd run during the long night was any desire to end this now.

What that meant, he wasn't sure. But he and Willow would figure it out together…if they could figure out how to have an actual conversation about it.

First and foremost, he had to know she was safe.

He took a deep breath and deliberately softened his tone of voice. "Please let him check you and the—" Tate was almost afraid to say it aloud. *A baby.* The emotions rolling through him left his throat tight. "Please."

Dr. D'Ambrosio smiled as if to reassure her. Tate had always liked the doctor. Even more so as he had softened with old age. His shock of white hair contrasted with deeply tanned skin that said he enjoyed being outdoors. He'd helped bring Tate and his brother into the world and tended to their sicknesses—and his brother's death—since then. They saw each other rarely, but Tate was certainly glad he could call on him right now.

"Why don't you just have a seat here," Dr. D said, indicating a chair at the breakfast nook table, "and tell me what happened."

Casting Tate another suspicious glance, Willow eased into the chair. She explained the barest of essentials about the past few weeks. The doctor glanced his way, and Tate confirmed with a nod. Yes, he was responsible. Tate found that knowledge scarier than anything he could dream up for his horror novels. Whatever happened here, he was responsible.

"And the dates?" Dr. D asked.

Had it really been four, no, five weeks?

The push and pull in his mind over Willow seemed to have gone on forever. He had made the decision to see where this could go, but as usual fate was prepared to goad him as far as absolutely possible.

The doctor took a seat in front of Willow, leaving Tate to observe.

"How are you feeling?" Dr. D'Ambrosio asked in a voice set to soothe.

"I'm not nauseated," she said with a frown. "Is that a problem?"

"No," he assured her. "I realize that's the most common symptom, but some women never have it. Anything else?"

"I'm really tired and everything tastes weird."

"Any cramps?"

"No. Not until I was in the water."

"Let's take a look at you." Using his stethoscope, the doctor listened to her heart and lungs and stomach before he asked, "So you went swimming?"

Willow nodded.

"And went under? Can you tell me what happened?"

She glanced at Tate, as if it made her uncomfortable that he was listening, then back down at the floor. "Everything was fine. But when I jerked up out of the water, I got a cramp."

Had his unexpected arrival set that off?

"Can you show me where?" the doctor asked.

Willow placed her palm flat on her right side, then dragged it down and across her lower belly.

Tate could feel his every muscle tensing. Regardless of where, cramping wasn't good. Was it? Even more surprising was the fact that he cared. Really cared. He didn't know where the emotions were coming from, but he did know his brain thought this was a good reason to freak out.

"I see." The doctor whispered something and Willow shook her head. Tate stepped closer.

Dr. D'Ambrosio leaned back. "Let's go lie down in the living room, and I'll take a peek. Would that be okay with you?"

Willow seemed to relax under his bedside manner. She'd been tense since Tate had yelled at her. No, *tense* wasn't the right word. She was tight to the point of breaking.

It was all his fault. If he hadn't been so ugly to her, hadn't let the high tension of his conflicting emotions get the better of him...

Dr. D'Ambrosio helped Willow up and guided her to the austere, old-fashioned couch in the living room.

"When did you find out you were pregnant?" he asked.

"I took the test last night, but I—" She lowered her eyelids while biting her lip.

"It's okay," he encouraged her. "Just tell me."

Tate understood her hesitation but was anxious to get past the interrogation. "It was a surprise because she took the morning-after pill," he said.

The doctor nodded and patted Willow's hand. "I'll be right back."

Despite his advanced age, he returned fairly quickly with a chest-high machine on four wheels. The bottom was a slick white and gray cabinet attached to a wide support post. Above that there were drawers, then a shelf with a closed laptop. The whole setup easily rolled across the hardwood floor.

"What's that?" Tate asked.

"An ultrasound machine. We'll take a look and see what's happening." He smiled down at Willow. "It may be too early. Maybe not. Okay?"

"Is it safe? Will it work?" Willow asked, her voice sounding small.

"Very," the doctor assured her. "And don't worry. Whatever is happening with you should show up. I only use the best equipment there is."

Tate moved around to stand near Willow's head as Dr. D'Ambrosio got everything ready. He opened the laptop and the screen flickered to life.

"Handy," Tate murmured, as impressed as he was surprised.

The doctor flashed him a grin, then focused on Willow. "Just relax. This won't hurt at all."

Dr. D'Ambrosio started rubbing Willow's stomach with the wand in slow circles, smoothing the clear jelly across her skin. The image on the screen just looked like shades of gray to Tate. Some spots were darker, some lighter. There was nothing that looked like a child, even a tiny one.

Finally, Dr. D'Ambrosio paused. There was a darker circle on the screen now. Along the lower curve was a small flashing light. "See that?" he asked.

"Yes," Willow whispered.

"That's your baby's heartbeat."

Willow gasped. Tate stared. His own heartbeat sped up, almost as if it were trying to match the rapid pace of the blinking light.

"It's too early to tell much," Dr. D'Ambrosio was saying. "But this is a good sign. We'll just monitor you both and see what happens."

Tate wasn't sure what other men felt when faced with the miracle of life, but he seemed to go numb. Everywhere except the beating of his heart. Even though they'd known since last night that Willow was actually pregnant, Tate felt like he'd been wrestling with nebulous what-ifs and his own assumptions.

The picture on that screen wasn't simply an object. A whole host of implications weighed Tate down. Fear. Dismay. After all, he'd told himself he'd never have children. That his family should end with him.

But as he stared at that little blinking light, the endless possibilities sparked a flare of hope inside of him. A foreign sensation, to be sure. But just like the love he felt for Willow, he recognized it without having ever felt it before.

Only he didn't know what the hell to do with either one.

The doctor swirled the wand around a little more, but Tate couldn't tell what he was looking at. Then he turned off the machine and started cleaning up the leftover gel.

Just when the panic reached a crescendo inside him, and Tate knew he'd have to leave before he did something stupid, a chilled hand slipped into his. He glanced at the sofa, but Willow wasn't looking at him. She watched the doctor intently as he finished, then helped her sit up. But her grip on Tate's hand didn't ease.

Tate found himself focusing in on her. How cold her fingers were. The slight tremble in her grip. The way she licked her lips and swallowed hard.

She's nervous.

"Will the morning-after pill hurt the baby?" she finally asked.

Then Tate realized she wasn't just nervous. She was scared. He could feel the same emotion creeping into the chaos inside him. Unsure what to do, he sat next to her.

He didn't put his arm around her. He wasn't sure she'd want that. But he sat close enough to lend his warmth and adjusted his hold on her hand to encompass more of her fingers.

"I'm hoping everything will be fine," Dr. D'Ambrosio said with a calm nod, "but we'll keep a close eye on you, just in case." He reached into his bag and pulled out a bottle. "I want you to start on these prenatal vitamins. That will help with some of the fatigue."

She nodded. "Why…" She licked her lips again. In that moment, Tate could only imagine how much worse her fear was than his. After all, she was the one it was happening to. He'd been focused solely on himself, how this would affect him. His demands were so selfish when viewed in that light. "What is the cramping all about?"

"Don't you worry. From the position and the fact that you had the cramp while you were exercising, I believe its source is very simple."

"What?" Tate demanded.

Dr. D'Ambrosio grinned. "Growing pains. As your belly expands, especially for the first time, your muscles have to adjust. Sometimes they don't like that. You shouldn't have to restrict your activities unless you have more severe problems. Simply rest when it happens and see if it goes away. If it doesn't, call me. I want to make sure you stay healthy, and that the pregnancy stays viable. That could be trickier if it turns out to be twins."

"What?" she and Tate almost yelled at the same time.

The older man grinned as if he found their shock amusing. "Well, there's been a set in every Kingston generation, hasn't there?"

Tate was stunned. He couldn't move. Couldn't think.

As he packed up, Dr. D'Ambrosio added, "Congratulations to you both. I'll check in next week unless you call me."

Tate mumbled something as the doctor left, but he and Willow remained locked in place, hands clasped.

Willow woke to find herself in Tate's bed. That was confusing because she was pretty sure she'd fallen asleep on the hard, uncomfortable couch downstairs as she lay there, desperately trying to process what had just happened. Tate hadn't been joking that first night when he'd said the furniture downstairs wasn't fit for sleeping. Or relaxing, even. She'd felt almost like she was on a real table in a doctor's office while Dr. D'Ambrosio had done her ultrasound.

Ultrasound. Incredible. That tiny flashing speck had actually been a baby's heartbeat?

Her hand wandered down to press against her lower stomach. How was she going to do this? She thought back to everything she'd seen Jasmine go through over the last year with Rosie. Rosie was adopted, so Jasmine hadn't actually had to go through labor, but even without that the load had been heavy. What if Willow sucked at all of that stuff?

Without warning, she started to cry. Big fat tears rolled down her cheeks. Thankfully her weeping was silent. She was mortified that it was happening at all. She wasn't a weepy sort of person. Then the bed shifted behind her and Willow realized she had an audience.

She pressed her face into the pillow, hoping to hide the reaction since she couldn't seem to stop it.

"Willow, are you okay?"

"Are you?" she mumbled, hoping to turn the conversation away from her own inner turmoil.

"What I am doesn't matter."

That stopped her tears quick. She twisted to face him. He sat on the opposite side of the bed. The rain must have finally started, because the room was dark, even without the shutters pulled. Still she could see him very clearly in this light.

"Since when?"

"I just don't figure the man has much say in these matters."

She sat up, too, feeling at a disadvantage lying down. She tried to wipe the tears from her face as surreptitiously as possible, hoping the dimness would protect her just a touch. "I don't know about other relationships, but in this one, you do. And I expect you to express an opinion...you know, when I ask for it."

In the light of the single lamp across the room, she saw him grin. At least they could still sass each other during this very awkward conversation.

"So this is a relationship, huh?" he asked.

That wasn't the question Willow had expected, but she refused to shy away from it. "Well, I thought that's where we were heading, but if you've changed your mind, I fully understand."

"No, Willow. I haven't changed my mind."

When she didn't respond, he went on. "I realize I lost control for a little while there. And I can't promise it won't happen again. All of this—" he waved between the two of them "—is new to me. Some of it is...scary."

"Even to renowned thriller author Adam Tate?"

"Yes, especially to him. I'm sure a psychologist would have a field day about why a man like me writes books like that, but the truth is, some of this will be scary. Please have patience with me."

"Me, too."

He raised a single brow.

"I've never done the relationship thing… At least, romantically."

"I find that hard to believe."

Willow shook her head. "I'm very close with my family, so I do know some things about relationships. But I've never dated much…never long-term. And I have helped a lot with my sister's adopted daughter, Rosie, so I'm not totally clueless about babies."

Even if the thought of having a baby of her own was terrifying. Exhilarating, too, but the fear muted everything else for the moment. The thought of doing it all alone didn't put her at ease, either. She didn't think Tate was into being a hands-on dad.

"I'm glad one of us will know what we're doing. You'll have to teach me."

Surprised, Willow stared.

Tate met her gaze for a moment, then turned away with an uncomfortable look on his face. "I'm warning you, I will probably completely suck as a father. But if nothing else, I'll be there for monetary support."

Uh, no. He'd already hinted at an interest in raising the child. She wasn't going to let him back down now. "That's not acceptable," she informed him.

His gaze snapped back to hers. "What?"

"You are a smart, sensitive man. Creative. Imaginative. I expect you to put all of those traits to work for our baby. The last thing we need is your ancestors having the last word and the child turning out like them, right? I'd much prefer he or she turn out like you."

Time seemed to freeze for a moment, then Tate gave a huff of laughter. "As I said, you're incredible."

"I'm just smart," Willow said with a shrug.

In the blink of an eye, Tate was across the bed and using his weight to bear her back down to the mattress. "And sexy," he growled as he buried his face into her neck.

Something had been bugging her since she woke up. Willow finally remembered what it was. "Tate, I really need to call my sisters."

"There's plenty of time for that," he murmured against her.

He was completely focused on one thing, so she added, "Before the landline fails."

"If you're really nice, I'll let you use my satellite phone."

Even as she giggled, she reached to his side and pinched him.

"Ouch!" he said, jerking back a little. "That's not nice!"

She gave him a big, cheesy smile. "There's more where that came from."

"Not if I sweeten you up first."

"Not happening," she teased, but had a feeling Tate would make her eat those words.

Easing her over, he started by removing her shirt and bra, then initiated long, steady strokes up and down her back. Just the right amount of pressure. Just the right speed. Willow felt like she was melting into the mattress.

Very few things had ever felt this good.

Then he started in on her arms, squeezing the muscles and massaging her hands. Her moans mingled with the sound of rain as it started to pelt the windows. He moved on to her legs after removing the rest of her clothes. Willow tried to lighten the mood before she completely lost her mind.

"Just for future reference," she gasped, struggling to form words.

"Yes?" he asked, but he didn't stop massaging her calves.

What was she saying? *Oh, right.* "Your talent in the bedroom makes up for a multitude of sins."

Finally he covered her back, surprising her with his bare chest against her. He whispered in her ear, "I'll definitely keep that in mind."

He turned her over, so they were face-to-face, and continued his gentle, thorough attentions. Willow soaked up his touch. His intensity broke through any physical barriers to stroke her very soul. Any hesitation she'd felt to this point was immediately burned away.

By the time he joined them together, Willow was lost. There was nothing left standing between them. Naked in every way possible, Willow opened up to him. She lifted to meet his every stroke. Tate's focus and intensity pushed her higher until she leaped over the edge without a second thought. His heavy thrusts and harsh cries sent her over again.

She resurfaced to the feel of his pounding heart beneath her palm and the knowledge that she'd never be the woman she'd been before. It was almost too much. Too raw.

Maybe for him, too. He rolled away, sprawling on the other side of the bed. To her surprise, he didn't break their connection, though. His hand came to rest on her forearm and he didn't pull it away. They lay for long moments, the only sound in the room their own harsh breathing.

Finally, desperate to break the silence, Willow teased, "I don't remember any sex scenes in the Adam Tate books. Where'd you learn to do that?"

Tate grunted, not quite as recovered as she was. It

took some time before he said, "I'm an author. I have a more vivid imagination than most."

As she giggled, he rolled back to hug her close. For at least a few moments, everything was right in Willow's world.

Sixteen

A bang, then muffled cursing woke Willow from her afternoon nap. Dr. D'Ambrosio had told her sleeping for a short while in the afternoons might help with the exhaustion. Luckily her employer had no complaints. After lunch, cleaning and a long three-way call with her sisters, Willow had lain down in her bedroom.

She still had to clean up some minor debris on the front deck and remove the lower-level shutters from the windows, but otherwise, they'd had very little damage from the storm. Not that they would have noticed if the house had come down around them. She and Tate had spent most waking moments during the stormy weekend in bed together. "Bonding time," he'd laughingly called it.

And she very much feared he'd created a bond she would never be able to break. This new, lighter side of Tate was a wonderful thing, beautiful and freeing. She knew better than to think the darker side had disappeared. She only hoped this happiness remained a part of him forever.

The room had gone silent again, but Willow could sense Tate's presence. She opened her eyes to see him staring at the floor. "What is it?" she asked.

He bent down and didn't come back up. The silence was too pervasive. After a few seconds, Willow sat up and stared at his back. "Tate? What's wrong?"

He stood up, then dropped something flat on the bed. The ledger. As her stomach sank, Willow had a feeling playtime was now over.

Without a word, Tate opened the book and leafed through the first few pages. His expression remained impassive when she'd have given anything to know what he was thinking. Then again, when he spoke she wished he hadn't.

"Is this another example of *I'm more than an employee so I can go wherever I want*?"

Ouch. But Willow couldn't fault him for saying it.

As much as she didn't think she was ready for this, there was no point in beating around the bush. "No, Tate. I found the keys you used to let the workmen upstairs."

"And just made yourself at home?"

"No, that wasn't—"

"What is this? Why would you want it?"

He flipped through the pages until he came to the one marked with a sticky note. Obviously those weren't around at the time the ledger had been written, so… He glanced up at her before reading the page.

"I still don't understand," he said. "Why would something like this be of interest to you?" He read some more. "It's just a contract for a random business transaction."

Willow stood up, seriously wishing she had on decent clothes for this confrontation rather than just her comfy shirt and shorts. "Actually, that date is very important. It's the day the McLemore ship was burned, with their male heir inside."

That gave Tate pause. He flipped back a few pages and read them. Then he flipped forward a few more. His jaw went tight. "So, this is a ledger of my ancestor's misdeeds? Why would anyone care about that in this day and age?"

Good question. "Well, that's a little complicated."

He braced himself, arms crossed over his chest. "Try me."

"My sister is pregnant with Paxton McLemore's child. The matriarch of the family was a little girl when her uncle was killed aboard that ship."

Tate frowned at that news.

"The people accused of perpetrating the crime were run out of town by the McLemores, who harassed them endlessly with sabotage of their business and personal threats. That family line is now continued in the Hardens. My Hardens."

She'd expected more questions, but Tate simply stared down at the open book before him.

Willow hurried to fill the silence. "I just didn't want my family, my sister, to be falsely accused. To be held accountable for something our family didn't do."

"But it's okay to implicate mine?"

Willow threw her hands up. "There's no good way to answer that, Tate. I've been struggling with the right choice since I found the ledger. I simply can't figure out what it is."

How could she explain this better? "At first, I only wanted to see if there was any information from that time out of curiosity. So we as a family could confirm what I found in my great-grandmother's journals. Some things Murdoch told me led me to believe…"

Willow could swear Tate paled five shades lighter. His expression went cold, just as his lips pressed tightly together. "You came here just to find this book?"

"Not that book specifically…"

"You came here to spy on me?" he clarified.

Knowing what he must be thinking made her ache inside. "Technically I had a job, but—"

Tate slammed the book shut, causing her to jump. In comparison, his voice was deadly quiet. "But you came here for this."

"I told you, I was simply curious, at first," she defended herself. "Then I found out my sister was pregnant, and things got complicated."

"I'll bet."

"Tate—"

She bristled at the way he held up his hand for silence. Even though she knew he had a right to be angry, his refusal to listen was totally ticking her off.

"My family lived off deceit," he said. "I told you from the beginning how they were, what they did. They didn't have very nice reputations, and the word *murderer* might have actually applied a time or two in the earlier generations.

"I told you I didn't want to live like that. Refused to live like they had. And yet deceit is exactly what you brought here."

She refused to let him brand her that way. "Tate, I did not know what would happen here. How life would change from the first moment I walked through the doors of Sabatini House. I love my family. I was trying to help them. But… I love you."

He picked up the oversize book with a white-knuck-led grip. "Then what is this doing here? If you loved me, why would you do exactly what I asked you not to?"

"Because I had decisions to make, Tate. I didn't know what to do. I wanted to hold on to the book until I could figure out what was best."

"Well, I'll make the decision for you, then," he said, dropping the book back onto the bed with a thump. The look he sent her had the hardest edge she'd seen from him. "Get out."

Tate sank into his office chair, dropping the stack of mail onto his desk next to the ledger. The stack was huge. He was used to having it brought to him every day and he'd forgotten that he now needed to go check the mailbox. It had been only a week, but it was long enough for him to see that both Murdoch and Willow had been culling the mail before bringing it to him.

Why in the world would anyone need so many advertisements?

He stared, feeling every bit of his irritation focused on the mail, even though logic told him that wasn't what was influencing his mood. Finally, he turned his gaze to the old, leather-bound ledger next to it. He'd found it on Willow's neatly made bed after she left.

He'd managed to stay away from the room for two days, but eventually couldn't keep himself from it any longer. He simply had to see if she'd left anything behind. And she had.

He just hadn't been able to accept her explanation. She knew how he'd felt about his family's actions. He felt so strongly that he'd cut himself off from relationships to eliminate the possibility of that behavior continuing through an heir.

To know that she came there for the express purpose of finding dirt on his family was just something he couldn't reconcile. At least, he didn't know how.

Since she'd been gone he'd been trapped in a kind of inertia, unable to motivate himself to work, or do much more than stare out that window…thinking. He knew he needed to hire a new housekeeper, and had even looked up a temp agency's phone number online, but he hadn't been able to make himself dial the phone.

The house was quiet, too quiet. He could feel the emptiness, but he had no idea what to do about it. Bringing in a new housekeeper wasn't going to change that.

And then there was the baby—the very last thing he wanted to think about. Did he want to have anything to do with the child if he couldn't have his mother? Did he need to just get over himself? Could he handle being nothing more than the person who sent a check once a month?

Hoping to shake off the endless rounds of questions he seemed to be stuck in with no answers, Tate sorted through the mail. His contract should be in soon. As he glanced through the various envelopes, one with familiar handwriting caught his eye.

Sure enough, in the upper right-hand corner was Murdoch's name. For just a moment, that feeling of emptiness lifted. Tate slit the envelope open and pulled out a card from inside.

A birth announcement.

Tate stared at the photo of the softly rounded baby face for a long time. It was the main picture on the front cover of the card; there were two other pictures to the side. One was of a man and woman holding the baby.

The other showed the baby and the woman with Murdoch standing beside her, his arm around her shoulders.

It was hard for Tate to picture his friend in such a happy familial setting. Neither of them had a lot of experience with it. But Murdoch seemed to be learning the ropes fairly quickly.

Finally, Tate opened the card and scanned the details of the birth announcement inside, but he kept returning back to that first large picture. A baby. So vulnerable, yet so indistinct. An unclear bundle of potential, containing the makings of the adult he would be some day.

How amazing.

To think back to that single little blip of light on Willow's ultrasound and know that it would one day be a baby like this one, a teenager like his brother had been, an adult like he was now, or a grandfather like Murdoch. Just the thought unlocked the inertia that had kept Tate cocooned from his pain.

To his dismay, a mixture of emotions started to seep through the cracks. Bad ones he hadn't wanted to recognize. Good ones he hadn't wanted to remember.

As he went to return the card to its envelope, Tate noticed a little piece of paper. He pulled it out and read Murdoch's scrawled note.

I was a fool to leave her for so long. Don't make my same mistakes. The past is what it is. But the future is all up to us.

Tate dropped the note on the desk. Restless energy forced him to his feet, got him moving. He crossed over to the arched windows and found himself staring down at the beach. He'd opened the shutters right after the storm and never closed them. As much as he wanted to say that overcoming his fear and aversion to the water had nothing to do with Willow, he knew he was lying to himself. Any thoughts of his brother still hurt, but simply looking at the water didn't anymore. And that was a miracle.

But as much as he wanted to believe Murdoch, to believe that the potential of the future was worth letting go of the past, Tate wasn't sure that he could.

Frustrated, he stalked back to the ledger. Why did she leave it? Didn't she need it anymore? It would just be her word against his if she took the information public. Did he even care about that?

He didn't know. Because he hadn't bothered to find out any answers past the accusations. Which was his typical MO with Willow. He'd pushed, but hadn't asked much. Heck, he hadn't even known her parents were dead for how long?

Idly he flipped through the book until he reached the page she had marked. He immediately noticed the sticky note was no longer blank. The brief message, in Willow's elegant handwriting, contained an address with the words: *If you ever need me, please let me know.*

For the first time, Tate looked at the long years ahead of him and wondered about the things that he could change, that he and his brother had always wanted to be different but couldn't do anything about. Deep down he knew it was time for action rather than hiding behind excuses.

It took Tate only a few minutes to change his clothes, and then he rushed down the stairs and grabbed his keys. He didn't want to give himself too much time to think, because that could lead to no action at all.

He fired up the Jeep, checked all the levels and backed out of the garage.

It wasn't until he reached the fork in the road that he acknowledged he had a choice to make. Left, and he would drive across the island to the hangar and stay safe and secure in his own little world. He could write his stories with their touch of danger while staying safely tucked away in Sabatini House for the rest of his life.

The path he always took.

Or right, and he could head down the hill to the bridge that led to the mainland. He hadn't crossed it since he was eighteen years old. He didn't even fly out that way. But he could today. He could find Willow and tell her he'd been a fool.

There was a big risk involved, especially for a man like him. One who didn't do risk. One who lived out all his adventures in the written word alone. But if he didn't take it, he would never again touch her silky skin or smell that soothing vanilla scent. Never bury himself in the heat of her body and forget the pain of the past.

Tate also thought about that soft baby face, and the picture of the mom and dad holding their child close. That's what he wanted for his child, and he hoped to God he was the type of man to give it to him. So he turned the Jeep right, took a deep breath and put it in Drive.

Seventeen

Willow finished up the beans and potato salad, while Royce took the last of the barbecue chicken off the grill. Cooking in the kitchen of the house where'd she'd spent most of her life made her foray to the island seem almost like a dream…though she was experiencing enough pregnancy symptoms to make it very real.

Auntie and Jasmine entertained the baby over at the table, while Ivy lay down after her long day searching for work. With two pregnant ladies in the house, Jasmine and Royce had been nice enough to come over a couple of times this week with dinner, instead of just the usual Sundays.

Plus, it gave everyone a chance to play with little Rosie.

At least these family dinners helped Willow not to feel so alone. A week had passed since she'd left Sabatini House. So many times throughout each day her mind was haunted by that moment of holding Tate's hand as they watched their baby's heartbeat. Even though they'd both had their own doubts and fears, in that one moment they had been united.

Instead she'd now be going it alone.

Royce came through the door from the back porch and set the platter of meat on the counter next to the stove. Then he walked over to the table and swept Rosie up into the air. Her high-pitched squeal echoed through the room. Just the reaction her daddy was going for.

Royce's transformation from cold businessman to loving father was nothing short of miraculous. Sometimes Willow could hardly believe it. If she hadn't really seen it in person, no one could have convinced her.

She and Ivy had discussed a couple of times how they were both a little envious of Jasmine, but they would figure out their relationship woes somehow. One thing was certain: the heirloom ring hadn't worked for either of them the way it had for Jasmine.

But Jasmine and Royce's path to happiness hadn't been the typical straightforward one, so Willow and Ivy weren't about to begrudge them the wonderful life they were now enjoying. It had taken a lot of effort to achieve.

To Willow, both the effort and the result were beautiful things.

As if she knew exactly what Willow was thinking, Jasmine met her gaze. "How are you doing?" she asked.

Good question. Some days she wasn't really sure. "I'm managing," she said, keeping it short and sweet.

What else could she say? She almost wished summer were over, so she'd have her teaching job to distract her. Instead she simply found whatever she could to keep herself busy, and she spent the evenings reading so she didn't waste hours wondering how Tate was and if he hated her still.

"Have you heard from Tate?"

"No. And I don't imagine I will."

"Give him time," Royce said. "He'll come around."

Willow wished she could believe that.

"Like you did?" Jasmine asked, grinning over at him.

"Yes, ma'am. We men might be slow, but we eventually recognize when we're missing a good thing." For good measure, Royce brushed a kiss over Rosie's dark, curly hair, and then did the same for her mama.

Willow wasn't so sure. Tate had barely been off that island in over twenty years. She had serious doubts about him coming for her now.

Jasmine headed down the hall to let Ivy know dinner was ready. They all gathered around the table as usual, bringing on that secure, comfortable feeling of having Willow's loved ones around her. The split was probably for the best, she thought as she looked around. Tate wouldn't ever want to be a true part of her family. He was too isolated. And her sisters and Auntie were something she simply couldn't live without.

Suddenly, the doorbell rang.

"Who in heaven is that?" Auntie asked, craning to see out the curtain-draped windows.

"I'll get it," Ivy said. She stepped out of the room for a minute and they all heard the front door open.

"Must not have been a salesman," Royce said with a secretive smile. "Last Saturday she about bit the head off one when he interrupted her nap with his persistent knocking."

"Better keep that in mind when you go to have a brother or sister for little Rosie there," Auntie said with a cackle.

Royce's brows shot up straight to his hairline. "Not anytime soon, I hope."

Jasmine just laughed.

Finally, Ivy came back into the room, her face flushed.

"You have a visitor, Willow."

"Me?" *Who would be here to see me?*

Ivy just nodded. "I think you'd better come."

Willow found herself reluctantly heading to the front parlor. Who in the world did she know who would bother them at dinnertime?

She gasped as she rounded the corner and saw Tate standing on the front porch. At first, seeing him was so out of context that her brain refused to register who it was. Then Ivy passed her with a glass of water. She stepped through the door, where she handed it over to Tate. He drew in a deep breath as if trying to steady himself before he tilted his dark head back and drank, giving Willow time to take in his olive skin and tall, familiar build.

As he finished, she could see he was deeply shaken but forcing himself to hold it together. She'd seen that expression a time or two before today. She'd be perfectly happy to never see him struggle this hard again.

The smile he gave her sister was really more of a stretching of his lips, but he murmured his thanks. Ivy stepped through the door and paused beside Willow. "He looked rough, so I thought he could use some water."

"Thanks, Ivy," Willow said, both for her thoughtfulness and for giving Willow a moment to gather her courage.

Then Ivy headed back to the kitchen, leaving Willow with no choice but to walk through the front door and stand face-to-face with a man she never thought would show up at her house.

"What are you doing here?" she asked, her voice trembling and weaker than she would have liked.

He stood with the glass in his hands, absently rubbing it like he was summoning a genie to make a wish. "I came to see you," he answered. His gaze, his voice, everything about him was direct. This was a man who knew what he was doing, even if he wasn't entirely comfortable doing it.

"Why?" Willow crossed her arms over her chest. The ache caused by the slight pressure on her breasts only reminded her how much unfinished business they had. Was the baby his reason for being here? His *only* reason?

Tate stepped closer, his grip tightening. "I need you, Willow."

"You what?" Of all the things she'd expected him to say, that wasn't one of them.

"You said if I ever needed you, this was where you'd be. Well, I do."

When she'd left that note, she'd been leaving open a door, but she'd never expected him to walk through it because of her. The baby, yes. Willow shook her head. "I guess this just isn't matching up with the Tate that I know."

"It's not the Tate I know, either," he said with a little grin. Then it faded as he swallowed hard. "But I can't do it, Willow. I can't live with the emptiness, the isolation anymore. Just me and the people who run around in my brain. I need you to make it all come alive, to make it worth doing. You and—" he gestured toward her stomach "—that little one that's beaten all the odds just to make it here."

It all sounded so good, but Willow had been burned before by him. "You said you can't live with the deceit."

"And when are you going to figure out the lie I told to protect myself? You're too smart for that." He set the glass down on the windowsill. His fists clenched and released as if he wanted to reach for her, but he kept his distance. "Claiming you deliberately deceived me was an excuse in the heat of the moment. Your actions disappointed me, so I lashed out, but I know you, Willow. You're nothing like my parents or my grandparents. If it wasn't for you pushing my boundaries, nothing would've ever changed."

"I know," she said.

"And now, so do I." His look held such longing, Willow felt tears prick her eyes. "I'm not going to pretend I don't have a lot of faults. We both know I do. But you bring out the best in me. I wouldn't be able to live with myself if I didn't take the chance that you could love me, at least a little."

Goodness, she'd have trouble holding back the waterworks if he kept talking like this. "Oh, I think I can manage a little more than that."

One step at a time he came to her, until he could finally bury his hands in her hair and study her face up close. "You really mean that?" he asked.

"Hasn't anything I've done convinced you?"

His kiss was sure, with a touch of reverence like Willow had never felt before.

"I promise to stop living in the past," he murmured. "I want a future, Willow. But the only future worth having is with you."

"We'll make it together, Tate. I promise."

"Your life will never be the same, buddy," Royce yelled out the kitchen window.

Tate and Willow turned to see a handful of faces on the other side of the curtains. She'd completely forgotten about her family, and she wanted to laugh. Eavesdropping was something she should have expected of them. But she glanced up to see Tate's eyes go wide. At first she thought he had a problem. Then she realized he was actually nervous. That was a new look for the forceful man she was used to seeing.

"Might as well get used to it," Willow warned. "We come as a package deal. You're stuck with them now."

He seemed to swallow down his nerves and nodded resolutely. "A new future. A new family. With you right at the center. Sounds like everything I didn't know I wanted. Now I can't imagine living without any of it."

"You won't. Not if you're smart." And she knew he was, or else he'd have never gotten this far. "But don't worry, they'll love you just as much as I do. As much as Murdoch does. All you have to do is let them."

Tate nodded. "I will."

It wouldn't be easy for him, not after all he'd been through, but she knew they'd get there.

Probably time to address the elephant on their front porch before Willow got too emotional. "How did you get here? Did someone bring you?" She glanced around for a taxi.

Tate took a few steps back and gestured to the Jeep parked along the curb. One she should have recognized, but didn't at first, just as she'd never expected Tate on her doorstep… "I drove."

"You what?" she whispered, shock still rocketing through her.

"I needed to see you," he said with a shrug. The explanation was so simple, but oh so profound. "Right then. I couldn't wait."

He grinned, that sexy, mysterious smile that sent shivers down her spine. On that night months ago when he'd caught her on the stairs of Sabatini House, she'd never imagined she'd be on the receiving end of something so special.

"Besides, you don't have a landing strip in your backyard, I'm guessing."

Willow laughed. "No. No, we don't."

"We might have to remedy that."

* * * * *

THE DOUBLE DEAL

CATHERINE MANN

To my sisters, Julie and Beth

"A sister is a gift to the heart, a friend to the spirit,
a golden thread to the meaning of life."
—Isadora James

Prologue

Naomi Steele wasn't naive.

Her life had brought enough challenges to make her wise—if not jaded. She'd expected pregnancy to bring changes too. Yes, hormonal upheaval. But also miraculous transformations, full of shimmering emotions and realized dreams.

She just hadn't expected to feel such a ferocious internal roar—a primal drive—to protect her child at all costs.

Or possibly children. Plural? Twins ran in her family and having used in vitro increased her odds of fraternal twins. A wave of nerves—and nausea—hit her.

Breathe. Breathe. Focus.

With a report from the private investigator to her left and her computer screen to her right, she compared notes on the world-famous research scientist who could bring her the business coup—the security—she needed for her child. Sure, she had a large, wealthy family, and she lived in the confines of their estate outside of Anchorage, Alaska. Her suite was large. The enclosed balcony offered her magnificent views of both the bay and the mountains.

But none of that helped her feel as though she had a real stake in the family business. A legacy to share with her child. And since her pregnancy had been accomplished by in vitro fertilization with a sperm donor, she was utterly on her own to create that legacy. That lasting piece of the Steele portfolio that couldn't be taken away.

Her family was in a state of upheaval. Her father's upcoming marriage to a former business rival and the resulting merger of their two oil empires meant everyone in both families were fighting for roles in the new company—Alaska Oil Barons, Incorporated. Naomi needed to contribute to the business in a way that was undeniably hers.

And research scientist Royce Miller was her ticket to making that happen.

She let the corners of the private investigator's report brush over her thumb like a flip book, information she already knew about Royce Miller, PhD, by heart. She let her gaze fall on her computer screen, where a rare image of him filled the space. He was a brilliant man, a reclusive genius. He was all compelling eyes and brooding good looks, his intelligence as evident as his strong shoulders.

She needed him to cement her value in the family business.

Was the anonymous father of her child half that smart? Half that strong? All moot musings. She'd chosen her path as a single parent, on her own.

Up to now, that independence had suited her just fine.

Since her battle with cancer as a teenager, she'd lived her life for herself, and with abandon. She'd embraced her competitiveness. In play, and later in her work as an attorney for her family's Alaskan-based oil business. She preferred no strings in all her dealings, outside the connection to her widowed father and her siblings.

Now, she was still going her own way, but the stakes were higher than ever.

She had seen often enough how quickly a successful company could crash. And with the tumultuous merger of the Steele oil holdings with the Mikkelson oil family—thanks to her father's surprise engagement to the Mikkelson matriarch—Naomi was more concerned than ever about the future of the business. Their competitor, Johnson Oil United, was hot on their heels, hoping to use the uncertainty during the merger as a chance to surge ahead in the market.

Naomi couldn't grow complacent. She couldn't back down.

Right now, her private detective and crazy good internet skills were her best advantages in tracking down her ace in the hole.

Finding the scientist and persuading him to bring his research on ecological advancements in oil pipelines to her family was paramount. At the very least, she needed to locate him and sneak a peek at his research. Aside from the benefits to her family's company, his research could be the key to reducing environmentally based cancers, a passion she shared with her ecologist sister Delaney. Doubling the stakes, really.

After tireless searching for Dr. Miller, Naomi finally had a lead on the sequestered scientist. He'd retreated to the mountains to work on his research in an isolated but luxurious glass igloo.

Now that she'd found him, she just needed to come up with a plan to meet him. Hang out with him. And use her creative maneuvering to wrangle an afternoon together where she could work her way into his good graces and secure the deal of a lifetime.

One

Research scientist Royce Miller didn't have a problem shifting from cerebral to alpha mode to save a woman from a hungry Alaskan grizzly that should have been hibernating.

But he needed to put on some clothes first.

Royce gathered up his jeans, boots and a parka to go over his boxers and T-shirt. Beyond the thick paned glass of his remote getaway, a shaggy brown bear stalked toward an SUV. Parked in his snow-piled driveway, the driver—someone in a blindingly pink parka—honked the horn repeatedly. The blaring would have alerted a couple of city blocks, except this happened to be the only cabin for nearly a hundred miles.

Well, not a cabin exactly.

Renting this insulated glass igloo out in the middle of nowhere had given him the irresistible opportunity to soak up some rare Alaskan rays this month as he

immersed himself in developing new safety measures
for oil pipelines. Not that he gave a damn about a tan,
but vitamin D from sunshine was in short supply this
far north and crucial for bone health, muscle mass and
strength. All of which could come in handy once he
stepped outdoors to say howdy to the massive grizzly
closing in on the SUV holding his unexpected guest.

The "guest"? An issue he would deal with later.

Just because he valued his privacy as highly as his
vintage Pascal's calculator, that didn't mean he could
let the angry bear take out the dainty woman behind the
wheel of the four-wheel drive. Her pink hood bobbed
left and right, fast, as if she searched for options. Or
help.

At least she was in a vehicle. That gave him a few
precious moments to prep rather than bolt out there in
the buff.

Bolting away from the glass wall, he sidestepped his
Saint Bernard. "'Scuse me, Tessie."

Tessie, as in short for the scientist Nikola Tesla.

The two-year-old shaggy dog lifted her block head
off her paws and tipped it to the side. She was worn-
out from their time playing in the yard earlier, a long
outing to stretch her legs since he'd known a blizzard
was imminent. Was that why this driver had stopped
here? Stranded on the way back to Anchorage? Spring
was just one breath from winter up here.

His Saint Bernard narrowed her eyes, studying him
intently. Sniffing the air, the dog let out a low whine,
standing. Perhaps catching the scent of the bear. Not
good.

"This isn't the time for curiosity, girl." Urgency
pumped through him as he tugged on his jeans, paus-

ing only to turn off his computer with a brisk click on his way by. Sensitive data secured.

From the bear and a lost tourist? Not likely.

Still, never could be too careful given the nature of his work. Patent-worthy research if all played out as he suspected. And when it came to his job, he was never wrong. The stakes were too high. Too personal.

His father had worked the old-school oil pipelines, like most of the population in the small Texas town where Royce had grown up. It had been a tight community. A loss of one sent ripples throughout that touched them all.

When his former fiancée's father had died in an explosion, Royce's world had been blown apart too. Then his fiancée miscarried their baby and left the country. Left him...

Shaking off the past, Royce dressed with methodical speed, shrugging into a fleece-lined flannel shirt, then tugging on a parka, and stepped into boots on his way to the door to deal with the massive curveball thrown at his day. This would have been the perfect secluded afternoon for productive thinking. He'd come to the wilderness retreat for peace, a slice of time with no distractions. No question, creating a safer, ecologically friendly oil pipeline was personal.

Corporations vied to get him on their payroll, but he preferred to work solo and, thanks to selling off a few patents, he had a multimillion-dollar cushion to innovate on his own terms. Such as working here. Alone.

So much for that plan.

Thinsulate gloves were all he could afford to wear and still use the tools at his disposal to rid them of the bear's threat. A flare gun and, as a last resort, a shotgun.

"Tessie," he said firmly, "stay."

She huffed in apparent irritation at being kept inside, but she didn't budge.

"Good girl." He tossed the words of praise over his shoulder.

Bracing himself, he unlocked the door that opened into a short igloo-style tunnel. A blast of frigid air whipped inward hard and fast, damn near freezing his breath in his chest. A painful breath, as the cold air crackled in his lungs. Steeling himself, he pressed into the howl of the blizzard wind, the blaring horn roaring almost louder than the bear.

Royce pushed forward into the full slam of storm winds. If he could steer the bear away before it reached the driver, or distract the bear long enough for the woman to bolt inside...

The grizzly ambled faster toward the SUV idling beside Royce's dual cab truck. Now that he was outside, he could see the SUV spewing sludge from the back wheels as the vehicle worked—in vain—to reverse out.

With a flying leap and roar, the beast pounded on the hood of the woman's vehicle, enormous paws taking swipes at the windshield. Even through the thick swirls of snow mixed with sleet, Royce could see the glint of long, lethal bear claws.

The time for finesse had ended.

Royce shouted, "Hey, you, teddy bear, check me out."

His voice got lost amid the car horn blending with the unforgiving blizzard. The grizzly's ears twitched but still he—or she—continued to rock the SUV, chunks of slush clotting in the shaggy coat. The blizzard dumped its fury faster and faster from the sky, wind carrying the flakes sideways in stinging icy bullets. Royce raised the flare gun and popped a flaming missile into the air, careful to avoid the frosted branches.

With a roar, the bear's massive head swung around.

"Yeah, Paddington, now we're in business," Royce shouted, gripping part of his unbuttoned parka and spreading it wide, making himself appear as big as possible.

Bears usually preferred easy prey, so looking large could help scare him off. But he wasn't counting on it. He kept the shotgun in hand even as he held his coat open. "Yeah, you. Back off, Baloo." Who knew there were so many jolly bears in literature? Kids should be taught to steer clear of them, not cuddle the creatures. "There's no food in my trash, and that little lady there isn't going to be dinner."

Or an appetizer, or canapé even, given the woman appeared to be more of a wiry sort.

The car horn pierced the air, long and loud, as the woman pressed the hell out of it. She had some serious mojo. No diving under the dashboard in fear for herself. She revved the engine, puffing thicker exhaust into the cold.

As the driver's side window eased down, a head peeked out. That pink parka shone, hood up, but a coal-dark ponytail trailed free along her shoulder. "I'm trying to back up, but either the tires are stuck or the bear weighs too—"

"Get back in there before Winnie the Pooh takes off your head with one swipe of the paw," Royce barked. Quick calculations told him he needed to get that bear away from the SUV within the next two to three minutes or the windshield would almost certainly shatter. The grizzly was big, but not too big to climb through the busted front glass.

"Of course I'm going to stay in the car," she shouted back. "I just wanted to know if you can think of some-

thing I should be doing differently. I have no intention
of budging until Winnie-the-Pooh bear trundles back
off into the Hundred Acre Wood—"

The bear's paw swiped off the side mirror, inches
from her face. Fat snowflakes quickly piled on top of
the shattered mirror, covering it in a testament to the
power and fury of the Alaskan storm. Also, a reminder
that Royce was up against more than just a grizzly.

Squealing, the woman tucked back into the SUV
as the bear rolled off the vehicle and landed on the
ground. On both back feet, wobbling but not down and
not retreating.

No more playing around.

Royce raised his shotgun.

Aimed.

The SUV lurched backward, then forward, snow
spewing. Apparently, the bear's weight had been keeping it in place, after all. Royce's shot went wild and the
four-wheel drive skidded on the icy ground inches past
him. The gleaming silver SUV was on a fast track to
bashing into his igloo hideaway.

Royce launched to the left, out of the vehicle's path,
while keeping eyes on the grizzly. The bear lumbered
off into the tangle of slick trees. Clearly Teddy-Baloo-
Paddington-Winnie thought better of tangling with that
pink parka.

Speaking of which.

Royce checked right and—thank God—found the
SUV at a stop in a puffy snowbank, the horn silent at
last. The driver? Already climbing out from behind the
wheel. Apparently unscathed.

And not as wiry as he'd originally thought. She was
petite, alright, but with just the right kind of curves
showcased in ski pants and a parka cinched at the waist.

A cute-as-hell—but still unwelcome—vision.

Now that the bear was gone, suspicion burned more than the frostbite threatening his face. Royce had to wonder. What was this woman doing out here in the middle of nowhere?

And what did she want with him?

Naomi Steele resented playing the wilting flower for any man.

She'd been born in Alaska, was a quarter Inuit on her dead mother's side. Growing up, she and her sisters had learned about survival in her harsh and magnificent home state right alongside her brothers. She could have handled the bear on her own with the flare gun in her survival kit.

But letting Royce Miller save her offered a golden opportunity to slide under the man's radar.

Shading her eyes against the fast-setting sun, Naomi watched the ornery grizzly hike back into the woods and out of sight. She turned slowly, careful to give her boots traction on the snow.

And…whoa, sexy snowman.

She'd seen press releases about Royce Miller during her internet search. She'd even sat in on one of his lectures a month ago, knew about his work from her background check on him prior to driving to his remote getaway. But no portfolio full of head shots, data or even back row auditorium viewing could have prepared her for his up close charisma. He was so much more than broodingly handsome good looks. The appeal was more than his leanly muscle-bound body on display in that open parka. And yeah, he got bonus points for the thick dark hair a hint too long like he'd forgotten to get a haircut, tousled like he'd just gotten out of bed.

All enticing. Sure.

But it was his eyes that held her. Those windows to the soul. To the man. A man with laser-sharp intelligence in his deep brown gaze that pierced straight to the core of her and seemed to say, *Bring it, woman. I can keep up.*

Raw sexual attraction crackled so hot in the air she half expected icicles to start melting off the trees.

Normally, she would have welcomed the draw, the challenge. But talk about poor timing. She needed to focus on her mission to wrangle a way to use that brilliant mind of his for her family's company.

And she happened to be two months pregnant. Those teenage years fighting cancer had seemed surreal at times, but she'd frozen some of her eggs before treatment, just in case. Her oncology specialist had called on a counselor to help her through so many decisions during that frightening experience.

Now she was ready to be a mother. She was through waiting around for a mythical Mr. Perfect. She'd started this journey with her career as a lawyer and her connections to her family as a solid foundation, but she'd since had her world turned upside down. With her father's engagement and the two rival companies merging, everyone was fighting for a place. And just as she had when she was a child, she needed to prove her place. For her child. For her sister who'd died. She blinked back tears.

Pregnancy hormones.

Of course. That must be the explanation for her off-the-charts reaction to a total stranger.

That stud muffin stranger adjusted his hold on the shotgun. "Let's get inside to talk before the bear comes back—or we're buried in a snowdrift."

"Oh, yeah, right." Another second staring at him and

she could well have drool freeze to her face. She needed a level head to stay one step ahead of him. Royce wasn't just smart. He was genius smart—and eccentric.

Locating the recluse at all had taken Herculean detective work, employing the best of the best private investigators she'd used in her legal practice.

Detectives known for their discretion.

If the search gained her access to his pipeline research, it would be worth every penny. If she could somehow accomplish the unimaginable and persuade this lone ranger researcher to sign on with her family's oil company, well, that coup would be worth more than any amount of money.

She would finally win her family's full approval by contributing more than her legal advice to the business. She needed this for herself and for her child, a stable future. Strategy mattered more.

Royce opened the door to the glass igloo—and a beast of another kind came bounding out. A huge Saint Bernard leaned into him, sniffing, taking in all the surroundings. The air was heavy with scents of pine, the lingering smell of the spent flare gun still carried on the blizzard breeze.

"Tessie," Royce commanded in a soft rumble, "inside, girl."

Panting, the Saint Bernard shifted away from the front stoop and let them enter.

Bracing a hand against the door frame for balance, Naomi glanced around the space and found it much like ones her family had vacationed in over the years. God, those were amazing memories, a time before her mother and sister had died in a plane crash. Before Naomi had gotten cancer. A time she'd innocently thought could last forever. But those times had ended prematurely, like a short Alaskan day.

She looked upward, tipping her face toward the sun's rays. The igloo's glass dome let in the last beams of light. Only one wall was opaque, a wall with a platform bed against it, and almost certainly the bathroom and closet tucked cubicle-style behind.

Half the room had a long, curved sofa along the glass. Tessie had taken up residence on the couch, watching Naomi and Royce with wide brown eyes. The rest of the room held a kitchenette and dining table that was currently being used as a computer desk. No doubt, the keys to his research kingdom were inside that computer. Not that she expected him to have anything less than the best security.

"So?"

Royce Miller's voice pulled her back around.

"Yes, well…" She searched for the right words. She'd spent so much time figuring out how to find him and get here, she hadn't given much thought to being here. With him. Alone. "Thank you so much for saving my life."

He unloaded the shotgun with a swift efficiency that shouted his Texas upbringing, and pocketed the ammo. "What in the hell coerced you to venture out in this storm?"

"Whoa, hostility check, big guy. Is that any way to speak to the person who brought your supplies?" she asked with the charm that had won over dozens of tough-as-nails juries. "Without my trek up here, you could have starved, not to mention run out of deodorant."

"Supplies?" He eyed her warily, shrugging out of his parka and shaking the snow onto the doormat.

He made flannel look good.

But she ignored that and kept talking. "Yes, that's what I said. You have contracted a delivery service for your supplies while you're isolated up here." And she'd slipped the driver a hefty tip to let her bring the supplies up to her supposed boyfriend. The driver had been an old softie, a real romantic, and was easily persuaded. Lawyer skills with word craft came in handy out of the courtroom too. "And I'm here to restock your pantry. I thought I'd left in time to beat the storm, but it came on faster and heavier than expected. And, well, here I am."

Sure, she'd quibbled, insinuating she worked for the rental company's supply business. Truth be told, she hadn't outright said so. She could talk her way around that equivocation later. Because if he knew she was a part of the oil mogul Steele family, he would have likely left her to the bear.

"And you are?"

"Naomi." She said just her first name carefully, toying with her parka zipper. Then catching the nervous twitch, she stopped. No outright lies to backtrack from, she reminded herself.

She studied his face closely to see if her name sparked even a hint of recognition. Nope. Nothing. She didn't doubt her read of him. She'd been top of her law school class and had yet to lose a courtroom battle.

"Naomi, thank you for the supplies that you drove here in the middle of a blizzard," he said tightly, "but what do you expect to do now?"

"I expect for us to unload the supplies in my car before things freeze."

Sighing, he reached for his parka and started toward the door. "Have a seat. I'll get everything."

She raised a manicured hand. "Don't forget the flare gun in case our 'friend' returns."

"Got it."

"I can back you up with the shotgun if needed," she added, already sensing he would insist *no*, *no* and *hell no*.

He paused at the door, hand on the knob. "I've got it," he repeated, then stepped outside.

Ah, and just as predicted, he'd assumed she was as defenseless as she looked. For a smart man, he had a weakness and she'd found it fast.

He coddled women.

Some would think that rocked, and soak it right up. But she valued her independence. Her strength.

Her health.

She'd fought hard for her life, battling cancer as a teen, then battling all over again to elbow free of her family's overprotective ways. And yes, she'd gone overboard at times asserting herself, pushing through boundaries, which gained her a wild child reputation. She'd been bold. She'd partied and lived every day to the fullest. And she'd let her reputation become larger than life, more risqué than reality.

A choice that was coming back to bite her now that she genuinely gave a damn about being a part of the family business.

Speaking of which, she needed to get her butt in gear before Royce returned. This window of time while he was unloading the supplies was precious. She could recon his cabin. She would need every clue at her disposal to get past his defenses.

Two

Head ducked into the wind that was picking up speed and throwing icy dartcicles, Royce carried the last box inside—his fifth trip. This Naomi was one hell of a delivery person. He had enough to make it through an apocalypse. Or thereabouts

Frankly, the hauling—while done on a day colder than the coldest day in hell—had given him a chance to air out his thoughts regarding this unexpected turn of events at a time when he needed unwavering focus.

A visitor at his private retreat. A woman.

A drop-dead gorgeous woman.

He stepped back inside, his dog there to greet him with a nudge of the nose and wag of the tail. Wide brown eyes seemed to ask about this new addition to their haven. Royce didn't have an answer yet. But he would.

"Hey," he said, "last box."

"Sorry the weather stinks so badly." She stood at the

kitchen cabinets with the other boxes at her feet, un-loading canned milk.

Naomi's parka was long gone and...damn, she was a sight for hungry eyes in formfitting jeans with silver studs and a red fuzzy sweater that all but shouted, *I'm soft—touch me*. Her dark ponytail swished in a silky glide as she reached upward to slide the can in place, then ducked back down to unload a jar of granola.

Eyes off her ass.

He set the last box on one of the two kitchen chairs, cushioned with leather for comfort and the kind of chair that could be used in his office or in the living area. Everything in the space was efficient and multipur-pose. "Isn't someone going to be worried when you don't return?"

"I texted one of my brothers while you were outside." She wriggled her toes in thick socks, stacking cans to make room for the granola container.

Texted? "How did you manage that? The signal up here sucks."

Sure, *he* could call out and email, but his equipment was top-of-the-line with a portable minisatellite dish.

"I have a really good phone," she answered simply over her shoulder, inky-black ponytail stroking along her back in a way that made him consider what it would feel like to trace her hair's path, then test the texture in a gentle fist.

"That's advanced tech equipment for a delivery per-son."

Stepping down, she faced him, smile bright, her full lips glistening with fresh gloss. "My family's generous. And, um, I was helping a friend by making the delivery since they were overwhelmed with storm purchases." She tugged at the hem of her red sweater, a slight flush staining her cheeks. "I don't actually work for the supply shop."

"You're a good friend, then, to make a trip in this weather." He still wasn't sure why he couldn't accept she was here to bring his supplies. It just seemed off that the store would send a woman out alone in this crazy-monstrous spring blizzard to deliver paper towels and canned goods. He should call, just to verify, which he would as soon as the supply offices reopened tomorrow...or after the storm.

A deep, shining smile plumped her cheeks, eyes dancing in the warm light. "We all have our reasons for doing things. Friendship is a treasure—and a hefty motivator."

"True enough." His parents and their next-door neighbors had been best friends, like family.

They'd been thrilled when Royce had started dating their friends' daughter, the girl next door, whose father worked alongside his. His parents hadn't been as excited when she got pregnant, since a baby would have changed his plans for a PhD. However, wedding preparations ensued...until a pipeline explosion rocked the town. His fiancée's father died.

Then his fiancée miscarried the baby.

Before Royce could process the grief over losing his child, Carrie Lynn had broken the engagement and left. For good.

Life fell apart for him. He didn't give himself over to emotion easily. It wasn't in his nature. Figuring out how to recover from that loss ten years ago had been tougher than anything he'd faced in his life.

But Royce had pieced himself back together with an unwavering focus on work and a dedication to reducing the chances of a pipeline tragedy happening to any other family again. Hell, he was better off doing what he did best.

Dealing with science and facts, not emotions and feelings.

His passion for his work had cost him relationships, but damn it, he wasn't interested in changing himself or his values for anyone.

Take him as he was. Period.

So, in reality, this woman wasn't a threat beyond being a physical temptation.

Reassured for the moment, he stepped out of his boots, his wool socks much like hers. Except his weren't purple.

Naomi closed the cabinet and settled in an empty chair, crossing her legs, purple-socked foot swinging. "Are you vacationing?"

"Working." A fact that shouldn't require elaboration.

She laughed lightly. "You don't look like a professional ice fisherman."

"I'm not."

"Then what are you working on?" she asked, drumming her fingers on his laptop computer, his abacus key chain resting beside on the table. "Your memoirs of life in the Alaskan wilds fighting bears?"

"Nosy much?" He moved the final box of supplies to the floor and sat in the other chair, eyeing her.

"I'm just making polite conversation. Unless you're going to cue up Netflix, we have time to kill waiting out the storm."

Damn, she was funny and sassy as well as hot. How long was this storm supposed to last?

"I have an extensive library on my tablet. You're welcome to browse. Make yourself comfortable over there on the sofa."

Out of his workspace and far enough away so that he wouldn't be breathing in the crisp scent of her, something like—he sought an intellectual answer to such an elemental scent—like the water, the ocean. Icy salt air. Did they make that into a perfume or was it just the scent of her? He focused back in on her words.

"While you work at..."

"I'm a science professor." He tossed out his generic answer, a truth. He did give the periodic guest lecture series.

"So, you have papers to grade?" she pushed without budging from her seat.

"Hmm..." He pulled his tablet out of his computer bag and cued up the library, while making sure the rest of his data was tightly password protected.

"You're not the chatty sort."

"Nope."

"You were talkative earlier, with the bear." She toyed with her ponytail, shiny black strands gliding through her fingers.

"Adrenaline." A chemical currently pumping through his body again as he watched her play with her hair. Was it his imagination or was she flirting?

And if she was, did he want to take her up on that offer?

Hell, yes.

She reached across the small teak table. "Is the offer for that tablet full of reading material still available?"

Three hours later, stars glinting overhead and a fire crackling in the stone hearth, Naomi curled up with a blanket and throw pillows, pretending to be engrossed in a mystery novel on the glowing tablet. She'd already read it a week ago, so if Royce asked questions, she would be able to answer. Meanwhile, she could study him and figure out how best to proceed.

Upon reflection, Naomi wasn't so sure this plan had been her best. After receiving the investigator's report, she'd moved quickly. Usually a strength of hers. Fast decision-making.

But given the upheaval in her family lately, she had to admit, she wasn't at the top of her game.

She'd rushed up here without considering all the outcomes.

Gathering a look at Royce's data would be easier said than done, and a few notes here and there would only have short-term benefits. Persuading him to join forces with the Steele and Mikkelson family businesses, which were merging into Alaska Oil Barons, was going to be a challenge. Especially with the tumultuous press her family had been generating since her dad had announced his surprise engagement to the Mikkelson widow—Jeannie. Stock prices had dropped.

Then her brother had gotten engaged to a Mikkelson and they were parenting a baby together.

Boom. No warning.

Stock prices dipped again. The board of directors rumbled there was too much chaos, too much emotional fallout and not enough strategy. They weren't sure how the merger would play out, and the board hated uncertainty.

She wasn't so sure she disagreed with them. She trusted her family. But the Mikkelsons? She'd been raised to consider them the enemy. Had that feud ended just because their patriarch had died? Could the entire contentious atmosphere be blamed on one person?

Not likely.

She needed to solidify her role in the company. She

was keeping a close eye on things from a legal perspective, but she'd need to win as many allies as possible to act on any discrepancies she found. She didn't know how the rival companies would be blended or how leadership positions would be divided. Nabbing Royce Miller for her family's team would go a long way in garnering loyalty and upping her professional profile.

But she would be a fool to think she could accomplish that tonight. She would settle in and watch his body language; she'd wait for that moment when he started to relax. Another courtroom tactic with a practical application.

Her stomach rumbled, reminding her how little she'd eaten. She'd only managed a few crackers in the morning and a cup of soup at lunch.

Now? She was ravenous. Yes, she had a job to do here with Royce, but she also needed to take care of her baby and keep track of what she ate. With her finicky taste buds lately, it was all too easy to skip eating until she was nearly dizzy, like now.

Setting aside the tablet, she stood and made her way to the kitchenette, sidestepping the table where Royce tapped away at his computer. He glanced up just as she opened the minifridge.

Royce tipped back in his chair, eyeing her with heavy-lidded dark eyes. "That's my food."

"I'll be glad to pay for my portion of this pudding cup and pear." She tossed the fruit in the air and caught it with a quick snap. "We're stranded. Do you intend to let me starve—or make me freeze out there ice fishing?"

He chuckled softly, a whiskey rich sound. "If you're hungry, help yourself to anything in the pantry."

"I am starving, actually. Bear hunting is quite exhausting." She crunched a bite of the pear and searched for a spoon. "Can I make you something, to earn my keep and all? I imagine grading papers is tiring."

"I'm fine. I ate earlier." He toyed with his abacus key chain, thumbing the beads back and forth. "Thank you though."

Inspiration struck and she sliced the pear instead. Suddenly, scooping the slices through the chocolate pudding sounded five-star awesome. Her taste buds seemed to vacillate between "no way" and "oh my God good," these days.

Settling across from him again, she scooped and crunched, savored and watched. A lot of oh my God good for the senses around this place.

Sighing, he finally met her gaze. "What?"

Blinking fast, she smiled widely. "Sorry. Am I bothering you?"

"I'm used to working alone, in quiet." His gaze homed in on her snack plate.

"Sorry the snowstorm didn't accommodate. Truly. It could be days, so honestly, it will be easier if we make nice, perhaps talk a bit. You can't work *all* the time."

He closed his computer again and scooped up the key chain. "Fine. Let's talk. Aren't you worried I'm a serial killer?"

In a whisper, she asked, trying to ease him into a conversation. Tease him a bit. She had enough brothers to know this tactic would probably work. "Are you?"

"My answer isn't going to matter." The abacus beads clicked under his fingers. "You know that, right?"

He had a point, but he didn't know she wasn't operating blind here. She wouldn't be able to carry this off long without risking alienating him altogether. "I'm an incredibly insightful person."

"From meeting so many people at work."

She looked up sharply. "Yes, actually."

"Well, lucky for you, I'm not a serial killer. I'm just an antisocial scientist."

"That must be tough to maintain in the classroom, Professor."

"Works fine in a lecture hall." He set his key chain down again.

Her mind zipped back to the first time she'd heard him speaking to an auditorium full of students and even professionals who'd joined the class to hear him. He saw the oil industry through revolutionary eyes. He walked a difficult line in making all sides of the spectrum happy, upping production while finding ways to increase safety and decrease ecological impact. His brain was every bit as sexy as his body.

O-kay.

Her distraction level was peaking.

She shot to her feet, tossed her empty pudding cup in the trash and popped the last slice of pear into her mouth.

"I thought you were going to eat and read?"

"I think I'm just going to turn in. Since you're not a serial killer." She winked.

He lifted an eyebrow. "Do you need some sweats?"

"I think I'll be fine in my thermal leggings and undershirt. Although I may need to take you up on that offer of sweats tomorrow when wash time comes." Guilt tugged at her. She really wasn't playing fair. "Thank you for being so nice about letting me stay here."

"Don't be so quick to thank me. I may not be a serial killer, but that doesn't mean I'm giving up my bed for you."

And there he went being funny again, like with his litany against the bear. "I didn't ask you to give me your bed."

Although she couldn't deny the raw attraction crackling tangibly in the air. The fire of it filled her mind with images of sharing that bed with him. Something must have flickered in her eyes because his widened, then narrowed, holding hers.

His head tipped to the side.

Nerves tingled along her skin, an unusual occurrence. She wasn't one to back down. Ever.

Perhaps she could call this a retreat. She swallowed, trying to recover from the heat in his dark eyes. "The sofa's more than fine. Thank you."

His chair legs lowered to all four on the floor again. "It's okay, Naomi. Take the bed. I'll be working late, anyway."

"But—"

The words died on her lips as he shook his head. "My mama wouldn't have it any other way. Manners and all. I'll sack out on the sofa. Good night, Naomi."

Good night?

Sleep felt like the furthest thing possible.

Naomi woke up, legs tangled in the tan satin comforter.

It was dark overhead, but that didn't mean anything in Alaska. She checked her watch and…holy cow. It was already five in the morning. She'd slept for nearly nine hours, out like a log. She shoved her hair back from her face.

When would she get used to these pregnancy hormones owning her body?

She was grateful for her baby, but she sure hadn't expected so many physical changes in a couple of months. Slowly, she sat up, wary, but her stomach stayed steady.

Scanning the studio area, she looked for Royce but found the space empty except for the dog snoozing under the table. The computer was nowhere in sight. Apparently, Royce wasn't leaving it unattended any longer.

Behind the wall that housed the headboard, she heard the shower running. That explained where her "roomie" was. And even though they'd both been in and out of the bathroom area last night, this was different. Thinking of him there, without his clothes, in that tiled shower sent a tingle down her spine clear to her toes.

She needed to distract herself. Pronto.

Naomi flipped back the covers, her fleece-lined leggings and undershirt soft against her skin. Thank goodness Alaskan weather meant layers. That left her with extra clothes while she stayed here longer than she'd expected.

She would sneak a call to her brother while she had privacy. Her backpack held the basics, just enough to seem normal on a day trip, and she refused to vainly wish for her closet full of clothes and makeup.

Focus.

She fished out her phone with the booster signal and dialed up her oldest brother, Broderick. With their dad in the throes of new love and planning a wedding, Broderick had become the de facto head of their family with orders from their father to make peace. Their dad had demanded that the Steeles and Mikkelsons unite as a family and a company. Get along—or sell their shares and move on.

Broderick had been charged with aligning the finances of the two companies, along with rival CFO Glenna Mikkelson. They'd surprised everyone by resuming their brief college romance...and now they were engaged and raising Glenna's daughter together.

If Broderick and Glenna could balance romance and work, why couldn't her father and his new "girlfriend" tend to the business angle, or at least participate more in the transition? The rest of them were barely treading water keeping up with the abrupt changes, keeping board members calm—and watching their backs as siblings on either side of the merged family jockeyed for top-dog position. The only Mikkelson son who seemed to be out of the running was Trystan, who managed their family's ranch and insisted he wanted no part of anything that required a suit.

Naomi kept one ear on the shower and another on the phone. The call rang and rang, then went to voice mail. She tried again with no luck.

Looking at the one bar of connectivity, she knew her chance to phone out could be limited. Sighing, she quickly dialed her sister Delaney. She wasn't as in-your-face as their brother about the business. But Delaney had a stubborn streak a mile long, especially when it came to ecological protection.

Perhaps her sister should have been her first call instead of Broderick.

Two rings in, Delaney picked up. "How's it going?"

Naomi wandered to the curved sofa lining part of the igloo wall for a better vantage point to monitor the bathing area for the second Royce stepped out. "I'm getting to know him. But he's not chatty. His dog's a better conversationalist."

Her sister laughed lightly. "But you're talking to the great Dr. Royce Miller. That's more than anyone else has managed to accomplish. I'm impressed."

"I've got crazy-good lawyering skills." She injected punch in her tone, more than she was feeling. She was fading fast energywise. What a strange, unexpected turn her expedition here had taken.

"That you do."

"Was that an actual compliment?" Naomi teased, relaxing into the familiarity of a normal conversation with her sister. She was lucky to have a large family, three brothers and a sister. They were such a great support.

And as she thought of her family, she couldn't help but think of her mother and her sister Brea, who were gone. Losing them had left such a hole in her heart—and a need for stability.

"Hey, was that insecurity, Naomi?" Delaney's tone was anything but teasing. More like stunned.

Few knew that shy Delaney had far more fight in her than Naomi did. Delaney chewed up corporate types who showed disregard for the environment. Delaney's latest target for scathing letters to the editors had been bigwig investor Birch Montoya, which did prove a bit problematic since the family business could use his financial endorsement, especially if they were to take on something as big as making Royce Miller's style of changes.

If Naomi won Royce Miller.

"Insecurity?" Not that she would admit. "Never. It's just nice to hear affirmation." Especially at a time when she was questioning herself. So many changes. So many hormones. And she still had to face telling her family about the pregnancy. "Things are strange in the family right now. How were Dad and Jeannie at dinner last night? Sorry to have crashed early." Pregnancy had made her so sleepy.

"Dad and Jeannie are the same. They're like teenagers planning their wedding. Not that they're waiting on the ceremony. That day Glenna and Broderick found them in the shower togeth—"

"Stop," Naomi said fast, half laughing. "My brain is on fire with the image."

"Imagine if we'd actually been there." Delaney chuckled softly, then the sound dwindled. "The thing that's starting to get to me though…if this was our mom and dad, we would think it was romantic. Granted, no one needs the full Monty."

"Can you please stop with the naked references?" Her eyes drifted back to the shower area. To Royce. There was a sauna there too. Oh, the possibilities heated her thoughts.

Her warm forehead rested against the cool glass wall. Lights around the property barely pierced the blizzard.

"I never would have pegged you for a prude."

Ouch, that stung, not that she intended to let Delaney know. "Well, it's not like you're in the middle of some torrid affair, either."

Silence stretched between them.

Putting Naomi on alert. She straightened. "Are you?"

"My love life is tame. I'm too busy with work. You're just imaging things after all that time you spent helping your friend revamp online dating profiles."

Naomi sensed something in her sister's voice beyond the simple teasing, but with a crackly cell phone reception, perhaps now wasn't the best time to push on personal stuff. Though she couldn't deny she was curious. "How're things going with smoothing Birch Montoya's ruffled feathers?"

"I'm working on it. It's just...not that simple for me. I feel like we would be taking money from the devil, given his stance on protecting the environment."

"Then that makes it all the more important for me to bring Royce on board to balance things out." Naomi chewed her lip for a moment before adding, "It's all so complicated."

"The business as much as the family." Delaney's words carried a hefty sigh. "It's not that I don't want Dad to move on. I'm just having trouble with him choosing a life with *her*."

And from all indications, Jeannie Mikkelson's kids were having a difficult time with the shocker romance, as well. Sure, Jeannie's husband had been dead for two years—of a heart attack. But the families had been at war for so long. So many harsh words and character assassinations had taken place. And the gossip. Someone went so far as to hint the Mikkelsons had played a part in the fatal plane crash that killed Brea and their mother—completely unsubstantiated and unbelievable. But investors were going to find it tough to overlook divisions so deep and public.

Naomi toyed with a lock of her hair. "Broderick is marrying a Mikkelson. Are you saying that's a problem?"

"I'm just saying it's not easy."

Back in college, Broderick and Glenna had indulged in a poorly hidden brief affair, then split up. Glenna had married someone else and become a widow before reuniting with Broderick very recently.

"And now they have a precious baby." A baby con-

ceived when Glenna's husband had an affair shortly
before he came down with pancreatic cancer and died.
And yet, Glenna and Broderick still loved Fleur un-
conditionally. They were in the process of making the
adoption official after the baby had been abandoned
by her mother.

Naomi's hand slid over her stomach and she wondered if her child would have a father's love someday.

"Fleur's pretty awesome." The smile in Delaney's
voice was unmistakable. "You should see her wave her
fists. I'm certain she's bumping my fist on purpose."

"Of course she is," Naomi joked right back. "Sing
her an extra lullaby from Aunt Naomi."

"You can't carry a tune."

"That's why you're going to sing it for me." The
shower silenced in the bathroom. Naomi's heart did a
flip against her rib cage. She really needed a game plan
for dealing with the sexy scientist before he emerged.
"Gotta go now. Love you."

She thumbed her phone off fast and bent over to
shove it in her backpack, making sure the security code
locked the screen. The hair on the back of her neck
prickled, as if she was being watched. She checked the
dog, but Tessie was sound asleep and snoring which
could only mean...

Naomi straightened slowly and turned to find Royce.
Big and awake and sexy, he stood in low-slung sweatpants, towel-drying his hair. He watched her with so
much heat in his eyes, she barely resisted the urge to
drag a finger down the glass windows to check for
steamy condensation.

Delaney Steele had a secret.

Sliding the cell phone into her coat pocket, she hoped

what she'd been doing—was about to do again—wouldn't wreck her sister's plan with Royce Miller.

But she just couldn't bring herself to tell Naomi.

Stepping out of her SUV into the snowy parking lot, Delaney braced herself for the walk into the Steele family headquarters. Wind whipped hard off the mountains, bringing a frosty bite against her cheek until she yanked up the deep hood of her parka.

Maybe Delaney was too adept at keeping things hidden, until it just became instinct. Such as how she wasn't as shy as she pretended to be. Or how she'd kissed her sister's boyfriend in high school. Or that she was scared of everyone's dogs, but didn't want to hurt their feelings.

Or how she fought survivor's guilt every day of her life.

She'd pretended to have the flu before the fateful flight that had shattered her family. Her mother had discovered the faked fever. Delaney had begged her mom not to go. Silly really. She'd just wanted her to stay to go shopping for makeup. Naomi had offered to accompany Delaney instead. Case closed.

Their mom and sister, Brea, had left for the flight—late. If they'd been on time…

What-ifs could rule a life.

Messenger bag tucked under her arm, Delaney put her head down and trudged forward, boots crunching through the icy crust that no amount of salting and shoveling could clear on mornings like this one. Forward was the only way she knew, after all.

These days, with so many regrets, she lived each day determined to grasp what she wanted and not add a single new item to that list. So hell no, she wasn't even close to being the crusader, the good girl her family believed. She'd only wanted to somehow make a mark, somehow help other families not suffer the pain hers had experienced.

She just hoped her current secret didn't torpedo all of Naomi's careful plans. Because Delaney was in so deep now, she wasn't sure she could stop herself if she tried.

Three

Royce never would have imagined silk thermals on a woman could look sexier than any lingerie.

Not that he could think of any woman other than Naomi at the moment. This one was filling his every thought.

Which wasn't a wise idea when they would be sharing a one-room studio igloo-cabin for an undetermined amount of time. It wasn't like he could jog off his pent-up sexual tension outside. The snowstorm was still raging. Even getting his dog to make the requisite "nature's breaks" outdoors was tough. Tessie bolted out into the igloo tunnel, had her moment and sprinted back into the shelter in record time. She shook snowflakes off her shaggy coat, creating a mini flurry indoors.

Too bad they couldn't all just hibernate.

Last night, he'd kept his eyes averted when Naomi had come out of the restroom, because just the sound of her movements, the scent of her, was distraction enough. And yes, once he'd given up and stretched out on the sofa, he'd watched her sleep. The covers had been pulled up to her shoulders, but the moonlight had played over her face.

It had been a long time since he'd slept with a woman. More than a year. There were offers, but lately work had consumed his life. He didn't have time for a relationship. This was a turning point in his research, everything coming together at just the right time.

To be honest, he was racing to finalize his work because the Alaskan pipeline production through Canada and into the Dakotas would ramp up sooner rather than later. If anything, the Steele-Mikkelson merger had accelerated the program since their major Alaskan competitor, Johnson Oil United, was sending signals of speeding their plans while the Steele-Mikkelsons were preoccupied with the merger.

And the more the businesses raced against each other, the more Royce worried. This wasn't the type of industry to rush, and the Johnsons already showed some hints of corner cutting. Even minuscule miscalculations could prove deadly or leave long-lasting contamination concerns. He couldn't afford distractions.

And no question, this woman was a major distraction.

There was something about Naomi…something he couldn't identify that tugged at him, a feeling that he couldn't shake. That there was more than met the eye with her. In a good or bad way? He didn't know.

Although he did know he needed to be on his toes around her until he figured her out.

He looped the towel around the doorknob and reached for his Massachusetts Institute of Technology—MIT—

sweatshirt, mulling over the best way to learn more about her. He needed to find a chink in that spunky facade, to see who she was on the inside and discover if a quirk of fate had truly brought her here. Or if there might be another reason she was holed up with him. Regardless, she intrigued him.

Tugging on the thick fleece, he stepped deeper into the room, aware of her sharp, analytic eyes. "So, you grew up in Alaska?"

"I did." She curled her toes in her socks and sat on the edge of the sofa.

"Could you have handled that bear on your own?"

"Maybe. Okay, probably," she said, smiling, her nose crinkling, knees bouncing nervously. "But I enjoyed watching you take over."

"How magnanimous of you." His dry tone cut her smile. She exchanged it for a wink before readjusting on the couch, a shift that revealed her curves more fully.

"Your ego seems solid." She looked at him squarely, but her twitching increased.

He dropped to sit at the end of the sofa, searching her deep brown eyes. "What's really going on here with you showing up?"

She stared back for a solid, sparking sixty seconds or so before shooting to her feet. "I have to go to the restroom."

And just that fast, she bolted away, the bathroom door slamming and locking behind her.

Naomi had never been so glad to take advantage of a pregnancy symptom.

She had to use the bathroom at least twice as often these days, which made the one-facility situation here a tricky element she hadn't considered in driving up to the secluded cabin. But as Royce had pressed her with questions, she'd been glad for the excuse to leave the room.

Brushing away morning breath went a long way too in clearing her sleep-fogged mind. Now that she'd had time to fully wake up, she had a plan.

She had decided to take a calculated risk.

Royce was a man of logic, a scientist. So, she intended to throw him for a loop, knock him off balance. Opting for outrageous remarks had worked well for her in the past in getting people to say things they might not have otherwise. And then with laughter and the sharing of even a little secret, they relaxed, revealing more as the rapport strengthened.

Such a tactic might well work in her favor now.

Naomi left the bathroom cubicle and leaned against the archway leading into the studio area. Royce moved efficiently in the kitchen, cooking bacon, sausage, and popping large slices of fresh wheat bread onto a toaster slab that fit in the fireplace.

Her mouth watered and her senses tingled on high alert. Because of her pregnancy or because of the man?

She reminded herself of her mission. She tugged the hem of her boring thermal shirt and asked, "Wanna play strip poker? I'll trade you clothes for first dibs on that food."

He glanced over his broad shoulder. "Do you always proposition strangers?"

"Only you." She fluffed her dark hair, a seductive challenge in her subtle moves.

He turned his attention back to the meal at hand. Unfazed. A low, rumbling chuckle. "Ah, you're being outrageous to get me to stop thinking and reveal—something?—to you."

He was smart, quick-witted, not easily fooled. "Very insightful."

"So sarcastic." Facing him, she couldn't help but notice the solidity of his chest beneath his MIT sweatshirt.

"But you're talking to me now rather than hiding behind your computer." He raised one brow and for a moment, almost too brief to register, a flicker of amusement danced across her face, smiling, bowing in...interest?

Dragging his attention from her back to the breakfast food seemed to be no easy task. He scrambled and flipped the eggs once more. His hands moved with such precision, the mark of a man with an ingrained attention to detail. Her mouth dried up at the vision of those hands paying precise attention along her body.

"True enough." He stalked quietly toward the kitchen area, pulling out plates for each item.

His eyes met hers, and there it was—that pop of electricity, something warming her to her core. The fluttering in her stomach intensified. Not pregnancy related, but a reminder of what her future held.

Royce dumped the sausage links and bacon onto a plate, arranged them neatly in a row. He fished out the four pieces of freshly toasted bread. The yeasty smell mixed with the savory smell of bacon and sausage.

He met her gaze, held it before he spoke. "Keep your clothes. I could stand a big breakfast too. What do you want to discuss?"

Naomi scratched just behind her ear, collecting her cool after spending even more time drooling over the man than the food. Deciding her strategy as he set out fresh jams on the small counter in front of her. The spread was vast, especially given their minimalist setting.

Bacon, sausage links, fluffy eggs, toast. All things she didn't even realize she was craving until now. Might as well feed one hunger pulsing through her and hopefully rein her thoughts in.

Tilting her head, she continued, "Since strip poker didn't get a rip-roaring endorsement, let's go with something more practical." She sat back on the edge of the bed and hugged her knees. "I would enjoy hearing more about your work."

"I told you. I'm a science professor." His smile was taut, tense.

And his response? Vague as ever.

But his eyes sparked with something else when she held his gaze. Her pulse quickened…at the game of wits or at something else entirely?

Food. She needed to eat.

"Well I figured you weren't a communications professor. Science is a broad field though. Care to narrow it down a bit? I assume you're passionate about your career given how intensely you concentrate."

With a sigh, he piled food on his plate. She watched him close his eyes, seeming to weigh his next words carefully. What felt like an eternity passed before he spoke again. His low voice a welcome rumble.

"I'm an engineer, actually. I work on oil pipeline construction and upgrades."

"A mathematical as well as scientific field. Interesting. What do you enjoy most about the pipeline angle? I'm having fun envisioning you out there in the wilds, the bear master flexing his intellectual chops."

"Still nosy." A smile—well, a half smile—pulled at his lips. He arranged the spread on the table, down to the precise position of both of their plates. He gestured for her to join him.

"Why does it matter if I know what you do?" She walked over to the table, settling into the seat closest to the glass. The snow still poured down, muting the minimal rays of sunrise, giving the breakfast a hazy, romantic glow.

Brushing knees with him under the table only added to the intimacy.

"I've shared with you," he dodged. She reached for the toast and then scrambled eggs as he continued, an edge of sarcasm tinging his tone. "Tell me more about being a delivery gal. How long have you had the job? Why did you apply to drive around in awful weather? Why did they hire you?"

"I told you, I'm a friend." Stick with rule number one: keep the story as simple and unadorned as possible. Too many details would complicate things. She tucked her knees closer to her side of the table. "I volunteered to help him out."

"Ah, right." He shoveled a large bite of eggs into his mouth.

Either he wasn't listening to her or he was trying to trip her up, which meant he was suspicious. With good reason.

Guilt pinched. Hard. He seemed to be a genuinely good guy and she wasn't being totally up-front with him. It had all seemed so simple back home, the stakes for her family so high. And none of that had changed. She wanted security for her baby and she believed in her cause. She wasn't as active as her sister on the issue of the environment, but her family's company truly was the one most open to what Royce had to offer.

Bottom line, she deeply believed research like Royce's helped reduce environmentally caused cancers, and the thought of saving others the grief she'd been through? She had to forge ahead.

"Tell me more about you? Family? Friends? Girlfriend who won't be happy to find out I've been here alone with you offering to play strip poker?"

"I'm an only child," he said, taking the bait as she shifted the topic. "My parents had me later in life and are retired. Girlfriends aren't your concern."

"Efficient answers. Sparse. But efficient."

Like he was with serving up portions on his plate from the platter in the middle.

"I grew up in Texas around the oil fields. My father and mother worked hard. We had a comfortable life. I studied hard and it paid off with a full ride to college. I made good with some patents, which enables me to afford to hide out working in a luxurious glass igloo and pay for delivery of supplies," he said simply, adding butter to his bread while it was still warm, the dab melting over the sides.

Kind of like her senses. He was eccentric, sure, but sexy as hell. The intensity in his eyes had disarmed her for a moment. She needed to press on while he was warming up into an unusually chatty mood.

"Texas to Alaska. That's quite a leap geographically, not to mention the weather."

"Oil. Pipelines. Common thread." He lifted his mug of coffee.

"Ah, yes. Oil."

"Hmm." He offered up the nonanswer while adding jam to his buttered toast.

She was losing him here. Or maybe she was losing focus, because all she could think about was him in the shower. His buff chest, his strong arms. "Tell me about your childhood growing up in Texas?"

He glanced at her, that strong jawline causing her heart to quicken. Something like a crackle of awareness passed between them, something that seemed to hang in the air. "Growing up in Texas was a lot like growing up in Alaska, I imagine, but without the snow."

"Since the snow is everywhere, how about spell it out for me more." She bit into her own toast, indulging in the freshness of the blueberry jam.

"Both places have fishing, hunting, rugged living... and oil."

"I applaud your concise way with words." And yes, she was starting to struggle to keep her thoughts reined in with the sensory overload of savory food and muscle-bound man.

He shrugged one shoulder. "Concise."

Royce's attention wandered for a moment, eyes roving her, stopping at her mouth. His sudden movement caught her off guard as he reached across the table and thumbed the corner of her mouth. "Jam."

He slowly licked his thumb clean. But his eyes didn't leave hers.

Her heart did a flip. Her thoughts scattered like snow from the roof in a squall. So much for staying on her toes around him. About the only way she could envision being on her tiptoes involved arching up to kiss him.

Royce wasn't sure why he'd opted to play with fire by touching Naomi. But damned if he regretted it.

Angling across the table, he skimmed his mouth over the corner of her lips, right where he'd grazed her with his thumb a second before. The taste of jam lingered.

As did the spark of attraction as he settled back into his seat.

She hadn't objected. She wasn't running. Granted,

she appeared a hint shell-shocked with wise eyes. But her pupils widened with attraction. She was stunning, potent.

And he was drawn to her like a magnet.

He studied her through narrowed eyes. "You're—distracting."

"I'm sorry about that." She sat back in the chair, and he couldn't help but notice the way her spine arched and her breasts pressed against her shirt.

Distracting was an understatement. His normally targeted linguistic skills seemed to fail him. She was… intoxicating. That might be more accurate.

"I didn't mean it in a bad way." He held her gaze, watching the way her lips moved, parting ever so slightly. The touch a moment ago, the taste of her, had left him wanting more. Much more.

"Oh, thank you." She exhaled hard. "Well, I guess there really isn't any use in denying the sparks, is there?"

Her bright eyes searched his, an eagerness dancing there. One he wanted to act on. Damn the logic.

"Attraction is what it is. Even my scientific mind knows it's not logical—but it is tangible." He leaned forward on the table, his knee brushing hers. She stared at the point of contact, the place where electricity seemed to build, coursing through him.

"I'm not a judgy kind of person." She lifted her head, fixating now on his mouth. But her knee didn't move from his. The warmth of her body teased him as she continued, her voice lower as if confessing a secret, "but I've also never indulged in a one-night stand."

"From the looks of the storm and the piles of snow out there, we'll be here for far more than one night. If you're so inclined to…indulge." He eased from his chair and leaned a hip against the table, taking her hand, surprised for a moment by the softness of her skin, the strength in the way she squeezed him back.

"Logical point." Her breath hitched audibly, her pulse speeding in her neck just below her diamond stud earring.

Were they really discussing this without ever even having kissed other than sharing a smudge of jam?

Although holding her hand, watching her reaction to that simple touch, turned him inside out with need.

"And I am a responsible man. I always have protection."

Her husky laugh washed over him. "You carry condoms to an igloo in remote Alaska?"

"Did you hear me? I am a practical man. And a careful man." He paused, looking down at his feet before continuing, the words heavy on his tongue. "My former fiancée got pregnant. We lost the baby, then broke up. If I'd been careful, I could have saved us both a lot of pain…"

Her hand rested on the back of his neck. "I'm so sorry for the hurt that caused you."

"Thank you." Pushing back against the memories, he glanced up at her again. "It was a long time ago. And damn, I don't know why I brought it up at all. What a total mood buster. I just wanted to say that I have condoms."

"Safe is always good." Her fingers moved lightly along the back of his neck, both soothing and arousing.

His direct nature had sent him off course with people before, and he wondered if that was the case now. "So, have I totally wrecked the mood?"

"Wrecked the mood?" She angled back, toying with the tip of her ponytail in a way that totally set his senses on fire. Did she know what she was doing to him? "Dampened it perhaps. But I think the moment could be easily salvaged."

Yes. Victory surged through him. "How so?"

She gave him an unmistakably sultry look. All thick lashes and parted lips. She raised an eyebrow, voice taking on a sweeter intonation. "You're a smart man. Guess."

Angling toward her, he slid his hand up her leg, watching her move into him with anticipation. He drew his head closer, lips a breath apart from hers.

The logical stuff? He would deal with that later. Because right now, nothing seemed more important than fully, thoroughly kissing Naomi.

Four

The moment Royce's lips fully brushed hers, Naomi leaned into the kiss, unable to stop herself from soaking up the muscular feel and earthy scent of this man she barely knew. Throwing herself at a virtual stranger. Which was atypical for her.

Sure, she'd cultivated a wild child reputation for the past few years. Totally unearned other than dressing flamboyantly and being outspoken. But she'd felt compelled somehow to prove to her family she was vibrantly alive. Independent. She'd even stopped waiting around for Mr. Right and embraced the possibility of motherhood.

And now when she was well out of the public eye, she was about to do the most reckless thing of her life jumping into bed with Royce Miller—who she should be winning over in a more practical fashion.

However, she was feeling anything but practical or logical at that moment.

The stroke of his tongue, the feel of his sure touch along her shoulders, down her back, brought her senses alive. Everything became more vibrant. The rasp of his beard-stubbled face. The coarse texture of his hair that she'd thought needed a cut and now found perfect. The smoky scent from the fireplace mingling with the musk of man.

His kiss was intoxicating.

Although, worry still niggled. What if sleeping with him compromised her goal of cajoling him into taking a job with Alaska Oil Barons, Incorporated? She certainly hadn't been able to snag so much as a peek at his work, which actually made her feel less guilty now. However, if they followed the attraction through, sex would complicate things. He might well believe she'd used sex as a means to persuade him.

Except damn, the draw between them was so tangible, undeniable. Hopefully he would know the truth of that.

If she revealed the truth of why she was there, this sexual exploration would end. She wanted to experience him first, no matter the consequences.

And she'd done so little real living with all those years devoted to recovering from cancer. Her future would be filled with putting her own needs aside for her child's welfare... This was a window of time for her to indulge in what she sensed would be a most memorable, delicious experience.

She was going to sleep with Royce Miller.

It was crazy on the one hand.

And totally logical on the other.

The attraction to Royce reached deep within her, and this could well be her only chance to pursue it. Once business officially intruded...

She had to seize this moment now.

Thankfully, he seemed to agree. Even Tessie somehow knew to grant them privacy and trotted off to curl up in her dog bed in the closet area.

Naomi gripped his fleecy sweatshirt in her hands. "This is insane."

"I know." He rested his forehead against hers, his breath ragged. "I apologize if I overstepped in moving so fast."

She laughed hoarsely. "I'm the one who mentioned strip poker."

He smiled, his fingers playing down her spine. "I'm the one who brought up condoms."

"You sure did." Her fists unfurled from his fleece and she palmed his chest. Oh my, his chest.

The desire in his eyes echoed the flame inside her. She wasn't sure who initiated what, who moved first. It was all a blur of motion and want. Her arms looped around his neck as he scooped her up, carrying her to the bed, lowering her with gentle strength. As he released her, his hand skimmed around her hips, grazing her stomach.

Her heart lurched to her throat for an instant as she thought of her pregnancy. The other layer of withheld information...

If she managed to persuade him to join the company, he would eventually learn about her baby. Although it wasn't like she expected them to be a long-term couple. She wasn't looking for that. She had plans. Goals for her career, goals for her family and, more important, goals for her life with her child. Royce didn't fit into those plans. He wasn't her type, when it came to relationships, and she was fairly certain she wasn't his type, either.

But they were attracted to each other. That was clear

in the deep eye contact, the way his hand grazed her skin. And her days for having a no-strings fling were numbered. *Casual* would take on a different meaning once she had her child. On a practical level, having a wild, torrid affair with him—right now—made complete sense.

No question about it, she did want him, so much.

She wriggled against him. "I assume this means you're sure?"

Royce angled back to look into her eyes, stroking her hair in a long sweep of his hands. "Aren't I supposed to be the responsible, honorable man asking you that question, if this is what *you* want?"

Her hair tingled all the way to the roots from the rasp of his callused touch. "Then ask me."

"Are you sure this is what you want?"

"Are you kidding me? I very much want this. And all the evidence points to you wanting me just as much," she said. "You're quite the scientist." Eyeing him, she took in the hard panes of his chest, the way his chin raised in confidence.

"It's biology." He eyed her right back with a gaze that drank her in, launching another wave of excitement through her veins.

Anticipation swirled through her until her face heated with a flush. "Biology? I would call it chemistry."

"Ah, how right you are. Good distinction." A lopsided grin graced his lips. He reached into the bedside table and pulled out an unopened box of condoms.

Morning sunshine pushed through the snow on the glass roof, dappling them with light as she tugged at his shirt and sweatpants. His skin was impossibly warm, the hard muscle shifting under her touch while she skimmed away his clothes. The expanse of his muscled chest sprinkled with hair wasn't that of a sedentary man. His sinewy planes spoke of activity, of a love of the outdoors.

She wanted to feel him, all of him, against her. Inside her. She'd never been so hot, so hungry, for any man. She reveled in the graze of his fingers as he bunched and swept aside her silk thermal shirt, sliding around the strap of the simple cotton bra she'd never planned on anyone else seeing. His avid gaze practically sizzled the fabric away. Her breasts beaded to aching points by the time he freed her. She shivered as he scraped down the thermal and underwear, until at last they were skin to skin.

The warmth of him, pressing flesh to flesh as he kissed her, ramped up her need—higher, hotter. He skimmed his mouth to the curve of her neck and she caught a glimpse of the heat in his eyes as he stroked her with his gaze. She felt it as tangibly as his caress along her breasts. Then he moved lower, kissing the inside of her thigh, then the core of her. Circling, plucking. Teasing a tingling flame higher and hotter until her hands gripped into fists.

"You're absolutely…gorgeous. But you have to already know that."

His intuitive touch made her feel like a schoolgirl. Carefree. The reality of who they were and why she had concocted a scheme to meet him seemed to fade away, melt like sun-soaked snow.

They were just man and woman, caught up in a feverish attraction. She'd had no idea how powerful that could be.

"You're making me blush."

Royce planted slow, deliberate kisses on her collarbone. "That sounds like an invitation to make you blush all over."

Oh. My.

Breath seemed impossible as he pressed against her. Still, somehow she managed to whisper, "As long as turnabout is fair play."

"Yes, ma'am." His confident chuckle heated her flesh and he angled up to graze his mouth along her ear, her jaw.

"And by the way?"

"Yeah?"

"You're too chatty." She nipped his bottom lip.

His slow, sexy smile gave her an instant's warning before his mouth closed over her breast, one then the other until the tingles gathered force within her to a tight urgency.

She grabbed for the box of condoms and wrenched it open, fumbling to tear into a packet. He reached for her hand but she nudged him aside. Wanting, needing to explore him. She sheathed him and his groan of pleasure brought an answering groan from her.

"Naomi, there are so many more ways I want to touch you, to—"

She pressed her finger to his lips. "And you can. We will. Right now, though—"

She didn't have to finish the thought. He slid inside her, filling her as her legs glided up and around his hips, her ankles locking. In synch, they moved. She didn't know how to explain the strength of sensations already swelling inside her, the way his caresses ignited her, knew her so instinctively. Being with him was insane and somehow so damn right all at the same time.

Passion built and she felt that flush inching over her, all over, the rise of impending completion. So soon.

And as much as she wanted to hold it back, she also thought of the next time, and there would be one. How much more they would share here. Together. For however long the storm lasted.

Just when she thought she couldn't bear the wait any longer, his hand slid between them and teased her the rest of the way over the edge. The stars sparked behind her eyelids like the northern lights splashing streaks of color across the sky's palette in a van Gogh–esque magnificence.

She savored the moment and sensations in a slow return to reality. Flames crackled in the fireplace, adding a hazy glow and the scent of wood smoke to the one-room space.

One room.

In the middle of nowhere.

Total escape.

And as she looked into his eyes, she saw he was every bit as close and, yes, as flushed with need. Her release rippled through her in rays of heat and bliss just as his ragged shout of completion mingled with hers.

His arms wrapped around her as he rolled to his side, cradling her to him. She buried her face against his chest, breathing in the salty scent of him, listening to his racing heart. Trying to take in the intensity of what had just happened, so much so soon.

Her family was depending on her to persuade Royce to join their company or at least share his research. Most important, they absolutely did not want to alienate him and risk his going to the competition, especially now when they were trying so hard to woo major investors like Birch Montoya.

And yet, she was here indulging in a reckless passion, living up to the party girl reputation she'd never earned when she should be focused on her family's business and her baby's future.

Rolling to her back, she stared up at the snow piling on the roof, listening to Royce's even breathing beside her. He was awake though, like her, which gave her a little while longer to relish this moment.

But soon, too soon, she would have to check in with her sister again and, even more daunting, return to reality.

Delaney wasn't sure how much longer she could keep her affair a secret. She'd built her career—her entire values system—on improving the environment for generations to come. Her sister Naomi had nearly died of cancer, and watching helplessly as she'd suffered had left its mark on Delaney. Her crusade for a cleaner environment was personal. Deeply so.

Being part of an oil family dynasty made her stance tough enough, but she liked to think she brought balance to the business. Besides, the oil tycoons she knew were relatives. She loved them. When it came to friendships and romance, she opted to spend time with people who shared her common interests and causes.

Until now.

Until Birch Montoya—a man with his eye on profits more than on the survival of an ecosystem.

Although, right now, he had his eyes firmly on her, and Delaney didn't want to resist.

She leaned across the desk, her breasts sensitive with arousal along the lace of her bra as she stared at her secret lover in his fitted boxers. She'd given up trying to understand how they could argue—how they could be such total opposites—and be so turned on at the same time.

But that's how it had been between them since they'd

sparred in a board meeting and ended up in a broom closet. Tearing each other's clothes off.

Like they'd done the second he'd arrived tonight. As if she hadn't known that delivering paperwork was just an excuse. An excuse that had barely held until she locked the library door behind them. An hour later they'd finally turned their attention to work in the book-lined room, fire blazing in the large stone hearth.

Work was always better in their underwear. The view made them less likely to fight about how he wanted to chew up the environment to add to the bottom line. If she thought about his ecological stance, her head would explode and their evening alone would be wrecked.

How could she want him so much and disagree with him on everything at the same time?

Her eyes were drawn to his thick dark hair falling over his forehead, his high cheekbones from his Native American heritage. All of him handsome and brilliant and, yes, infuriating.

Birch pushed aside an architectural schematic and clasped her hand. "If the company goes bankrupt from your *requests*—" he kissed her wrist, punctuating each word "—then you'll have nothing left to win at all."

Her head lolled back at the sensations spiraling through her as he kissed and nipped. "And don't you want to be on the cutting edge of innovation in the oil world?"

"We have Royce Miller for that." Birch glanced up at her, his dark eyes meeting hers, smoldering.

"He's a scientist." Delaney tried to find her logical side, but each word came out breathy, her blood turning to liquid fire in her veins. "I'm an activist. It's different."

Birch muttered, "Tell him that."

"What?"

"Nothing." He stepped around to her side of the desk,

scooped her up in his arms and sat in the massive office chair, settling her into his lap. "My point is, with Royce on board, we're already ahead of the race with other companies in being eco-friendly. Good luck getting Johnson Oil on your side if Alaska Oil Barons goes under."

"Dad's company is not going under," she retorted automatically, her legs tingling from the bristle of Birch's bare thighs.

"It's not solely your father's company anymore."

"Thanks for the reminder." She tapped the platinum wolf charm Birch had given her. She'd been touched that he seemed to know her preferences and how she avoided diamonds unless she knew exactly how they had been mined.

He'd been a welcome distraction.

The past few months had been stressful as hell since her brother Broderick and his fiancée, Glenna, had walked in on their business rival parents in the shower together, in Jeannie's office bathroom, no less. Their whole world had been upended with the Steele patriarch and Mikkelson matriarch laying down the law. They were merging their two companies and their offspring needed to get on board or move on.

So much change. So fast.

But now, Birch leaned forward, his mouth covering hers, scattering her thoughts and sending her body into motion. She swung her legs around to straddle his lap and wrapped her arms around his neck, scooting forward, which brought the core of her deliciously against the hot length of him.

Yes, she needed this diversion in her life. She needed him.

A growl rumbled in his chest. "I want you so damn much I could barely keep my hands off you in there."

"I wanted to tear your clothes off with my teeth." She nibbled at his bottom lip for emphasis, then flicked her tongue along it to trace away any sting.

"Your teeth?" He narrowed his eyes, envisioning. Fantasizing. Liking.

Just the feel of his dark eyes on her body made her breathless. Needy.

She laughed, kissing her way down his chest. "I'll be happy to show you."

"Save the thought for when we can linger." He tucked a knuckle under her chin and guided her face back up and tasted her, once, twice. "Next time you're at my place, we can play that out. In detail." He cupped her breasts, his thumbs stroking over each pebbling peak.

Desire sizzled over her skin, driving her need higher. Had she ever wanted anyone the way she wanted Birch? The way she craved him?

"Fair enough," she purred. "Can you hurry up though, so I don't finish before you're even inside me?"

"Why do you have to be so hot?" he asked, his mouth skimming along her jawline.

"Why do you have to be so insatiable?" she teased back, even as she knew their differences would one day drive them apart.

"I *definitely* don't want to fight with you." A smile creased his handsome face, his mouth brushing hers.

She forced aside worries to focus on the heat. The want. The undeniable need. "I agree one hundred percent with you on that."

In all the ways Royce had calculated and planned this solitary research excursion into the remote wilderness of Alaska, he had never accounted for this variable.

How could he have ever anticipated a research distraction like Naomi?

It was one thing to be led astray with faulty formulas—quite another to be distracted by a dark-haired beautiful woman with chocolate-brown eyes.

Royce sprawled beside her, his sweatpants a minimal barrier between his knee and her leg as she settled back into bed. She'd made a phone call in the bathroom to reassure the outside world she was here safe and sound. He gave a brief thought to her insistence on making the call privately, but then who was he to cast stones? A recluse by nature, he enjoyed his privacy too.

Although right now, he had his sights set on enjoying Naomi. The bed captured enough warmth to justify his half-clothed state. He thumbed the edge of the square plate settled on his lap and took a moment to soak in the vision of her again.

Her damp hair was piled on top of her head in a ponytail tied into a loose knot. His sweatshirt hung off her slender body, allowing a glimpse of her bare shoulder. She too sat cross-legged on the bed, plate balanced on her bare knees and thighs. They'd puttered around the kitchen for food, him piling on cold cuts while she surprised him by choosing a peanut butter and jam sandwich for herself.

For a moment, as he bit into his sub, the last few hours replayed in his head. How they had made love not once, but twice in the bed. And then another time in the shower. How in tune their lovemaking had been.

Tessie let out a hefty sigh. The giant Saint Bernard was a terribly vocal sleeper. The dog had wandered back to join them after Royce had brought the sandwiches from the kitchen area. The intensity of his and Naomi's passion had left them both hungry and tired.

The power of what they had shared rocked Royce's carefully calculated world. That level of connection was something he hadn't felt in years. But as intrigued as he was by what they'd shared, he knew he needed more information about her. Hell, he didn't even know his mystery woman's last name. He was missing something. And as much as he wanted to continue in this sexual bliss, he needed some answers.

She traced his mouth, his head tipped to the side as she eyed him. "I should have known that bear was a sign."

"What do you mean?" He struggled to follow her meaning, given her touch was distracting as hell.

"My maternal grandmother was Inuit, and she made a point of sharing mythology as bedtime stories."

"And what do bears have to do with that?"

Sighing, she settled back. "Supposedly, in our dreams, we're able to go places we would normally only experience in the afterlife. And certain themes have common interpretations."

"Like bears?"

"Exactly. The polar bear can signify a number of things, from purity to death, rebirth—or even sexual overtones." She bit into her sandwich, jam oozing out of the side. She flicked it with her tongue, winking at him.

Laughing, he reached for his sub. "What about grizzly bears?"

"I'm not sure. I'm going with a loose interpretation here." She licked a smudge of blackberry jam off her lip. "Thank goodness we didn't see a weasel."

"What would that have meant?"

"Trouble."

"Be wary if I have a dream about weasels. Got it."

"Royce, I have to know." Naomi set her sandwich down on the square gray plate. She looked at him sidelong. "Is there a femme fatale girlfriend due to show up here and fillet me for being around her man?"

"Around her man" was an interesting way to describe the last few hours. "Are you asking me if I'm single?"

"That's what I said." She picked the PBJ back up and bit into it.

"Not quite. 'Are you single' is three words. Your convoluted question was more like nineteen words that included someone getting cooked over the fire."

Chewing, she seemed to carefully consider his words. After swallowing, she shook her head. "I said filleted. That could have been sushi-style, you know." She winked at him, and a genuine smile revealed her straight teeth. "My mother was half-Inuit. I'm quite handy with a seal knife, just in case you have some vengeful girlfriend looming on the horizon."

"I'm single or I would have never propositioned you. No lurking girlfriends. Just an ex-fiancée who is now happily married to another guy." But he didn't want to think about Carrie Lynn.

"Ah, okay." Naomi shrugged and then leaned against him to whisper in his ear, "Me too. About the single part, not about the broken engagement."

Her nearness set him on edge again and he ached to kiss her, to pull her in close and feel those subtle curves against his chest, coax a husky moan from her throat. But he still needed more information before he'd allow himself to do that again.

"And we're snowed in here together."

Naomi set the sandwich back down, scooting around to face him on the bed. "How long do you plan to stay after the storm passes?"

"I'm not sure. Depends on when I finish my work. This was meant to be a retreat."

She nodded, playing with the plate edge, eyes downcast. "Your research."

Damn. There was something larger at play here. He angled his head and studied her eyes, or rather the way she avoided his gaze. "You know who I am. What I do. More than what I've told you."

She picked at a ragged bread edge on her sandwich. "What makes you say that?"

In another effort not to engage with him, she brought the sandwich to her full lips, took another bite.

Setting the plate to the side, he let out a long sigh. "I'm a smart man. That's not ego talking, a mere fact of a genetic lottery. Still, it took me a while to put the pieces together because you're such an incredible distraction. And you're good at dodging answers. Like now. You're not denying outright that you know me. You brought me the supplies, so you knew where you were going. But it's more than that."

She picked at the crust, making a veritable snowdrift of torn bread. "I do know who you are. Royce Miller, wizard of the pipeline upgrades."

"And you know this how?" His heartbeat quickened, waiting for the mystery to unravel, the pieces to fall into place.

She lifted one shoulder, wincing. "I heard you lecture once."

She had asked him more than once about his job and never let on that she knew he was a professor when he told her.

"And that's all?"

She finally fully met his gaze, those chocolate-brown eyes sharp, honed. Determined and brazen. Too much for a delivery person. "What a curious question."

"Curious that you're dodging the answer. Again.

You're not a delivery person. You sound more like a lawyer— Ah, hell, you *are* a lawyer."

He couldn't miss the confirmation in how Naomi braced her shoulders defensively.

"Wow, Royce, once you figure something out, you're on a roll."

"My question would be, what's a lawyer doing pretending to deliver goods for a friend?" Synapses firing, he pressed on.

"I didn't pretend." She gestured to the plate of food, to the pantry and the two boxes still stacked by the counter, all a result of her so-called delivery.

"You're quibbling."

"And you're a difficult man to meet."

He met research colleagues frequently. Corporations, on the other hand, seldom could get ahold of him. Which could only mean one thing. A chill coiled in his gut. "You're with an oil company."

She nodded slowly.

"No." A feeling he couldn't quite name—betrayal, maybe—gnawed at him. Of course. Was this just a new, base tactic in the bid for his brain?

The thought rocked him, causing him to reevaluate that connection between them.

She touched his arm lightly, warily. "At least listen to me, please."

The pleading in her voice might be a nice rhetorical strategy in the courtroom, but it would not sway him now. He shut down his emotions. He couldn't afford to be swayed now that he knew what this was about. Cold disappointment weighed on him that Naomi could be so calculating.

His logical side powered to the fore. "I'm not signing my life away."

"We have so many different ways this could work."

"'We' who?"

"You haven't figured that out?"

His patience for guessing had been replaced with a demand for answers. This same feeling—the one guiding his speech right now—was what made him a brilliant researcher. He pushed. "Enlighten me."

He could see the wheels of her mind churning, could almost hear the rustle of thoughts battling in her head. And he knew, this was about more than listening to some lecture he'd given.

She'd played him. And he'd been too attracted to her to see it.

"Okay," she said, her cheeks puffing with an exhale. She thrust out her hand. "I'm Naomi Steele, officially representing the newly formed Alaska Oil Barons, Inc."

Five

So much for her no-strings affair with Royce.

The horror on his face after her announcement spoke volumes. But she couldn't outright lie to him. She'd already been fibbing by omission. That lawyer brain of hers could only justify quibbling so far.

Sleeping with him had been impulsive and, in hindsight, had actually jeopardized her chances of bringing him into the company.

Except something crazy had happened inside her since she'd met him. Business had become more and more difficult to consider. She could only think of him.

And now she'd made a huge mess of things. The happy endorphins buzzing through her after the incredible sex began to fade.

"I assume from the horrified look on your face that you heard me and you're not happy with who I am."

The need to check in on him—to make sure she hadn't dealt something like a killing blow—overwhelmed her.

A tinge of guilt pushed at her, knotting in her stomach. Her instinct was to touch him, to reach out. But based on the way pain and shock twisted his dark, handsome features, she wasn't sure if her touch would be welcomed. So, she sat there on the bed and reached for the oversize comfort of Tessie instead.

The Saint Bernard woke up at Naomi's gentle scratch. Blinking, Tessie looked back and forth between Naomi and Royce. As if she understood the full depth—and unease—of the space and words between the humans, she slunk off the bed, landing on the ground with a decided thunk. The dog knew trouble was coming as surely as Naomi did.

"Let's just say, Naomi, that I'm…confused." Scrubbing his stubbled jaw with one hand, Royce leaned forward. Dark eyes trying to read and extract something from her.

He was still talking to her. He hadn't completely shut down. Not that there was a place to retreat from each other in this igloo. But he could ice her out and ignore her. The fact that he was still talking gave her hope.

"By what, exactly?"

She watched Tessie circle five times before plopping down on the bearskin rug in front of the crackling fire. The orange flames cast warm light on the dog's shaggy fur.

The rugged domestic scene was idyllic actually. So long as the tension between Naomi and Royce was ignored. The tension she'd introduced so soon after their lovemaking. But ignoring the reason she was there wasn't an option anymore.

And ignoring it wouldn't be fair to him, she'd realized somewhere during the conversation over sandwiches. When she'd made her grand plan to deliver the supplies and convince him to work for the company, she hadn't known anything about him that wasn't on his official bio. But Royce was so much more than a sharp mind or a valued corporate asset. He was a warm-hearted man with protective instincts too strong to let a woman fend off a bear alone. He was an intriguing mixture of the methodical and the spontaneous, a science-loving genius with a wild streak all his own.

"Royce? Confused by what?" she asked again, wondering if he would just refuse to answer.

"What the hell are you doing here? I assume since you're a Steele, you don't need to moonlight as a delivery gal."

"I wanted to meet you. Your work is fascinating to me. I did attend one of your lectures, but you have to admit, you're tough to find for chitchat."

"Yet you managed."

"I'm resourceful?" She paused. "You're not smiling."

"What we did here this afternoon? Not chitchatting." He looked down at her bare legs.

His attention and vague accusation left her feeling exposed. No—overexposed. She wrapped her arms around her waist, his sweatshirt enveloping her body like a hug.

"Yes, well, this chemistry caught me by surprise." She raised a hand to stop him from talking. "And I swear, if you dare accuse me of sleeping with you for ulterior motives, I will seriously hurt you."

"It wouldn't be an unreasonable assumption."

"Actually, it would be a very unreasonable conclusion. My sleeping with you was a bad idea because it was a surefire way to make you suspicious or turn you against me once you found out who I am. I'm a lawyer—I should have been more logical."

"A lawyer. You're *that* one of the Steele family?"

She bristled at the way the description—the accusation—rolled off his tongue. "Yes, I'm *that* one."

In that normally unemotional, unreadable face, Naomi saw a twisting of anger glimmering in those rich brown eyes. His mouth closed tight as if containing harsh words. There was more though. The way he exhaled heavily through his nose, the way he continued to examine her like a witness on the stand... Naomi, who knew how to read people as well as she knew the law, could feel a hint of something within him that looked like frustrated disillusionment. Her meal grew heavy in her stomach, the joy of the day fading.

The buzzer for the dryer echoed in the small room. Tessie's ears twitched, and then she swung her head around to look at the dryer before chuffing in vague annoyance at being woken again. Truth be told, Naomi sent up a silent thank-you, eagerly exiting the bed to reach for her now-warm clothes. The small distraction might just give her a much-needed moment to regroup.

Still stunned, Royce didn't move from the bed when Naomi walked toward the compact stacked washer and dryer tucked away in the closet. Actually, *stunned* didn't even cover it.

He studied her, attempting to decipher the intentions of their afternoon burning up the sheets. A helluva introduction. Naomi pulled her clothes from the dryer, but seemed to linger a moment more than necessary at the machine.

A flare of anger rose in his chest. Threatened to bubble to the surface.

Most of all because being with Naomi had been good, damn good. There'd been an instantaneous chemistry there, more powerful than anything he'd experienced with any other woman. And yeah, he wanted to find some way through this mess and back to that.

For now, though, he would execute the most logical plan possible. Which involved putting on clothes. Attempting to shut down the physical connection between them.

Hoisting himself off the mattress, he rummaged in the drawers under the bed, digging for clothes. The house's space-saving drawers and its overall functional economy had appealed to him—like everything else in this utilitarian space. Because there was no waste. No BS.

Until, of course, Naomi arrived. Then the BS factor exploded exponentially.

Pulling out a long-sleeved T, he dared to add another sentence to the now-uncomfortable quiet. A sentence to gain clarity. "Tell me why you're here."

Glancing at her, he watched as she slipped into her panties, the slight flex of her slender legs pushing the reality of their situation to the corners of his mind.

That connection—it still rocked through him. But that was a distraction he couldn't afford. "Well, Naomi? Use your words, please. You've been damn well pushing me to use mine ever since you strolled in here."

"Fine. I'm here to convince you to work for my family's company." Naomi placed her hands on her hips, standing in nothing but her panties and a gray shirt.

Damn. Damn. Damn.

"And that's it?" he pushed, shelving his attraction for the moment, knowing a moment was likely all the restraint he would be able to muster with her in the same room. "That's all you're hiding?"

"Isn't that enough?" A tinge of regret deepened her words.

He stared at her silently. Waiting. Needing…more? Of what, he wasn't sure. She messed with his mind in a major way.

Naomi stepped into her silver-studded jeans and shimmied them up, her dark hair falling out of her loose ponytail. "And yes, we want you in the company because of your research. Don't you want to see it used by a company that cares?"

Working with an ethical company—one that gave a damn—was the end goal. But he would never, ever release his work until it was fully developed. And even then, he wanted to be involved. "I want to make sure it's ready to be used. And I want control of it. So do you just want the research, not me?"

Naomi sighed, pink lips parting. "Of course we want you, because research is always going to be evolving and you're the best. But…if you're not interested in working for a company, then yes, we would settle for an exclusive on what you've developed."

He tugged on his shirt, one arm through the sleeves at a time, processing everything she'd said—and what she hadn't. "And you haven't been here trying to gain access to that?"

"I'll be honest. If it fell under my nose, I wouldn't look away."

The hits just kept coming. "Why are you going to such extremes?"

At least she'd shared her actual intentions. A strange sort of victory, considering everything up until now had been lies. Well not lies exactly, but half-truths.

"Seriously, Royce? Your work is that good." She looked at him through long, sooty lashes.

The fact that they both were fully dressed now evened out this conversation.

"Nice try." He shook his head. "There's something else going on here. I'll ask again, and keep in mind how precarious my mood is right now, what made you go to such extremes to meet me?"

She paused for so long he thought she might not answer.

Naomi sank to sit on the floor next to Tessie and stroked the dog. "I had leukemia as a teenager."

A stab of surprise hit him. When he'd been growing up, a kid in his elementary class had gone through chemo and radiation. Memories of that coupled with the thought of Naomi being that sick… Damn. "I'm so very sorry you went through that, especially so young. And I'm glad you are sitting here today clearly glowing with health."

Naomi leaned into the Saint Bernard. Tessie lazily licked her right hand, clearly enjoying the attention— perhaps offering her own endorsement. "You're the first person who ever put that positive spin on things. They usually focus on the sympathy."

"You survived." He knelt beside her. "That couldn't have been easy."

"A lot of people don't. I had great medical care and was also lucky it was caught early. But yes, it was rough."

Her throat bobbed, suppressing emotions—and memories, no doubt.

Royce attempted to find the thread that brought this all together. But cause and effect with people was a lot harder to discern than with scientific research. "I'm still not making the connection. What does that have to do with you being here?"

"The toughest part was my dad."

"What do you mean?" He reached out to pet Tessie, aware of the way Naomi's hand shied away from his.

"My sister and mom died in a plane crash, so he'd already lost one child. I was so scared of what would happen to him if he lost another."

"That was quite a burden for you to carry so young. And what a time not to have your mother." His parents had been a bedrock of support for him growing up. He couldn't help but think about how his ex-fiancée lost her way when her dad died.

"You're intuitive for a man."

"I think that's supposed to be a compliment."

"It is."

"I'm only drawing logical conclusions."

"Not everyone makes those connections. And yeah, I needed my mother so much then. My grandmother was around and she was great..." She shook her head. "I'm here. And trust me, I was pampered to pieces... still am."

"It's reasonable that your family would be even more protective after so much loss."

"I guess what I'm trying to say is I am a strong person. I can't take being smothered. I need to be valued for who I am and the work I do, like my siblings. I'm a lawyer. I graduated magna cum laude. And somehow, it's never dawned on my father that I could play a major role in the company beyond litigating legal issues. I know he loves me and that I'm not a replacement for my sister who died, but somehow our relationship got stuck in those teenage years. It's like if he can freeze me at that age, he can keep a piece of her alive..." She pinched the bridge of her nose, clearly holding back tears.

A slow understanding dawned on him as he made the connections. Understanding the broader implications of what she said. In a softer voice, he continued, "And that's why you're here."

She nodded slowly. "Well, that's why I'm here at your retreat. But it's not why I'm—" she pointed to the bed "—*here*, here."

"Heard and understood." He tucked the hair that had fallen in front of her face behind her ear, the need to touch her inevitable, irresistible, like a force of nature. "You don't have to prove yourself to everyone."

"Easier said than done when people don't have faith in me. You sure could help with that if you would at least meet with the heads of Alaska Oil Barons. Just listen, no obligation. I need to prove myself. You're my key. If I can get you to give our company an exclusive on your research—"

He shook his head. "I'm not ready."

"Whatever you have for safety upgrades is already better than what's in place."

"And the time I'll lose putting those in place will be time and energy better spent getting to the answers I want. Committing too soon will cause a delay in the long run. I have my eyes on the big picture."

Tessie moved from under his hand, running to the door, emitting a slow but insistent whine. She pawed at the door, scratching against the white paint. Turning her big head back to Royce, Tessie let out a low bark.

"We can give you people—"

He shook his head, the emotional pressure too damn much. He wasn't her answer. Couldn't be her answer. He had to end this conversation. "Stop, Naomi. We're done talking. I'm taking Tessie outside." He shot to his feet and closed the distance between himself and the door. He pulled on his boots and grabbed his jacket.

Maybe for the first time ever, he was thankful to head out in blizzard-like conditions.

Royce's sudden move to the door set Naomi into motion. She sprang up from where she'd been seated. Practically tripped over her own two feet as she too made her way to the door. Stuffing her feet into her fluffy lined boots and shoving her arms into the pink parka's sleeves, she readied herself for the freeze-out—both from the Alaskan wilderness and from Royce.

She couldn't just leave things this way between them. She'd mishandled the situation and she needed to do her best to set things right.

Making her way out the door, she put her suddenly cold fingers into the gloves that she'd stuffed into her parka's pocket.

She was surprised he hadn't evicted her altogether, or at the very least banished her to sleep in the bathtub. She was mad at herself over the way she'd handled this, the way she'd lost control.

How frustratingly ironic that in working to be taken seriously, she'd done the most reckless thing she'd done since she was sixteen and snuck out of the house to joy-ride with friends after curfew the day she'd received her license. Not because she hadn't been allowed to take the SUV if she'd asked. But because she wanted to prove she was invincible. Naomi had wound up spinning out and driving into a snowbank that day—and she never forgot the anger in her father's face when he arrived on scene, reminding her of how many lives she'd put at risk.

And how many people would be hurt if something happened to her.

Since then, she'd cultivated the image of being a

party girl—in appearance more than reality. Sure, she enjoyed flaunting convention, but she actually preferred her confrontations and emotional drama be contained to the courtroom.

Snatching up his gloves, she made her way to him and Tessie. Snow collected on his shoulders. A lot of snow for the relatively short amount of time he'd been out there.

Twenty feet between them, but it might as well have been half the globe. As her boots sunk into drifts, she accepted the possibility that maybe he wouldn't work with her because he believed the sex between them was motivated by business. The thought sickened her. Naomi didn't want to disappoint her family, but she also didn't want Royce to think she'd use their lovemaking as a strange kind of leverage.

Taking a steadying breath of ice-cold air, she felt awake, at home and grounded. Ready to try to talk to him, to make him understand the stakes of her offer and her attraction to him were not one and the same. Tall trees cast her snow-crunched walk in shadow. Glancing behind her shoulder, she looked back to the glass igloo in the clearing, appreciating the way it stood apart from the woods. The small building didn't intrude on the natural surroundings. No—the economic igloo seemed to mirror Royce's outlook. Understated yet impactful.

Turning her attention back to the path to Tessie and Royce, she let out a deep breath she hadn't realized she'd held. He turned, snow spilling off his shoulders. Dark eyes met hers, and that spark of familiarity and excitement danced in her.

She gestured to his dog, currently walking in circles sniffing the ground. "Tell me about Tessie."

"Tell you what exactly?" He broke eye contact, his gaze focused somewhere along the tree line.

"I was hoping my open-ended question would lead you to reveal things I didn't expect." She thrust his coat and gloves toward him.

"Open-ended questions, huh?" He pulled his hands from his pockets and slipped on his jacket and gloves. "Showing off those lawyer skills of yours?"

A small joke. The ease warmed her core. "Not showing off if it didn't work. How long have you had her?"

He held out his hand, holding it steady while snow gathered in his gloved palm. "Since she was a puppy. A backyard breeder got busted, and the shelter needed to place nearly a hundred puppies, all different kinds. The little breed ones went fast, but it was tougher to place the larger dogs. Tessie also had a broken back leg. So, I picked her and headed straight for a veterinarian's office. She spent her first six weeks of 'freedom' wearing a cast. Luckily though, she healed up just fine. No lingering effects."

She smiled and, yes, her cheeks were already starting to sting from the blustering cold wind, but she couldn't resist the allure of his sweet story. "You have a soft heart."

"I like dogs." He shrugged, more snow falling from his broad shoulders. "That doesn't make me a softhearted individual. Just human."

"You've had other dogs?"

"Yes." His gloved hand clenched the collected snow into a ball that he then tossed toward Tessie.

The Saint Bernard pounced with two large paws, sending a shower of white powder poofing upward.

"Just 'yes'? I'm glad you're not on the witness stand." She knelt to pet Tessie with one hand and started gathering a snowball with the other. "I'd have to ask the judge for permission to treat the witness as hostile."

He looked at her sidelong, brow arched. "Not hostile, just guarded."

"I could have kept quiet and we would be playing in the snow, then warming up in the shower before eating supper by the fire."

"Almost makes me wish you'd kept quiet."

"We could pretend." She scooped at the snow absently. "But pretending is what got me in this position. And for that I am so very sorry. I never anticipated the powerful attraction between us. I only hoped to learn something insightful about what it would take to appeal to one of the finest minds in the field, what it would take to lure him into working for the company."

He hissed between clenched teeth. "I want to believe you."

"Then do," she said simply, and lobbed a snowball for a square hit at his chest.

"Damn. You're good at that."

"I have three brothers." Standing, Naomi took a mock bow. "I had to be good if I wanted to survive snowball fights."

"You're competitive." He stepped toward her, eyes narrowing.

"Very." The wind practically pushed her into him. Not that she put much effort into resisting.

Skidding forward a bit, she found herself pressed into his chest, his arms suddenly around her. Silence echoed between them as his eyes held hers. Heat built inside her and she saw it returned in his gaze. The cold air seemed to lose its potent punch—

A rapid succession of cell phone chimes split the air. She couldn't make herself move.

Royce patted her coat pocket. "Now your great equipment makes sense."

"That's the ringtone I use for calls from my brother. I don't have to take it if it bothers you. I realize I've thrown a lot at you today…"

"Naomi," Royce whispered, the warmth of his breath on her cheek. "Take the call."

She shook her head. "No, I'm here with you. We're talking and playing with Tessie. I'm enjoying myself and I think maybe you are too. I'm not letting a phone call mess with that."

He smiled in a slow, confident way that lit all the way up to his brown eyes. He squeezed her tighter, and she melted into his touch. Aware of nothing but the glint of promise in his eyes. The way his face moved to meet hers. A thrill tingled along her skin, so intense it was almost like flesh coming back to life after frostbite.

She would only have to move a whisper more and they would be kissing, except she needed him to make the move this time, to know that he'd found some sort of resolution to how she'd played with the truth in her reasons for coming to his cabin. Their breaths puffed white clouds in the cold air, the bursts mingling, making her ache for that connection to be real.

Royce shook his head slowly. "Ah, hell, Naomi Steele."

His arms went around her and he sealed his mouth to hers, fully and confidently. Sighing, she leaned into him, heat rekindling through her. Her thoughts about practical reasons for being here scattered like the snowflakes swirling away as she and Royce toppled backward. The warmth and weight of him was intoxicating and she wanted more, so much more—

An insistent ding sliced the air. The sound of her text

messages. But she was here. In the moment. Whatever her brother needed could wait.

Ding.

Ding.

Royce elbowed up, the strong lines of his handsome face only inches away. "Someone's eager to get in touch with you. Maybe you should check."

Another *ding* echoed. The insistence was unmistakable.

She sighed in frustration. "I'll look at the messages, then turn the phone off."

Naomi, call me.

Call back. Important.

Call ASAP. Emergency.

Not something I want to text, but you need to call me. Dad had a horseback riding accident. Spinal injury.

Her whole body went numb. Except for her eyes. They burned with tears. Her father. Dread weighed her deeper into the snow, her mind filling with horrific scenarios.

As she tried to process what she'd read, a wave of nausea slammed into her, roiling hard and fast. With her tear-stained eyes, she thrust her cell at Royce and made fast tracks toward the igloo.

Not an outright run, but a lifetime of Alaskan winters gave her sure-footed steps along the icy path. Fear propelled her, along with an untimely round of pregnancy sickness.

Inside, she ripped off her parka on her way toward

the bathroom, leaving a trail of gloves and boots behind as she—thank God—made it in time.

After there was nothing left and her stomach settled, she leaned against the cream-colored wall, eyes closed. Naomi set her hands over her mouth, taking a few deep breaths before forcing her eyes open.

Adjusting to the light, she blearily registered Royce in the doorway, concern in his eyes, in the way he crossed his arm. He moved toward her, sliding into the small space between her and the sink. Royce set her cell phone on the countertop, exchanging it for a washcloth. He ran the warm water, dampening it to put on her neck.

He sat next to her, leaning against the door frame. "Food poisoning?"

Weary and drained, she scrounged for the will to shrug off the question. But fear still snaked around her—fear for her father.

Staving off panic, she took a deep breath. Exhaled. Then another until she realized this was the end of the road for her games and her plans to win over the reclusive scientist.

The business just didn't seem so important, considering what had happened to her father. She'd wanted stability and, instead, what she'd gotten from the universe was even more uncertainty. An attraction so big it frightened her. A man who didn't trust her. Plans that came apart. And now her dad…

She surrendered, spilling her last secret, one she hadn't even told her family yet. "It's not food poisoning. It's pregnancy."

Six

Stunned, Royce processed the twelve letters Naomi had spoken.

A breath tumbled out of his nose as he scrubbed a hand over his windburned cheeks. Slowly, he looked around the small bathroom. Feeling like they needed more space than an efficient bathroom like this could provide. He blinked. Once. Twice.

She buried her face back in her hands, collecting herself.

As Naomi drew in deep, measured breaths, Royce wished he could find some of that ease for himself. He was reeling.

His effort to view the situation from an objective— indeed distanced—lens proved more challenging than he cared to admit. So Royce did what came naturally. He cataloged the world around him, made sense of existing order and structures. The bright light in the stainless steel fixture drew his eyes up to the glinting white tile that surrounded them. Huge squares were arranged in a pattern on the walls, and on the cool ground beneath his fingertips.

This was the only room in the studio igloo without a full skylight. Instead, the slanted roof was kissed with stripes of glass panes. He'd never noticed that the quality of natural sunshine had a dizzying effect.

This mental exercise of grounding always left his mind refreshed, ready to tackle a difficult theoretical or mathematical problem.

Hopefully, that would also extend to this particular situation. "You're pregnant."

"Yes. Two months along. And I haven't told anyone about the baby yet. I certainly wouldn't have expected you to be the first I told." She swallowed hard, something like pain twisting in her beautiful features.

A gut punch rocked through him. She was pregnant? And the father? There was no ring on her finger and no hesitation in the way they'd slept together. Still, so many questions. He didn't want to risk upsetting her and unsettling her. She looked so pale already.

He would tread warily. In a softer voice, he began again, "Naomi."

"What?" Those dark eyes of hers, red rimmed, made her seem worn-out.

How had he not noticed her fatigue before? "I'm worried about you."

"My doctor says I'm in perfect health. Morning sickness is normal and, yes, I've been dealt a shock too."

Events from a lifetime ago scrolled through his mind. He recalled another time—when he was another person—with his former fiancée.

Carrie Lynn had been so upset after her father's funeral. The day after, she'd gotten in a car wreck on her way home from the grocery store and lost the baby. The cops had ruled it a no-fault accident, but she'd blamed herself, sunk into a depression and broken things off from him. He didn't blame her for the accident, even for a second, but he did blame himself for not being there to help her more. If he'd been driving that day, things well could have turned out differently.

Tamping down thoughts of the past to deal with the present, he took Naomi's hands in his. "It's not about your health. It's about you being careful. For your child. You went barreling off into a blizzard by yourself. Anything could have happened."

She tugged her hand back, eyes narrowing. "I don't answer to you."

So much for offering comfort. All he could do was nod. "Fair enough."

Silence passed between them. He glanced at the counter where he'd laid her phone. Reaching forward, he grabbed it and handed the device to her.

A half smile of a thank-you. She looked down at the still-dark screen. Without looking up at him, and in a voice uncharacteristically small, she asked, "Did you read the texts?"

"I assumed you meant for me to read them since you gave me the phone rather than stuffing it back into your coat pocket."

She clutched the device. "I should call my brother."

"Yes, you should, but I need to tell you, right after I read the messages, the storm picked up. The connection is down again."

Her face scrunched with frustration, her eyes blinking fast against pooling tears. His gut knotted and he wished like hell there was something more he could do for her. He reached for her and she held up her hands fast.

"No, thank you though. I'm pretty sure if you hug me, I'll fall apart. Nothing personal. If anyone were to offer me sympathy right now, I would lose it. Hormones, probably, because I am *not* the weepy sort."

"Okay, space granted. For what it's worth, even my tech isn't getting a call through on my cell—I checked for a signal. I'm sorry. And I'm sure one of our phones will be back up soon." He took her hand. "So how about giving yourself a second to catch your breath and gather your thoughts." He stroked her wrist. "Your pulse is still too fast."

"I wish I could joke that's because of you." Naomi's grin didn't quite reach her eyes.

No, Royce could see the weight the news about her father put on her. "Me too."

Tessie nudged his back in a hello, then lay down, pressing against his side. Filling the bathroom floor to max capacity.

Naomi slumped to rest against the shower stall door. "As for being careful, I've been driving in snow since I could reach the pedals. But the storm did roll in faster and heavier than anyone expected. Not that I answer to you," she repeated.

"It's okay to be cared for."

"Cared for is one thing. Smothered is another."

"I assume you're referencing your fight against cancer as a teen."

"More like my family's reaction afterward."

A thought came to him, and normally he might not have presumed to ask, but talking seemed to help distract her, so hell, he could talk. "And it's safe for you to be pregnant? Even after having had cancer and treatments?" He held up a hand. "Not smothering. I want to know."

She lifted a shoulder, tracing the grout in the floor tile, nonchalantly. "I had eggs frozen as a teenager—"

"Hold on. Not to be invasive, but are you saying this was an in vitro?"

Her eyebrows raised. "You're asking about the father."

He shrugged. "As your bed partner a few hours ago, I am curious."

"In vitro. Anonymous sperm donor," she said clearly, succinctly. "I have no lurking boyfriends or baby daddies."

Relief, too much, rocked through him. It shouldn't matter this much to him. But it did. "And so you decided on in vitro fertilization."

"I did. Granted, I made the decision before my family changed. Before we learned about Dad and Jeannie and the merger, which has shifted the world for all of us. But I want to be a mom. I've dated some great men, but never quite The One. I have a steady career, and my health scare has always made me aware of how important it is to embrace the day. I decided to have my baby now."

"And if Mr. Right comes along?"

"If he can't love my child, then he's not Mr. Right."

"Fair enough," he said, the subject of children making him itch between the shoulder blades. The shadowy image of a lost baby he had never seen still haunted his dreams some nights. He knew that loss would follow him always. But this wasn't about him. This was about her, and a grief no one should have to endure. And to face it so young? "You were talking about having cancer as a teen. I'm sorry to have interrupted you."

She thrust her hands in her hair, scraping it back. "It was such a surreal time, wanting to hope for the future but feeling like time was running out. When you're a teen, the future is getting invited to the prom. But because my sister died, I felt like I had to grasp every chance to experience life I could, cancer or no. I still feel that way."

This woman. Damn. Her tenacity humbled him. To have been through so much—faced so much tragedy—and still be this strong. A helluva fighter, that was for sure. But for now, she didn't have to fight alone. Royce wanted to take charge, fix the past for her, find solutions to unsolvable problems. The jut of her chin made it clear she was a woman who fought her own battles. And he admired that in her. Still...

Unable to resist, he cupped her shoulder, hoping she would accept that much comfort at least. She swayed a hint, as if she might lean against his chest and take the solace he ached to give her.

A ding sliced through the moment. Naomi looked down at her phone in disbelief. The signal meant a break in the storm. She nibbled on her bottom lip, took a steadying breath. Then, as if she was channeling all her strength, he watched her spine straighten, the composed lawyer taking over her body. "I guess that means the phone connection's back for now." She pushed to her feet. "I should call right away before we lose connectivity again."

In an instant, he watched her spring to her feet and blur past him. Angling over him and Tessie, she made her way to the living area, leaving Royce seated on the tile floor.

Curled up on the sofa, Naomi scrunched her warm toes beneath the thick chunky blanket Royce had unearthed from the closet. She clutched the cell phone, pressing it hard against her ear as if the mere pressure would ensure the connection's strength.

It had taken her three tries to get through to her brother Broderick. During that time, Royce had brought her the blanket, steaming hot chocolate and an assortment of crackers.

"How is Dad?" Was that shaky voice really hers?

"They have him immobilized until the neurosurgeon decides exactly how to proceed." Broderick's steady voice grounded her, even if the news sent her nerves skittering.

"Immobilized?" Her mind reeled, attempting to imagine a force strong enough to keep her father down for any length of time. "Neurosurgeon?"

"He broke his back…two bones in his neck, actually." The words thundered through the cell speaker, piercing her heart. Stunned silence. Broderick must have sensed her tension. His hurried reassurance came next. "But he's still able to move his arms and legs."

"He broke his neck?" The words felt foreign to her tongue, like she'd been tasting a strange reality. Her eyes sought Royce across the room, craving that connection. Damn it, how had she let herself lean on him already?

"He cracked the top two vertebrae, the C1 and C2. Actually, the C2 has a peg on it that goes through the C1. That peg is broken. Right now, there's no nerve impingement and he's able to move his legs."

She tried to call to mind anatomy textbooks to envision what Broderick was talking about—a diagram of her strong father's frame inside a force of personality that had always been indomitable.

Broderick's textured and overwhelmed sigh filled the speaker. "But he has to stay in bed, in a brace. He can't move his head and, God knows, he can't fall. And he must—" his voice cracked for the first time, and then he cleared his throat "—he must survive through surgery. It's risky, but there's no choice."

Naomi absently reached for the hot cocoa on the end table, needing the feeling of warmth, of something, as she turned over her brother's words. Better to reach for that than the appealing man across the room who had offered her the comfort she truly craved. The steam danced around her face, and she blew on the beverage, scattering the steam into the studio's air. "I can't imagine—" her own voice hitched this time, but she cleared it "—a world without Dad."

"Or a world where Dad's paralyzed."

A gut-sinking feeling anchored her to the sofa. "Did the surgeon give any more details about the surgery? How is surgery going to fix the break?"

"Apparently, there's a small screw they can put into the peg on the C2 that will hold it in place. Then he wears the neck brace for six months, but there's not as much risk as letting it heal on its own, which could take months and a halo."

"That sounds good." She grasped at the hope.

"The surgery is done so rarely, the screw isn't in stock and has to be special ordered. Most people who have this kind of break don't survive."

"Okay, scary, but also a relief he's alive." Naomi's thoughts drifted from her own anxieties to Jeannie, her father's fiancée. The former rival matriarch of another oil company. Heat found Naomi's cheeks as she recalled how resistant she and her siblings had been to the family and corporate mergers. Family feuds were meaningless right now. Jeannie had already lost a husband to a heart attack… To lose a fiancé too… "How's Jeannie?"

"She's putting on a strong front, but underneath it all, I can tell she's a mess."

"That's understandable. This type of accident is... incomprehensible. Dad's such a sure seat in the saddle. He's the last person I would have expected to have a riding accident." Her hands shaking, she sipped the hot cocoa, the sweetness giving her an unexpected boost. Throwing a glance over her shoulder, she looked to the kitchen area where Royce meticulously cleaned the counter.

"They have staff with him, but we don't want him left alone. So, we've already started making out a schedule to rotate through."

"Do you think he'll allow that?" Another question—a more terrifying one—intruded on her thoughts. "God, is he even alert enough to know?"

"He's mighty clear considering the hit to the head he took. Clear enough to be frustrated, but he seems to be scared enough to be compliant." A dark laugh blasted through the cell speaker. "And honestly, he's not going to have a choice. We're as stubborn as he is. We figure we'll talk about business. He'll let us hang out as long as we want." Silence echoed through the phone. She could practically hear Broderick's gears turning as he shifted topics. "How are things up there with you?"

"Still snowed in, not sure when I'll be able to leave. I pray it's in time for Dad's surgery." She paused, weighed her options, then decided she needed to update her brother. "I, uh, decided it was best to be upfront with Royce and tell him why I'm here."

"Royce? You're on a first-name basis?"

Brother, if you only knew.

"We have been stuck here in a snowstorm, and for longer than I expected." She looked back at Royce, his dark features calling to her. That crackle of desire dancing along the air between them like static skipping over the rustled blanket. Excitement quickly gave way to sadness—to the reality of their situation.

"And what came of the meeting?"

Such a tricky question. She scavenged for her best lawyer voice. "We're still in discussion."

"You didn't get him to sign on at Alaska Oil Barons."

"He hasn't signed on with anyone else. And honestly, I can't think about that right now."

"You're right, of course. I guess I was just looking for a distraction."

Thank God, she'd managed to shut her brother down on the subject of Royce Miller, because she had very little chance of getting her head on straight about him with the news of her father's accident knocking the ground from under her. "I promise if there's something to announce, I'll let you know."

The day had passed in an insignificant blur for Royce as he tried like hell to control his thoughts. He didn't want to think of Naomi's pregnancy. It could too easily drag him into a pit of memories about his ex-fiancée and their lost baby. He definitely didn't want to think about Naomi's ties to her family's oil business and how that complicated their undeniable chemistry. So he concentrated on the weather.

The storm had let up in time for an Alaskan sunset. The open night sky above them—kept at bay by a layer of weatherproof glass.

From the kitchen, he'd watched Naomi sitting curled up in the thick blanket, her hair tumbling past her shoulders, framing that elegant face, making her dark eyes seem more inviting.

Since the retreat was so small, there was no way to give her privacy while she was on her phone call. He could tell the gist of what had happened to her father by her answers and reactions. Yes, he was still angry at her, but that had taken a backseat to what she was facing with her father's accident. She had to be in hell right now, wanting to see her dad and being stuck up here.

Royce looked at her, sitting on the sofa, clutching the red mug of hot chocolate he'd given her. She absently stared forward, seeming lost in her own world. She'd spent most of the day like that, since the phone call. He'd replaced her hot chocolate twice between working on some reading material in the kitchen.

He cleared his throat. "From what I've seen via the internet, the weather is supposed to lighten up tomorrow. Hopefully it'll be clear enough for me to drive you into town."

She looked up sharply. "I can drive myself."

"I thought you wanted to spend more time persuading me to join your company." An offer to help. Damn clear she wouldn't take it outright.

She set her mug of hot chocolate down and stood up, hand on her hip. "You're the one who said I shouldn't have driven up here on my own. It's clear your 'offer' to drive me has more to do with machismo protectiveness than any inclination to hear a business pitch." Her words rolled out faster and faster, her pitch getting higher. "Which—by the way—happens to be the last thing on my mind right now—"

Her words choked off and she bit her lip. Hard. Her jaw trembled.

Protective urges churned inside him. He charged over to her and hauled her to his chest, cupping her head. A shudder rippled through her along with a near-silent sob.

He held her tightly, hoping his grip meant something. He stroked her back, smoothed her hair and couldn't help but wonder how she'd come to affect him so much in such a short time. Her pain slashed right through him. He could damn near see it flashing through his brain.

Then he realized the northern lights were beginning a path across the night sky.

"Naomi," he said softly against her hair. "Let's lie back and watch the lights through the ceiling."

As if her voice no longer could be persuaded to work, she angled back to look at him and nodded, her eyes red with worry and fatigue. She pulled off her shoes, letting them drop to the floor with a thud. Tessie stirred from in front of the fire as he took off his boots. Naomi had already started scooting up the bed. He hurried to meet her, brought her close to him as they leaned back as a unit.

Perfectly synchronized.

She laid her head on his chest, and they watched the sun wink out, exchanging the mundane orange of sunset for a crackling display of stars. Pristine for lack of light pollution. In this moment, in the quiet of it all, it was easy to forget there was anyone else in the world but them, especially as the radiant green oscillations of aurora borealis painted across the sky.

Words retreated from him. She could likely use something to distract her, something else to occupy her thoughts besides her father in his hospital bed. He couldn't find the precise thing he wanted to say to her. Every half-rehearsed formulation sounded clunky in his mind. So, he decided to share why he didn't want her to drive off alone.

With a deep sigh, he began, his head pressing down into the feather pillows. "I was engaged. She and I grew up next door to each other, both were grades ahead in school and started college early. We became friends—at first because there weren't many other seven-year-olds who wanted to talk about Pascal's calculator. In our late teens, we started dating."

He stroked her shoulder, unsure of how to proceed.

"You had a lot of history, then." She shifted, her hair dragging across his chest as she flipped to stare at the cosmic show above them. "That had to make the breakup even more difficult. May I ask what happened?"

He swallowed. Hard. Concentrated on the crackle of fire, the sound of Tessie's light snore. He found moments in the present to focus on. It'd be too damn easy to find himself stuck in the past. In those hard spaces. "The week before we were to get married, she lost the baby in a car accident after her father's funeral... She pulled away after that. And I lost her too."

"I am so sorry."

He closed his eyes, anchoring himself on the feel of the white sheets, the soft flannel texture beneath him. "She said I was emotionally unavailable when she needed me most. She wanted a partner she could count on."

"I can't claim to know everything about the situation since I've never met her, but I can say, if you knew each other for eleven years, then your reaction—whatever it was—couldn't have been a surprise to her."

"You're good at spinning things, Counselor."

"I'm just examining the facts." Naomi traced her fingertips on top of his.

And now he needed to focus on the shimmering of

the overhead aurora borealis to keep himself from giving in to temptation. To resist drawing her to him for a kiss they could explore at leisure. She followed his line of vision. Out of the corner of his eyes, Royce watched a smile tug at her lips as her eyes beheld the natural light show overhead.

"Naomi, I'm trying to explain why I can't help but be protective, of you, of anyone in a similar situation. But I also want you to understand why I am the way I am, who I am."

Her fingers trailed up his arm; sincerity and empathy seemed to radiate from her touch. "We've both been through a lot in the past and it shaped who we are. I don't expect you to be anyone other than who you are. But I need for you to accept who I am."

"And you're independent."

"To a fault, yes, I am. You need to give me some breathing space."

He couldn't hold back a bark of laughter, in fact found he welcomed it right now.

"What did I say?" Her knee slid over his calf.

His body throbbed in reaction. Damn poor timing with her face still pale. "Forget it."

"Not a chance. What's so amusing?"

"You promise you won't go hormonal on me?"

She lifted an eyebrow. "Seriously? Did you just say that?"

He held up his hands. "Never mind."

"I can't decide if you're trying to be funny or if you're serious. Either way, I want to know and I will keep my infamous temper—which has nothing to do with hormones—in check."

"I just found it ironic that you want less attention. I've never met a woman who wanted space."

"That's stereotyping." Her lips went tight and prim, totally at odds with her sweater slipping off one shoulder.

He remembered well the taste of that creamy patch of skin. "Yes, it is. And you're anything but a stereotype."

Her mouth softened, delectably so. "I think you just complimented me."

"Maybe. But either way, you can be damn sure, you're not driving out of here alone." He'd barely survived the guilt after his fiancée's accident. He wouldn't make the same mistake with Naomi, no matter how much she wanted to call the shots.

And no sooner had the words fallen out of his mouth than her smile went tight.

"Sure," she said, inching away. "I really need to get some sleep."

While he knew he sometimes fell short on gauging the emotional component of a conversation, he could tell loud and clear she'd shut him down. He just wished he understood why.

Seven

Naomi woke, blinked, confused for a moment about her surroundings. The warm weight of a masculine arm over her stomach grounded her, the stream of acknowledgments flooding back as an information wave.

She was with Royce. Her father was in the hospital. Careful not to wake Royce, she eased out from under his muscled arm to retrieve her cell phone from the bedside table. She thumbed the screen…and no messages, no signal.

Sighing in frustration, she smacked the phone down onto the comforter. The snow was so thick she couldn't even see the sky anymore.

She turned her head on the pillow to look at Royce. He'd been so much calmer than she'd expected when she'd told him everything. Although it was clear he was angry, and she'd almost certainly blown any chance of getting him to join her family's company, he'd still offered his compassion and protection. He'd still insisted on taking care of her. She should have tried to talk to him more, but...

She'd just fallen asleep. Out like a light so fast. She'd read that pregnancy would make her sleepy, but she suspected her exhaustion had more to do with the emotional outlay of her fears for her father and her confrontation with Royce.

The hell of it all? She'd really enjoyed her time with him—and the amazing sex—and she wished she could lose herself in that now. But her fear for her dad had her heart in a vise. Only the comfort of Royce's arm around her, the warmth of his body beside her, kept her from bursting into tears altogether.

Tears were something she'd always had trouble setting free, a facet of her personality forever linked to her teenage years. To holding back her grief over losing her mother and sister because everyone else was hurting so much. To battling cancer and trying to spare her father more pain.

Those circumstances grated on Naomi, made her internalize her fear into a decisive, deadly logical blade. It was what made her a damn good lawyer. Fear of losing pushed her to assemble a facade of brick in the courtroom. As a teenager facing down the likelihood that her disease just might beat her, she had chosen to emulate the wild abandon of her environment.

She'd done it for her family's sake, even though every fiber of her being shook test after test, treatment after treatment. For her brothers, sister and dad, she learned to bury the urge to cry or to express fear. Instead, she adopted a carefree air.

There had been one time she'd really let the reality of her treatment get to her and it had been the last time she'd given herself permission to lose her resolve in front of her family. A moment etched forever in her memory. The day her hair had started to fall out as a reaction to the chemo.

Naomi's hair had always been a point of pride—something that connected her to the mother she'd lost as a preteen. Naomi's mother had spoken of the way it shone with night—radiant, like a character in the old, oral stories her mother's grandmother had shared by firelight. So, when the first chunk of the hair her mother had brushed—and the hair so like her mom's that it had prompted a look into her mother's heritage—fell out, teenage Naomi had privately crumbled. Not out of vanity. But over yet another loss—the tie to her mother, her sister too.

Tears had burned in her eyes as she brought the lock to her father and siblings. Her sister Delaney had done her best to cheer her up, but even as a teenager, Naomi knew her condition wore heavy on them. Too much grief in one family only two years after that fatal plane crash.

She'd resented her body for putting them all through this. And she'd wanted her mother so much.

She still did.

Her hand slid over her stomach.

In her mind's eye, she imagined her unborn child. Names spoken by her mother during the stories she'd passed down danced silently on her tongue now. The love she already had for the baby steadied her, reminding her of the importance of connection. Of family. When she'd opted for in vitro, she'd had such plans for bringing up her baby here in Alaska, her big family surrounding the child with love too. She would embrace the future, have a family of her own, on her terms.

Right now, she couldn't help but wonder what it would have been like to have a man like Royce at her side when she'd decided to become a mother. Even thinking about it made her go weak on the inside.

A reaction she couldn't afford with her life in more turmoil than ever.

She'd seen the determination in his eyes when he'd said he intended to drive her into town. And the lawyer in her recognized that arguing with him on that point would be futile. She'd failed to win him over to the company, and she'd lost whatever romantic connection they'd shared. Both threatened to send her knees folding.

Once the snow eased and roads cleared, she would be spending a few awkward hours with him in an SUV. After that? She doubted she would ever see him again.

How was it that her brain—a legal mind that always served her well in thinking on her feet—was on total stun now? She needed a plan B. She always had one.

Except for now. Somehow, this one man had changed everything.

Royce's hands gripped the wheel of the SUV, his abacus key chain swaying. He'd surprised the hell out of himself by offering to drive Naomi to Anchorage to be with her family. They had chemistry, sure, but she was also a Steele.

And she was pregnant.

His gut went icy at the thought. Yet even as the thought chilled him, he couldn't ignore the need to see her safely home.

Despite the freezing temperature, the palms of his hands slicked with sweat as he navigated the vehicle on the still-snow-covered Alaskan back roads. The moisture had little to do with the warmth produced by the car's heated seats. No. It had everything to do with his beating chest, his concern for the beautiful woman seated next to him. He needed to get her to her father.

The storm had let up enough for them to leave. He knew better than to let this break in the weather pass them by, even if a selfish part of him wanted to return to the bed and just hold her. Be near her.

Flicking his eyes off the road to see Naomi, he watched her absently catalog the thick snowbanks and snow-drenched trees. Her head casually rested forehead to glass, the thick tangles of her hair obscuring most of her face.

She clutched her phone in her manicured hand, an exhale sending her body moving. "Uh-huh... Yes... I understand."

Her half whisper was so soft it stoked over Royce's senses. Dangerous on more than one level.

He gathered his attention back to the icy road, ahead and behind.

Glancing in his rearview mirror, he took in the lay of the land covered in the thick blanket of new snow. The roads were passable with careful speed and four-wheel drive, but he still needed to be on alert. They'd been driving for about a half hour and they'd yet to encounter another living soul. Even the wildlife seemed subdued, hidden still after nature's onslaught. Too bad that same peace was nowhere near echoed inside him.

"Okay. Okay. I just—" Naomi's voice mingled with the weather station on low that filled the spaces between her silence.

"Can I say hi to the baby?" Naomi asked, her tone lighter than a moment before.

From his peripheral vision, he saw her move her

hand cautiously to her own stomach. Royce scratched a hand along his jaw. Damn, but this was all complicated.

"Hey there, princess. Auntie Naomi misses you."

The affection in her voice couldn't be missed. He thought of the child he'd lost. The life he'd almost had with his ex-fiancée. The secret Naomi was keeping from her family. His hands clenched around the steering wheel at the urge to keep her safe. To not let the past repeat itself. To put safety first.

Cricking his neck from side to side, he worked to ease his grip on the wheel before his fingers numbed. The road back to Anchorage always ramped him up, but not necessarily in a good way. Too much activity, noise, business clogged creative thought. It's why he'd chosen the rental igloo outside of Anchorage. The oscillation from chunks of ice moving in the water on one side and mountains on the other stimulated his brain, somehow helped him situate his thinking and calibrate his equations for a safer pipeline procedure.

To temper the desire for Naomi until he had her settled—and figure out what the hell to do next.

The scientific process, for all its precision, owed something to the humble power of nature. Still, that thought didn't keep him from noticing how the light refracted off the snow and illuminated Naomi's face as she readjusted her seat.

Tessie let out a long sigh from the back, refocusing his attention from his wandering thoughts to the present moment. Another glance in the rearview revealed an ecstatic Saint Bernard, one clearly excited to be out of close quarters. Tessie wagged her tail, head bobbing, taking in the rush of scenery, the layers of snow and ice that made their home so pristine and beautiful.

For the first time since they began their trek back to the city, they passed another SUV.

The sudden intrusion of other people jarred him for a moment and made him realize she'd stopped talking. Even though Naomi had been speaking on the phone to her brother, there'd been a way to feel as though this part of the world belonged to them and them alone.

Royce glanced over at her. "Any news about your father's condition?" She cradled the phone in her lap.

"The doctors are waiting for his blood pressure to stabilize before surgery. He's otherwise stable, stuck in bed in a neck brace, but awake and as clear as anyone with a major concussion can be."

"We'll arrive as soon as I can safely get there." His primary objective was a safe journey for her and her unborn child.

"I wanted to hear the surgery had already been done. That all had gone perfectly, and Dad was ready to jog down the hall."

"Jog?" His attention returned to the road as he navigated along a patch of ice. The tires skidded for a moment. For a Texas boy, Royce had learned the nuances of driving in these conditions like he learned everything else—relentless experimentation and practice.

She laughed softly, the sound an enticing curl between them. "Maybe that was optimistic, but it sounded good when I was thinking it."

"I wish I could tell you everything's going to be fine, but life isn't always fair."

"If that's supposed to be a pep talk, you're not doing so hot." She gathered her hair into her fist and twisted a hair tie from her wrist to make a ponytail. Her diamond stud earrings caught the light.

"You would have known blind reassurance was a

lie. I was going to finish by saying he has the best care possible and a reputation for being strong as an ox."

"Much better that time." She gave him a small laugh. But more important, a genuine one.

Victory pumped through him—over eliciting a simple laugh. He really needed to get his head on straight. "Good to know."

She tapped on the window glass, as if she was locating Anchorage with her fingertips. Her shoulders sunk as she leaned forward, eyes attentive on the snowy landscape. "I realize he has lots of family support. I just wish I was already there."

"Three siblings, right?"

"Four actually…four living, that is. Two older brothers, a younger sister, a younger brother…and my sister who died with my mother in the plane crash."

He gave her hand a quick squeeze. "I'd heard Jack Steele had a lot of kids, but that sure is a large family."

"Going to get even bigger now that he's marrying Jeannie Mikkelson. She's got four kids—two sons and two daughters—who have a claim to the company."

"The merged company, you mean."

She rolled her eyes. "Yes, merged. Which is easier said than done. Believe it or not, I care about preserving the way business is done, and I worry about this. There are so many ways it can go wrong. Even if we do work out our differences, if there's a dip in power and Johnson Oil United uses that to their advantage…"

"Which is why you wanted to bring me in, because you love the land and not because you're a lawyer jockeying for a stronger power play for your family in this merger."

She didn't speak for a moment, the blast of the heater

and crunching ice under the tires the only sounds. He glanced over quickly.

Her lips were pressed in a tight line, the pink straining to blanched white. "It's okay to care about both. Although right now, business is the last thing on my mind."

"Are you okay? I mean, do you feel alright?"

"I'm fine," she said tightly, "but thank you for your concern. Do you have siblings?"

"Nope. Just my parents, older, I was a surprise." A surprise and an anomaly.

"Sounds…quiet. Is that why you're so quiet sometimes?"

He looked hard at the road in front of him, assessing the slight snow increase. Explaining why he was quiet was like trying to explain his DNA. "I'm an introvert. A scientist. I was always three grades ahead in school. It's who I am."

"And I brought all this mayhem to your life."

"I'm a willing participant, and I have the ability to retreat to quiet as needed." Squeezing her hand again, he hoped she could feel his urge to get her to Anchorage safely.

"We're very different."

"Yes, we are. Is that a bad thing?" It hadn't seemed like such a problem back at the retreat when they'd landed in bed together.

"Depends." Her head dipped and she seemed intent on studying his hand.

A wall of snow flurries intensified, forcing his attention back to the road. He loosened his grip from her, needing both hands on the wheel. It was time to focus on the road. To get her to safety.

In the ensuing silence, broken only by the weather

station on the radio, a gentle snore from Tessie in the back. And in the pensive quiet he couldn't ignore the obvious any longer.

He didn't want to say goodbye to Naomi once they reached Anchorage.

Hospitals always made her stomach churn with apprehension. The too-white lights beat down on her, settling on her skin like an unrelenting sun. In all her years, a visit to the hospital had never been quick or easy.

Glancing right, she looked at Royce, who stood cross-armed, and she had the feeling he wasn't leaving anytime soon. When they'd stopped for gas, he'd called ahead for a place to board Tessie. She'd tried not to read too much into that beyond the fact he wasn't going to toss Naomi out at the hospital door, a place the dog wasn't welcome.

Royce was plastered to her side, one hand on her back every step of the way. As if she hadn't been walking on icy sidewalks her whole life.

Broderick leaned against the arm of an industrial-looking green couch, guardian-like over his fiancée, Glenna, who sat next to her mother, comforting Jeannie. Normally, Glenna's blond hair fell in fairy-princess waves around her shoulders. But today her hair was drawn back into a sloppy bun.

Jeannie's expression was obscured by her hands over her face. Even from here, as Royce and Naomi closed the distance from the entrance to the hospital, she could see how her father's former rival was racked with worry and grief.

They weren't the only ones there in the waiting room. In fact, the place was packed. As Naomi scanned the scene, she realized her family and the Mikkelsons—who she supposed were also family now—had taken over much of the waiting area.

Her sister Delaney paced the floor, darting around her youngest brother, Aiden. Poor Aiden. Normally he seemed so grown-up. Responsible. But today he looked like the teenager he was, lines of worry cutting into his face.

Delaney, nurturing as ever, rushed toward Royce and Naomi.

Trystan, Jeannie's youngest son, the rancher, had been standing off in the corner, but as Naomi came closer, he moved to the other side of his mother, eyes narrowed. "What's *he* doing here?"

The words dripped with a defensive, protective quality. She hadn't had much exposure to Trystan, but she knew he could be hard to handle, preferring the solitude of managing the ranch to family business.

Royce glanced quickly at her before extending his hand to Jeannie's son. An attempt to diffuse the tension, perhaps? "Royce Miller."

With a calculated, thin-lipped glance, Trystan stared at Royce. He held his head high, the longer hair over his forehead revealing something about his no-nonsense behavior. "I know who you are."

"Naomi and I were discussing pipeline business when your call came through. The weather's so bad, I drove her over," Royce offered by way of explanation.

Trystan Mikkelson leveled a surprised stare at Naomi. "You got an audience with the elusive Royce Miller? While you were working miracles, did you manage to convince Birch Montoya to invest a few million more?"

Broderick choked on a cough. Others looked skyward. Trystan wasn't known for his diplomacy. Thank heaven he wasn't the mouthpiece for his family's side of the business.

Royce put a hand on her shoulder, and she tried not to lean into his touch. "Naomi, I'm going to find coffee. I'll bring back enough for everyone."

As Royce turned away, Glenna sprung up from the green couch, wrapping her future sister-in-law in a tight hug. "I'm glad you're here because I really need to get back to the baby. Let's talk later. I'm going to head home and make sure there's food and fresh beds for everyone."

"Glenna? Broderick? Where's Marshall?" Naomi had only just registered that her middle brother wasn't here, a fact that surprised her. Marshall worked with the landholdings. Much like Trystan did for the Mikkelsons. Except Naomi suspected people found Marshall easier to deal with than the gruffer Trystan.

"Marshall is on his way. He was a few hours away doing a property survey and got held up by weather like you."

For the first time since she'd arrived, Jeannie unburied her face from her hands. Eyes tired from tears, dark circles attested to lack of sleep. The woman's clear pain tore at her.

The Mikkelson matriarch held out her hands to Naomi without standing. "Naomi, it's good to see you. Your father has been asking. He was worried about you out there driving in this weather."

The PA system echoed softly with a call for a doctor.

"I'm fine. Royce drove me." Naomi leaned over to give Jeannie an awkward hug. They were still getting to know each other and now they were in the middle of such a huge crisis.

Jeannie managed a half smile. "I have high hopes all will be well with your father." She drew in a shaky smile. "Of course, we've put a delay on any plans for the wedding until we know about possible surgeries. We need to focus on him getting well."

Naomi searched the woman's eyes, wondering at her motivations, wishing she knew her better. Was this delay something to be accepted at face value? Was Jeannie's love real? Or was it a shallow thing, more financially motivated?

Voicing those questions, however, would serve no purpose either way. So, Naomi just asked, "Can I visit my father?"

She hated having to ask at all, but Jeannie was his fiancée. It seemed the right thing to do, especially if the woman truly did love Jack. And if she ended up as a part of their family. Everything was still so...surreal. The engagement. The accident.

Her own attraction to Royce Miller.

Jeannie tapped her own chest, right over her heart. "Of course you should go see him. He will be glad to see in person that you're here safe and sound. You know how much he worries."

Naomi winced. "I do."

Jeannie gestured to a hospital room three doors away, past an orderly wheeling a patient down the hall on a stretcher. "Your father's talking to his brother now. Conrad is doing his best to reassure Jack that the business isn't going to implode."

Conrad had helped keep the company afloat when Jack had struggled with grief over losing his wife and child, but Conrad was more deeply invested in his own business these days. It was doubtful he could step in again. And there was also the concern of the Mikkel-

sons having to sign off on things… Definitely complicated. "I'll do my best to calm his concerns."

In five steps, she'd managed to leave the waiting
room filled with a family learning how to talk to each
other. Entering her father's room, she felt a strange sort
of relief to see her uncle Conrad sitting next to her father. He looked at her with sympathetic eyes, although
he had to be very upset, as well.

A memory flashed through her mind of her uncle sitting with her during a chemo treatment, watching some
teenage show with her that he surely had no interest in,
but he'd been there to support her. Her whole family
had come out in full force for her. Right now, she fully
realized for the first time how much it sucked to be on
either side of this kind of health crisis.

Her uncle motioned for her to come closer, and
Naomi made her way to where her father lay.

Oh God. She knew, logically, that her always dash-
ing father with his dark hair and bravado would look
rough. But all the imagining in the world could not pre-
pare a child to see their once superhero-like parent so
horribly broken.

A neck brace pushed her father's graying hair up,
seeming to highlight the massive deep blue-and-pur-
ple bruise on his forehead, his face swollen from the
trauma.

Jack Steele's eyes flicked to her, and she took in
the sight of the IV in his arm, the constant data rolling
across a blood pressure monitor. A heart monitor too.
And some other screens she couldn't readily identify.

"Hey, baby girl." His voice still sounded strong, a
small comfort. Uncle Conrad moved to the sofa in the
room, giving them space.

Naomi reached out her hand to touch his, feeling like she was in a nightmare. "Hi, Daddy. I didn't mean to wake you."

"I'm not sleeping. All I do is lie in this bed, staring at the ceiling." He'd never been a good patient.

She tried to joke, looking around the room at the many flowers already taking residence around the recliner chair with the pillow and all the available counter space. "I could have sworn I heard you snoring."

"Nah, not a chance."

"Well," she said, glancing at the neat handwriting on the board that charted her father's progress and medication schedules, "the nurse has written there that you're well past the time you can have a sleeping pill."

"I hate taking meds." His gravelly voice sparked with irritation.

She understood that feeling well after having had her body pumped full of poison for months. She empathized with the frustration of being out of control, of being trapped in a broken body.

"You need to rest so you can heal. We want you as strong as possible for surgery."

"Uh-huh. If I'm in pain, I'll let you know to call the nurse." He looked at her with intense eyes, and though he couldn't move much, Jack still had a way of commanding attention.

"When have you ever admitted to pain?"

He mock-scowled. "If you're here to nag, you can go home. Call Delaney to babysit me."

"You just want her here because she's a pushover."

His laugh wheezed a bit and he stifled a wince. "You're your father's child, for sure."

"That I am. So, no underreporting pain. I'm watching your blood pressure. Your secret is out. It's the quiet indicator of your discomfort."

"Duly noted. But enough of that serious talk." His fingers moved on the bed, causing a rustle on the blinding-white sheets. "It's been a long time since we had a campout."

"Once you're better, perhaps we can institute family campouts again." She hoped. God, how she hoped.

"Sounds like a good idea."

"Mom loved those times away from everything." Her throat closed with emotion over memories of her mother. Mary had been more like Delaney, soft but with a quiet determination under it all as she'd balanced a larger-than-life husband and six children. "Looking back, I realize you both took us on those trips to give us a sense of normalcy, to teach us to be more than trust fund babies."

"And it worked," he said proudly. "You all turned out damn good. Your mother would be so pleased."

"Thank you, Daddy, it means a lot to hear you say that." She squeezed his hand. "We'll be camping by this summer. I'm certain of it."

"Jeannie's top-notch at fishing. Maybe we can plan that for after the wedding. I wish we didn't have to delay the ceremony…"

Glancing back at the door, Naomi thought of what now constituted family. And the new addition to the family that she'd yet to tell anyone about except Royce. "We'll need a caravan if we're including both sides of the family for that camping trip."

She couldn't help but wonder if he really would be able to take those trips again. Would he play with her child the way she'd dreamed? Her throat clogged with emotion and restrained tears.

"It would be a nice chance for all of you to get to know each other better, like at the little bachelorette party you girls had at the house for Jeannie. Thank you for that."

She felt a hint guilty for the frustration she'd felt over arranging that party, the shock of her father's engagement to their business enemy still so fresh.

She nodded, looking at her father. In a choked voice, she continued, "I only want you to be happy."

"You have to know there's nothing I want more than for your mother and sister not to have been on that plane. But I can't change the past. Your mother loved us. I've never doubted that for a moment. She would want us to be happy."

"Change is difficult. And quite frankly, you couldn't have come up with a bigger way to upset the applecart." She winced the instant the words fell out of her mouth. She shouldn't be bringing that up right now. Grief must be getting the best of her even though she was supposed to be calming her father.

"Truth. But let's not talk about the accident. I can't believe I let a horse get the better of me. Not his fault. Want to make sure everyone knows that. Now let's talk about something else before my blood pressure has people overreacting," he said with a hint of teasing in his bloodshot eyes.

"Sorry about that." She kept herself positioned to lean over his bed, to stay in his line of sight. "Back to happy talk."

"Tell me about Royce Miller." Ever the businessman, even immobilized in a hospital bed.

She should have known he'd already heard about her impulsive trip.

An image of snuggling on Royce's bed watching the

aurora borealis filled her mind's eyes. With her dad's blood pressure already on the rise, there was no way Naomi would be sharing details of her relationship with the sexy scientist.

Eight

The visit to the hospital had taken everything out of Delaney.

Seeing her indomitable father laid low terrified her. She'd lost her mother. Her sister. Then there'd been Naomi's cancer scare. Delaney couldn't deal with the idea of losing her father.

But what kind of woman was she to use that fear to justify being with Birch now?

She'd broken speed limits to get here. Broken faith with her family every time she hid her relationship with him. Seeing her sister working so hard to bring Royce Miller into the company made Delaney feel all the more like a traitor to her beliefs by having an affair with Birch.

Still, she needed this. Needed him.

She snapped the band of his boxers. "You should get rid of those."

Birch trailed his fingers to the front clasp of her bra and with a deft flick, the cups parted. Air swept over her breasts, her nipples pulling tight and tingling. Every nerve hummed to life, her senses on overload, breaths full of patchouli, her gaze drowning in the whiskey hues of his eyes, luxuriating in the muscular planes of his chest. How could one body store so much heat in winter?

And she wanted more.

She tugged at his boxers, but it was tough to pull them off while she was sitting. In a smooth move, he locked his arms around her and lifted, her feet dangling just off the floor as she kissed him. Or he kissed her. She wasn't sure, but somehow their underwear landed on the plush wool rug.

Delaney slid a condom from the pack they'd set on the desk earlier when they'd had frenzied sex in front of the fireplace in his home office. She rolled the condom down the length of him, slowly. His eyebrows lifted at how very much she took her time. Angling forward, he captured her mouth, catching the moan.

Biting her bottom lip, she raised up on her knees, her breasts rubbing against his chest. His pupils widened with desire just as his eyes narrowed. A shiver of awareness rippled down her spine. She slid over him again, taking him inside her, slowly, fully.

His fingers dug into her bare hips, guiding her as he thrust, again and again as she met his rhythm, his pace. The crackles in the fireplace echoing the snaps of electricity traveling through her. Her neck arched and he covered her pulse with his mouth, hair sliding along her spine as she savored the way he knew just where… just how…to touch her.

The rasp of his late day beard was a delicious abrasion against her tender flesh. His ragged breaths heated over her skin, her gasps accelerating along with his. They were always in sync that way. Maybe some of that had to do with the hidden nature of their affair. It added an edge to their time together.

Or perhaps they were both afraid it couldn't survive the harsh light of their differences, leaving them frenzied to take all they could before this connection imploded. Every time she pondered the thought it just made her more determined to stop thinking. She wanted to feel, to savor, for as long as they could because being with him was...

Incredible.

Just the memory of their other times together was enough to send her orgasm unraveling inside her in wave after wave of bliss. Birch thrust his hands into her hair and kissed her, taking her cries of release into his mouth, his own low growls of completion mingling with hers.

Sagging against his chest while her galloping heart slowed to a trot, she breathed in the scent of him. Of them. Perspiration and sex and a musky blend unique to the two of them.

Birch swept aside her hair and stroked her back, the calluses on his fingers a sweet, sandpapery abrasion. "When are we going to stop sneaking around?"

She kept her face buried in his neck, avoiding his gaze. "Aren't you having fun?"

"You know the answer to that." He dropped a kiss on top of her head.

"Then let's just keep things the way they are."

The disappointment on his face stung her with guilt. But she flinched away from saying anything. Confrontation was not her strength. A weakness in a family full of pushy extroverts. Passive aggression was more her speed.

And she intended to keep this sexy pocket of happiness all to herself for just a little longer.

Royce's boots thudded on the hospital tile as he made his way to Naomi, careful to avoid the wettest spots on the recently mopped floor. For the past few hours, he'd parked himself in the waiting room amid the Steeles and the Mikkelsons. The tension had left him uncomfortable, but not as uncomfortable as the two merging families had seemed with each other.

He'd left and made a trip to the store, waiting to return until late enough that the hospital would have quieted, the families would have left.

A time when Naomi would be alone and perhaps need him.

All that time sitting had left him restless. Ironic, perhaps, because he'd grown accustomed to long stretches in front of a computer or whiteboard doing research and solving equations. The fundamental difference between those scenarios and this one was that he had felt productive in those instances. Like he was doing something.

He'd never suffered idleness well.

His hand closed tighter around the bag of food he'd brought, all too aware that stress had kept Naomi from taking care of herself.

As he balanced the juice and snacks in his hand, he made his way to her. He knuckle-rapped the door. From the other side, he heard the sounds of footsteps padding against the tile in a hurried fashion.

The door swung open. Damn.

Even rumpled and weary, Naomi looked beautiful. Her dark hair fell in a ponytail wave over one shoulder.

She wore a hoodie with tights, a casual outfit that still hinted at her curves. Adjusting her weight from one socked foot to another, her eyes danced with something that looked like grateful relief. Seeing she was happy to have him there…that gripped him. He didn't want to think about what his reaction to her might mean.

She looked around, poking her head outside the door frame. "How did you get past the nurse's station?"

"No worries on that. I'm here. I've been in the waiting room actually. I wanted to be sure you had snacks if you're not sleeping—and you weren't." Peering into the room to the sofa with the still perfectly folded blanket. No signs of rest.

"I can sleep tomorrow. I'm afraid to take my eyes off him."

"That's understandable." He held up his offering—cheese, crackers, juice and two slices of pizza. "I thought you might be hungry. Sorry, but the pickings are thin this time of night."

"It looks amazing, actually." She nodded toward the two simple straight chairs—wood with worn maroon cushions—left over from earlier visitors. She sat down in one, patting the seat of the other, inviting him to join her. He did, satisfied to accept a stolen moment with her.

She took the food and dug in with clear appreciation.

"You know you can call me or text me if you need anything."

She chuckled softly, swiping a cracker crumb from the corner of her mouth. "Do you realize I don't even have your phone number?"

That fact had escaped him. "Well, hell. We need to rectify that."

He fished his cell phone from his pocket, sheepishly handed it over to her. Naomi's face lit up as she entered her contact information and slid it back to him, chewing on the corner of her lip. He sent her a message—just a smile. Her cell vibrated in her pocket. Connection official.

"Thanks." She gave him a shaky smile back, then glanced toward her father again, worry furrowing her brow. "The surgery seems eons away, every second so scary even beyond concerns of a stroke from his high blood pressure. What if he sneezes? And jerks and paralyzes himself?"

"There's nothing you could do about that one. That imagination of yours is working overtime."

"Part of my job, imagining all the possibilities so I can plan accordingly. You should understand that with your work too. It's not like we can shut down our imaginations after hours."

"True enough." He lifted her feet, started rubbing them through her socks.

She moaned softly, some of the tension easing from her face. "That feels amazing. Thank you." She popped another cracker into her mouth. "You're incredibly thoughtful."

"Is it working?"

She tipped her head to the side, her dark ponytail swishing. "What are you trying to accomplish?"

"Winning you back into my bed again once things settle out with your dad," he said simply, honestly.

"Winning me into your bed again? Did you really just say that?"

"I did." He leveled a stare her way, the spark between them intensifying with each second that passed.

"Do you really think having an affair is possible? Especially if you're working for the company?"

"Fine. Then I won't consider working for the company."

"You're considering working for the company? When did you…? Um, how did you…?" she stuttered.

Hell, he hadn't known he was considering it until the words fell out of his mouth. But admitting that would sound far too illogical. So he settled for, "I've been mulling over your offer. I still am."

"Care to share more about your…mulling?"

Sliding an arm around her shoulders, he let his thoughts shuffle and move around like puzzle pieces in search of a possible fit. "Consider this. What does it matter if we're sleeping together while I'm working with your father's company? You won't be my boss. I won't be yours. There's nothing you could say to change the results of my work. So, after hours are after hours."

"Have you thought about the fact that I'll be as big as a house in a few months?" She leaned in. "There's a baby growing in this belly."

"So I hear," he said, doing his best to hide the gut kick of those words.

"And that doesn't bother you?"

He weighed his response carefully, because yes—hell, yes—the thought of entangling his life with a baby's scared him spitless. But he wanted her that much. "I think you and I have talked enough for one night." He stroked her hair back from her face. "I'm going to leave now. You should get some rest."

To make sure she didn't have enough time to press him further, he leaned in to kiss her, and damn, the feel of her lips, the sweet stroke of her tongue, made him wonder how long he could wait before he had to see her again.

* * *

Naomi paced outside her father's door while the nurse gave him a bath. Exhaustion soaked into her bones, and the fact that she still had the ability to walk without breaking down in tears seemed like a helluva surprise. Sleep hadn't been possible in her last twenty-four hours, and the pregnancy had drained her additional stores of energy.

As much as she wanted to be present for every moment of her father's hospital stay, she knew she needed rest. If not for her sake, then for the sake of her unborn child. Soon, the next family member would come to relieve her and she could get home, crawl into bed and sleep. Hard.

Her insomnia had more to do with the late night conversation with Royce, along with the foot massage and his kiss, which tempted her to lean on him.

She heard a commanding, brusque voice echoing down the hall, pulling Naomi away from the fantasy of sleep—and questions about Royce.

Trystan Mikkelson approached, flanked by Jeannie.

He gave Naomi a curt nod as he approached. His gaze was intense, brows furrowed, everything about his body signifying distance and the need for space.

She did her best to smile at him, to feel like they were family.

The attempt was unsuccessful, judging by the way his focus returned to his mother, away from Naomi and the realities looming behind the door to her father's room.

Jeannie, normally so smoothly professional and composed, looked like she hadn't slept in weeks. She hugged her bulky sweater tighter around herself, a tissue clutched in her fist. "How did he do through the night?"

"We had a nice chat and then he slept well. His breakfast just arrived." Naomi's stomach lurched at the olfactory memory. Just another item of food that made her ill during this pregnancy. The weight of the world slammed into her a little bit more. Focus. She needed to focus. She thrust out her hand to her future stepbrother. "Trystan, hello."

Trystan's rugged exterior showed nothing of his emotional state. Probably why Charles Mikkelson Jr. had become the face of the company since his father had died. Always right there helping his mother.

Trystan tapped the brim of his Stetson. "Hello, Naomi. No offense, but you look exhausted. Mom and I have this."

Naomi had to confess, "I could do with a shower and a nap."

Jeannie touched her wrist lightly, a gesture that still came off a bit awkward and uncomfortable, given how long their families had been enemies. "How are you going to get home? You're so tired it can't be safe to be behind the wheel." She turned to her son. "Trystan, you should—"

Naomi cut her short. "Thank you, but Broderick and Glenna arranged for a driver to be on call at the hospital at all times. The car should already be downstairs waiting for me."

Jeannie smiled, looking more than a little weary herself. "Okay, then, sweetie. Take care."

Naomi reached in for a hug, half bumping into her future stepmother in the process. Damn. She anxiously awaited the moment when this sort of contact felt natural.

She waved over her shoulder at Trystan, hurrying to

get to the outside of the hospital and to the Suburban Glenna had sent for her.

As she entered the backseat of the SUV, she counted her blessings for at least finding a decent connection with one Mikkelson.

The ride to the Steele compound passed in a whir of snow. Naomi practically forgot that a chauffeur was present and driving the car. His deep rasping cough called her attention out from a nebulous nowhere, plopping her down in the present, her eyes roving over her family's spread.

As a child, her home had seemed like a castle on the outskirts of Anchorage. The mansion stood on a cliff, overlooking mountains. Tall pine trees formed a protective circle around the building proper, and a slate path led from the main house to the stables. Hours were spent there as a child, among the horses. It was where freedom had first felt possible to Naomi. Even though Brea had been Marshall's twin, she had been the sister closest in age to Naomi. They'd been close. Only a year apart in age. Inseparable. Losing that connection had been—still was—devastating.

She rested her head on the cool glass window, thankful for the marked contrast from the hot nervous sweat on her nape.

Her eyes fixed on the barn, on their horses—the love of the animals her father had passed on to her and her siblings. A wince of pain shot through her as she thought of his riding accident. Such a fluke as he was so sure-seated in the saddle.

Tires crunched along the ice and the Suburban slowed to a stop in front of the main doors. She hopped out, barely two steps into the great, gray building before her sister Delaney emerged from the room adjacent to the foyer, her dark hair contrasting with the cream walls where large paintings of Alaskan brush hung.

Delaney leaned against the glass table on the farthest wall, chewing her lip. "How was Daddy?"

"Feisty as ever. The doctor's supposed to come by this afternoon to discuss a possible surgery date. We'll want to be back there by then."

"Yes, of course." Delaney drew in a shaky breath. "Just so you know what you're walking into. We have an issue that needs discussing. Just with the family. The Steele family."

The prospect of having to perform family duties at this moment seemed damn impossible. "Now? I can barely stand up, much less think."

"You have to. We need you. You're the family lawyer."

Naomi waved a hand. Dismissive. Firm. Knowing she needed sleep for the sake of not only her own sanity, but for the baby, as well. "The business has a team of lawyers—"

"Yes, but you are our lawyer, a Steele. Your opinion carries the most weight."

Family first. That old mantra churning something in her.

"Thank you," Naomi said, a faint blush dusting the apples of her cheeks.

"Just stating facts. You're a damn good attorney."

And those lawyer instincts told her that her siblings had sent Delaney with this request because she was the most mild-mannered of the bunch. But she also wasn't to be underestimated.

Naomi gestured to a nook in the foyer, the one that seemed unassuming—an oversize windowsill to the un-initiated. But this was the spot where as kids, Naomi,

Brea and Delaney had snuck away to talk. It seemed appropriate now. "What is it you feel the family needs to discuss?"

"We have two issues at hand. First, Dad's clicking along well mentally now, but if things go south at any point we may need to make medical decisions for him. With all due respect to Jeannie and Dad's engagement, they're not married. So, if he's incapacitated, she has no say. Am I correct?"

True, but God, her dad would go ballistic if he knew they were having this conversation. Still, they needed to look out for his best interests and they did know him. "Legally, you are right as far as me having the power of attorney. But it will be a delicate balance. When Dad recovers, he'll raise holy hell if he thinks we shut her out."

Although, knowing they'd shut Jeannie out might just force him to recover faster. Not another soul on earth could rival her father's strong will.

"True about the power of attorney. But it's still the day-to-day stuff that worries me. As much as they may have feelings for each other, does she know his medical wishes? Does she know him that well?" Delaney asked tentatively. She'd always been more of a peacemaker, not an easy role in their family of volatile personalities.

"I have told you the law. We'll handle the diplomacy if the situation arises." She prayed it wouldn't. Shoving the thought away, Naomi found it hard to stay objective. To stay purely in the lawyer mind-set. Too raw. "Let's take one crisis at a time."

"If it needs addressing, that will fall to you."

"Why me? Why not Broderick?"

Delaney blinked at her, drawing her slender legs to

her chest, looking much younger, recalling a time before life disrupted their happy family—their peace. "Your legal skills with words. Broderick's more a bull in a china shop. And in case you haven't noticed, he's been off his game from lack of sleep since Fleur's going through that bout of colic."

True. And he had Glenna to share the parenting with. Naomi touched her stomach lightly. How would she manage this on her own? Her plan had seemed so right before everything changed in her family, but now she feared coming up short for her child.

All of which she would have to worry about later. Right now, she needed to focus on her father.

"Fine." Exhausted, terrified for her father, the tight response was all she could manage.

"Broderick is busy playing host to everyone. Marshall is barking orders. Aiden's a kid. And me? I'm not pushy enough, but I'm good at patting hands."

"Okay, okay, I agreed. You said two issues. What's the other?" Naomi sighed, steeling herself. Yep. Her siblings had definitely selected subtle, gentle Delaney to win Naomi's cooperation.

"If the surgery doesn't go well and Dad's incapacitated—or worse—we need to have a plan ready to roll. We can't afford for the Mikkelsons to step into the power void. Things are all the trickier as Broderick and Glenna have started sharing the CFO responsibilities—and of course he trusts her. God, things are getting muddy. Start thinking. After we finish at the hospital, we're going to meet tonight after supper while Jeannie's with Dad and Glenna's feeding the baby."

And just like that, unrest threatened the tentative peace they'd brokered with their longtime rivals.

Before Naomi could respond, the doorbell rang.

Saved by the bell, quite literally. She leaped to her feet and peered through one of the windows flanking the door to find...

Royce.

He stood outside, snow gathering on his parka, Tessie at his heels.

Nine

Royce had intended to go to his place and sleep. Or work. But somehow, he'd ended up here.

Even though he knew stepping into the Steele lair meant stepping away from his quiet, solitary realm of research and facts, where he worked long enough to keep nightmares about the past from haunting him, he hadn't been able to stay away. Being here, with this large and looming clan, placed him that much closer to becoming a part of their team. Being a part of other peoples' lives, people to care about.

But saying goodbye to Naomi—well—just not an option.

So here he was. With his dog. Awkward as hell. Social nuances sometimes slipped past him, his head stuck in the scientific world of black-and-white. There were so many people in this rapidly blending family, he was going to need some kind of pneumonic device to remember all their names.

Naomi bounded up to him, her dark hair swaying as she approached the archway between the hall and the great room. "What are you doing here?"

Damn, she made jeans and a lamb's-wool sweater look like runway glam. And her knee-high leather boots sent his pulse jacking upward.

"I understand you're looking for a consultant." Thank God Tessie was on her best behavior, sitting like a princess beside him.

"Now?" she whispered. "You want to talk about that *now*?"

He breathed deeply, taking a moment to stabilize his emotions. Reaffirm that coming here—to this mansion with soaring ceilings that reminded him of grand cathedrals—had not been some terrible miscalculation. In that breath, he surveyed the space, his eye catching on the great room beyond Naomi, the gathering space full of multiple sofas and seating areas large enough for such a massive family.

A blaze hungrily crackled within the gray slate fireplace. His eyes traced upward to the sprawling moose antlers mounted above.

Royce noted the way the decor pulled together sophistication with an air of a bygone time in Alaskan history. Rustic, rugged elegance. The nods to the hunt—the deep, rich colors of burgundy and brown—reminded him a bit of Texas, another place of possibilities and open land.

A blonde woman—Glenna Mikkelson, most likely—rocked a baby in a thickly padded rocking chair. She attentively cooed at the sleeping baby. A Siberian husky puppy lay over her feet, ears and eyes alert to Tessie, but staying blessedly still.

Beside the blonde, a man sprawled on the wide

leather sofa but quickly stood and took hold of the husky pup's collar. Naomi's brother, no question. He stared at Royce with ill-concealed interest.

Royce shifted his focus back to Naomi. "If that's what your family wants, but that's not why I've come. I realize you're in the middle of a crisis." He held up his hand. "I brought pastries. I'm a Southern boy. My mama always said bring food."

The blonde woman slid off the rocker, rising to her feet. She carefully adjusted the infant onto her left shoulder, a smile resting easy on her face. "That's very thoughtful of you," she said. "This is the apple of Broderick's eye—our daughter, Fleur."

"She's a heart-tugger," he said simply, thinking of the child he'd lost…of Naomi's baby on the way. He'd avoided children for so long and now there was no more hiding.

Broderick thrust his hand out. "Welcome. Thank you for the pastries. We can never have too much to eat around here, especially with the whole crew in town. We appreciate you stopping by."

"No problem," Royce continued. "I'm sorry to intrude and sorry about having my dog along—"

Glenna stopped him short. "No need to apologize. I adore my Kota." She reached down to scratch the Saint Bernard's ear. "I'm glad you didn't leave—"

"Tessie," he supplied, looking down at his massive pup. The dog seemed to wink at him, a tongue lazily sliding out of her mouth into a light pant. She nuzzled his hand with her great head.

"Yes, glad you didn't leave Tessie in the car." Glenna adjusted the baby on her shoulder, rubbing a soothing hand along her back. "Thank you again for the, uh, pastries."

Thin excuse to show up. Busted. "I also wanted to make sure Naomi arrived home safely from the hospital." Another lame excuse, he knew. He could have called. For a genius, he was coming up aces in the "too obvious" department.

Naomi lifted an eyebrow. "Oh really."

"Yes, really."

A willowy, dark-haired woman stood. "I'm Delaney Steele, by the way." She raised a hand absently, a softer, quieter version of her sister. "I truly would love to chat with you, but I need to help Trystan and Jeannie."

Delaney Steele. The name clicked in his mind. She was a well-known conservationist crusader with a reputation for holding her family's feet to the fire on safety issues. Someone he could consider an ally if he chose to sign on.

And yes, he was seriously considering Naomi's offer, though he couldn't quite believe it of himself. Maybe Naomi's words had sunk in, about the cost of waiting too long to implement the schematics he had so far for upgrades.

"Nice to meet you, Delaney. I've read some of your blogs."

She flushed and blinked fast. "Thank you, I'm honored." Her smile faded. "But I do need to get back to my father. I know the hospital must feel overwhelmed by so many of us, but we can't imagine leaving him alone…or missing the chance to see him if…"

She swallowed hard.

Broderick gripped her shoulder and turned her to face him. "He's going to be fine. We're all here for support, not on a death watch. We're all too stubborn to let that happen. Marshall's flying in now. Uncle Conrad and Aiden have gone to the water to meet the seaplane." He glanced at Royce. "Marshall and Aiden are our brothers."

There were so many people in this family, Royce wondered if they'd ever considered keeping flyers by the door, complete with a family tree as a cheat sheet.

No sooner had the thought about the large family crossed his mind than the space cleared out with excuses of dog running and baby feeding, leaving him and Tessie alone with Naomi.

"For a family that wants to win me over as a business partner, they sure did bolt fast." He leaned in, his voice low.

She touched his arm, looking up at him between thick dark lashes. "You made it clear you're here for me. You couldn't have been any more obvious."

The spark rattled his system. Yep. Busted. "Guilty as charged." He held up the bag. "Hungry?"

"Always." Her lips parted slightly, that electricity passing between them like static on winter air.

"Should we stay here or go to the kitchen—" His eyes locked with hers.

"I have a suite here, like my own loft apartment." Naomi seemed to move even closer to him, the distance between them feeling minimal, flimsy. "Let's go there. It's a little quieter."

He gestured ahead. "Lead the way."

Anticipation and a splash of apprehension quickened Naomi's steps as she led Royce to the elevator. Peeking her head around the corner, she checked for lingering family members in the hallway.

The house, surprisingly silent for the amount of family present on the compound, seemed to aid her on her surreptitious mission. Not that, as an adult woman, she had to justify her time with Royce.

But she didn't want the complications of the questions her siblings would launch at her if they saw her inviting Royce into her private quarters. Soft steps across the dark wood floors, her hands trailing behind her, close to the rustic-inspired walls textured with paintings of the wilderness.

The heat in the elevator had nothing to do with the temperature of the mansion, but everything to do with the heat of him radiating into her back. So close.

An indulgence.

She was allowed that.

When the door opened to her loft in the east wing of the house, her stomach somersaulted. She couldn't tell if it was nerves or from her pregnancy. Possibly both.

Naomi tried to recall the last time a man had come into this space—her sanctuary. So different from the rest of the house, which boasted old Alaskan charm. Her narrow, long loft took inspiration from her eclectic spirit.

Royce motioned for her to precede him out of the elevator, such a quiet man full of old-world manners. His hands tapped lightly along her trinkets that populated the built-in wood bookcase at the far wall of the loft, which separated her bedroom from the main living area. As if he was cataloging the knickknacks as a means of learning more about what made her tick. Certainly, the clusters of framed family photos spoke of her love of the outdoors—skiing, fishing, horseback riding.

And a cherished photo of her mother, another of her sister Brea. Those losses never stopped hurting.

That wall, past the sofa and coffee table where a

smattering of photography books framed a pottery vase that had always been her favorite. Different sculptures from her travels were showcased and she found herself seeing them all through new eyes. His eyes. How surreal to have Royce in her space, in her home. So different from the stark igloo in the wilds. Having him here, where he could see some of who she really was, made her want to know more about him.

"What does your place look like?" She knew from his file that he'd bought a condo on the outskirts of Anchorage.

"I bought it already decorated."

"Oh," she said, deflated. Not much to learn there.

"Easier than hauling a bunch of meaningless furniture from Texas. I donated the old stuff to charity."

"That was really kind of you." She was touched. Truly. But still, she wondered. "You brought nothing from Texas?"

"Actually," he said, "I did bring my vintage Pascal's calculator."

"Oh wow, that's really cool." She envisioned him traveling with that seventeenth-century treasure, placing it in his generic condo along with his Saint Bernard.

He was definitely an original.

She walked deeper into her suite. During the day, her loft didn't need any artificial light. Huge windows allowed the Alaskan sun to poke through, permeating the living area.

Their footsteps were muffled as they strode along the Inuit rugs—gifts from her grandmother when Naomi had gotten her first college apartment, another cherished touch in this space.

From the rough-hewn beam on a slanted, arched ceiling hung a crystal chandelier that sent prisms dancing on the cream-colored sofa, brightening the quarters.

Tessie bounded ahead, examining the L-shaped kitchenette around the corner. Short-lived attention to the kitchen though. As soon as Naomi opened the sliding glass door to the glass-sealed balcony, Tessie padded over on fat paws, making herself comfortable outside.

She circled three times, clearly enjoying the sun as she plopped down, rolling her back out. The dog seemed blissful.

After such an emotional night watching over her father, Naomi needed comfort, needed a distraction. She'd always prided herself on being independent, but had to confess, the way Royce had shown up at the hospital, the way he was here now with his dog and pastries— so eccentrically wonderfully himself—she was on the verge of tears.

He touched something in her soul. And as much as that scared her, it also drew her in.

He held up the bag of pastries again. "Are you hungry?"

"Yes," she said, "for you."

With a growl of approval, he tossed the bag onto the black marble table tucked in the corner of the L between her kitchen and living area.

His hands slid up to span her waist with a bold, large grip. She cupped his shoulder, ready, eager to step into his embrace.

In a smooth move, he lifted her and set her on the edge of the table. She gasped in surprise as the stone chilled through the denim of her jeans.

"Okay?" he asked.

"Absolutely." She clutched his shoulders and pulled him to her for a kiss, mouths and tongues meeting in the familiarity of lovers who'd explored each other thoroughly. Well, as thoroughly as they could in such a short time. Breaking off with more than a little regret, she touched her tender lips as if to hold in the sensation of him.

As she leaned away, she heard a rustle beside her and realized he was opening the pastry bag. She eased back to see... Royce tearing off a corner of the pastry and stirring it through a cup of berry jam.

Hmm... Her senses came alive at the scent and at the playful glint in his intense eyes. He was such a delicious contradiction, never ceasing to surprise her. How much more was there to learn about this man?

He brought the bite to her mouth and she opened, but then he popped it into his own mouth playfully. As he chewed though, he pinched off more for her and offered it up. She angled forward for the taste, teasing her tongue along his fingers. Her eyes slid closed at the burst of flavor, sweet fruit and salty him. His pupils widened in response to a last flick of her tongue.

She thrust aside the pastries and tucked her hands into the back pockets of his jeans, digging in her fingers. *Closer*, she willed him. Needed him. Until he stepped between her knees and kissed her again, openmouthed and fully.

Her senses sharpened, the taste of him, the scrape of his unshaven face under her fingers. The crisp scent of Alaskan air on a man filling her every breath. Hmm... And thinking of him filling her sent her mind reeling again.

His hand slid under her sweater, his touch warm and raspy along her flesh. He tunneled farther, sweeping the lamb's wool up and over her head. He growled low in appreciation, cupping her breasts, his approval of red satin quite clear. Her nipples went hard, her skin everywhere tightening with a need for more of this touch, more of him.

Clamping her legs around his waist, she locked him nearer, lost in the connection she'd been aching to recapture. Arching toward him, she pressed for a fuller joining and, yes, thank goodness, yes—he took the hint. His hands slid behind her and freed her bra in a deft sweep.

She made fast work of the buttons in his flannel shirt, sweeping it off his broad shoulders. She flung the body-warmed fabric across the room to rest on top of her sweater. Her fingers trembled, her ache for him so intense. She fumbled with the top button and zipper on his jeans while he tugged her jeans over her hips, lifting her briefly, then pulled the fabric along her legs.

She took the moment to soak in the sight of him.

His washboard stomach gleamed in the sunshine. She reached to trace down, down, down farther still, following the crisp sprinkling of hair in a narrowing trail to his freed button, the V of his open zipper.

Royce flung her pants to the floor and stepped closer. The marble felt cool and slick against the backs of her bare legs. Only her satin panties separated her from total exposure. Her eager hand freed his arousal and his eyes slid closed. He flattened a palm on the counter for a second as if to steady himself.

A surge of feminine power curled through her as she stroked him, her thumb rolling over the first pearly glisten. His throat worked in a long swallow before he opened his eyes. The intensity, the raw passion in his gaze left her breathless.

With slow deliberation, he swiped two fingers through the cup and traced a small swirl of jam over one of her nipples, following to clean the fruit away with his mouth. The warmth of his tasting tongue and the cool air on her wet skin provided the most delicious contrast. He nipped the last taste, sending sparks of pleasure crackling through her. Then he scooped more of the jam, eyeing her lower, lower still, with only a hint of warning that he intended to...

Yes.

He eased her back to lie down on the table, her legs dangling. He twisted the edges of her panties in his grip until the satin snapped. Cool air swept over her heated core. Kneeling, he guided her legs over his shoulders. Then... Ahh...

The touch of his finger circled her tight bundle of nerves for tantalizing moments before he replaced the sensation with his mouth. Desire spread throughout her body. Her head fell back as he laved, his undivided attention on her. The gentle sucking along her skin, the light rasp of his tongue, sent shivers of pure pleasure down her spine. She gripped the edge of the marble tabletop, her fingernails sinking in deep.

Her release came hard and fast, rocking through her. She bit her bottom lip to hold back the cry of release as shower after shower of shimmers spread through her.

"You," she gasped simply. "I want you."

Standing, he nipped over her shoulder to draw on her bottom lip. "You are a fantasy come true."

His words sent a thrill along her spine. Her heart tripped over itself in anticipation of more. Of him.

He inched her hips nearer to the edge. "Condoms or no condoms? I'm clean. There's been nobody in a year."

A year? His words, along with the thick pressure of him, right there, so close teased her perilously near completion again.

"Go ahead," he urged, "surrender. I'll take you there as many times as you wish."

His bold confidence sent a charge through her, reminding her of how he'd coaxed her to let go before. And she realized he was in complete control of this moment between them. A thought that called for contemplation when she wanted nothing less than to think.

She banned all other thoughts from her mind but the here and now.

"There is no need for a condom. None. It's only you and me."

Growling, he leaned over her, his hand flat on the table by her ear. Her fingers dug deeper into his flanks as he thrust inside, his low growl of possession echoing through the spacious kitchen. Clamping her legs around his waist again, she urged him deeper, faster. Still she wanted more of him, no holding back. She whispered her wants, even her fantasies, into his ear, delighting in the feel of his throbbing response to her words.

She lost herself in the frenzy of the moment. Nothing could compare to the intensity she felt now in his arms. For a moment, she could forget there was an outside world, concerns for her future in the company, for providing stability for her child.

Royce brought her just shy of release again and again until their bodies slicked with sweat. The musky scent of them together blended with the sweet stickiness of the raspberries and sugary fruit juice.

Locking her ankles tighter behind him, she inched closer and rolled her hips against his. They'd lost the isolation of the retreat, but for this moment at least she had him to herself again. She didn't have to think about all the chaos and fear in her life.

His pulse throbbed in his neck. He dipped his head

to her breasts, increasing her pleasure with a flick of his tongue. The tingling in her veins gathered low and pulsed, tighter still until she gasped. Then again.

She couldn't hold back the moan and, thankfully, he quickly kissed her, took her cries of release in his mouth. She bowed upward and into his arms as he thrust again, again, again, until finishing with a hoarse shout muffled against her neck. Her arms went limp with exhaustion around him. She tried to hold on, but her body had melted with weightless bliss. Royce's hold on her tightened and he swept her into his arms.

Sleep pulled at her, pushed her eyelids down. In waves, she faded further and further away from consciousness. The exhaustion from all the stress finally catching up to her, making her bone tired, worries racing to catch up with her again.

Naomi felt Royce carry her to bed for a nap, and the flashes of reality melted into her dreams.

In Alaska, late winter sunsets never ceased to dazzle as if to make up for the fact they came so early half the year. But this? Damn. He'd have a helluva hard time beating this one.

Tessie walked up to the glassed-in balcony, sniffing the air three times before losing interest and setting off in a half prance to explore the rest of the suite.

Royce felt content on the reclining cream sofa at the center of the temperature-controlled sunroom. A dance of vibrant oranges and reds soaked the mountains, casting the landscape in a fiery blaze.

And while the view was damn impressive—breathtaking even—it was the woman in his lap that made his pulse quicken. Instilled that sense of wonder. Naomi curled up against him, a silk black robe draped over her curves. He adjusted it slightly, careful not to let the strands of her dark hair catch under his arm.

Making love to her again had seriously complicated things between them. But then he suspected nothing with Naomi would ever be simple. Protectiveness hampered things too, given her independence. And if he did act on the impulse to work for her family's company, he would have to figure out what to do about their relationship. Quickly.

He stroked her long hair, letting the silky strands glide between his fingers. "Is your family going to come looking for us?"

"No, we live separate lives here, each of us with our own quarters. We're all adults, who happen to be related. The lodge feels like condos. We all come and go as we please, but the communal areas still make it easier to have business meetings here if need be."

"Sounds like an efficient setup."

"It is." She angled back to look at him. "Were you serious about considering joining the company?"

"I'm considering it," he answered simply.

She nodded, looking away again. "I know our setup here may seem strange to you since you come from a small family. But we're all close, for so many reasons."

He stayed silent, sensing her need to talk. Her family had been through so much, and they were going through hell now.

Naomi toyed with the belt on her robe. "When all of us were kids, Dad would wake us up early on Saturday mornings. He would caution us to be extra quiet, to tiptoe so we didn't disturb Mom. We'd all bundle up and go to Kit's Kodiak Café." Her tensed muscles relaxed against him with every word. "Best food in the world. We kids would order off the Three Polar Bears Menu. We always ordered the same thing—reindeer sausage, eggs and tall stacks of pancakes served with berry syrup."

He pressed a kiss to her temple. "Your dad sounds like a great guy."

"Yes, he is, very down-to-earth in spite of his wealth. Mom and Dad were emphatic about wanting us to grow up with values, no silver spoon. We had to make our own way in the world."

For a moment, he wondered if she was still working to win him over with stories about her rich but "regular folks" family story. Yet, with all the stress she was under, he couldn't bring himself to confront her on that. "Your father is quite a legend around here. I look forward to meeting him."

"He really is a good man. A little gruff sometimes, but good. After Mom and Brea died, he struggled though. Uncle Conrad stepped in to run the company. Dad became…lost. And so terrified something would happen to us. We had bodyguards, nannies…"

"And then you got sick."

"I was so scared. He'd only just started to come back to us."

"You were scared about him? You were a teen with cancer. You had every right to be scared for yourself."

"Oh, I was. And the staff was great in helping me deal with that. They helped me keep myself together around the family."

"Naomi… I'm sorry. You should have had your mom, your dad, everyone around you."

"I'm here, and I'm tough." A twist in his arms and suddenly, her face was inches from his, lingering in the space between a kiss. With a wicked grin resting on those plump lips, she kissed him once, twice, nipping and even teasing a hint.

He cupped her head, deepening the kiss.

The kiss held the promise of something more. Or would have. If not for the sound of the elevator bell. And damn, the privacy door had been left open. Two distinctly masculine coughs echoed through the open door between the sunroom and her sitting area.

The separate suites in her family's lodge-style mansion afforded a certain level of privacy, but bottom line, much of her family did still live in the same house. He was so used to a solo life, this blended lifestyle felt alien to him.

Bracing for a confrontation, Royce glanced up fast to find… Hell. Naomi's brothers Marshall and Aiden closing in fast.

Surprise glinted in Marshall's eyes as he tucked his hands into his jeans pockets, his plaid shirt untucked. "Sorry to interrupt, sis. I came to say hello. I didn't realize you were, uh, entertaining."

Naomi gasped, rushing to stand.

And promptly swayed, her knees folding. Royce rushed to brace her but her eyes were already closing as she passed out. She eluded his grasp, collapsing back onto the sofa.

Panic pumping through him, Royce knelt beside her, checking her pulse, stroking her soft face. "Naomi? Naomi, honey…"

Marshall moved to the end of the sofa, swinging her feet up and placing a pillow under them. Teenage Aiden shuffled back and forth in a youthful fidget of indecision.

The million reasons for her fainting entered Royce's head—all of which focused on pregnancy complications. More panic burned in his veins. He looked to Marshall. "Someone call a doctor."

Her older brother sat on the armrest, a hand on his sister's propped feet. "Let's give her a second to wake up before we go all ballistic."

Sighing at the inevitable, Royce knew he would have to betray Naomi's trust. "You don't understand. She's pregnant."

Ten

Royce wanted to focus all his thoughts on Naomi, but logic was tough to find with his brain on fire with the image of her fainting.

Having all her relatives swarming around him didn't help. Neither had his impulsive revelation about her pregnancy. She would be mad as hell at him, no question. But they needed to know.

Naomi was coming around, sitting up on the sofa, hand resting on her forehead. Royce sat carefully beside her on the cream-colored sofa.

His Saint Bernard was the only mellow one in the room, sprawled out by the wall of windows, soaking up the sun. Naomi's brother—Royce searched for the name of the guy who'd just flown in—Marshall walked forward one thudding step at a time. "What the hell? You knocked up my sister and have the gall to come here, like this, now when our family is going through personal hell?"

Broderick clapped a hand on Royce's shoulder, leveling a laser stare at him. "I think we need to have a... talk."

Aiden hung back watching, quiet, but clearly the teen was ready to throw himself into the fray with one word from his brothers.

Royce stood, keeping an eye on Naomi even as he addressed the trio of brothers. "I realize you're under stress, but you should seriously consider removing that hand. Now."

"How about this?" Broderick's voice rose with every word. "I'll remove any job offer that may have come your way."

Glenna squeezed her husband's elbow. "Broderick, stop. Think of your sister."

Broderick winced, guilt in his eyes. Royce nodded tightly and returned his attention to Naomi. She still looked foggy but she was coming around fast. Fast enough that he could see her fiery temper filling her eyes.

Royce rubbed her shoulder. "Naomi, relax, I've got this."

Naomi shook her head and dark thick hair swished against black silk. "No, *I* have this. I have my life." Her chin tipped as she faced her family. "I'm pregnant because of in vitro fertilization from an anonymous donor. I wasn't ready to tell the family yet since it's still early, just two months along. Royce had nothing to do with this. Our, uh, relationship came as a surprise to both of us. And that's all you get to know."

Broderick extended a conciliatory hand. "Naomi, I'm sor—"

Naomi silenced him with a glare. With a lawyer's precision, she broke their gaze, turned to Glenna, eyes softer now. "Glenna, could you please deal with my Cro-Magnon brother? He's yours now, after all."

"Of course I will." Glenna placed a hand on Broderick's elbow. "But we did come to your suite for a reason. We wanted to let you know that your father's surgery has been set for tomorrow morning."

Royce turned quickly to Naomi just as she all but deflated, her face filling with concern. The scientist in him didn't miss a beat. He put his arm protectively around her shoulders.

No matter what all this family had to say about it—or even how much Naomi might protest—Royce wasn't going anywhere.

For the first time since she woke up from fainting, the jumbled unease in her stomach wasn't from her pregnancy. Too quickly, fear for her father had come back to the fore.

How could she have forgotten for even a moment?

Unable to resist, she curved into the comfort of Royce's hard-planed body, his steady breaths soothing.

She lost track of how long they sat in silence, Tessie stretched at the base of the sofa. For a moment, Naomi allowed herself to imagine Tessie here long term, running headlong in the pasture below where a bay horse galloped now, kicking up snow and leaving trails of hoofprints.

But then her gaze strayed from the pasture to the water, where the family seaplane bobbed in the waves, tied to the dock. A reminder that her brother Marshall had rushed home. She wasn't ready to think about her father or the mess of everyone hearing about her pregnancy just as they'd discovered her relationship with Royce wasn't all business. She just couldn't go there in her mind. Not yet.

As if sensing the loop of her thoughts, Royce pulled her closer, his arm wrapping around her chest. "I imagine it's tough to think about anything except tomorrow, but let's try." He massaged her shoulders, his jeans warm against her fleece-lined leggings. "I want you to imagine we can go anywhere right now. Where would you want to go? Don't think too hard. Just answer."

Her mind took flight. "Kayaking with whales."

"Seriously?" His laugh rumbled against her lightly. "You wouldn't pick somewhere warm to laze by the beach in the sun?"

"Is Texas boy freezing his toes off in those boots?" she teased.

His laugh—the feel of it tangled up with hers— lingered. "I'm just surprised."

"I love my home state." And she did. So deeply it was a part of her. She glanced back to the Inuit rugs on her floor. Her thoughts went to her heritage, to her mother and all that was already lost.

"Yes, but you're also a glamour girl." He stroked her loose hair.

"Winter clothes are fun too, and more layers to peel away." She tunneled her fingers between the buttons on his shirt, stroking his T-shirt underneath.

"True enough." He slid a palm beneath her loose tunic with deft familiarity that stoked fissions of warmth through her.

"Honestly, I get to travel wherever I want, and I've enjoyed the trips, but I still always look forward to coming home. Maybe part of that is because my family's all here. There's nothing I wouldn't do for them." Her family was woven into her soul, into the fabric of this community and the way she understood the world.

"Clearly. You braved a bear for them."

The bear. A helluva stunt. And one that felt like a distant memory, despite being only a few days ago. Tragedies were funny things like that. Compressing the weariness of years and months into moments. "That seems a lifetime ago."

"A lot has happened in a short time." He drew her closer. "Your father is going to be alright. Just relax and let the doctors do their work. Let me be here for you."

"Releasing control is easier said than done." A sigh tumbled free.

"Control over anything?"

"What about you? You want me to trust you, but that goes both ways. We've rushed so much and still have so much to learn about each other."

He tensed against her as if it was all he could do to stay on the sofa. But she'd already seen how determined he was to remain by her side. With her father's surgery looming, she doubted Royce would go anywhere.

But afterward?

She shoved aside that thought. "So, do you mind if I ask more about you?"

"What else do you want to know?"

"I'd like to hear more about your former fiancée."

He cricked his neck from side to side, pulling his arm from along the back of the sofa. "She was the girl next door, but also an outsider like me. We both were a few grades ahead in school and, being younger than the rest of the crowd, that made it natural for us to hang out together, eat lunch together, walk home from school together."

"That's quite a history to have...and lose."

His dark eyes went distant, as if he was somewhere else, another place, another time. "When she put the pieces of her life back together again after the miscarriage, she decided to sever all ties to the past. She said she was too dependent on me. Which is damn ironic because I always knew she carried me through life, taught me how to navigate the world, from school onward."

"I'm so sorry." Naomi paused, searching his eyes, unable to resist asking her question, nervous about how important his answer would be to her. "Do you still love her?"

"That's irrelevant. We've been apart for ten years. She's married with three kids."

She couldn't help noticing he'd dodged her question. "Alright, so she's moved on, but that doesn't answer my question. Do you still love her?"

"I can't love anyone who would turn their back on me."

"That's very clear-cut."

"I'm a scientist. I deal better in facts. You should understand that as a lawyer, a person of reason."

"I see so many shades of gray in my job it defies description." A yawn interrupted her. Exhaustion tugged at her after her long night at the hospital and everything that came after.

And she knew Royce wouldn't miss the telltale sign of her tired state. Still she insisted even as her eyes drifted closed, "I want to visit my father again later, when everyone's not vying for his attention."

"I'll wake you."

Surrendering control wasn't easy...but her body won over her will.

For now.

Royce knew that his place was not inside the room with Naomi and Jack Steele, the patriarch of the Alaska Oil Barons dynasty. He knew that. Logic screamed it.

Naomi needed time with her father to talk before his surgery.

But damn. He found it hard to stay at the threshold of the hospital door and not be there physically beside Naomi when he knew she needed support.

So he'd settled for the next best thing. Standing at the doorway to eavesdrop.

Not that he coded it that way. Royce preferred to think of it in more scientific terms: *data collection*. Since he couldn't be in there with her, Royce would make sure he knew how to best attend to that beautifully strong-willed force of nature after she left the room.

Jack had a voice like a gale force wind. Even sick and worn, his cadence demanded attention. "I hear from your brother that you're pregnant?"

"Domestication has turned Broderick into a blabber-mouth." Though her back was to him, Royce could hear the eye roll in Naomi's assessment of her brother. "But yes, Daddy. I am." She sat in the chair at his bedside. "I'm sorry you didn't hear it from me. I had planned to tell you myself tonight. I wanted you to know before the surgery."

"This guy, the scientist with you? He's the father?" Jack Steele's gaze went to the door where Royce stood reading his cell phone, tamping down a wince over the assumption he was the father.

Broderick hadn't told his dad the details? Apparently, he only spilled part of secrets. Or maybe Jack's concussion was messing with his memory.

"No, Dad, he's not. I went the in vitro route. You're going to be a grandfather. That's good news." Naomi squeezed her dad's hand. "This wasn't how I'd planned for you to find out, but I'm glad you're happy."

"Yes, baby girl. I am. I'm just surprised, and the concussion has me thinking slower than usual. I'm happy for you, for all of us."

"Thank you." Silence echoed heavily before she continued, "I'm sorry I couldn't be the conventional daughter you want."

Naomi's words gutted Royce.

"Whoa, stop with that." Jack lifted a shaky hand to pat his daughter's cheek.

"I didn't mean to upset you. Just rest." She kissed his forehead. "Love you, Daddy."

"Well, just so you know, I like that scientist. Now could you find Jeannie for me?"

Royce could see a hint of resentment sneak past her defenses. But she smiled anyway. "Of course. I'll let her know you're ready for her to come back in."

She stood, tightening her ponytail, then flipping it over her shoulder in an attempt at normalcy. Royce could see her hurt and disappointment in the way her face tightened. The line of her smile and her dark brown eyes said everything, betrayed her disappointment at her father's lukewarm reaction to her news. He couldn't help but think about her apologizing for not being the kind of daughter she thought her father wanted.

And damn if Royce couldn't help but wonder if that had played into why she'd thrown herself in front of a grizzly bear just to meet him.

Eleven

Wind whipped around the corner of the hospital balcony, covered but not enclosed, stinging Naomi's exposed skin. Wrapping her arms around herself, she tried to push more warmth into her body. The thick cable knit of her green sweater valiantly sheltered her from much of the wind's relentless impact. A day in the thirties in Alaska felt downright balmy.

Normally she embraced the support of her large family, but right now she felt a hint of understanding for Royce's need for solitude. The waiting room had been so packed with people and riotous emotions, everyone worrying about how Jack's surgery was going. Not just family, but friends, as well. People from work. Even a surprise visit from Birch Montoya. He'd quietly kept his distance, while offering support by keeping everyone supplied with coffee.

Naomi's brain and heart were on overload. She'd

made sure they knew where to find her and she had her cell phone.

As she inhaled, drinking in the wind, an acute sharpness wedged into her chest. Palpable, locatable fear and unease from a legion of sources.

She needed this moment. This space away from everyone. Part of the allure of Alaska that struck true to Naomi's heart was the iced aloofness of the landscape. Though a delicate ecology existed, there were ways in which the Alaskan brush protected the individual's need for sovereignty and solitude.

Which she needed now more than ever. Waiting for news of her father's surgery had set her on edge, then to feel she fell short of his expectations yet again? That hurt and she didn't know how to reconcile the pain. Heaven help her if something happened to her dad before she found peace with him.

She'd retreated out here since all her siblings had channeled their anxieties over Jack Steele's surgery into a discussion of her pregnancy, with sidelong glances that insinuated she'd gone off on a lark.

No wonder she hadn't told them ahead of time.

The attention felt suffocating. But then her siblings were likely falling into old habits out of stress, focusing on her health and her father's as if their concern could somehow keep death from lashing out prematurely at their family yet again.

From behind her, the rustle of an opening door intruded on her thoughts. Out of the corner of her eye, Royce approached, clothed in a warm jacket, a rough five o'clock shadow taking up residence on his angled face. Her attention remained ahead, extending to the mountain range in front of her that watched over deep sapphire water.

A feeling of conflict rose as a lump in her throat. On one hand, she wanted to melt into Royce's embrace. Cast her fears of intimacy aside and believe he'd be there to support her. He was here listening to her with unjudging eyes when the rest of her family wasn't. But leaning on the railing, she chewed her lip, the fear for her father coalescing with the fear of depending on Royce.

"I just needed some air." She put on her best smile to keep him from whipping out a five-course meal here on the balcony, which was actually kind of sweet. If she could just believe he had faith in her ability to stand on her own. "I assume you of all people understand about the need for some quiet."

"Here's your jacket."

"Thank you. That's thoughtful, but it's actually a fairly warm day for us Alaskans, Texas boy."

"If you're sure." He didn't sound convinced. At all. "Food? Whatever you're craving, I'll find it."

"I'm too upset to eat, but thank you." She couldn't help but notice how he was standing there holding her jacket for her, at her side when no one else in her family was. "I appreciate your effort, but can we just relax?"

"I'm worried about you. Is that so wrong?" He walked toward her, a dusting of snow packing with each step. He stopped beside her, leaning against the railing. Face so near to hers.

Again, Naomi felt torn by the urge to reach out coupled by the urge to run. "You're concerned and that's kind of you. But there's nothing you can do to help my father. Just being here is comfort."

"You've been running yourself ragged with the trip up during the storm and now with your dad's injury." He tucked a windswept strand of her hair behind her ear.

While she recognized he had a point, his observation grated on her nerves, sparking a different kind of fire between them. "I am an adult—" she waved her hand as if gesturing to all of her family members "—with lots of support. And I do mean a lot." Although so far, they hadn't been as supportive as she'd hoped. She wanted to think it was because of distraction over their dad's accident. Time would tell.

"I realize that, but you're tired and stressed. It's icy out here." He had a point, but the way he said it… "What if you were to slip while you're alone?"

"Royce, could you please just—"

The doors swooshed open, cutting her short. Trystan Mikkelson burst through. His rugged, usually reserved face shone with a smile. "We tried texting you."

She patted her sweater pockets and realized… "I, uh, I must have left my phone inside."

How could she have been so careless? She braced herself for the news, almost afraid to accept the hope Trystan's smile brought. Royce moved closer, squeezing her hand in support.

"So I gathered. I am actually the bearer of good news. Your father's surgery went well. He's out. Moving his toes. He will be allowed visitors in about a half hour." Trystan's shaggy hair lifted with a gust of wind that rocked through the balcony.

Naomi's knees went weak, and if she hadn't been leaning against Royce she probably would have slid to the ground. "Thanks, we'll be in shortly."

Trystan nodded, folding back into the hospital, leaving her alone with Royce once again.

Naomi tipped her face into the coolness of the breeze, relief warming her down to her core. "Thank God."

Royce palmed her back. "That's great news."

His touch left her vulnerable at a time when she was clinging to calm by a thread. That's all Naomi had been clutching for days, and that thread rapidly frayed. She couldn't so much as stumble. Not in front of him.

As a child, Naomi rambled when nerves overpowered her. That old habit manifested again as she desperately tried to gain a firmer grip on her emotions. "Dad's recovery will take about six weeks, then rehab, but it's so much better than the old days of needing that metal halo for six months."

"Let's go to the cafeteria and get something to eat while you wait to see him."

She bit back the urge to snap at him, frustration firing deep inside her now that the pressure from her father's surgery was gone. She was tired and cranky and, yes, still irritated with him for telling her family about her pregnancy.

What right did he have to do that? To take that moment away from her? Somehow, she'd lost sight of the impact of that when she'd been groggy from fainting. Afraid for her child. Terrified for her father.

She couldn't let that pass. He couldn't take over her life this way.

This wasn't the time or the place to tell him, with her emotions still too raw for logic, her feelings bubbling to the surface. "Royce, I'm not hungry." She stuffed her hands into the sleeves of her sweater, refusing to admit that, yes, she was getting cold. "I don't mean to snap, but I'm an adult. I'm not going to fall off the balcony, and I can feed myself. Drive myself. Keep myself upright."

Royce drew in a deep breath, his jaw tight before he spoke, "And you have a reckless streak."

Her eyebrows shot upward.

"Excuse me?" So much for resisting snapping. Logic, reason, calmness—all lost somewhere on that breeze. He'd laid down fighting words. Same ones she'd pushed against her whole life.

"You're impulsive."

"Perhaps it just feels that way since you're so methodical— Forget I said anything. I'm going back inside." She wheeled away from him.

And her feet shot out from under her.

Royce caught her just shy of her hitting the ground. "See, you do need me. Think about your baby."

Anger fired hot inside her. She loved her baby. How dare he insinuate otherwise? "That's not fair. Do you plan to stay plastered to my side for the next seven months?"

"Calm down. You're being irrational."

She leveled her best courtroom gaze his way—and yes, she had inherited more than her fair share of her father's bravado. "Oh, so I'm impulsive and irrational?"

"You're playing lawyer, twisting my words."

"If you ask me, you're the one whose emotions are out of control. You blurted to my family that I'm pregnant. You stole that once-in-a-lifetime chance for me to tell them about my first child."

"I was worried for you." He shot back.

"I'm not your fiancée." The woman he'd loved. A thought that burned through her, bringing an ugly green jealousy to the fore. "This isn't the past."

His head jerked back. "That's a low blow."

"I can't help how I feel, or how it seems that you're using our relationship to reconcile what happened before."

"And I think you're overreacting because of how your family treated you when you had cancer. Maybe you're even pushing me away because of the people you've lost, or some fear of trusting the future. Hell, I don't know for sure. I'm not the word expert like you are."

"Wow, well, you're certainly off to a great start." She crossed her arms tightly. "It's clear we've made a mistake. The storm is over."

"You're pushing me away. Point proved."

"If that's the way you want to see it." She braced a hand along a rail and backed away from him. "I'm going to see my father. I can find my own ride home."

Angling past him, she made her way inside. Just in time to see her father being wheeled past on a gurney by a middle-aged nurse. He groggily sang lyrics to old '50s songs, his tone loopy. On another day, Naomi's heart might have burst with laughter at the goofy display.

Instead, tears burned in her eyes and an ache filled her heart. She wanted to cry her eyes out over the realization that the fear she'd felt when she'd *wanted* to lean on Royce, the stab of jealousy she'd felt, was for a reason... She'd fallen for the man she'd just shoved out of her life for good.

Delaney raced down the hospital corridor to catch Birch before he made it to the elevator. Keeping her eyes on his broad shoulders in the crowded hallway, she angled past a nurse pushing a vitals monitor down the hall. She could still hardly believe he'd shown up here.

At first, she'd been afraid he would push the issue of sharing the truth about their relationship when she was feeling too scared and vulnerable to resist. But he'd kept his distance, hadn't given so much as a hint of their affair, simply stating he'd come because he respected Jack.

Birch had been such a steady source of support as she waited to hear about her father's surgery. Although every now and again, she could have sworn his eyes had broadcast his frustration at keeping his distance. Others wouldn't have seen it. But she knew him too well now.

Once the doctor had told them Jack was out of surgery, in recovery but not awake, Birch had said his farewells. Relief had taken the wind right out of Delaney so intensely, she'd almost missed the chance to catch him. And that made her feel guilty as hell after the way he'd come to check on her.

At the elevator, she rested a hand lightly on his arm as he pushed the button. She kept her touch neutral, too aware that someone could see them, but needing to thank him for being so thoughtful. He was a good man in many ways. "That was nice of you to stop by the hospital to check on my father."

"It's what people who care about each other do," he said tightly, pointedly.

She shifted, guilt pinching. Looking around at the people gathered at the elevator, she tugged Birch's elbow, leading him with her to a tucked away corner with two chairs. Thank goodness he didn't resist, only gestured for her to sit first and then took his place beside her.

"You have something to tell me?" he asked simply.

"I know you wanted something more from me back there, but it just didn't seem like the right time to…"

"To what? To let people know we've been together for over two months? Although I'm not sure what to call whatever we have going on. What are we exactly?"

Tension pulled tighter inside her, shoulders bracing.

"My father just went through a life-threatening surgery. Cut me a little slack."

"That's why I am here. To support you. You can't intend to keep us a secret forever."

"Of course not."

"Good. Let me be here for you. I can get coffee, we can sit with your sister and Royce."

The possibility of such a gathering sounded…happy. Good. She bit her lip against the hope.

Birch continued, "Maybe Miller might have worked a miracle with some kind of modifications for the pipeline that won't bankrupt the company."

She knew he meant it as an attempt to ease the tension with a joke, and maybe her emotions were too sensitive at the moment, but just that fast, Birch dashed her hopes of his ability to see her side of things. "Sure."

"You mean that?" The skepticism in his tone told her he'd heard the undercurrent in her voice. The pulling away.

"When the time is right." She'd been using the same delay tactic for weeks, knowing it wouldn't last forever.

"We've been sleeping together for over two months." His dark eyes flashed with a new fire. "We've known each other for a helluva lot longer." He took her hand in his. "When's the right time?"

She swallowed past the fear, wishing she could fall into the promise in his gaze. Knowing that would be beyond foolish. Licking her lips, she peered around to make sure no one they knew was nearby while they held hands this way. "Be honest. Where do you see this relationship going with how very different we are?"

He let go of her, his jaw flexing. "I thought I made myself clear. I want us to go public, to meet each other's friends and families." He paused. "But I can see in your face that's not something that interests you."

Panic made her stomach ache. She hadn't wanted

things to end like this, but she couldn't lie to him about a future together, either. "I just can't envision how we'll blend our worlds."

"You're dumping me because I would embarrass you in front of your friends?"

She flinched at the word *dumping*. She'd known this couldn't last forever, but thinking about ending their affair was tougher than she'd expected. "I'm saying I can't imagine how we'll blend our very different beliefs."

"Let me get this straight. If I don't agree with you on everything, we can't be together. Look at your sister and Miller."

"It's not that simple. Not for me, at least."

"Then explain it to me."

"Of course, people in a relationship can disagree about a lot of things. But there are some core values we can't compromise on." She searched his eyes and could see he still didn't understand. "What if I asked you to give up your holdings in companies that are harming the environment?"

She held her breath, knowing he'd refuse. But then again…what if he didn't?

"I wouldn't ask you to give up your job." His dismissiveness chafed.

Still, she gave it another chance, reframing her position.

"I'm not asking you to give up your profession. Just a portion of your holdings."

"It's not that simple—"

She couldn't help but notice how his words echoed hers from earlier.

"—people count on me with their futures," he continued. "If I do what you suggest, unrest could ripple through the investors, causing my whole corporation to collapse in a stock market sellout."

His position was expected. But the disappointment that came with it burned so much deeper than she ever could have imagined just a few weeks ago.

"I suspect you're smart enough to figure out a way around that. If you wanted to. But I can see that you don't."

She couldn't compromise on something so intrinsic to her values. Images of her sister's teenage body ravaged from cancer treatment haunted her to this day. Her family had taken one hit after another. She couldn't give Birch a way to hurt the Steeles too. Not when she had it in her power to keep him and his business practices at arm's length. And she couldn't string him along, either. She cared too much to do that to him.

The time had come to walk away from Birch.

Even if it cost her a broken heart.

Somehow on her way to check on her father, Naomi had found her steps slowing as she spotted Jeannie. An urge to stop, talk, comfort the woman had flooded through her. Crazy. Probably. Jeannie Mikkelson had four children of her own ready and eager to hold their mother's hand.

But Naomi had felt drawn to something in the woman's eyes. Something that sure seemed to echo a feeling taking root in Naomi's heart for Royce Miller.

To hide the renewed sting of tears, Naomi pulled her hair clamp free and re-secured her ponytail. The past two hours since Jack's surgery had been emotional, to say the least. Each member of the Steele family had filtered in and out, followed by the Mikkelsons, all eager to see him post-op, a sea of concern and relief washing through the room.

Naomi had decided to wait until the end by Jeannie's side since Glenna had left to make sure the house was ready for everyone to crash. Everyone was exhausted. Even Delaney had disappeared. And yes, maybe Naomi was afraid to go home to her solitary suite, where she feared she would fall apart amid the memory of her time there with Royce.

Jeannie touched her arm, calling Naomi back to the present. Leaning forward, the older woman's blond hair fell on her pink sweater, making her seem younger somehow. Much more together than Naomi felt. "Thank you for hanging out with me, you've been so kind. I'm really okay." She paused, then looked at Naomi with a narrowed gaze. "But are *you* okay?"

Ha. Loaded question for sure. "I'm fine. Just a little tired. This is a day to celebrate."

"Yes, we've had a miracle here with your father's surgery and the wonderful news about your baby. I know that no one will ever replace your mother, but I hope you know I am here to listen if you need me. Family is there for each other."

Family? Naomi sat stunned as the word shifted around in her mind and realized, accepted, yes, this merger—a blended family—was going to happen. And before she knew it, words tumbled out of her mouth. "How did you juggle it all? Kids, work, a happy marriage?"

Jeannie laughed, rolling her eyes. "Who said I juggled it?"

"I've heard about you for years, seen the features in magazines." Read them as a teen, poring over the perfect family photos, wondering what it would have been like if her mother had lived. "You had it all, career and family."

"Charles and I loved each other, but make no mistake, we argued," Jeannie said. "All couples do. I made mistakes at work. Heaven knows there are so many things I wish I could go back and redo as a mother, times I wish I'd slowed down to cherish."

"But you still did it all. No one's perfect."

"Exactly, honey. No one's perfect. Quit expecting perfection from yourself—and from Royce."

Naomi leaned forward in the chair. "It's scary to think about, um, failing."

That last word tripped her up, hung in her mind, resonating at the core of so much. Fear of imperfection. Fearing she'd failed her family. That she would cause them more grief. She'd known that cancer wasn't anyone's fault, but to see her father broken all over again so soon after losing his wife and a child?

Naomi's teenage mind had felt the guilt. Clearly some of that had leaked into her adulthood, pushing her to overcompensate.

Jeannie leaned back in her chair, nodding. Considering. Heartbeats of silence passed before she spoke again. "Not trying is scarier."

"Perhaps we're more alike than I realized." Damn straight, Naomi was scared of failing. But Royce? He was worth facing her fear. She realized now that she wanted to fight for him with every ounce of her soul. If only she had some sort of courtroom-style strategy to win him back.

But as experienced as she was in that arena, when it came to love, she could only follow her instincts.

Twelve

Royce had spent the better part of an hour behind the wheel of the SUV, trying to clear his mind after the fight with Naomi yesterday.

Like Texas, Alaska offered pristine roads, perfect for driving and thinking.

He didn't know how to approach this problem. There was no scientific method to apply. All the variables and moving parts made the situation with Naomi feel impenetrable and unapproachable.

For a man who prided himself on his critical thinking skills, he'd come up empty-handed.

Which was how he ended up back at the Steele compound. Sure, he needed to collect Tessie. But really, he had to admit, he didn't want to leave Naomi like this.

Emerging from the car, he started toward the looming main house, feeling dwarfed beneath the towering architecture. Perhaps it had to do with nerves.

Helluva mess here. His fidgeted with his abacus key chain in his parka pocket.

Trystan Mikkelson intercepted him on the way to the house, nodding. Jeannie's younger son, the rancher, sported cowboy boots and a tall black Stetson, a jacket—wind resistant—designed for riding in this weather. He motioned for Royce to follow him. "Let's nab a couple of Steele horses."

"Sounds good to me."

They walked in silence to the twenty-stall barn, a large red building trimmed by slate stones. Trystan was known as a rugged guy, his lack of polish earning him a behind-the-scenes role in the family.

Making their way to the barn, Royce passed a few of the Steeles and Mikkelsons on horseback, heading out toward the mountain trails. Marshall led the small group. Naomi, he couldn't help but notice, was not a part of the group. Heaven help him if he or anyone suggested she might not want to gallop around while pregnant.

Trystan's somber features seemed more pronounced in this setting, his Stetson shadowing his face. "You do ride, right?"

"I'm from Texas." To his mind, the math was obvious. "I live in Alaska. I ride."

"Let's saddle up, then."

"Wouldn't you rather drive? I would think after Jack's accident you might not be too eager for a horseback ride." Royce looked to the line of stalls. A variety of horses poked their heads out, a seeming perpetual murmur of nickers echoing in the modern barn facility. He wondered which horse was Naomi's. He looked the length and saw sleds, skis and even a horse-drawn sleigh parked in back.

"It wasn't the horse's fault. It was an accident. That

could have happened in the car or fishing or walking. Things happen. We can't let accidents keep us from living our lives." Trystan led a sorrel quarter horse with a blaze out of the stall. Handing the animal's leather lead rope to Royce, he gave the horse a pat on the neck. "I've met Phantom before. Shouldn't throw you on your ass."

"Thanks for the vote of confidence." Royce let the sorrel sniff his hand, the whiskers of the gelding tickling his palm. Leading the horse to the cross ties, he looked over at Trystan, who pulled a dapple gray from another stall and led him to another set of cross ties.

Trystan pulled out two currycombs and a hard brush for them to use. Royce grabbed the currycomb, rubbing sinewy shoulders and flanks in circular patterns, loosing dirt and warming up Phantom's muscles.

"Once things settle down with Jack's recovery, I would like to schedule a meeting to speak with both families together. Just to talk." Royce brushed the loosed dirt off Phantom and used a hoof pick to clean out his hooves.

"Naomi was persuasive, huh? She's always been a top-notch negotiator." He took them into the climate-controlled tack room and hoisted an intricate Western saddle, saddle pad and bridle for Royce to grab.

"Actually, it was seeing the Steeles and the Mikkelsons pull together. That integrity made me want to know more about your operation." He'd been considering the move since they'd arrived here, but now... How awkward might it be to work in the company if he and Naomi weren't a couple?

As they exited the tack room, Royce placed a hand on Phantom's haunches, letting the horse know he was there. In a quick motion, he placed the saddle pad and saddle on the gelding and cinched the girth. Keeping one hand on Phantom's neck, he moved up to unhinge the halter from the cross ties. Eschewing the halter, he slipped the sorrel's head into the bridle.

"Let's ride and talk." The dapple gray let out a low nicker as Trystan led him past Phantom and Royce, moving from the barn to the open field.

"Is this a business test of some sort? And if so, shouldn't we be in a boardroom?" Royce followed, clicking his tongue to command his horse to follow. The quarter horse responded with a spirited toss of the head and a prance forward.

They made their way into the open space. Trystan, already seated in the saddle, looked at ease. He leaned on the horn, tipping his Stetson. "I'm not the boardroom sort. Let's call this more of a challenge."

Staying silent, Royce pulled himself up into the saddle adjusting his weight.

"A rite of passage, really—" Trystan urged the dapple forward "—if you expect to be a part of this motley crew."

"I think you have that backward. I'm the one deciding if I want to share my research with your company or another." Squeezing his calves, he prompted Phantom into a working trot.

"I'm not talking about business. I'm talking about the way everyone's blending all these families together. I may not be as diplomatic as the rest of them, but since Naomi's not my sister, I'm also less likely to punch you in the face. So I got nominated to take measure of you. And, well, I guess you'll do." With that, Trystan and the dapple surged forward, kicking off into a headlong gallop. A challenge indeed.

At Royce's whoop, Phantom lunged into a gallop, gaining ground on Trystan. Each stretch of the stride seemed to melt some of the tension away. It'd been too long since his last ride.

After a quarter mile along the beaten path through sprawling trees, Trystan slowed his horse into a loping canter and then a slow trot. Reluctant to disengage from the speed, but eager to see what Trystan meant by his comment, he slowed Phantom down.

"Hmm?" The nonanswer hung in the horse-length distance between them. The sounds of the others riding carried on the wind. The roar of a snowmobile hummed as Aiden drove just ahead.

"What?" Trystan asked. "Nothing to say?"

"I didn't hear a question." A technicality on Royce's part.

Trystan cast a glance backward at the family they'd left behind, then shifted forward in the creaking saddle again. "Are you and my future stepsister seeing each other?"

Such a loaded inquiry. One that made Royce reel. The fight from earlier flashed before his eyes, the fear of losing the woman in his life again, a woman pregnant with a child he was already learning to care about. "No, we're not."

"Man of few words. I like that. But it's obvious to all of us that the two of you have some kind of connection."

"You're a little old for the overprotective stepbrother routine," Royce said drily, stroking Phantom's neck as they slowed to a walk.

Barking out a laugh, Trystan shot him a look. "Clearly you don't have siblings."

"Touché."

"Well, if you are seeing each other—or plan to be seeing each other again—be careful with her. I've been around horses enough to get a sense of things. Naomi's more softhearted under that tough exterior than people think."

"I noticed."

"And there's the baby to consider—as you told everyone."

Royce scratched along his neck, remembering Naomi's pain over how he'd shared her secret before she was ready. "I'm an intelligent man. This is all obvious."

Or rather it should have been.

"Okay, then there's this. Be very certain before you start a relationship with her. My brother Chuck, my future stepbrothers and I outnumber you five to one. Not to mention my baby sister is quiet, but can hold her own in ass-kicking."

Unlike earlier, Royce realized he wasn't looking at data or science at all. He was hearing the words, the way he'd learned from Naomi. He tuned into the nuance. To the way data was framed. The word *outnumbered* echoed in his mind. Outnumbered positioned him as a threat, sure, but also signified to his mind that even as a fully capable and dynamic adult woman, her brothers thought of her in the framework of the teen who was sick with cancer.

Well-intentioned, just as he'd been earlier by insisting she eat, insisting she rest. No wonder her reaction had been so severe. So sharp. She constantly worked to not feel smothered. To not be pampered. She wanted to be taken seriously and seen as strong.

He knew she was strong.

So what could he do to win her back? To prove he could be the man a strong woman like her needed and wanted in her life?

This time, it couldn't be about the numbers or logic. He was going to have to dig deep for what came tougher for him, the part that—because of Naomi—he was learning was crucial.

Because Naomi was his future and if he wanted to win her—and God, he did—then he knew.

He would have to lead with his heart.

Pacing around her loft, Naomi couldn't seem to work out the problem that had nagged at her mind for the past few hours. Guilt over how things went with Royce, how she'd snapped at him, tore at her soul. And yes, it had something to do with the fact that scared her down to the core of her being.

She loved him.

There. That certainty swelled in her chest. It ought to give her relief. But there was still the issue of her needing to be an equal partner, cared for, sure, but not smothered. How could she make things right while ensuring he understood?

Could he understand?

Of course, all of that was contingent on him even wanting to see her again after their fight.

Another turn about the room didn't bring on the inspiration of a plan. Nope. She came up empty again. Every apology sounding horrible as she imagined the conversation in her head.

Those thoughts would have to wait. Her cell, which she'd clutched as she paced the room, screamed to life in her hand. Glancing down at the screen, her heart beat out of time.

Royce.

For a moment, she'd forgotten he'd placed his number into her phone. And it wasn't just a phone call. He wanted to video chat.

So much for having her plan smoothed out.

She stroked back her hair, breathed in and out to steady herself, then tapped the screen. His dark eyes smoldered, struck into her.

Naomi wished she'd taken in a couple more of those bracing breaths. "Hello. Did you leave something here?"

He gave her a lopsided smile. "As a matter of fact, I did."

Her heart sunk. She'd been hoping… "What is it? Let me know where to look and I'll leave it with one of the staff."

"It's not something you can return, actually."

She searched his face, hoping, and yet still wary of voicing as much. "I'm not sure I understand."

His smile—full-on shining now—made her heart skip a beat.

"Look out of your window, Naomi."

Her window? She walked to the enclosed balcony and…her heavy heart leaped right into her throat.

Royce stood in the snowy yard, with Tessie by his side. Just like something out of a movie. He'd come to her, tall and handsome against the background of glistening trees. She looked at the phone image of him again and wondered why she hadn't recognized the surroundings before. She could hardly believe he was here, after the way she'd pushed him away at the hospital.

Tessie barked once, twice, pulling Naomi's attention back to the phone, back to Royce and the hope that they could rediscover what they'd found at the retreat. "Are you going to stay out there or are you planning to come inside?"

"I could, but actually I had something else in mind. Do you think you could come down so we can talk more about what I left at your place? I would come up there, but I'm fairly sure we'll end up in bed together and there are some things we should discuss."

He was reaching out and from the roguish grin on his face, what he wanted to say was most definitely something she wanted to hear. "I'm on my way down."

She practically tripped over her own two feet as she tugged on her pink parka, snow boots and sheepskin gloves. A blur took her from loft to elevator, barely registering the rest of the compound as determined footfalls led her outside to the chilled air. To Royce.

Flipping up her hood, she raced to where he stood. An enchanted prince against a snowy backdrop. Tessie bounded in the fresh powder to Naomi, tail wagging with anticipation and excitement. Naomi tilted her head, gesturing to the landscape. "Where have you been?"

"Here, actually. I came to get Tessie and ended up going riding with Trystan. It gave me some time to think, get perspective." He extended a hand to her. "Would you like to go on a sleigh ride so we can talk?"

Joy shimmered inside her at his magical offer, all the more special as it was unexpected from the reclusive scientist who claimed his life was all about work.

"You know how to handle a horse and sleigh?" A rhetorical question, really. She was more taken by the fact he'd arranged this for her, for them.

"I've driven a wagon in Texas." He shrugged a shoulder, confidence glinting in his eyes as he stepped closer. "I'm hoping it's the same. But if it's not, I trust my Alaskan companion can teach me how."

Was he serious? He'd been worried about her falling off a balcony, for crying out loud. Would he give her that kind of control?

"You're willing to let me drive?" She said it slowly, wanting to be sure he understood the underlying issue.

She needed to feel like he trusted her to be strong. Capable.

"Of course. I'm trying to send a message here, but in case you haven't noticed, I'm not always as good at emotions as I am at science." He extended his hand again. "But I am trying," he repeated.

This time, she took his hand, and together they made their way toward the barn, snow crunching beneath their feet.

Off to the left was her father's old-fashioned sleigh with two draft horses—Mars and Jupiter—already hitched. Mars shook his head, the rustle of bells filling the air with a hint of holiday cheer in an Alaskan spring.

Climbing into the sleigh, she grabbed the plaid blanket he'd placed on the seat, then waited while he unhooked the horses from the post. Anticipation mounted in her chest. That determined heart of hers no longer feeling heavy, but alive, pounding with excitement.

Stepping into the sleigh, Tessie close at his heels, he passed the leather reigns to her, an earnest gesture.

His gloved hand touched hers in the exchange, that electricity once again growing between them, warming her from the inside. She clicked her tongue, urged the two draft horses forward. The sleigh gained momentum, gliding in the yet untouched snow.

Royce sat next to her under the blanket, his leg touching hers, maintaining contact that almost threatened to distract her from driving and the scenery of a slowly sinking sun behind fresh white land.

Her land. Silence stretched as she enjoyed the view, this pristine beauty that stole her breath as fast as the man beside her. Chunks of ice breaking loose in the water caused the family seaplane to bob, seeming to nod approval at their journey. She could see tracks where her brothers had ridden earlier today. As she passed the tree house she and her siblings had used as children, her heart nearly burst. So many memories here, in this place.

"Naomi." Royce's low voice rumbled like a river through her thoughts, drawing her into the present. The beautiful present. "How's your father doing?"

"Sleeping well, as of when I spoke to Delaney an hour ago. The last nurse's check showed all great vitals. No recurrence of the high blood pressure." She couldn't ask for more. Family was everything, a blessing she hoped to expand with the baby she carried.

And with Royce?

The possibility warmed her far more than any blanket.

"That's good, really good."

Her grip tightened on the reins. "I'm sorry for the way I spoke to you at the hospital."

"You have nothing to apologize for. While I was out with Trystan, I realized something."

"What's that?" She pulled on the left rein with a tug-tug, signaling a change of direction to the horse team, striking out for the trail leading through a bower of snow-laden trees. Her favorite path.

"We moved so fast that while we got the basics, we don't know each other enough to instinctively understand where the other person is coming from," Royce said, resting a gloved hand on her knee.

His touch and words pulled her gaze back to him and she realized no way could she keep her attention on driving any longer. She slowed the horses until they came to a stop with a snort. Tessie, who had been on Royce's other side, hopped out to tunnel through piles

of snow in that way of hers that was becoming familiar and dear.

Naomi shifted in her seat to face Royce. "Okay, I
can see that. Is that your way of saying you understand
I was on edge at the hospital?"

"More than that." He took her hand and linked their
fingers, squeezing lightly. "You told me your family
smothered you, and I didn't listen, not really."

"You were being thoughtful. I realize that now. And
you have your own fears from your past."

"You know those facts, just like I know the facts of
what you went through. But fully trusting each other?
That takes time." His voice, so strong, filled the cold
air with warm puffs.

"Are you saying you want us to take that time?" She
needed to hear him say it outright, to be sure she hadn't
misunderstood. And yes, maybe she wanted to savor
the words, as well.

"Yes, that's what I'm saying." Simple words, but honest and up-front—as this man had always been with her.

She had to clear up one last, but vital, question.
"Even though I'm pregnant?"

"Yes. In fact, I seem to recall that I told everyone,
when that should have been your news to share. I apologize for taking that joy from you. I have the reputation
as a recluse for a reason. Relationships and communication? Not my strong suit."

"You're doing really well right now. And to be fair,
I started things off on the wrong foot between us, not
being honest." Guilt pinched her even more than before,
now that she knew him, respected him. Loved him. "I
should have been honest with you. Now you've been
more than fair in how you've dealt with my family. In
how you've forgiven me."

"You've had solid reasons for your actions. I understand logic."

She laughed lightly, relieved and glad she'd trekked up the mountain to meet this man on that snowy day. "Thank you. You've made me so very happy."

"It's that simple to make you happy?" he asked, his brilliant eyes a hint bewildered.

"It's a good start." She took his hands. "But what makes you happy?"

"Loving you."

She blinked, swiped snowflakes from her vision and wondered if perhaps she'd heard wrong. No one other than family had ever said that to her. And certainly no one in the romantic sense. She'd given up thinking she'd have this kind of love. She would have never imagined this kind of happiness when she went to that clinic alone to start trying for a baby.

She swallowed down a lump of emotion and asked, needing to hear it again, "What did you say?"

"I said that I love you, Naomi Steele. You blindsided me from the moment I first saw you in a snowstorm shouting down a bear." His smile dazzled her. "I'm still working on the details of how we fit as a couple, but damn it, I know we have something amazing here. Once-in-a-lifetime amazing, and I want us to work together to build a future together, with the baby— Am I going too fast for you again?"

"Not too fast at all. Just perfect. Absolutely perfect." She stroked his strong jaw. "I'd been making lists of possible names, but I'm wondering. Would you like to do that together?"

He kissed her hands clasped in his. "I would like that." A wealth of emotion shifted through his deep coffee-brown eyes. He tucked her close, a perfect fit. "What are you thinking?"

As he held her against his side, his arm around her shoulders, she felt at peace for the first time in longer than she could remember. Like she no longer had to run or throw up guards. No. Right here in his strong arms, she felt...at home.

"Actually," she said, blinking back happy tears, "I was just thinking how I wish I had a beautiful speech to offer you in return. I'm the wordsmith, the litigator, after all. But the only words that come to mind are how much I love you too."

Sketching a kiss along her temple, he whispered in her ear, "Sounds like the perfect formula to me."

Epilogue

Two weeks later

Naomi Steele wasn't naive. Her life had brought enough challenges to make her wise—and thanks to knowing and loving Royce Miller, she was no longer jaded.

Curled up beside him on the sofa at the glass igloo where they'd met, she typed on her computer, complete with reliable internet thanks to the permanent satellite Royce had installed when he bought the place. Apparently, those patents of his opened up a lot of choices when it came to where they lived. They'd found this the perfect nostalgic retreat for when the Steele compound noise proved too much for Royce. Sunshine streamed through the roof, casting prisms along Tessie's fur as the dog slept at Royce's feet.

Naomi and Royce were finding their way through

building a relationship and a future. His consulting work for Alaska Oil Barons was invaluable. His strong-willed independence made for a good balance with her family's big personalities.

He'd even accompanied her to her doctor's appointment yesterday and wanted to attend the ultrasound appointment in two weeks. His enthusiasm about the pregnancy was genuine and made her love for him grow.

Royce stroked a lock of her hair, before sliding a hard-muscled arm around her shoulders. "How are you feeling?"

"Like I'm gaining weight at the speed of light." She looked up from her laptop to smile at him. "But so happy."

"It's good to see your father walking around."

Her dad was a bit of an impatient patient, but he was devoting his full effort to rehab. Jeannie had proved to be a godsend in gently but firmly teasing him out of his frustration. Delaney had also stepped up, taking time off work to devote her full attention to their father. There was a hint of sadness in her eyes. But then, the scare with Jack's health had been hard on all of them.

Naomi stroked Royce's bristly cheek. "Have I told you how much it meant to me having you at my side lately?"

"Being with you is clearly no hardship." He tipped her chin and kissed her, his touch, his mouth, launching tingles to the roots of her hair. Easing back, he tapped the edge of her keyboard. "What are you working on?"

She pulled her thoughts off taking that kiss further— for now—and clicked her computer screen back to life. "Broderick forwarded me an invitation our company received to be featured at a wildlife preservation fund-raiser this summer."

"Whoa." Royce whistled softly. "That's quite a coup. It'll be super press as the merger moves forward. There will be a lot of movers and shakers there, a lot of investors like Birch Montoya."

"Which could bring more capital for your initiatives." She tapped the abacus key chain in his hand. "They just want a commitment from us on a face for the company since Dad's recovering and Jeannie's not leaving his side."

"There are plenty of Steeles and Mikkelsons to choose from." He set aside the key chain on the coffee table. "Although Aiden's clearly too young. And I can't imagine Trystan Mikkelson would want any part of it."

"Thank heavens." She shook her head, then tucked her loose hair behind her ear. "He's great at what he does, managing their family's ranch outside of Juneau, but he's more than a little rough around the edges. He would need an intense makeover to pull off that kind of public role for the company."

"We all have our niche in getting the job done."

"That we do." She looked into his bourbon-brown eyes, the intensity of the man setting her senses on fire.

Her cell phone rang, expanding the world around her. She angled over to read the screen. Her doctor's name scrolled across it.

A hint of concern skittered up her spine. She answered, turning on the speakerphone, then clasping Royce's hand. He squeezed firmly.

"Hello," she answered.

"Miss Steele? This is Dr. Odell's office. I'm his nurse."

"Yes…" She paused, thinking back to her appointment. "Is there a problem with my blood work?"

"Not a problem at all," the nurse continued, a smile in her voice. "We would like to bring you back in for an ultrasound. Your blood serum tests lead us to believe that you're carrying twins."

"Twins?" Royce echoed.

Stunned, Naomi couldn't even speak. Swallowing hard, she looked up at Royce—and found him grinning. The shock eased, joy and wonder sliding in after.

Her hand slid to her stomach and she finally whispered, "Twins."

She shouldn't have been surprised. With twins in her family and having used in vitro, it was a possibility. But she'd been so afraid it wouldn't take at all, this double blessing. Her heart swelled.

The rest of the phone call passed in a blur as the doctor's nurse gave her an appointment time. Which Royce noted in his tablet, thank goodness.

Once the line disconnected, he set aside the device and moved her laptop. "This calls for a celebration."

Excitement over the news mixed with a thrill at his touch skimming down her arm. "What exactly do you have in mind?"

His fingers trailed from her hand to her thigh. "Ice cream."

Her breath hitched in her throat as he stroked up her side, grazing the curve of her sensitive breast. "Ice cream?"

"Together. In bed. Naked. Double scoops for the double deal celebration."

"Hmm," she sighed, arching into his caress. "Lead the way."

He lifted her into his arms and turned toward the bed. "My pleasure."

* * * * *

LET'S TALK
Romance

For exclusive extracts, competitions
and special offers, find us online:

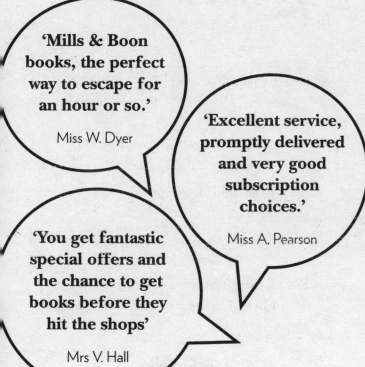